CW00926221

THE HUNTERS

ALSO BY DAVID WRAGG

The Black Hawks
The Righteous

DAVID WRAGG

HARPER
Voyager

Harper*Voyager*
An imprint of
HarperCollins*Publishers* Ltd
1 London Bridge Street
London SE1 9GF

www.harpercollins.co.uk

HarperCollins*Publishers*
Macken House
39/40 Mayor Street Upper
Dublin 1
D01 C9W8
Ireland

First published by HarperCollins*Publishers* 2023
1

A catalogue record for this book is available from the British Library

ISBN: 978-0-00-853372-4 (HB)
ISBN: 978-0-00-853373-1 (TPB)

Typeset in Sabon by Palimpsest Book Production Ltd, Falkirk, Stirlingshire

Printed and bound in the UK using
100% renewable electricity by CPI Group (UK) Ltd

This book is produced from independently certified FSC™ paper to ensure
responsible forest management.

For more information visit: www.harpercollins.co.uk/green

For Adam, who is responsible

ONE

The woman who called herself Ree saw the feather of dust coming up the trail long before she heard the riders. The morning had been hard, as usual, and thankless, as usual, but her glow of small achievements was undimmed. She had greeted the dawn – the sun dances seemed harder each day, but she persevered – and done her rounds of the pens with Edigu, her foreman, checking and feeding the animals, before beginning the day's tasks in earnest. The feed store was half done now, and by mid morning she'd dug out the last of the red earth where the stable would go. There was plenty of time left before winter, as the battering heat of the high sun gave joyless testament. Her pride at the construction milestone blunted some of her hissing frustration at the kid's persistent dereliction. Once again, she'd drawn the morning's water herself.

She was sipping tea on a battered stool in the shade of the half-stone, half-timber cabin at the stockade's centre as the riders crested the last rise from the direction of the town, kicking plumes of dust into the streaky sky. Half a dozen riders, heavy-footed. She could guess who.

They loped straight through the open gateway of the stockade and reined in before the house. Six of them, all men, in their familiar long, split-tailed coats, bracers and greaves, their Guild-stamped breastplates grime-streaked, and dust masks pulled up almost to the broad brims of their helmets.

Ree leaned back against the timber wall and blew the steam from her tea as the lead rider edged his mount closer with a heavy nudge of his spurs. His little trophies rattled and jingled amongst his tack: ears, mostly, shrivelled and blackened, others impossible to identify but nonetheless tufted with hair. He tugged down his dust mask to reveal a square-jawed smirk.

'Dawn's fortune to you, Ree.'

'And good morning to you, Kurush Mawn-Hunter. What brings you so far from the delights of the paradise terrace?'

'*Guildmaster* Kurush, may it please you.'

'My apologies, Acting Guildmaster.'

His smirk was undimmed, but a muscle in his cheek twitched. His eyes dropped to the mug in her hands. 'You care to invite me in for tea?'

'Sorry,' she said with a small smile, its precise width calculated to hit the mark between deference and defiance. 'This is the last of it.'

The smirk was indelible, as if carved into his blocky features. 'Caravan's due any time, maybe I can keep some back for you. You know I'm a man of influence. Just another reason to be nice to me.'

'I wouldn't want to put you to any trouble. Was there something urgent you needed to tell me? Six armoured riders at my threshold, must be important.' Ree kept her eyes low. Where was the kid? Ridden off again? Her pony was missing from the corral. Was this about that?

Kurush sat back in his saddle and scratched at his helmet, revealing a line of trail dust across his brow and a pale stripe of thinning hairline. He caught her glance and pulled the helmet firmly back into place. 'Word's reached us at the Guildhouse that you've been . . . dealing . . . with the nomads.'

'I've traded a few animals – they know their horses, as you'd expect. What of it?'

He leaned forward again, affecting concern. 'Ree, my dear, those people are savages. They're thieving murderers, and they'll be coming back one day soon to slaughter you and steal all of this.

It's just a matter of time. That old fella you're keeping around, he'll be the one to cut your throat in the night.'

'Edigu isn't Mawn, Kurush. The nomads aren't Mawn. No matter how often you harvest them.' She dropped her voice. 'Gods know they've suffered most of all.'

He continued over her. '. . . Now, if you were to let the Guild staff your little farm properly, provide you with adequate security, we could see to it that you and that kid of yours were kept safe from any . . . untoward incidents.'

'So that's what this is about. Guild encroachment, again.'

Kurush put one hand on his dust-streaked breastplate, a picture of offence. 'My motives are nothing more than a pure-hearted concern for your safety and that of your child.'

'She's not mine.'

'Your relation aside, you should be taking care, yes? A lot of bandits in these hills, a lot of people who find robbing easier than working. Many of the other smallholders are happy to receive an enhanced level of protection, in exchange for—'

'Kurush, do I need to fetch my writ of property? You know full well this land is titled to me, and the Guild has no claim on it.'

Kurush's bonhomie fell away, and he fixed Ree with a steady glare. Behind him, the other riders shuffled and fidgeted, their horses swishing away predatory insects. 'You're still kinda new here, so maybe no one's yet explained to you how things work. See, this ain't the protectorate out here, this is the edge of the world. This is Guild territory. Now the governor down in Mahavrik, he and the Guild have an understanding. His outfit writes the titles and collects the taxes, but that's as far as it goes. The Guild has what's called a "free hand" in its matters domestic. And the, uh, protection of citizenry, that's a matter domestic.'

'Meaning what?'

'Meaning you should think about things a little harder, Ree. You and I, we could help each other out. Not every man would look past that scar of yours, especially at your age, but . . .' He tailed off, affecting a wistful gaze into the middle distance, but Ree could see the hard lines beneath his eyes, the checked anger at her resistance. She quelled the urge to snap, 'And what age would that be?', and kept her hand from reaching up to trace the line of the pale, jagged scar that ran from temple to cheek. She was past forty now. She supposed this kind of nonsense was inevitable.

'Place like this, no one for miles around,' Kurush lowed on, 'no one in earshot. A band with ill intentions could do terrible things out here, and it might be months before anyone found the result. Only then would the Guild investigate, of course.'

He leaned forward in the saddle, fixing her with his mock concern once more. 'It would be a real shame if my next ride out here was on the long-cold trail of your murderers, wouldn't it, now?'

His coat hung open; one gauntleted hand gripped the hilt of the sabre slung from his belt. If he chose to ride me down, she thought, that would be it. No one would stop him – not his riders, not Edigu, not the kid . . .

From the corner of her eye she could see the fearsome crossbow leaning where she'd propped it against the water barrel beside her. Strung, loaded and cranked, she could snatch it up now, and give the Acting Guildmaster a first-hand taste of her enhanced level of protection.

. . . And not me.

Because, said a dark and cowardly voice at the back of her mind, you need this wretched man. You need his indulgence, and that of his blasted Guild. Glorious as it would be to punch a bolt through that little tin breastplate of his and out into the clear blue sky, his goons would hack you down and this place would be aflame by noon. You need him.

For yourself. For the kid.

Kurush leaned further forward in the saddle, yellowed leathers creaking. A bulbous fly had landed on the brim of his helmet, vile and iridescent in the sunlight. 'So maybe,' he drawled, '*maybe*, you want to think again about your level of protection?'

She let her gaze drop. 'You're right, of course. I must be prudent.'

He nodded slowly, his shoulders bobbing with the movement. A hint of the smirk had returned to the corners of his mouth, but she could feel the heat of his simmering anger at her impertinence. 'Indeed you must, Mistress Ree. Indeed you must.'

The fly departed Kurush's helmet and launched itself at his horse's eye. The animal shied and he yanked the reins with a snarl. 'Boys,' he said, looking around at the restless riders, 'we have here a reminder that mares can be troublesome and . . .' he snapped the reins again as the horse tried to turn '. . . unpredictable.' He cuffed the horse and it stilled. 'They need a firm hand.'

Ree's gaze flicked to the spur-rakes that marred the animal's flank. She spoke before she could stop herself. 'I find they merely respond to how they're treated.'

She saw Kurush's nostrils widen. He spat into the dirt and hauled his horse around. 'We have other stops to make this morning, I'll leave you to think on what we discussed.' The smirk returned with a gleam of malice. 'But you might not want to dally, Mistress Ree. Not with so many intriguing types asking after you and your child in these parts.'

'What? What do you mean?'

'First of the caravan's outriders came in this morning, full of questions. Questions about a fine-looking, white-haired woman, and a child in her care. Can't think who they meant. Maybe you'll bring me a prompt answer yet, eh?'

They spurred their mounts back beneath the gateway, raising dust into the air, leaving Ree staring open-mouthed in the cabin's shadow, unable even to call after them.

He couldn't have—

That can't mean—

Fuck.

She swallowed hard, balled her hands into fists to stop their trembling, and ran to fetch her sword. Moments later, she was mounted and riding hard for the gate, the sword at her hip and the crossbow on her back, and one thought alone in her mind.

Where are you, Javani?

* * *

Javani considered Behrooz a stupid man, which made him both great and terrible as a stooge. Such was his reputation, few would suspect him of the mental capacity to play the tiles well enough to gamble honestly, let alone under nefarious instruction. This was a man who had lost one foot to an avoidable mining collapse and an ear to a snakebite, and there were rumours that the snake had caught him sleeping naked and taken more than his ear. Javani disregarded the rumours; as long as he did as she'd told him, his body parts or lack thereof were no issue at all.

But now, suspended in the dark of the teahouse wind tower, perched on the little seat she and Moosh had carved, her legs braced, she was having second thoughts. She still had a perfect view of the game table, including the tile hands of most of the players, and although the rush of chilled air past her was distracting, it wasn't altogether unpleasant, even if the wind's moan in the tunnel stole away most of the conversations below. The morning outside was already bright and fearsome, and feeling her skin prickle in the tower's cool gloom was as welcome as it was unfamiliar.

The problem was that Behrooz hadn't looked up, even once. Not to check she was there. Not to ensure he didn't play too early, or win a hand he shouldn't. Not even just to stretch his ridiculous neck. Javani had the sinking feeling that he'd simply forgotten why he was there, why she had staked him, why she'd spent two hours the previous day drilling him in the plan. Why she'd pressed her aunt's one true treasure into his grimy palm and made him swear not to lose it. He looked as though he was playing tiles, drinking and having fun. Either he had settled into the role like a master chancer, or her plan was buggered.

It had been such a good plan, too. The timing was perfect, catching the last of the overnight crowd once the triers and losers had been peeled off, when the hours spent in the cool of the teahouse and the musty spirits it served were beginning to blunt even the keenest sharp. There were always plenty of players overnight: off-duty miners, of course, some freemen, others bonded convicts, their crimes and sentences tattooed on their faces; Guild enforcers and resting caravan guards, awaiting the next departure; and the occasional itinerant professional gambler, chased out of every other venue on their inexorable path to near-exile. The tables were already piled with bundled scrip, some coin and even the odd miner's treasure – a nugget of turquoise glinted in the lamplight on one, and another boasted a chunk of what one of the Guild heavies had loudly declared was 'baby gold'. All Behrooz had to do was be Behrooz, right up until she gave the signal and he suddenly wasn't. But for that to work, he had to *see* the signal.

A creaking and rattling above her announced another arrival, as did a shower of mudbrick dust. Moosh was coming down the little ladder. She hissed and waved at him to go back up, to get out before he made enough noise for everyone below to notice.

He either didn't see or ignored her gestures, but fortunately the sounds of his arrival were covered by a commotion from the far side. One of the robed and bearded sect that plagued the main street had descended the teahouse steps and was attempting to drag out one of the players on another table. The wind and Moosh's arrival blanketed most of their argument, but Javani gathered that the player was another member of the sect, and they were supposed to be heading out into the literal wilderness, not the moral variant. The younger man disagreed, but his fellow players were of the opinion that he had resigned forthwith and set about dividing his stake. Furious and ashamed, the zealots left.

'Is he winning?' Moosh whispered from beside her, his voice far too loud in her ear.

'No,' she growled back, more quietly.

'So it's working?'

'I don't know yet, dipstick.'

Moosh settled down on the perch beside her. His legs were shorter and he had to stretch to brace himself. 'My dad was a sharp,' he said, now matching her level. 'Back in the city, before they made him give everything up. He made stacks of coin, but the big families didn't like it and they made him promise to stop.'

'Uh-huh.' Javani kept her attention fixed below, her eyes on the 'deserter' tattoo on Behrooz's cheek. He'd have to look up soon, if only to yawn. The smell of Confined Men was getting overpowering in the vent, and her eyes were starting to water.

'In the end, he gave all the coin to the temple – he didn't have to, but he didn't want to make a fuss,' Moosh went on. 'And he promised not to gamble again, which was fine because he'd already won all the competitions, even the underground ones, so he didn't need to do it any more. But that's why he never came to the teahouse here.'

'Uh-huh.'

'But they still made him leave because he was really the lost son of the old Keeper, and the new Keeper was afraid he might try to take over, so that's why we came north in secret.'

'Moosh, your dad was a stonemason,' Javani sighed. Moosh was an orphan, like her, although he'd at least had a chance to know one of his parents. His father had brought him north after his mother died of a fever in Moosh's infancy, then he had perished a year before when a scaffolding collapsed at the Guildhouse. Moosh was now a ward of Terbish, the teahouse keeper; it was through Moosh's unrelenting explorations that Javani had discovered the wind-catcher as the perfect venue for her scheme.

'Exactly, that's what he wanted everyone to think.' Moosh paused, his babyish face scrunched in effort beneath his tangle of mudbrick-dusted hair, presumably thinking up his next tale. In the time Javani had known him, Moosh had claimed his father was a former commander of the Golden Lancers, a champion pit-fighter, and an assassin who had worked to topple the corrupt church of the Sink. He didn't appear to see any contradictions. She didn't begrudge him his invention; she'd been inclined to invent fantastical narratives for her own parents more times than she'd care to admit. All her aunt would tell her was that they'd been killed by Mawn, and in Javani's weaker moments, the void of knowledge pained her.

'What are you going to do if you win?' Moosh asked, chewing at one finger. Javani suspected he still occasionally sucked his thumb. 'It's not like we can spend the scrip, we're minors, not miners.' He giggled.

'Behrooz can spend it for us, and so can Ree.' If it came to that, which she hoped it wouldn't. 'It's not the taking part, Moosh, it's the winning.'

'It's probably forged anyway, you know what these gamblers are like. My dad once said—'

'Hush, this could be it.'

Behrooz yawned hugely, leaning back in his chair and issuing a silent howl. Javani tensed, ready to signal or wave, just to make contact, remind him that she was there. Her legs were beginning to tire and her backside was numb. He'd just lost another hand. His scrip was gone, the bleached and pitted blackwood of the table before him now vacant of stake. His fellow players were an odd-looking bunch, long-stayers, a couple wearing mail. They had fat bundles of scrip before them as well as loose coppers and a sliver of silver. She saw no Guild colours; Javani took them to be freelance muscle, probably waiting for the next caravan to pass before heading back south. One was due any day, this was the perfect time to pluck them. It was *such* a good plan.

And then, at last, the still-tilted Behrooz opened his gummy eyes and beheld Javani. She gesticulated wildly, mouthing furious curses, transmitting her orders with the ferocity of her expression. The light returned to his eyes as they widened.

'Finally,' she muttered. The wind had shifted beyond, and the moaning in the tower had mostly died.

Behrooz clomped back down on the forelegs of his chair, gave a theatrical swallow, and began patting his patchwork clothes. 'Fellas,' he said, 'you just about cleaned me out. I've nothing left for food and board, won't you show a little mercy on a luckless sort?'

Javani gave a narrow smile. That much was probably true.

'Should have considered afore,' one of the other players growled, one of the mail-clad. 'Man shouldn't risk what he can't lose.'

'You want any back,' another snarled, 'you play for it.'

'But I've nothing left,' Behrooz said, withdrawing his hand from his jerkin, 'save this old stone my mama left me.'

The players leaned forward as the blue jewel clonked onto the table, and Javani leaned with them. She could feel their excitement.

'Guess we could play a few more hands,' the mail-wearer said. 'If'n you cared to wager the stone.'

'Now, boys, this here stone is worth more to me—'

'We'll stake you. Saba, deal 'em out.'

Javani checked her view of the players' tiles as Behrooz glanced up in apparent consideration. She met his gaze with a smile of triumph.

'Let's spring this trap,' she whispered.

TWO

The shaded alley between the teahouse and the tatty chapel next door wasn't exactly cool, but compared to the scorching street beyond it was almost temperate. The more Behrooz capered, the sweatier he got, but his look of joyous triumph remained undimmed.

'We did it!' he cried. 'I did it. I tricked 'em. I tricked 'em good.'

'It's *called* a gambit, Behrooz.' Javani bunched her share of the scrip in her fist, tucked the blue stone into her shirt, and tried to calm the cavorting one-footed goon. He was a lot taller than she was, even bent on his crutch. Behind them, Moosh was making his way down the rickety ladder they'd laid against the wind tower, chattering to himself. 'Let's not make too much of an actual song and dance now.'

Moosh hopped from the ladder and dusted his palms. 'I can't believe that worked.'

Javani feigned mortal offence. 'How dare you? My gambits always work out, sometimes.'

He put a skinny arm around her shoulders, stretching up on his toes. 'Forgive my error of speech, I meant, of course, that I never doubted you for a moment.'

'That's more like it.'

They looked down at the bundled scrip in her hands. 'Shame it's useless, eh?' Moosh murmured.

'It would never have been enough anyway.'

He glanced up at her, a drip of sweat gleaming from his eyelashes. 'Enough for what?'

Javani's own gaze had travelled upwards, past the spreading lemon tree that swayed from the teahouse courtyard, past the mudbrick town walls, to the stark umber crags of the towering Ashadi mountains to the west, their looming face like the rucks of an unmade bed. The distant peaks wore a cloak of brilliant snow, even in the height of summer. 'You know what's on the other side of those mountains, Moosh?' She didn't wait for him to answer. Behrooz was still capering somewhere behind them, working himself into a triumphant frenzy. 'Arestan, they call it. Paradise. Adventure. Opportunity.'

'What's so good about the other side? Isn't it just like this?'

Javani shook her head. 'This is the dry side. Ree explained it: on any mountain range, you've got a wet side and a dry side. Over there it's lush with vegetation and plantations and olive groves and fruit trees and anyone can make a life for themselves away from this dirt and heat and squalor.'

'I do hear they grow really good olives there,' Moosh supplied.

'A proper life,' Javani murmured. 'Not like this gods-forsaken hole.'

Moosh tweaked her ear. 'Hey! That's my hole you're talking about, pay it the respect it is due.'

She wrestled him off her, fighting back giggles. 'I've no wish to discuss your hole, Moosh! It's far too close to lunch.'

He gave her a gentle shove. 'Besides, you know what they say . . .'

'No one gets over the Ashadi,' Javani intoned with a sigh.

'Too right,' Moosh replied with a fervent grin. 'There are tigers up there.'

'There are not.'

'There are! In the high forests. Great big stripy—'

'There are not!'

'I bet your aunt could handle a tiger anyway, that sword of hers, slash-slash! Tiger steaks!'

'Not a chance. She'd run a mile – "*we must be prudent*",' she mocked. 'That sword of hers is an antique, probably doesn't even have an edge. And she doesn't even use her crossbow for hunting these days.' Javani shook her head with a smile. 'Come on, we should move the ladder before someone—'

'Hey! You!'

Figures stood at the mouth of the alley, silhouetted by the glare of the dusty street beyond. Four figures, wide, tall, or both, two of them evidently in mail.

'Oh, shit,' Javani whispered. Behrooz had ceased his capering, and was sweating more than ever.

The men advanced down the alley, the widest in front. He was heavily bearded and wearing a sheet of dirty mail, and had a wide-bladed hatchet at his belt. He walked with a conspicuous limp, and his face bore the marks of convictions, perhaps robbery; those behind him were equally marked. He gestured at the ladder, at which Moosh had frozen. He was missing two fingers from the gesturing hand. 'What's this? You playing some kind of trick, one-foot?'

'It's *called* a gambit,' Behrooz said reflexively.

'You ran a rig on us? You cheated the Guvuli brothers?' The men were very close now, close enough to smell their reek. 'A man should think more than twice before pulling a play on Movos Guvuli.'

Javani stepped out from behind Behrooz. 'You two go. I'll handle this.'

Moosh and the cowering Behrooz stared at her, incredulous. She nodded firmly, and gestured for them to make themselves scarce. Moosh mouthed, 'Are you sure?' but she only increased the intensity of her dismissive hand-waving. Behrooz scarpered, capering away on his crutch without a backwards glance; Moosh departed with a look of deep suspicion. Javani held fast in the path of the menacing Movos Guvuli, not meeting his fierce gaze, waiting until the others were out of sight at the alley's end. Then, finally, she looked up, and nodded to him.

'Guvuli.'

'Urchin. This nonsense your doing?'

She cracked an easy grin, one peer joshing another. 'Sorry, Guvuli, had no idea it was you down there. Should have paid closer attention.

Here you go.' She reached out and pressed the bundle of scrip to his mail-clad chest. 'No harm done, eh?'

He let it hang there a moment, then took it with his truncated hand. His eyes hadn't left her, and his expression had not softened. 'And the stone?'

'Hmm?'

'That blue stone. We won that, fair and square. Seems you should be handing it over.'

Javani's smile was beginning to fracture at the edges. He was an awful lot taller than her, and his brothers filled the alley. A tiny half-thought began to assemble itself to the tune of perhaps she had overreached herself a tad, but she crushed it with sheer mental force. 'I'm just surprised, that's all,' she said, her voice loud and ringing from the mudbrick alley walls, 'that you'd have been gambling in the teahouse. I thought you would have been *preparing*.' She added a meaningful nod.

'We're prepared,' he growled, keeping his voice low, his brows lower. 'The final pieces are arriving with the caravan. And . . .' he licked his lips '. . . your contribution?'

Javani gave an arch nod, and reached a hand into her jacket. Movos put up his damaged hand. 'Wait. Boys!' With a quick set of gestures and whistles, he dispatched two lumbering Guvuli brothers to each end of the alley, waiting for the confirmatory nods before allowing Javani to continue. If Moosh had been peering from the teahouse courtyard, they'd have chased him away now. That didn't make Javani feel any safer.

'Continue, urchin.'

She withdrew a nub of charcoal from her faded jacket. Movos stared at it, then at her. 'Are you fu—'

'Do you have something to draw on? I was going to mark it out on the wall, but I suspect you might want to take it away with you.'

The lead Guvuli began patting at his mail, which jingled sadly. 'You ain't drawn it out already? When you were there?'

'How would that have looked? Me taking sketches of their architecture while wandering around?'

His eyes were narrow, dark brows lowered like thunderclouds. He pulled a roll of canvas from a pouch at his belt, but kept a tight and jealous hold on it. 'And you think you can draw it out from memory?'

'Yes.' She plucked the canvas from his grip and shook it out. It was already covered with markings.

'Hey! Careful with that!'

'What is this? A map?' She stared hard at the canvas. 'Is this what I think it is?'

'Never you mind. Use the other side.'

The other side was blank, or as blank as a scrap of rough material that had lived close to Movos's person for so long could be. It even smelled like him. She laid it gently on the sandy ground with the tips of her fingers.

Ignoring the pungent reek, she began to sketch with the charcoal. 'Here are the outer walls, here's the main gate, here's the ore-train entrance. Strongroom is here, beside the cells. This is the servants' stairway, the main stair would be off over here somewhere on the other side of the courtyard. Water pumps and garden terrace not shown, of course – I'm only drawing in two dimensions.'

She glanced up to check he was following. The burly tough was staring down at her, bearded mouth hanging open. 'Is this . . . is this accurate?'

'Course.'

'How?'

'Ree's in and out of there all the time working various schemes, and I trot around after her like a little pup.'

'But how . . . how do you remember?'

She tapped the charcoal against her temple, then regretted it and wiped at the mark. 'It's a memory game Ree and I used to play down south – we'd walk around a place, she'd ask me questions about it afterwards. How many floors, how many rooms, where the guards were, where the servants came and went, that sort of thing. Later she'd get me to draw maps, tell me how far wrong I'd gone.' She looked away wistfully. 'Used to give me a little sugared fruit if I didn't make too many mistakes.' She released a long breath. 'Not done it since I was small, but I've still got the habit.'

'You're still small.'

'Small*er*, then.'

'So where do we . . . you know. Put it?'

She stabbed her sketch with a grimy finger. 'Here. The cell block was the original strongroom, but when they built the new one they reused one wall and a lot of stone, carved out these little windows for a bit of light and air. Then, later, they built the terrace on top, and filled it with pools of water.' She added some flourishes to the sketch. 'There's far too much load along here. If this pillar were to, you know, *become weakened*, there should be enough pent-up force to bring down this outer wall, leaving here—'

His voice was almost reverent as he interrupted. 'A whole new entrance to the strongroom.'

'Damn straight. The key thing is acting on the shift change after the caravan arrives – the big doors will be open for loading and unloading, the place will be full of people milling around, if that wall comes down they'll scatter in panic and you can fill your boots. Should be at two bells.'

He was watching her closely, one finger on his bearded chin, the reverence of his gaze mingled with a glimmer of incredulity. 'How old are you, urchin?'

'I'll be fourteen next year.'

'When next year?'

She cleared her throat. 'Winter.'

'Huh.' The reverential moment had passed, and the mocking glimmer had returned to his gaze. 'I guess we won't be needing that blue stone after all, eh, little girl?' He snatched up the canvas and began to roll it, awkward with his maimed hand. She looked away, feeling her cheeks burn, resisting the urge to tuck the stone further under her shirt.

'No,' she muttered through gritted teeth. 'You pull this off right, Guvuli, we'll be drowning in ore and uncut gems, and whatever the smiths have worked through on site. You won't miss that one.'

'It sure was a nice stone, though. Where was it you said you got it?'

'*Speaking of which*, we need to talk about the exit.'

'The exit?'

'Guvuli, how are you going to get it all out of there, then out of the town before they hunt you down?'

'It's taken care of.' He straightened, the rolled canvas tight in his grip, and started walking back towards the alley mouth. Javani hopped up to keep pace.

'You're sure? I've allowed for confusion buying some escape time, but—'

'It's taken care of.' His irregular strides had become a swagger. The glare of the dusty street beyond lit their faces as they neared the alley's end, the buildings' shadows knife-edged black. Javani felt as if she was being left behind.

'And my share – I'll meet you on the trail outside? You need to give me enough time to get to the farm and back, bring my stuff.' She swallowed, her throat dry. 'And tell Ree. She won't be happy, but it'll be too late by then. She'll have to come west.'

Movos put his fingers to his mouth and whistled. In the whistle's echoes, Javani heard a rumble of approaching hoof-beats, heavy and jingling. Her next urgent question was stilled by the arrival of a giant vehicle at the alley's end. A wagon, at least in form, but low-axled and seemingly plated in steel beneath its canvas ribbing. Eight small, sturdy horses were hitched to its ludicrous frame. It was so massive it seemed to block out the sun.

'What in the name of all gods is that?'

Movos reached out and rubbed an appreciative hand over the flank of the nearest animal. 'The exit.'

The other Guvulis ambled past and began hauling themselves aboard. Javani tried to take in the sheer scale of the wagon, feeling her eyes trying to leave her head. 'But . . . But what *is* it?'

Movos Guvuli chuckled and scratched at his beard. 'Converted ore wagon. Once used for hauling precious goods through bandit territory down the southern road, 'til they realised barges don't guzzle barley the way these fellas do.' He patted the horse again, and nodded to the man on the wagon bench, a surly, skinny-looking type in a hooded cowl despite the day's punishing heat. 'Our friend Shantar made some modifications, of course. Knows a few things about the scientific arts.'

The hooded man tutted and tossed his head. 'I have told you more than enough times, you ursine coprophage, that my name is Abishantarayan.' He spoke with weary petulance and an odd accent. 'Not Shantar, not Abish, not Shantaran. You remember this? Of course you do not . . .'

Movos jerked a thumb at the driver's bench and grinned. It was a grin that had a lot of history behind it. 'Has a word with ways, does our Shantar.'

'. . . Because you are barely sentient muscle with the brain of a pubic louse,' the hooded man muttered behind him.

Javani was still staring at the four pairs hitched before the creaking monstrosity. 'What kind of horses are these?'

'Plains ponies, from the distant north. Mounts of kings.' He chuckled again. 'Took a sight more stealing than the wagon did. These fellas can run for days, haul this beast fully laden up a mountainside if need be. Good, strong boys.' He patted the nearest pony again, which snorted in a vaguely appreciative fashion. The pony looked like a mare to Javani, but she didn't press the point.

She took a step closer, risking a noseful of Movos Guvuli's musk. 'But it won't come to that, right? You've got a plan. Once they realise what's happened, every brass-fronted rider in mining country will be on us. So you have a plan, right? To escape? To get west over the mountains?'

'They get too close on the trail, Shantar's packed a few surprises in the back to, uh, discourage excessive proximity.'

'. . . My proper name, you piss-fingered necrophile . . .'

'You know the kind of reach the Guild has – we'll be hunted by every bugger with a mount and a sharp object!'

'Mind you listen, urchin. Too few understand the merit of listening.' Movos leaned over, his thick beard still stretched into a grin. 'You want to know how to shake a chaser? Simply make them think you're already dead. Our old lives die away, and we are reborn – like a butterfly.'

'More like a dung moth,' muttered Shantar.

Javani rubbed at her eyes. 'What? How? That isn't good enough!'

The grin vanished, and Movos Guvuli loomed, wide-eyed and bristling. 'Told you, urchin, it's taken care of, and no concern of yours.'

'There we disagree,' Javani squeaked, hating the rising pitch of her voice in the face of his growling bass. 'I need to know the details! Where to go, where to meet. The way west! I have to get ready, to get Ree.'

The heavy-lashed eyes narrowed to near slits, and from the corner of her eye she saw his grimy knuckles whiten. 'Your ma won't go running to the Guild types about this now, will she?'

'No, she won't, because by the time I tell her it'll be too late to do anything. And she's my aunt, not my ma.'

Movos Guvuli appeared to relax, a glimmer of white appearing in his glare. 'That's what I like to hear.' He swung himself up beside Shantar on the driver's bench. He whistled again, short and sharp.

'Don't fucking whistle at me,' the man beside him snapped. 'I told you before, if you must—'

'Just drive, Shantar, before my patience thins and I'm forced to castrate you from sheer exasperation.'

Still muttering, Shantar flicked the reins, and the groaning wagon began to move.

'Hey!' Javani called up, walking with a rising pace to keep up. 'What about me? How do we get over the Ashadi? Is there really a secret pass? Is that what the map was for? Where do I *meet* you?'

Movos looked serene, his eyes on the road ahead. 'You'll see us when we need you. You do your thing, urchin, we'll do ours. And all will be peaches.'

'You know that's really not any kind of—' she called up, breaking into a jog, but Movos whistled again and the wagon roared away from her, sending up a great wash of pale dust in its wake. She fell back, coughing, hands on her knees, eyes streaming with grit. By the time her vision had cleared, the wagon was long gone, leaving nothing but deep ruts in the powdery dirt and a lingering cloud of shimmering dust.

'Shit,' Javani said.

THREE

Six weeks ago, far to the south

Siavash Sarosh did not like to call himself a wealthy man – he preferred to have others do it for him. Few things, however, gave him greater pleasure than wandering through the stalls and stores of the north road's caravanserais, the travellers' way stations, sampling their myriad delights, while his own caravan rested and reassembled.

Stallholders greeted him by name as he shuffled through, proffering their wares – roasted pistachios, dried and candied fruit, various broths and local wines. Some even displayed a surprising variety of silks and carpets, all the more impressive given the collapse of the region's silk production a decade before. Siavash rested his hands on his pleasingly expanding paunch, the most visible signifier of his success, and nodded in benediction. He loved this caravanserai most of all: the last before the fort line, the last before the boundary of civilisation passed and there lay only the plains, the wild expanse, the land of opportunity.

Tearful farewells mingled with the honks of pack animals and traders' calls, the delicious scents of roasting and grilling sporadically overpowered by the matted stink of camels and dung. What opportunity it had proved, gods be praised! Not many merchants of his stature made the trips all the way north in person, but he was a happy minority. The contacts he had made, the accounts he had recorded, the connections built . . . all had coalesced into a most auspicious position and the promise of ever greater riches. Who would have thought a boy from such humble beginnings as his, growing up in a remote farming community in a backwater of the protectorate, could one day—

A shadow swept over him, blocking out the punishing northern sun. Siavash blinked in the sudden darkness, squinting up at the obstacle that now blocked his path.

'You are merchant?'

The voice was low and accented to an almost absurd degree. The thing before him was a person.

Siavash resummoned his gracious aspect. 'Ah, ha. I would say that I *employ* merchants, gods be praised. Perhaps my clerk can find someone who could—' he began.

'You go north?'

Siavash's eyes were adjusting to the pool of gloom that encompassed him. The figure towered over him, clad in a sweeping, thick cloak despite the day's heat. Beneath the cloak he thought he saw armour, and a lot of straps. Eyes narrowed, he peered up at the figure's head, haloed by the white sun it blocked. Braided cables of pale hair flowed from a large, lumpen head, its skin almost as white as the sun behind. It was not smiling.

'You're . . .' Siavash swallowed. 'You're of the Horvaun?'

The Horvaun. Even thinking the name almost brought Siavash out in a carpet of sweat. Bloodthirsty, pale-skinned savages of astonishing cruelty from the distant south, who had raided and plundered the furthest coasts of the Sink until they had been all but abandoned by what passed for civilisation down there. From the stories he had heard on the road, the Horvaun made the hated Mawn look like temple tutors. Why in the name of all the gods would one of them be here?

'You go north,' the figure repeated. This time it was not a question, and Siavash found himself nodding. He had no wish to irk a mighty reaver of the distant south. He had stared long enough to deduce the Horvaun was female, but he had no idea if that made things better or worse.

'You need . . . guards,' she said, and relief bloomed in Siavash's innards. Nothing more than muscle in search of work! His munificent smile returned.

'Ah, indeed and in truth,' Siavash said, gesturing for his aged clerk to scuttle up to join him. 'Of course, yes, my caravan will be guarded on the road north – we could hardly transport our cargo there and back without the pitted shield of protection, eh?' The smile widened with indulgence. 'But, kind visitor, I am Siavash Sarosh' – how he loved to use his name in public – 'and my caravan is an official conveyance of the Serican protectorate. We have a veritable abundance of guards, supplied and outfitted by the Miners' Guild.'

The giant Horvaun frowned, not in anger but in thought. Siavash was sure he could hear her armour creaking over the noise of the caravanserai. A tattoo marked her face, not a conviction but something decorative that bisected one brow and cheek. Something long and thin with a pointed end, perhaps a spear? 'How many?' she growled.

'How many?'

'How many . . . guards.'

Siavash waved a hand at his clerk. 'Do you consider us well-guarded, Ulfat?'

'Incontrovertibly so, master,' the clerk replied, his own accent still thick despite more than a decade north of the gorge. 'Plentiful guards both mounted and on foot, with archers placed among the wagons.'

'You see, blessed visitor?' Siavash had recovered himself now, although he had made a mental note to keep a couple of guards with him in future when wandering the caravanserai. 'We have no need of further help.'

'We number five,' the giant countered. 'We have business in north. Important business. Urgent business. We travel with you.'

Siavash offered a tight smile. 'A thousand apologies, gracious visitor. Guild caravans may permit no travellers by regulation.

Mining equipment and supplies, too precious a cargo, you understand!' Not to mention the crates of semi-legal weaponry and alchemical precursors he was transporting. 'I wish you every favour of the gods in your journey.' He began to shuffle past, the clerk at his heel.

'My gods grant no favours,' the woman rumbled as he passed, but she did not follow.

Siavash continued his tour of the retailers, skirting the glare of the courtyard and doing his best to stay upwind of the few camels kept in the far stalls. Camels were uncommon on the north road, but occasionally an enterprising type might bring some this way having crossed from the east. They were always kept separate; their stink upset the horses more than it did the merchants, and that was saying something.

When Siavash stopped to sample a frozen delight of syrup and saffron, declared fresh from the ice pit at the caravanserai's rear, he looked back across the baked and bustling courtyard. The big Horvaun was on the upper balcony, leaning on the rail in the slanted shade of the gallery. She was staring right at him.

Siavash told himself that his shiver came from only the ice.

Siavash was completing his handwashing in an ornate basin when Ulfat the clerk approached at a trot. It was a little ritual he enjoyed in advance of departure, especially after eating a lot of sticky plums, and it gave him something to do while his clerk settled their levies with the gate officials. He hated to involve himself directly in the necessary backhanders, and having clean hands was pleasing in both a literal and figurative sense.

'Ulfat! Are we all paid up and ready to leave?'

'We are master, but there is . . . a complication.'

Siavash wiped his hands on one of the finer cottons reserved for caravan heads. 'What is the complication, Ulfat?'

'We are short in number, master. A number of guards have not rejoined the caravan.'

'What? Which? How many?'

'Denk and his brothers, and their cousin Erol.' The clerk scratched at his collar. 'Five in all. I have sent men to check the stalls and upper floor, but there is no sign.'

Siavash pursed his lips. 'Possibly they have made local friends, but we cannot wait for them to sate themselves and slither back. Gods grant us favour! Five is too many to travel without.'

Something enormous blotted the sun and cast Siavash into a familiar darkness.

'You need . . .' came the rumble '. . . guards?'

Five weeks ago, still far to the south

Siavash was pleased at the progress the caravan was making. They had left behind schedule, he knew, but it had been worth the wait for the last of the lesser-advertised goods to catch up and be loaded aboard the hidden compartments of his larger wagons. If they arrived a few days late at their final destination, he suspected he'd hear little complaint from those he intended to serve.

The convoy made good speed across the plains, travelling in the flattened footsteps of the countless thousands who had gone before, including, of course, Siavash himself on several occasions. This time, however, he enjoyed their sedate pace from the comfort of his own wagon, beneath beautiful silk coverings, watching the sparse country roll by while shaded from the punishing sun. It was a civilised place from which to enjoy some candied apricots and quince juice. Ahead of him, the scouts ranged over the ridges on their ponies, watching for bandits and ensuring water and resting locations, while his guards kept stride alongside the wagons, both mounted and afoot.

Ah yes, his guards. They were well out from the fort line now, into the real wild country, and it would be many days before they would see a town again. It was common, even for seasoned guards and mercenaries, to be constantly on edge, mindful of the capricious weather and terrain as much as tales of bandits or rampaging

Mawn. Even those among his staff who had made the trip with him several times were conspicuously vigilant, the riders closest to his wagon alert and upright in their stirrups, spears never out of their hands.

But those they'd collected at the final caravanserai were different. There were five of them, as the Horvaun had promised, walking with an easy swagger near the head of the column. The other four were not of the same size and scale as the giant southerner, but none was small: the shortest in height was almost a cube, with a chest like an aurochs'. Despite the heat, they wore their cloaks at all times, and beneath them Siavash imagined they wore fearsome and prodigious armour. They rarely spoke, even to each other, and sat apart from the rest of the caravan guards and staff when they stopped at night. They never took part in overnight watches, and growled when approached.

They looked truly menacing, and Siavash was delighted.

Four weeks ago, to the south

The servants were heating the water for Siavash's bath and constructing his bed when Ulfat entered the tent. He looked more nervous than normal.

'Ulfat?' Siavash was down to his robe, polishing off the last of his dinner, saffron rice with dates and salted lamb. The further they were from towns, the smaller the portions became, he rued. 'Gods grant me peace, I prefer not to be disturbed at this hour.'

'I am aware, master,' the old clerk mumbled in his appalling accent. 'There's trouble outside.'

'Can't you handle it? Your purview encompasses—'

'It's the guards, master. And those . . . mercenaries.'

'Ah.'

Siavash pushed his last mouthful aside with a sigh, took a swallow of lemon juice, then followed the clerk.

The last red drips of sun had bled away into the black western horizon, and the sky to the east was already a deep indigo of prickled stars, as rich and glittering as one of Siavash's most prized silks. He knew they were the same stars he watched from the south, from the safety and comfort of his thick-walled home (thick-walled, yes, but large enough that a visitor might be more dazzled by the high ceilings, or the colonnaded courtyards in which Siavash would hold forth on his adventures), but out here they had a magical quality, somehow more boundless, infinite, unfathomable. The sky always seemed bigger out on the expanse, more alive with possibility. He sighed again. What was life, after all, without a zest for adventure?

He made a mental note to have Ulfat bring his journal before he retired to bed. These thoughts were too important to be lost to the desert wind.

The wagons were pulled up alongside the trail, the horses corralled, fed and watered, the working staff likewise, around two large fires. As the sun dropped behind the mountains, the temperature did the same, and Siavash shivered in his robe. Ulfat led him towards the second fire, but the rising noise rendered the old clerk's guidance redundant.

Those guards who were not on watch were sitting around that fire, or should have been. Instead, they were gathered, with increasing discontent, a few strides from where the mercenaries sat with their own meal, their backs to the rest of the camp.

'They think they're too good to eat with us!' One of the guards was a little in front of the others, half addressing them, half the seemingly oblivious mercenaries. Siavash was disappointed, but not surprised, to see it was Mehrez, one of his least favourite Guild hires. A wiry, bulb-eyed man who was rarely still, he had every hallmark of a leaf-chewer bar the bulging jaw. Siavash would cheerfully have waved him off onto fresh ventures long ago, but one of his cousins was just high enough in the Guild's bureaucracy to make things prickly.

'They think they're too good for watch duty!' Mehrez went on. 'They think they're too good to dig latrines!'

Ulfat was struggling to keep up as Siavash quickened his pace. 'I came for you as soon as it started, master,' he managed in a breathless whisper.

Mehrez spotted Siavash's approaching silken bulk. 'And here's the caravan-master. Going to tell us how much more these foreigners are being paid to do half the work?'

Siavash raised a palm in both greeting and placation. This was a thorny one. For a start, the guards he normally relied on as his personal protection were among the mass behind Mehrez, and their faces weren't radiating an abundance of unquestioning loyalty. Beyond that, he hadn't actually discussed rates with the big Horvaun; he'd rather assumed that they'd be paid the standard rate per way-stop, and their refusal to engage in some of the less pleasant duties could perhaps be addressed come the settling-up, when he had many more guards around him. It would be a little indelicate to attempt that explanation now, in front of all the interested parties, while dressed in his bed robe.

'What troubles us this blessed night?' he said, in place of anything helpful. Perhaps making Mehrez restate his case would sap some of his indignation. The Horvaun and her crew had yet to move, still sitting off to one side with their backs to the growing scene.

Mehrez was unsapped. 'We're out here, risking our necks for basic Guild rates, travelling across deserts and mountains and waterless plains, facing storms and insects and—'

'Was that not what you considered yourself signed up for?'

'—away from our families for months at a time—'

'Forgive me, I wasn't aware you had much family, Mehrez.'

'—paying our dues, serving time, doing everything asked of us—'

'And how is your cousin in Administration?'

'—while these savages swan on in and take the head of the column, swerve all the shit-work, and take triple rate for it!'

Siavash frowned. 'They're not getting triple rate.'

Mehrez wasn't listening. 'They're only on the job in the first place because they killed Denk and his brothers! They're killers!

Justice for Denk!' He pulled his dagger from his belt and advanced on the mercenaries. A few others took up the chant behind him.

'Mehrez, stop!' Siavash was losing control of the situation. He searched the faces of the guards, looking for his personal detail, his seasoned campaigners, his stalwarts. No eyes would meet his.

Mehrez was within a few strides of the mercenaries when the Horvaun rose to her feet and turned. She did it so quickly – a single, fluid motion – that he actually stumbled in his approach.

'You wish . . . speak?' she said to him. She was a head taller, still in the great dark cloak, her hands lost somewhere within it. Siavash was sweating all over. He had to stop this, before blood was spilled. Losing caravan guards to bandits, sickness or terrain was unfortunate, but considered unavoidable. Internecine struggle, on the other hand—

Mehrez raised his dagger. 'You're hired killers, assassins. You shouldn't be here. Kenan recognised you, says he knows who you really are.'

'You wish . . . kill us?'

'If that's what it takes. Or you and your lackeys walk into the salt and let the desert take the credit.'

The Horvaun raised her head, surveying the other guards behind him. Most still wore their armour and weapons, even when off duty. Unlike Siavash, they did not have tents and baths.

'Others . . . agree?' she rumbled. The other four mercenaries were still sitting with their backs to Mehrez and the guards. Siavash thought they might be playing dice, or something with small bones. Their lack of interest terrified and electrified him.

'They do,' Mehrez snarled.

'Come, then.' The Horvaun gestured with a great white hand, signalling Mehrez forward. Mehrez hesitated for a moment, the dagger heavy in his grip. Siavash tried to speak, but could find nothing to say.

Mehrez lunged. The giant's arm flashed out from the cloak, catching his hand and driving it wide. The second hand slammed into his throat, staggering him, then snatched the dagger from his spasming hand. The dagger punched four times into his torso, once into each eye socket, then finally whipped across his throat, before the woman released him and let his gurgling, twitching body fall. The dagger clattered down next to it, quickly swallowed by the blood soaking into the rocky earth.

Nobody moved. The giant swept her gaze over the stationary guards.

'Others . . . agree?' she said again, and as one they turned and shuffled back to the fire, resuming their meals and chatter as if nothing had occurred. The Horvaun stood for a moment longer, then sat back down with her crew. Mehrez convulsed and bubbled for a little longer before falling still.

Ulfat was beside Siavash. 'I'll have the servants bury the body later, master, once they finish their other duties. I'll record his death as . . . natural causes?'

'Mm. Yes.' Siavash nodded, staring at the spreading patch of darkness around the body. He wondered if it would be glossy enough to reflect the twinkling blanket of stars above.

'Your bath is probably ready now, master.'

'Indeed, Ulfat. Indeed and in truth.'

Later, as he relaxed in his bath and contemplated, Siavash concluded that in many ways, the evening's outcome had been rather good.

FOUR

Four weeks ago, far to the east

Anashe kicked her brother awake, sending him sprawling from his bed of sagging crates and onto the cracked and salted flagstones of the dock. 'Get up. Get up, you worthless fool.'

'Mercy of the heavens, my sister!' He bounced to his feet, rubbing an injured elbow. 'What manner is this to wake your brother from his reverie? I was having the most extraordinary dream, a vision of truth and distance. A message from beyond. And I know that—'

'Aki,' Anashe warned with a growl, her fist raised.

His grin spread like a slow dawn, despite his bleary eyes. 'I have seen it, my sister – the Goddess will provide. She wills it. We must persevere.'

Anashe let her fist fall. Above the shadow of the rotting warehouse beside them, the sun climbed overhead in a crystal sky, wheeling seabirds sparkling in its light. 'What we must do today, brother, is find a ship that will grant us passage back south for the meagre coin in our purses.'

'My sister—'

'Once we are back in Arowan, there will be work more suited to our skills. We are not sailors, Aki, and nor are we dock-loaders.'

'There is coin to be made here, Anashe, but—'

She held out a hand. 'And where is it? Where is the coin you made with your tavern tales, that kept you out until dawn?'

He looked pained. 'It was a bountiful harvest, my sister, but there were others there whose need in the moment was far greater than ours. There will be more coin to be made with my stories, but that poor young thing had—'

'By the Goddess, Aki! You gave it to a girl again, didn't you?'

'Her family had deserted her! She had—'

Anashe raised her hand, silencing him. When she spoke again it was with the low, quiet voice their uncle had used when they had disappointed him. 'Today we will find a ship, one that will at least grant us permission to board. We can work to earn our place if necessary.' She flicked a glance at her brother. 'Or one of us can.'

Now Aki snorted and stood tall. 'Nonsense, my sister. We will persevere. We will cross the plains, not turn back.'

'Without supplies? Without mounts? Without coin for either? No caravans travel that way from this place, Aki, there is nothing to stow away on. We will never garner the necessary here!' She leaned close, her voice a whispered hiss. 'There is nothing to steal, and nowhere to fence. We have been here for weeks and never even made it all the way over the Ucrali, and they barely count as mountains.' She gestured to the low, muddy peaks that climbed behind the port of Kermastar, basking in the morning light. 'We *must* turn back.'

She began to walk away from the warehouses, towards the teeming wharves. Aki trotted to keep up with her, still rubbing his elbow.

'I know the way. I will cross on foot if I must.'

'Cross the plains on foot? The salt desert? You will die of thirst.'

'I can smell water.'

'I can smell goat dung.' She stopped at the edge of the weathered dock, toes gripping the edges of the water-softened boards through her thin boots, cool sea breeze blowing salt against her cheeks. 'You will die of something else then, something absurd. Something that will reach people only as rumour, as legend, and they will not dare believe anyone could have been so foolish.'

Aki's indignation puffed him up like a bull turkey. 'Then leave me to do so, and we shall see who is right! I will depart at dusk.' He turned to stalk away.

She caught his arm. 'Aki! Brother!' Her voice softened. 'You know I cannot.'

Some of his righteous inflation eased, and when he spoke it was with raw emotion. 'I will not give her up, my sister. I will find us a way. The Goddess will smile upon us, as she smiled on Qhodis and welcomed him home to the heavens. I will find us a way. She wills it.'

Anashe tried to sound mollifying. 'Please, Aki, it is time to start—' she began, but he was looking past her.

'What kind of ship is that?' he said.

Anashe and Aki wandered down the dock towards the strange new vessel. Aki greeted Bilig, another daytime dock-sleeper, who had roused himself from the warehouse's far side. He was a slight, hunched man of Mawnish heritage, afflicted by a creeping corruption that had already taken half of his face and a few of his teeth. Anashe did not like the way he looked at her. 'Bilig, my friend, what kind of ship is that?'

The ship tied at the closest pier differed from the standard merchant sails, their bellies groaning with cargo and the occasional transit bond-holder. This one was smaller, stranger, single-masted and bore odd colours.

'A Shenakar coast-hopper,' Bilig said, whispering spittle. Bilig knew about ships; as he told it, he'd spent a good number of his years plundering coastal traffic before the sickness had taken him. 'Look at her curves.' He'd no doubt have whistled if he still had the lips for it. 'Could be she came all the way from Shenak!'

'Shenak is a thousand miles on a short course,' Anashe snapped. 'All that matters is where it will head next, and whether the captain will deign to let us aboard.' It had funny little notches down its flank. A sound from the vessel gave her a start. Her head tilted. 'Is that—'

'Horses,' Bilig said with a grotesque smile. 'She's carrying horses.'

Anashe leaned against a mooring post. She could feel the excitement radiating from her brother. 'Madness to carry beasts at sea,' she murmured. 'There are plenty of animals to be traded here.'

Bilig grinned his vile grin again. 'Could be they're special horses. Very *valuable* horses. Worth a closer look, for anyone of an enterprising mind . . . and moral flexibility . . .'

The gangways were down by the time Aki and Anashe reached the ship, dock-types already rolling barrels and kegs down to the pier. Those that recognised the pair gave them a wide berth; they were too friendly with Bilig, and those that worked the docks feared his sickness more than sharks.

'She *is* from Shenak,' Anashe murmured, watching a barrel pass at speed. 'All is grapes down there; wine and brandy and . . .' She tailed off, fighting against a tide of surging memories. Memories she'd worked hard to suppress.

Aki had moved ahead of her and she stepped to keep up. The first of the horses was coming down the gang, led by a man in a fine half-cloak that barely reached past his belt. A beautiful creature, tall, glossy and muscled; the rider was equally arresting. A second horse followed, its uncertainty on the gang tempered by the firm confidence of the calm-eyed woman leading it. Anashe watched with calculating eyes. The horses were indeed special, but the chances of separating them from their escorts seemed vanishingly small.

She studied the group at the far gang as more horses descended, fourteen in all, to eight humans. Aside from the brevity of their cloaks, they wore unremarkable coverings, but their equipment beneath gleamed, and their hair was oiled and coiffed despite the length of their voyage. On the lead man, a dazzlingly handsome type with a long, groomed moustache, she caught a glimpse of a jewelled scabbard. She nudged Aki.

'Our horse-traders do not lack for displays of wealth,' she murmured, eyes fixed on the glimmer. 'Perhaps they have brought a few more trinkets than they can track. If we were to—'

The man was approaching, walking with an unsteady sea-gait

down the pier. The calm-eyed woman followed at his shoulder. She had strange markings down her forearms, dots and lines, and Anashe spotted a long Shenakar sabre sweeping beneath her half-cloak. They all looked reliably, casually armed. This was an opportunity that demanded patience and a delicate touch.

The man hailed them, or seemed to, but whatever words he used were nonsense to Anashe. At her blank look, he shot a disarming grin and tried again. On the third attempt, he managed some fairly decent High Serican. 'Blessings of the gods and saints to you, master, my lady. Forgive my impertinence, but might I request some information?'

Anashe paused. She'd expected the man to go past. He and his crew, freshly arrived, would go in search of lodgings and livery, and would become relaxed and stationary for a time, while Anashe and Aki seized on the chance to make up for their relative poverty of opportunity. Patience and a delicate touch. But the newcomer had perhaps mistaken the berth the dock-types gave them for respect, and taken them as figures of local importance. Maybe it was Aki's beaming smile, or her own calculating stare – it was possible they'd been taken for tax officials. Whatever the cause, it was a complication: you were not supposed to talk to those you planned to rob. Humanising them seemed like bad manners.

'How may we serve, sire?' she replied with an uncharacteristically bright smile, all too aware that her own Serican, High or otherwise, was a little short of flawless.

'The grace of the gods and a thousand thanks to you both. In the light of the sacred fire, my name is . . . Lazant,' the young man said, running a hand over his moustache and offering them his broad grin again, 'and my friends and I must travel west and north, as fast as we can. I understand that there are few ways through these mountains,' he continued with a nod to the hazy brown peaks beyond them, 'and yet fewer ways across the plains and desert beyond. Forgive the imposition, but can you aid us in finding a guide? We can offer generous payment and expenses. Our need is dire.'

Anashe worked hard to keep her expression in check. Wherever this young man needed to go, he would be carrying his means of payment – for supplies, for services and lodgings, for whatever business he intended to conclude – with him. His undergarments had to be stuffed with silver. It was staggering he didn't clank as he walked.

Aki had surged past her. 'Master Lazant, did you say west and north? May I ask the name of your destination?'

Lazant withdrew a small roll of something that could have been paper from his cloak and glanced at what was written within. 'To mining country. The furthest reaches of the protectorate, a town called Kazeraz. As fast as possible.'

Anashe's mouth fell open. She turned to Aki, tried to raise her hands to stop him, tried to say something, the right thing, a quick thing, but she was far too late.

'Master Lazant, truly the Goddess shows us her favour today,' Aki beamed, near-glowing in the sunlight. 'My sister and I are expert guides, she to the mountains, I to the plains. We would be honoured to guide you and your friends in your travels.'

The young man beamed in return and signalled for the other horses and riders to join them. 'Most auspicious news, praise be to the Highest.'

Anashe was still flapping her jaw, in danger of catching flies. She scrambled. 'Master Lazant, the . . . the . . . the plateau is vast, it is a journey of . . . *ludicrous* proportions!'

The young man nodded, his eyes earnest, his smile firm. 'I understand, but duty commands. We shall, of course, cover the necessary mounts and provisions for yourselves. Please, give us a short time to collect ourselves, and then we can be away.'

'But *why?*' Anashe cried, then caught herself. 'If you'll permit me to ask the nature of your voyage, Master Lazant.' She glanced at the magnificent animals being led down the wharf towards them. 'You'll have to trade in your horses en route, several times, and what you get back . . . may not be horses.'

Lazant took the bridle of his mount from a rigid subordinate. 'I have to find someone,' he said. His eyes fixed on the mountainous horizon and his smile faded. 'It is vital I find them before others do, and something terrible happens.'

Anashe looked to her brother, seeking some acknowledgement of the incongruity, the improbability, but he merely bounced on his toes, exulting in his triumph.

'You see, my sister?' he said in a low and joyous voice. 'Kazeraz. She wills it! The Goddess provides!'

Three and a half weeks ago, still far to the east

Anashe did not like the mountains. Perhaps it was her heritage, something ingrained in her bones; perhaps the years of her life spent out in open country, where the only limit to your vision was the eyes you were born with. They built tall on the plains: tall tents and shelters, tall lodges and clan-halls, reaching up to the rolling skies. She didn't mind the cities, for the most part – as long as the masons were good and the stench somewhere short of overpowering.

But everything was wrong in the mountains. Sloping walls of rock rose on each side, even through the shallow pass that she and her brother by now knew so well. Dwellings, where they saw them, were squat, embarrassed things, low and wide, as if ashamed of their existence before the soaring peaks crowding overhead. All she saw each time they crested a ridge or emerged from a furrow were more mountains.

These weren't even the worst of them. Despite its name, the plateau was not flat; it was riddled, infested with ranges, shot through with mountainous spines like a curse victim. Those to the plateau's east, those through which Aki and Anashe were leading the Shenakar nobles, were the smallest, most sedate of the lot, the Ucrali; their route rarely raised them above foothills. The nobles' stated destination, however, the mining country to the far north-west, was the most accursed ground of all: nestled between two ranges, the Ashadi and the Ascori; the first towering and savage, the second merely unpleasantly high. Between those ranges, the miners and other parasites burrowed into the earth to plunder its treasures, scurrying beneath the teetering fury of monstrous rock, at any moment ready to collapse and crush them to paste. Anashe shivered at the thought.

The sound of an approaching horse raised her attention: Aki was returning. He offered his wide smile to the waiting Shenakar before reining in beside Anashe.

'I have scouted,' he said in a loud voice. 'There is a trading post at the foot from which we may purchase supplies for the next stage of our journey.'

'Very good, Master Aki,' Lazant called back. 'And you saw no sign of bandits? I understand that ambushes are common in these lands.'

'We are accredited guides, Master Lazant. You have nothing to fear.'

Anashe was still thinking about the mines, the tunnels, the sheer weight of earth over the miners' heads. It was against the teachings of the Goddess, to dig like that. They'd stir up the demon spirits of the earth, the minions of Usdohr, drive them to vengeance with their avarice. Mining country. She spat down at the rock underfoot.

Aki gave her a sidelong look, then pulled his mount closer and murmured, 'Please do not spit in front of the clients, my sister. They will think you uncivilised, and may insist on teaching you the ways of polite company. While I would delight to see such a thing, it would delay us on our onward journey, which is a cost I am not prepared to pay.'

'Aki,' she murmured back, 'is this wise? We are no more accredited than a desert hedgehog, and far more likely to attract predators.'

'My sister, we have been back and forth across these hills more times than I can count—'

'As many as three?'

He snorted with exasperation. 'We have never once had trouble with unwanted attention.'

'When every time it was just the two of us, running wide from anything that moved. This group cannot run, it cannot hide in gullies, it cannot tread soft and quiet below moonlit ridges. These birds will be plucked before we reach the foot, and us along with them – when it should have been us doing the plucking!'

'Cease your worry, Anashe. The Goddess has provided, and I will not refuse her gift.'

Anashe shook her head, the muscles of her jaw sharp and hard. 'You're the worst plucker of all.'

Three and a bit weeks ago, still very much to the east

'But how do we know that words come from the head?'

'We see from the head. And hear, and smell, and taste.'

'I smell from other places.'

'I do not disagree, brother.'

'But we feel with our skin, with our whole bodies! Could we not also make our words with our bodies?'

'Words are expressions of ideas. Ideas are formed in the brain. Think of the injured brains we've encountered, and the effects on the thoughts of their owners.'

'I disagree. I know what I feel.'

'And what is that, Aki?'

'I feel my words in my soul. It is from my soul that my poetry springs.'

'And where in your body does the soul reside?'

'In my heart, of course, sister.'

The wind that rustled the spare shrubs sounded exactly like a sigh.

'The next time we encounter an open chest cavity, shall we dissect the heart within? Perhaps, like you, it will drown us with words.'

Anashe sighed and looked over to the trading post, a battered wagon with some barely functional guards lounging alongside it. The lead Shenakar, Lazant, the handsome one with the long moustache and charming smile, had dismounted, as had his calm-eyed lieutenant. Anashe had been trying to work them out on their ride through the pass. He seemed in charge, and in possession of the best gear, but he seemed to defer to her on nearly everything. If they were some kind of military force, she couldn't work out a chain of command. Perhaps they were married.

Her eyes travelled over the wagon, the low wooden stalls set either side, the shape of the rough canvas tent pitched just up the slope, and suddenly her eyes went wide. Anashe didn't recognise the traders, but she did recognise the bloodstains and fresh graves.

'By the Goddess,' she breathed, sitting up straight in the saddle.

Aki, midway through a discourse on the emotional resonance of the words of the true poet, glanced to her. 'What is it, my sister?'

Anashe scanned the scene before them. If you knew to look, you could see the outlines of the clubs and bows, just hidden from view or tucked beneath canvas, ready to be snatched up when the signal came. Anashe knew where to look. These people were nowhere near the most convincing merchants she'd ever seen. They were barely convincing bandits.

The other Shenakar had likewise dismounted now, all six of them, and the hoods were doing their best to look like the kind of people with enticing supplies. Anashe had only seen the shallow diggings from her vantage at the top of the slope. The Shenakar were blind to them.

'Aki, these people are murderous thieves,' she whispered. 'Your birds are about to be plucked!'

Aki gasped. 'We must warn them!' He snatched up his reins.

She shot out a hand, grabbing his wrist. 'Wait. Wait, brother. Distasteful as it is, if we lend a hand to those doing the plucking, we can claim a share. Enough to get back to the protectorate, to Arowan. Enough to pick up where we left off.'

Aki flexed in her grip, his teeth bared. 'For what, for why, my sister? We know what the Commodore told us, and we know where we must go. The truth of our hearts lies in Kazeraz. She wills it! What good is coin in a life without understanding, without meaning?'

Anashe squeezed harder, dragging his attention back to her. 'You are mad, brother, the plains or the desert will claim us all, coinless, meaningless, bleached bones in sand. And what will we have achieved then? What great mark will you have left on this world? Aki, I want to go home to Arowan. I want to be *comfortable*!'

'Then leave, my sister,' he hissed. 'But I will not give up.'

She flung his arm away. 'One day I will leave you to die.'

He shook out his arm, then snatched up his reins again. 'And I will be glad to leave you by dying!' He kicked the horse into a run, pulling away from her. 'Master Lazant, Master Lazant! These people mean to rob and murder you!'

Lazant stopped walking, as did his second. His eyes scanned the supposed merchants before them, suddenly alert and searching.

'Khalida,' he said slowly, 'I believe our guide is right.'

'I believe you are correct, Zakir,' she replied. She remained maddeningly calm, but raised one hand, fingers up, then pointed at the wagon.

'Mother always said I was too trusting,' Lazant said ruefully, his hand going to his sword.

A bandit threw the canvas off the wagon's side with a yell, and the hoods seized their arms. The Shenakar leapt into formation, swords flashing out from their cloaks, three making for the horses.

With a weary sigh, Anashe reached for her axe.

One week ago, a little to the south

The caravan was well into mining territory now, the mountains rising on both horizons as they made their way north. The western mountains were vast, brown-blue things, still capped with snow even as they travelled beneath fierce sun. They'd enjoyed successful stops at three of the fortified mining outposts – so much to trade, and the prices he could charge were simply outrageous – but Siavash was looking forward to their final stop most of all. The last of his goods were kept back for special purchasers, and the crowning glory of his fortune would come with them.

The increasing savagery of the terrain made the going harder and reduced the rate of progress, as did frequent stops to fix wagon wheels and axles, and occasionally reshoe horses. They mostly followed the rivers, minimising crossings and staying close to fresh water. The towns were far apart, which should have made Siavash nervous, but this far from civilisation he felt as if they were the only people in the world.

With the sun not yet at its peak behind fast-moving fluffy banks of cloud, the mercenaries stopped walking. Ahead, the terrain narrowed and kinked through a valley of bleached red rock, the ribbon of white river they followed the only colour not within a few shades of beige. The rest of the caravan kept moving, the other guards giving the five cloaked figures wary looks but no more.

Siavash's wagon pulled alongside, and he signalled for it to stop. The five were crouching off to one side of the trail, sharing a pouch of chewing nuts. It looked as though they were going to play dice again.

Siavash cleared his throat. 'Is there any particular reason why you've stopped?' he called.

The Horvaun pushed herself upright and walked with slow steps over to the wagon. Ahead, the leads had noticed that the caravan-master had stopped, and reined in accordingly. The day was bright and hot, the air still and cloying; it felt as if they were due a storm. The only movement in the valley seemed to be the swishing of horses' tails or the waving of sweaty gauntlets, each in service of batting away the persistent feasting insects of the land.

The Horvaun snorted then spat a great rattling measure of trail dust into a wiry shrub at the trailside. 'Ambush,' she said, with a half-hearted wave towards the steep rock ahead.

'What?'

'Your scouts . . . lost. Probably dead.'

Siavash blinked and rubbed his eyes, then leaned out of the wagon and stared up at the streaked crags. 'You're sure?'

She shrugged.

'And were . . .' He cleared his throat again. 'Were you going to say anything to anyone else?'

She shrugged again.

Siavash felt his cheeks grow hot. Without the gentle breeze of travel, it was getting warm beneath his canopy, but he was really quite upset.

'Now listen here, mercenary,' he said.

'Yes?' She looked up, straight at him, and he shrank back a little. The spear tattoo down her cheek was really very unsettling.

'Yes, listen here,' he continued, trying to keep the quiver from his voice. 'You're being paid to guard this caravan, and that includes protecting it from ambushes. You could start by mentioning it when you're aware of one! We may not have a contract, but this is part of the job! What were you going to do, let them attack us, then rejoin the survivors later?'

She shrugged again. 'What do, then?'

Siavash rubbed his eyes. 'I don't know, go up and ambush the ambushers? You're the professionals here!' He looked around, but none of the other guards had approached. After Mehrez, they wanted as little to do with the mercenaries as possible.

The woman put one white finger on her white chin, pondering, then nodded.

'You wait.'

She strode back to the other mercenaries, exchanged a few words, then the cloaks came off and the helmets went on. Siavash marvelled at the armour beneath; it wasn't gleaming or ostentatious, but it had the look of very well-made and well-kept stuff. The weapons were similar; axes and spears were hefted, bows were strung, then with an unseen signal they set off, jogging up and over the scattered rock, swifter and surer than Siavash had thought possible. In a few breaths they were out of sight.

He sat back on his cushions. It was getting unpleasantly warm beneath the canopy.

'Ulfat,' he said after a moment, just as the first cries and screams echoed from up the valley, 'we need to organise some new scouts.'

FIVE

Ree rode hard, her mind bouncing in time with her horse's gait. The kid had gone off on little adventures before without mishap. Ree trusted her enough not to do anything catastrophically dim, but also because she didn't want to be seen to mother her. There were two reasons for that.

The girl needs to know how to fend for herself, she told herself. Needs independence. Self-reliance.

But her mind was racing, galloping away over dark hillsides towards chasms of conclusion. Someone was asking about her, trying to track her down, but who? She cursed herself for not making more of an effort to disguise herself, to cover the scar, recolour her hair. It was so hard to stay hidden for ever. She'd told herself there were plenty of scarred, white-haired women in this part of the world, who'd notice another?

But the eyes. They always remembered her eyes.

Who, then? Who was hunting her? There was no shortage of candidates; she'd led a long and . . . interesting . . . life, and left a lot of people in her wake who might feel their business was unfinished. The focus on the kid, though – that bothered her. Who else knew about the kid? Surely nobody in the protectorate, even down to Arowan itself. She'd been gone from there before anyone . . . Further south, then. The Sink. Or across the sea?

Too many variables, too many possibilities. She had to find the kid, and fast. If someone had really tracked them down . . . They'd have to up sticks again, and she was just getting settled after the last move. A farm, this time, with horses, permanent structures, building plans. But where was left to go? Out into the desert plains with the missionaries? Over the great red mountains to the west? Kurush had been right, this was the edge of the world, the edge of nowhere. The prick.

Her entry into the town was delayed at the gates; another preaching expedition was heading out into the plains, its wagons piled high, but one had cracked a wheel-rim in a hard-packed rut on the way out and now lay blocking the gates, listing so far towards the broken wheel that the storm-blackened tree lashed to the wagon's front had almost torn from its mooring and flattened the rest of their supplies. As Ree reined in, a collection of wild-eyed types – long of hair and beard, where applicable, and decorated with whirling tattoos on their exposed arms and legs – were engaged in tense remonstration with the Guild-goons on the gate, none of whom seemed the slightest inclined to lift a finger to help.

Ree watched the argument for a moment, pondering her options. The other gate was reserved for Guild business alone, and even with her powers of persuasion she had no desire to run into Kurush on his way back in. She wiped a paste of dust-sweat from her brow. It was far, far too hot to be out in the sun's glare, let alone working to re-wheel a stranded wagon. For all their fervour, she couldn't see the Storm Children getting this wagon moving any time soon. The sight of them still unnerved her; she'd hoped this far north she'd be well clear of anyone keen to bend her ear about their latest messiah, but there seemed to be something about the 'untamed' nature of the expanse that attracted this sort of thing.

With a sigh, she dismounted and tied up her horse in what passed for the shade of the gatehouse, impressing upon the sweat-stained guard within that she would be returning shortly and was very friendly with the Acting Guildmaster. Then she slipped inside the gates on foot, just missing the gathering muddle of dust that was coming up the trail far behind.

* * *

Ree kept her eyes open for the kid as she walked down the shady side of the street, pausing at the trough in the square to splash the worst of the dust from her hands and face. She'd hoped she might see the kid's pony tied up somewhere as a giveaway, or perhaps spot her ghastly little friend scampering around, but the streets and alleys around were bright, hot and empty.

She checked all the usual haunts, the alleyways, the little hollow in the mudbrick town wall where she'd once caught her and the smaller one building their own fortifications. She thought she'd seen a ladder around the side of the teahouse on the way past, but when she went back to check, it was gone. She even steeled herself and descended into the teahouse's cool reek to ask in low tones if Terbish knew where the kid was. The woman at the bar denied seeing her, and Ree didn't feel it prudent to take her questions to those patrons still conscious enough to answer. Many of them she didn't recognise, and any one of them could have been on the hunt for the kid. Drawing their attention, however bleary-eyed, was a needless risk.

She returned to the streets, sweating, stalking. A commotion was rising from the gates downstreet, where the stricken wagon still blocked entry to the town. A plume of dust had risen into the air beyond the walls, thick and wide, and she caught the sound of horses and shouts, and was that the rumbling crunch of laden wagons . . . ?

The caravan had arrived. River of shit, as an old colleague used to say. She stared at the gates. The wagon was beginning to move.

She had to find Javani.

Siavash had been delighted to see the walls of his final destination appearing through the shimmering haze of the day. His imagination of the feasts and pleasures to come was so vivid that he actually salivated. The caravan had already attracted a swathe of hangers-on before they'd even sighted the town walls, first running children, then riders and delegations from the local farmsteads as news spread. The advanced scouts would have reached the town hours earlier to begin preparations; to Siavash's puzzlement, the big mercenary had spoken to them before they rode off that morning, private, urgent words that left his curiosity burning.

Their grand entrance into the town had been delayed while some kind of broken-down wagon occupied by people who seemed better at prayer than at vehicular maintenance had to be moved from their path. Earlier attempts to get it clear had failed, leaving the thing completely blocking the gateway. Siavash had been stunned when the Horvaun and her crew had charged forward and begun to drag the vehicle bodily out of the way. In a few moments, the gates were clear, and the caravan could at last enter the town.

Siavash savoured their arrival. It wasn't exactly a triumph – they'd lost a few staff on the way, and two of the wagons in a flash flood during a storm, and suffered the standard shrinkage in headcount of guards and scouts – but it was an achievement, to have travelled the length of the north road from the heart of the protectorate to its furthest extent. He still had the best of his goods, and intended to charge the most eye-watering prices for them. It was well-known quite how rich mining towns were, how little the miners, guards and clerks had to do when they weren't blasting chunks out of mountainsides, how disposable their income had become. He had great expectations.

The caravan began to unwind itself in the town square, the wagons rolling to a final stop, the horses and pack animals relieved and taken for stabling. Already the square was filling with townsfolk, faces at windows and doorways, including some bleary and staggering output from the teahouse. He'd need to keep the guards close for a time before letting them loose, just until things settled down and his various buyers had begun to make their arrangements. There was a nascent carnival atmosphere as the last of the wagons rolled into the square, growing excitement and intrigue, all the result of his caravan's arrival. A caravan-ival. Siavash chuckled to himself, and Ulfat offered him a reflexive smile.

He wanted to share his good humour, and looked around for the Horvaun and her crew. Siavash was most pleased with how they'd turned out, despite his disquiet at the Mehrez incident, and had decided to offer them a proper contract for the return journey. Their methods were unorthodox, but the results were unarguable. He'd need to have Ulfat make some additional pay-offs to ensure that the fallout from the Mehrez incident didn't settle anywhere permanent, and that his habitual workers weren't too slighted by the whole affair, but once his trades were complete he should have coin to burn.

She was not with the other guards, which was expected, nor anywhere close to the caravan, which wasn't. He spotted her at last, at the edge of the square, in intense conversation with what looked like one of Siavash's advance scouts. She looked urgent and dissatisfied, and moved quickly on to a knot of approaching townsfolk.

Siavash watched her, puzzled. Oh well, he thought. I haven't paid her yet. She'll be back.

SIX

Javani was stalking around the shaded courtyard at the rear of the teahouse, aiming frustrated kicks at the blameless lemon tree, when Moosh appeared, sliding down one wall from the building's flat roof, hanging for a moment from the projecting stub of a rafter before dropping to the dusty ground. Wrapped in her own mantle of grievance, Javani affected not to notice him.

'You're still alive then,' he said with a grin, ambling over. 'Thought those bruisers would have pulped you.'

'I'm not, I'm a spirit of vengeance from beyond the veil.'

'Then you have charcoal on your face, O Great Spirit, and an odour that would make a nightsoilman weep.'

Her composure cracked. 'Oh, piss off, you big piss.' Javani spat on her finger and tried once again to lift the mark. She gestured at the roof. 'Where have you been?'

He counted off on his fingers as he spoke. 'Well, first, I was going to spy on your chat with the bruisers with the ladder, but then they chased me off. Then I hung around to listen out for them murdering you, then I got bored, so I went to check on my puppies.'

'Your what?'

He locked her with what might one day have become a fearsome glare. '*Don't* tell Terbish. One of the stray dogs has had a litter round the back of the old bathhouse, I've been feeding the pups in secret. They're so cute, they lick my fingers and—'

'Moosh! They might be riddled with disease.'

'So? That's true of most of the people in this place.' He shrugged, halfway between defiance and indifference. 'They're not dangerous, just strays. Sometimes we all need a little looking after.' He yawned, stretched his scrawny arms over his head. 'And then after that I took the ladder round the square.'

'What? Why?'

He stared at her. 'The caravan's arrived, bum-brain. Place is heaving. How did you miss that? I was watching from the rooftops. It's madness out there, never seen so many people out for an arrival.'

She stared at her feet. 'Guess I was lost in thought.'

He regarded her from beneath raised eyebrows. 'Unfamiliar territory?'

She cuffed his shoulder. 'Gods, Moosh, that one's older than the hills.'

'Speaking of which, are you going to fill me in on what in hells you're doing cavorting with the Brothers Guvuli?'

'Cavorting? I was hardly dancing around out there. It's too hot for that.'

He paused, lips pursed in concentration. '*Consorting*, that's it. What are you playing at?'

'Just another gambit, Moosh.'

'But . . . but . . .' He gestured helplessly. 'With *them*? They're killers! You know, actual stick-a-knife-in-your-guts-and-go-about-their-day killers!'

'They're not that bad, once you get to know them. We have an understanding.'

'Jav, they are bandits and thieves. What kind of understanding do you think you've reached? What are you doing with them?'

Javani felt the heat of her frustration rising, the tight pain of nervous anger at the thought that she might be cut out of the scheme she herself had devised. The Guvulis would have achieved nothing without her ideas and her inside knowledge, they were just . . . just sentient muscle, like the wagon driver had said!

'Jav? I can hear your teeth squeaking. What are you into?'

'I can't tell you. Not yet.' She waved a hand. She had charcoal all over her fingertips. 'But it's going to change everything. They'll keep to their end of it. They will.'

'You can't trust anyone like that, Jav. My dad said they used to be miners, long ago, and miners are good for nothing but drinking and gambling. All the real work is done with blasting powder, they just come along after and sweep—'

She blinked at how close he'd got without realising it. 'It's not . . . It's . . .' Gods, what if he worked it out? What if he blabbed? What if the Guvulis really did cut her loose from her own plan? She felt heat rising in her cheeks, fresh sweat on her back.

'Whatever it is,' Moosh continued airily, 'you may as well just go straight to the Guild and turn them in. You might get a reward.'

'No!' The force of her own reaction surprised her. Moosh took a step back. 'No,' she repeated, quieter, calmer. 'First, I don't *know* they won't come through, it's just a feeling. Probably paranoia. Second, how's that conversation going to go? How was it you knew about this plan, young lady, and what size is your neck, would you say? Come on, Moosh, Kurush is desperate to get confirmed as permanent Guildmaster, Ree says he's been pushing for it since before the old Guildmaster was even cold. He'd leap on a chance like this to put some miscreants to justice.' She mimed being hanged, tongue projecting, arms swinging, one leg kicking.

Moosh looked wistful. 'I reckon he did away with the old man, you know, cleared the path for his rise to power.'

'Don't be silly. Although . . .'

'You're not going to the Guild, then?'

She put her hands on his shoulders. She was still taller than him, just, although that wasn't saying much. 'Listen. After today, I might have to disappear for a while, along with Ree. But I'll send word to you. You understand? I'll send for you.'

He was looking at her, one eyebrow raised, an infuriating mirror of her own sceptical attitude when he was in full tale-telling flow.

'I'm serious, Moosh! I'll make it right for both of us.'

'Uh-huh. Oh, speaking of your aunt, she was looking for you earlier. I saw her from the rooftop, marching round the place, demanding to know if anyone had seen you. Guess she didn't think to look back here. She seemed a little, uh . . . tightly wound.'

Javani sighed. 'Ah, foxshit. I "forgot" to draw the water from the well this morning. Stuff to do, you know. She's been on me like a buzzard about it all week. Guess I pushed it too far.'

He nodded. 'Yeah, maybe dodge her until she calms down a bit. She looked ready to cut someone.'

'Ree? That'll be the day.'

'It's funny how you never call her "Auntie Ree" or anything,' he said. 'Peri always calls her aunts "Auntie", and Terbish says I can call her "Auntie", you know, if I want, which I'm not sure I do. You know?'

'She won't let me. It's always just "Ree".' Javani paused, one hand still on his bony shoulder. 'You know, once we met a man on the road, further south, called her a different name and she answered without batting an eye.'

He mimed a sharp intake of breath. 'Deeply suspicious, very sinister. Want to go and see the caravan? Ladder's still up round the back of the little bell temple, get a good view from that corner. There are some mighty odd types on this one.'

The caravan . . . Movos had said the gang needed something from the caravan to complete their preparations. Maybe he'd be there, and she could finally get what she needed. Hope flared within.

'Let's go.'

Aki could barely contain his excitement. He rode upright in the saddle of his ungainly mount, bent as far forward as it would allow, his face radiating joy. What a journey it had been! The plains had been a sight, a false but welcome reminder of home, and the desert crossing had thrilled him in unexpected ways – to see the famous deadlake, even in the distance! – and now the rock ledges rose from the red earth, and ruddy, blunt-faced mountains glowered on two horizons. The town was in view; Anashe might have called it a sad, stumpy thing with dung-coloured walls and a gaping gate, but to Aki, it was perfect. It lay at the end of the winding, dusty trail, and beyond it, there was nothing. Nothing at all.

This was it. Kazeraz: the great destination, the target of their burning quest. Where all questions would find their answers, where at last they would complete the tasks the Goddess had set for them. As Ranu the Champion had so performed his duty and attained eternal greatness, thus would Aki. He could see the strands of the stories that bound them, that guided them, converging on the town, this modest brown lump on the landscape at the centre of a whirling vortex of fate.

'Do you see it, my sister? Our journey's end. Our destiny.'

Anashe rode slumped, or as slumped as she could be on her tiring mount. 'And such a sight it is.'

'Is it not? Rarely have I seen such wonder, such splendour! To think such a prize has lain here so long, awaiting our—'

'This reeking midden at the edge of the world?' she retorted, her lip curled. 'My expectations were not high to begin with, but somehow I am still disappointed.' Anashe shook her head with a weariness that was unlikely to be altogether affected. 'At least the Shenakar owe us a healthy fee for this insanity.'

Aki had indeed been as good as his word (although inclement circumstance had prevented him demonstrating his ability to smell water, to his great regret) and had navigated them safely, and swiftly, across the breadth of the expanse. He knew pride came off him in waves, but a little pride was hardly unjustified given his achievement. And the fact he had proved his sister wrong was something on which he would make no comment. For the time being, at least. Unless pressed.

'We must insist on immediate payment,' Anashe grumbled on. 'Let our noble clients complete their noble business at their leisure, find whoever it was they have come so far for, see whatever they intended to see. We will be counting our coins in an alehouse – there must be an alehouse, even in this armpit. And under no circumstances are you to give your share away to the first floozy who spins you a tale of woe!'

Aki straightened, one hand on his chest in outrage. 'My charity to those in greater need pleases the Goddess! While your shameful gambling—'

'If I choose to gamble,' she shot back with a voice like ice, 'at least I invariably increase the amount of coin with which I began!' She clicked her tongue in irritation. 'I hope only that this fee will be enough to cover our passage back south . . .'

'Let us not speak of returning, my sister, let us think only of what awaits us here, at this juncture of fortune.'

'Very well, brother. What awaits us? What will we do when we arrive?'

Some of his conviction abruptly ebbed. 'Well, yes, of course, when we arrive, we will . . . we will need to look around.'

'Look. Around?'

'We cannot expect our quarry to fall into our laps from the sky, my sister. The Goddess provides, but we must prove worthy of her bounty.'

'We are unworthy of her bounty, all of a sudden? When was this decreed?'

'Do not defame the Goddess in service of mere goading, my sister. She gave you more sense than that.'

Anashe sucked her lip against her teeth and kept silent.

'We will see our clients to their lodgings,' Aki went on, 'and perhaps enjoy the comforts of stationary repose ourselves for a while. Then we can begin our enquiries in earnest.'

'Aki, we have travelled a distance so great as to be measurable in the stars, and you are telling me we must go *searching* from here?'

His grin lit the morning. It was all so simple, if she would but let herself see it. 'We are hunters, my sister. It is what we were made to do.' He nodded at their clients, ahead of them on the trail. 'I will speak to young Master Lazant and tell him of our aims, perhaps he and his people—'

'Khalida, it is time,' Lazant called out. 'Quickly, now!' He kicked his plodding animal into a reluctant trot, the ever-faithful Khalida at his side, lolloping towards the town on their towering beasts. They should, of course, have changed mounts again as they left the true desert behind, but the young man hadn't wanted to stop again, adamant that they'd lost too much time already. So on they went, their inappropriate mounts thudding over the broken red hills in the shadow of gleaming, snow-capped peaks, their journey's end in sight.

A ruined wagon stood to one side of the gate, fussed over by a couple of robed figures who seemed more intent on shouting at each other and the gate guards than actually fixing whatever was wrong. Lazant and Khalida were pacing, their ungainly mounts swaying as they closed on the town, and Aki and Anashe had to urge theirs with force to keep up. Their aroma was not improved by further exertion, and the motion was clearly making Anashe queasy. Aki once more resolved not to pass comment, unless sorely provoked.

Lazant and Khalida went straight through the open gateway without slowing, and the startled guards made no move to stop them. Aki and Anashe followed, the remaining Shenakar in pursuit somewhere behind them. Something was happening in the town, a rising tide of noise washing from ahead; Aki could see faces at windows, people hurrying from their square mudbrick homes into the dusty street. Their clothes were spare, modest, simply made from hard-wearing fabrics, so fitting for the baking austerity of the surrounding landscape. A rough, straightforward populace, no doubt unsophisticated compared to Aki's own rich and worldly outlook, but most likely possessed of a refreshing, grounded perspective, and the perfect audience for his bursting stable of glorious tales. Excitement seized him, but he was just aware enough to quell it. Before all else, they had their mission. Their quest.

Lazant reined in, Khalida with him. 'Where are these people going?' He looked around, peering towards the square at the end of the street, squinting against the sun's glare. A few of the townsfolk did double takes at their approach and hurried from their path.

'Something in the square,' Khalida said. 'Perhaps a festival. Or an execution.'

Lazant was looking around with a vague smile. 'These people seem very able-bodied for a mining town; I heard accidents were common. I see few cripples and beggars, few of life's unfortunates. How reassuring!'

Khalida pursed her lips. 'As I understand it, most caught in accidents do not survive long in these places.'

'Ah.'

Aki pulled up alongside them, fighting to control the sway of his animal, his sister a pace behind and looking increasingly bilious. 'A caravan has arrived. In the square. Master Lazant, if I may, a word about—'

Lazant's eyes went wide, and he snapped his gaze to Khalida. 'Could it be . . . ?'

'Perhaps,' she replied with a curt nod, and her hand went to her sabre.

'Onward!' the young man cried, and the two of them spurred their sullen mounts off at a canter towards the square. The other Shenakar came racing past, flashing after their leaders in a great cloud of drifting powder.

This time, when Aki and Anashe tried to follow, Anashe's mount refused. It had made its decision; it had moved more than far enough, and would take not a step further. It sank down and gently tipped her from the saddle, sending her sprawling on numb legs. Aki dragged his mount around beside her, concern battling against his eagerness to follow the disappearing nobles towards the square. 'My sister, we must hurry! Our clients are escaping.'

She spat dust and looked up at her brother. 'Help me, then!'

He stared back, eyes flicking to his own surly mount, his unease growing. It was looking at its resting companion, and getting ideas.

'How?'

'Give me a hand up. We can share.'

'My sister, I believe that if I deviate more than a hand's breadth from my current emplacement, this animal will—'

'Give me your hand, you witless oaf!'

'My sister, be—'

A moment later, both of them were sitting in the dust. The now-riderless animals stood, stretched, and moseyed away down the street, back towards the open gates. Anashe glared after their retreating, dung-clotted rumps.

'I prefer to walk, anyway,' she muttered.

The caravan filled the square, horses, wagons, armed and armoured guards. From the nest of covered alleyways around the square swarmed the hawkers and stallholders, amateur metalsmiths and their gewgaws, mingling the bazaar with the caravan's market. The townsfolk were out in great force, and Ree could no longer bear the sheer number of humans around her. Any one of them could slip a blade in her ribs as they passed, she couldn't defend herself, she couldn't watch them all. She'd left the crossbow stashed with her horse, but the familiar weight of her sword at her hip did nothing to reassure her, nor did the trail-knife at her belt or the surprise-knife in her sleeve.

Her hair was stuck to her forehead with sweat. This place was too hot, too crowded. She needed somewhere with sightlines, somewhere she could see trouble coming. Somewhere she could see the kid. She didn't stand a chance in this crush.

She spotted the foot of a rickety ladder resting against a wall behind the little temple. A vantage! The gods were smiling on her at last. Blinking sweat and touching nobody, Ree threaded her way through the throng and retreated from the square.

'Where's the ladder, Moosh?'

'It's across the corner there, on the other side, alley behind the little temple. You can't see it from here. It's got a lot busier.'

The square had indeed got busier, and now the local merchants were weighing in, rushing to beat their rivals to the caravan's offerings, safe in the knowledge that however much they paid, those who bought from them would pay more. A few enterprising locals were already approaching the caravan guards with samples of trinkets and sweetmeats; it was a fair bet that their wages would be coming their way in the near future, and extracting wages from transient workers was something the town had in its mudbrick blood.

Javani tried to follow Moosh, but he was incapable of leading, buffeted by everyone who hurried past. At length, Javani called time on the attempt – they were getting nowhere, and she'd spotted a stack of weathered crates beside a drooping awning at the square's edge. A little sweaty scampering later, they clambered onto a creaking crate and surveyed the teeming square.

'I didn't think there were this many people in the whole town,' Moosh said, his voice weighed down with awe.

'There aren't, dung-skull,' Javani murmured absently, scanning the motley and multifarious crowd. The view wasn't as good as it would have been from the rooftops, but she was in with a chance of spotting Movos. 'The caravan's brought a load of people, and others have come in from the outliers as word's spread.' She had a sudden thought: was Ree somewhere in the square, still looking for her? Should she dodge her, or face her scolding? Should she tell her about the Guvulis and the plan, or was it still too early? Might Ree ruin everything, tell her it was unsafe, hold her back as she always did?

Javani squinted. The square was alive with noise and movement, and the heat, dust and smell rising off it made the air swirl. Horses whinnied and stamped, mules honked, and a breath of wind brought a pungent scent to her nostrils, some mixture of manure and old piss that she put down to the caravan's great unwashed.

Then she saw the figure. Once you noticed her, she was impossible to miss: she towered over the people around her, her head and shoulders clear in the wavering air. Her pale skin was sun-slapped, her long braids bleached almost white, and her face bore a long, dark tattoo down one side. She was talking to someone, her manner forceful, her gestures sharp. The sight of her filled Javani with sudden, visceral terror.

Javani swallowed. 'Who . . . ?' she managed, one trembling finger pointing.

Moosh craned to see. 'Ooh, who do you think that is? Looks like she's asking for directions. Think she knows the Guvulis? Do bandits have a guild? She looks southern, maybe one of those mountain-dwellers from the Sink. My dad said they were all cannibals, but—'

One of the small people around the big one turned and pointed. He pointed straight at where Javani and Moosh stood. The big figure turned, and Javani was certain that their eyes met across the swarming square.

Her throat was dry. She was fixed in place, one sweating hand on the yellowing wall beside her.

The big woman began to move.

'She's coming this way!' Moosh sounded excited. 'Maybe we can ask her where she's from, what language she speaks, if she eats human flesh. Shame the square's so busy, it's going to take her a while.'

Javani was still frozen. She could feel her heartbeat all through her body, thudding in her ears, her eyes, her throat. She was drenched in sweat and her legs were trembling.

The big woman advanced, shouldering the crowd from her path. A hawker stepped in front of her, brandishing a selection of crudely wrought jewellery, and she put one hand on his chest and hefted him out of the way. The whole time, she kept her eyes on Javani.

'Ah, she'll be across in no time.' Moosh at last noticed her stillness. 'Jav? You all right? You look ill.'

Javani was shaking. She wanted so desperately to flee but her legs were stone. Moosh tugged at her elbow but she couldn't respond. If she hadn't already sweated all the water from her body she was certain she'd have wet herself.

The enormous woman was halfway across the square now, and she raised one hand to signal. Javani's twitching eyes picked out other figures in dark cloaks, none as tall as the southerner, but all strapping, and moving with unyielding menace through the crowd. A few cries and shouts rose above the noise as townsfolk and traders alike found themselves shoved aside. Javani could only watch their approach, like five leopards carving their paths through the long grass of the plains, converging on their prey.

The foul smell was getting stronger. Maybe she really had pissed herself.

A caravan guard stepped in front of the southerner, checking her advance, and stood his ground. It looked as if he had something he wanted to say, some bubbling resentment that was surfacing after so long on the road. He raised one finger and opened his mouth when she backhanded him across the face, sending him tottering backwards, then he crashed down into the shouting crowd. Now there was space, as people scrambled back from the collapsed man and the cause of his upending. The human tide parted, and Javani found only clear earth between her crate and the huge, pale woman.

The noise fell away as more of the crowd turned to look at the growing scene. The woman ignored them. She sniffed, once, then threw her cloak back over her shoulder to reveal a muscular arm carrying a fearsome double-headed axe. Around the square, the other cloaked figures did likewise, uncovering swords, bows and hatchets. Finally, one-handed, the giant placed a black steel helmet over her head, her bleached braids hanging from its rear like ashen tentacles. The helmet had a snarling animal's face worked in the same black metal, but the woman's pale eyes burned unmistakably from within.

The great weapon hanging in her grip, the southerner resumed her heavy, inexorable steps. She was still staring right at Javani and Moosh on their crate. Nothing stood between them now.

'Moosh,' Javani gasped at last. 'Mooshie!'

'Hm? Gods have mercy,' he blurted, 'what is that smell?'

Javani wasn't sure whether she heard or felt it first, but from the street beyond there came the strangest thunderous rumble. Then, with a sound like a strangled man's scream, the camels burst into the square.

SEVEN

The camels galloped across the open space and charged the cloaked mercenaries, driving them backwards. The tall woman was almost taken from her feet, bowled sideways by the arrival of a great honking, stinking beast, ridden by a figure waving a gleaming sabre. Screams and shouts filled the air as the townsfolk scattered, running and colliding in their haste to escape the reach of the flashing blades and whirling hooves.

The big woman was up, and one camel was down, hit by a flurry of arrows from the retreating dark-cloaks. But one of their number was lost beneath its crashing form, and the rider leapt clear, sabre in hand, just as another three camels came thundering around the corner and into the square.

Someone started ringing the bell in the little temple behind the clay oven, and its sudden peal shook Javani from her trance at last. Her legs buckled, and Moosh pulled her down from the crate.

The big woman was up again, taking a wild swing with the axe at an onrushing camel, then ducking and rolling. From across the emptying square came the clang of steel and cries of pain, then the hoarse bellow of a wounded or angry camel. The southerner sprang to her feet, then ran at Javani and Moosh as they stumbled back into the street, her eyes wide and unblinking. Moosh was running, Javani's wrist in his grip, yanking her along. But Javani couldn't help looking over her shoulder as her legs flailed beneath her, couldn't help watching the giant's thudding progress. She was getting closer, catching them up. Each galumphing stride ate up more of the gap, until she was almost close enough to swing the axe. Her snarling visor was up; Javani could make out the tattoo on her face: it was a spear.

A camel smashed into the woman and ripped her from sight. From the rising dust cloud emerged the first rider, a handsome man with a long moustache, running clear of the square. His eyes seized on the two runners.

'It was you she was after?' he called in accented Serican.

A roar came from behind, not a camel but a very angry human. It was followed by a terrifying crash.

'Keep running!' the man with the moustache called, waving them on.

Behind him, one of the black-cloaked mercenaries ran clear of the drifting dust and took aim with a thick recurve bow. Javani felt like she could see right down the street and along the shaft of the arrow, a darkened thing with a savage barb. It had to be aimed right at her. Her foot caught and she stumbled, yanking Moosh off-kilter. They went tumbling to the earth as the mercenary loosed. The arrow hissed past the moustache-man's shoulder and over Javani's prone form, thumping into the mudbrick of one of the smaller chapels and spidering great cracks across its wall.

The mercenary snarled and drew back another arrow. Javani watched from the ground, unable to rouse herself, while Moosh staggered to his feet and grabbed for her. She couldn't breathe, her throat clogged with dust, her clothes soaked with sweat, all strength gone from her. She stared at the arcing bow, quivering with force, and at the arrowhead lining up with her skull.

'What did I do?' she whispered.

A camel barrelled from the dusty square, great hooves flying in an ungainly gallop, its rider hanging almost sideways from her saddle with sabre held high. The beast reached the mercenary in three strides and the sabre swung, cleaving into the man's unprotected neck and almost removing his head. The bow clattered to the earth, the arrow soaring harmlessly into the clear sky.

'Come on, Jav!'

Something came scything across the street from the square, whistling through the air, and connected with the galloping camel: the great double-headed axe. It swept straight through the animal's neck and this time the head came clean off. Such was the camel's momentum, it ran for another half-dozen strides and crashed stump-first into the corner of a two-storey boarding-house as its rider leapt clear. The wall crumbled then collapsed as the force of the impact spread, and with a rumbling crunch the entire building began to fall in on itself, flooding the street with a new rolling wall of choking brick dust.

'Javani!'

At last she felt strength in her legs, and she scrambled back as Moosh dragged her.

The man with the moustache had nearly reached them. 'Which one of you is she after?' he called, his half-cloak flapping over his shoulder.

Javani was still being dragged backwards by her friend, doing her best to push herself to her feet. No idea, she wanted to shout back, when she saw a dark shape come thundering out of the dust cloud behind them.

'Look out!'

He turned as the first throwing axe came hissing through the air and he flinched aside in time. The second he caught with his sword, batting it from the air with a flourish. The big figure was closing again, running on with great thudding strides.

'Khalida!' he called. 'Your assistance, if it please you!'

The woman they'd seen on the second camel came sprinting out of the murk with a cry, her sabre still in her hand. The southerner grimaced and turned to face her, drawing two new axes from her belt.

'Quick,' the man said, 'into the alley!'

Moosh dragged Javani around the corner and straight into half a dozen Guild guards coming running from the other direction, some with straps still loose on their burnished breastplates.

'What in the name of all the gods is going on?' cried one. From the street behind came a clang of steel suggesting that the southerner was being delayed, at least.

The handsome man came to a smart stop behind them, and beckoned them forward. 'Stout yeomen of the town! You see that giant pale woman there, duelling with my second?' he said.

The guards leaned forward around the corner. Cries and grunts accompanied the metallic ringing, while bellows and shrieks were still coming from the square, now muffled by the drifting blanket of dust laid over the street.

'That is the White Spear,' the man said.

'Don't see a spear, just axes,' one of the guards said, and the young man produced a smile that seemed almost manic to Javani.

'She is a notorious mercenary killer,' he said, his voice patient and clear, 'and her purpose in your town is to do it and its people great harm. You must eliminate her immediately or she will kill every man, woman and child in this place in pursuit of her aims. And we wouldn't want that, would we?'

The guards stared at him, then out into the street. They did not advance.

'Go! Do your duty to the gods and to your people,' he shouted, and nudged one of them out of the alley. 'Work together, and nothing can stop you!' With great reluctance, the others jogged after him. From the street, the shouts and clangs rose rapidly in both number and pitch.

Javani was back on her feet but trembling uncontrollably. Moosh held her arm tight. 'Mercenary killers, Jav? Gods have mercy, what's going on?'

At last she could speak, although her teeth were chattering despite the heat. 'I . . . don't know. But I feel like . . . it's my fault.'

The alley was empty but for the two of them and the handsome young man with the moustache. Javani found herself warming to him – something about his bearing seemed to command respect, but when he spoke to her and Moosh she could see concern in his eyes, feel the weight of the worry he had for them in his voice. The noise from the street had become, if not remote, then quietened.

'My name is Zakir Lazant,' the man said, putting one hand on his chest and affecting a mock bow. He wore quite a swish breastplate beneath his stained half-length cloak. 'To whom do I have the honour of speaking?'

Javani wanted to say something, but Moosh got in first. 'Who are these mercenaries? What company are they from? What are their rates? My dad always said—' Javani nudged him with an elbow. 'Oh yeah, and why are they after us?'

Lazant frowned. 'Not both of you, I believe – just one. You don't know which?'

'We . . . didn't stop to . . . ask,' Javani muttered through rattling teeth.

The short-haired woman, Lazant's second, entered the alley. She was limping but seemed otherwise whole. Shouts still came from the street, and a tramp of boots suggested more guards had finally arrived. Javani was beginning to relax now, her heart rate reduced to a mere canter. She really, really needed to urinate.

'They have her?' Lazant asked his second.

'More have come, maybe a score now. They are attempting to subdue her.'

'Then we should move fast.' Lazant turned back to Javani and Moosh. 'Let us move away from here, just in case.'

They shuffled down the alley away from the street, some of them surer on their feet than others.

'Who are you?' Javani said as they ducked around a corner and against a wall. 'What's happening?' More footsteps, seeming to come from all directions. Javani felt faint. I think I'm in shock, she told herself. Ree had told her of shock. Ree had told her of a lot of things. Where was Ree?

The man's hand returned to his chest. 'As I said before, my name is Zakir Lazant. That is Khalida. We come from a place called Shenak – have you ever heard of it?'

Moosh nodded energetically, which proved nothing – he'd never admit to not knowing something. Javani just leaned back against the rough wall and let the waves pass over her.

Lazant crouched down before them, his handsome face earnest. His long moustache was brittle with dust. His gaze rested on Javani, and she felt a tiny shameful thrill from the focus of his attention. 'Shenak is a kingdom, far from here, across the sea or around the Sink. It is ruled by a king, called the King of Kings, and his family, or house. Great misfortune has befallen the ruling house of Shenak in the years since the last of the wars of the Sink, and the ascension of the king below and all that followed. Do you know what, and who I mean?'

Moosh nodded again. Javani, again, did nothing, but she realised she'd heard of these places, and these people. Ree had told her a lot of things.

'In the last ten years,' Lazant went on, his eyes sombre, his voice grave, 'every heir and direct family member of the King of Kings has met their end, and some of these endings were most premature. Whether it was this that broke him, or merely his years, now our ruler's own time is at hand; he is in his last days. The issue of Succession has paralysed the court, and whispers and rumours, plots and mischief abound. Do you understand me?'

Ignoring Moosh's incessant nodding, his gaze rested on Javani, searching, appraising. Convulsively, she shook her head, and Lazant gave a rueful smile in return. 'The king is dying and has no heirs,' he said, 'and nobody can agree who the next king will be.'

'Or queen,' said Moosh, to which Lazant nodded vaguely.

'And that's bad,' Javani said, almost a question, her voice still a little wavering.

Lazant's smile returned with warmth. 'It is. Uncertainty is the biggest problem of all. Too much of it, and a kingdom can fall apart, make war with itself. Just look at what happened in the Sink.'

'But why are there mercenary killers trying to get us?' Javani squeaked, her cheeks flushed, a taste like blood in her mouth.

Lazant nodded, a quick, almost furtive gesture. 'The Shenakar court is full of stories, full of . . . ideas. One of these ideas relates to a forgotten nephew of the King of Kings – the eldest child of his first sister – a man who lived and died across the mountains in a place called Tenailen, in Vistirlar.'

'In the Sink? And he's already dead? How does that help?'

Lazant put up a hand. His fingers were very neat but stained from his gauntlet. 'The . . . story . . . that has fascinated the court relates to a, ahem, dalliance he had with a passing diplomat, some time in the early days of the wars of the Sink, and not long before he died himself. The diplomat was, as the story goes, a Serican noble travelling in disguise, and she swiftly returned to her country and bore a secret child in the aftermath.'

Javani's heartbeat had been slowing, but something about how he spoke set it scampering again.

'Because the diplomat knew that the child was of royal blood, she went north, away from Arowan and civilisation, into the backwaters of the protectorate. There she resolved to raise the child in secret, away from the schemes and machinations of the court, until it could come of age and . . . stake its claim.'

Javani's mouth was dry. Surely it wasn't . . . It couldn't mean . . . Her parents had been killed by Mawn, hadn't they? That's what Ree had always told her. But who had they been, before? She suddenly wanted to speak to Ree very much.

'I knew it!' It was Moosh. 'We only came out here because my parents were hiding something from the posh types in the big city. Stands to reason it was me.' He was beaming.

'Um, Moosh—' Javani tried, but had to stop to swallow. Her throat was so dry.

Lazant's eyes were on Moosh. 'Your mother? She's a noble? A diplomat?'

Moosh was already inflating, ready to go with another tale. 'Weeell, my mother passed away when I was smaller, at least if you believe the official story. But I'm pretty sure she could have faked it, and that she's still out there, in secret. You see, my dad—'

'Um, Moosh—'

'Please, young man, step into the light, let me look at you. You say both of your parents are dead?'

Moosh stepped forward, out of the shade, preening.

'Oh yeah, completely. My dad was a big deal down south, someone really important, but then—'

Lazant was looking at him sidelong, turning his head this way and that. 'It could be,' he murmured, 'it's possible. Khalida?'

The short-haired, calm-eyed woman approached, then stepped behind Moosh, who was still chattering away. Something about the way she stood gave Javani a sudden rush of apprehension, the hairs on her arms leaping to attention.

'Moosh, you need to—'

The woman reached around Moosh and dragged a knife across his neck.

'MOOSH!'

She let him fall, right away, his eyes bulging, as blood flooded from the tear at his throat. He was still trying to talk, gabbling and gurgling, his hands patting at the wound, as he slumped gently forwards into the darkening dirt.

'MOOSH!'

Screaming, Javani had found her full voice at last.

'Be silent, please.' Lazant stood over her, no longer an iota of warmth to his expression. His hand was back on his sabre. 'You may grieve your friend, but his death will save the lives of thousands. Uncertainty can burn a kingdom to its bones, and this will bring certainty. There will be no puppet prince. The viziers of Shenak will attempt no regency.'

'But he was *lying!*' Javani screamed. 'It's what he does!'

Lazant went very still, and his gaze punched into her like a lance. Behind him on the ground, Moosh gurgled and gasped with decreasing urgency. 'What did you say, girl?'

Javani's thoughts arrived, too late. If it wasn't Moosh, they said, then it's you. And he's thinking the same thing. And at this point, why take any risks?

'Khalida?' Lazant said.

Oh, shit. Oh, Moosh. Oh, shit!

A great roar from the alley's mouth drew their attention back.

Khalida was at the corner in two quick steps, her own sabre in her hand.

'The beast has freed herself. She is coming.'

Lazant nodded. 'Delay her.' He put one hand to his hilt and began drawing his sabre, his eyes fixed on Javani. Javani wanted to look at Moosh, wanted to check him, wanted to see if he might still live, but she could not drag her eyes away from the beautiful, imperious, murderous man before her, his sword emerging smoothly from beneath his half-cloak. Thudding steps came from around the corner, shouts and cries, seeming to echo from the rooftops above.

Lazant's blade was out. It gleamed.

'I regret that one of you,' he said with a look of almost-convincing remorse, 'will deserve my apologies.'

Oh, shit, Javani, think!

Something vast and black barrelled down the alleyway, smashing from one narrow wall to the other as it came. Lazant leapt back as Khalida flung herself aside, then screamed a challenge and launched herself forwards. Shouts and bellows came from the alley's mouth as Guild troopers came charging after their quarry. For a moment, everyone was scattered, and at last Javani's legs responded. She turned and bolted, breath halting, racked by sobs, her eyes flooded with tears, running in hot tracks down her cheeks. She hurdled a bundle of rotting carpet at the alley's far end and skidded around the corner – straight into the arms of Ree, coming the other way.

'Javani? Javani! Thank the gods!' Ree wrapped arms around the kid, who buried herself in her shoulder, her little body sodden and shuddering. 'Was that you screaming? I thought I saw you across the square, but before I could—'

The kid pushed her back with a jolt, reddened eyes flashing wide, and swung a look back over her shoulder. Her breath was coming in heaving gasps, clear snot running free from her nose. Her legs and boots were crossed by a delicate, dark splattered arc, matted with dust. Ree knew it was blood.

'They killed him,' she croaked. 'They killed Moosh.' She took a great rattling breath and stumbled forwards.

'Gods. Come.' Ree grabbed her hand and turned to flee.

'Not that way!' the kid squeaked, and yanked her in the opposite direction, down a narrow alley strung with drooping canvas awnings. Ree ran with her, the crossbow bouncing on her back, the sword beneath her coat thudding against her hip, an electric urgency jolting through her in a way it hadn't for years. She should never have gone back to her horse for the crossbow, she should have gone straight after Javani the moment she'd spotted her. Stupid, Ree, stupid. That boy's blood was on her hands as well as the kid's boots.

So many questions she could have asked, could have demanded answers to. Who killed him? Why? Are they chasing you now? How many, how armed? The truth was that right now, it didn't matter. Running was instinct. But the deeper truth was that she wasn't ready for some of the answers.

They dodged through the souk, ducking low-slung awnings and hangings, dodging abandoned stalls, twisting down one winding alley after another. Across the roofs came the sounds of continued combat and chaos, the rumbling shudder of another building collapsing, screams of panic and pain. They were not the only ones fleeing. Her horse was no doubt gone, snatched up by a panicked citizen, and the gate . . . the gate would be pandemonium.

'We can't get out,' the kid moaned as they ran, Ree's hand still clamped around hers. Clearly she'd had the same thought. 'The gate will be rammed. It might even be shut!'

'Then we need to get somewhere safe,' Ree said, changing direction and pulling the girl after her. 'Somewhere defensible.' They turned another corner, and above a snatch of sagging mudbrick wall she saw it: the gleaming pale stone of the Guildhouse.

Ree led Javani at a run towards the towering bulk of the Guildhouse, its carved sandstone outer walls dwarfing the mudbrick structures around it. It was the only fortified structure in town; even the town walls were packed mudbrick, like the bulk of the buildings within them. Ree had expected more stone, given the volume the mines quarried in their quest for precious stones, but mudbrick did the trick, as the local masons liked to say – although it precluded the more ostentatious architectural instincts of some of the more enthusiastic members.

The walls of the Guildhouse certainly could not be accused of lacking architectural enthusiasm. The carvings had spread since Ree's last visit, a little oak scaffold leaning against the wall marking the limit of their progress. A small, white-haired man was chiselling away at the yellow stone, partway through the creation of a magnificent griffin. They were big on griffins up here, wingless and crested, and already a family adorned the Guildhouse walls. Ree had always wondered at the term for a group of griffins. Probably a 'pride', but she could see merit in an 'abomination'.

The Guildhouse tower peeked over the top of the wall, gleaming in the sun. It, too, boasted scaffolding, and Ree was still shocked to see why. Before his death, the old Guildmaster had lost his mind: he'd been having the dome coated in turquoise. The carvings were one thing, but this was something else. He might as well have dispatched heralds across the expanse proclaiming his prodigious embezzlement.

The outer doors to the Guildhouse were open, the liveried guards absent, no doubt called to the carnage in the square. Ree dragged the kid along the shadow of the wall, scanning every window and alley's mouth for movement, for danger, for camels. At last they were close enough and darted inside, chests heaving, into the cool dark of the anteroom.

Keeping to the shadows, Ree advanced to the wide, carved staircase that dominated the outer hall, listening to the strange sounds from the distant square that filtered through high, latticed windows, while servants and Guild guards occasionally scuttled along the hallway beyond, looking wide-eyed and harried. The opulence of the interior always took her back. Sometimes, after a visit, she'd dream of it, and lost times from her past, triggered memories. The dreams made her melancholy and furious.

With a gesture to the glazed Javani, she reached out and grabbed a scurrying seneschal by the collar. 'Kid, get those doors closed and find some way to barricade them. You,' she turned the force of her gaze on the stunned flunky, who recoiled in her sweating grip. 'Fetch the Acting Guildmaster. Now!' Her expression brooked no dissent.

Kurush wanted to extend me his protection? she growled to herself. *Now's his fucking chance.*

EIGHT

Kurush was pleased. By the time he and his boys had come riding in, Nilam – his only credible rival for the permanent Guildmaster position – and her crew had done much of the heavy lifting in gaining control of the town's situation, and been pulped in the process. But now the instigators of whatever strange violence the square had witnessed were either dead or subdued, the corpses dragged aside in the pale, settling dust, the survivors bound and hauled off towards the cell block at the barracks. Even the monstrous Horvaun was in chains, restrained at last by Nilam's survivors just as Kurush and his riders felt ready to lend a hand.

He watched her led away at spear-point with his hands on his hips and a glow in his chest. He was aware of the faces in dark windows, those townsfolk peering into the declining carnage from positions of relative safety. They'd all have seen him take command, ordering the sealing of the gate, the rounding up and imprisonment of any outsiders who looked like they might have been responsible for the chaos, and setting the clean-up underway. And all from the towering saddle of his horse, framed in the brilliant sunlight and drifting dust clouds. He reckoned he looked pretty heroic.

This was ideal; Nilam was down, possibly for good, and Nilam's crew were either likewise distressed or on cell duty. His only real competition out of the picture – surely his confirmation for the post couldn't be far away after today's events. The gate guards and relief who'd come rushing were looking to him for orders. And Kurush had orders for them aplenty.

'You are in charge here?'

The voice that seemed to read his thoughts came from the street below, accented but confident. Kurush looked down.

A bloodied, dusty man in fine armour beneath a stained half-length cloak regarded him from beneath the watchful eye of a handful of Guild heavies. Behind him stood another figure, armed and dressed likewise, a cold-eyed woman with a sabre hanging from her hip.

'That I am,' Kurush said, sitting back in the saddle with what he hoped was a visible swagger. 'And who might you be, outsider? You part of this untidiness today?'

The man bowed his head. 'A regrettable part of this tragedy; would that we had only arrived ahead of the caravan, this blood-shed could have been averted.'

'You admit it freely? Your part in this inclement violence?' Kurush made ready to give the order to disarm and imprison these outsiders too.

The man met Kurush's accusatory stare with a confident gaze of his own. He was a fine-looking man, with a full, thick moustache that Kurush gazed at with no small envy.

'Perhaps I should introduce and explain myself,' the man said, his bearing relaxed, almost . . . regal. 'My name is Zakir Lazant, and I represent a very wealthy kingdom called Shenak.'

Kurush listened, and as he listened, the warm feeling in his chest began to grow.

'Why are we in the cells?'

'We're not in the cells. We're by the cells.'

'Seems a pretty slim distinction.' The convulsive sobs had passed, but Javani's legs were shaking. They'd started trembling the moment they'd moved out of the searing daylight and into the welcome cool of the Guildhouse, from what she'd initially taken to be the chill of the air. But the trembling wouldn't stop, even when she'd hugged her knees to her chest, and she was still sweating all over. Her teeth kept chattering too.

Ree had noticed the teeth. 'Just breathe, kid. Nice and slow. You're in shock. What you're feeling now is normal, and it will pass soon. Just breathe.'

'But why are we here?' Javani said through the tremble of her jaw.

Ree looked tired, too tired for this early in the day. She'd propped the crossbow on a stack of empty wine barrels in the nook where they had taken refuge, opposite the row of cells built into the old walls. Light came narrow and piercing from thin, barred windows in the upper wall. Somewhere on the far side, Javani knew, was the Guildhouse strongroom, packed to the gills with a god's fortune in metals, stones and ore, waiting to be shipped south where it would be processed into ever vaster wealth. Outside, the sounds of chaos and destruction had faded now, or were distant enough to be lost beneath the clamour of twitchy people just trying to get away from whatever it was that had happened.

'For our protection,' Ree muttered. She was counting out her bolts. There were still six.

'When's Kurush—?'

'Hells, kid, I don't know. They said he's on his way. They said to wait here, where we'd be safe. Now you know as much as I do.' Ree took a long breath, then the hard edges of her face softened. 'Are you feeling better? Are you able to tell me . . .' Her voice faltered for just a moment, a catch so small that Javani thought she must have been the only person in the world who could have noticed it. '. . . What happened?'

What happened. Javani felt only detachment, as if she were floating above herself, her thoughts of Moosh and his murder calm and logical, untainted by emotion. Moosh was dead, killed before her by agents of Shenak. If she chose to, she could still picture the moment the knife met his neck, recall the exact feeling of dread and escalating horror.

She did not choose to.

Who had they thought Moosh was? And who, in turn, was she? And Ree? And what of this White Spear, the giant southern mercenary, who had seemed no less keen to join in their killing? Why had she fought the Shenakar?

What happened. She shook her head, expecting Ree to grumble and snap, but instead her aunt put one arm around her trembling shoulders. 'Take your time, kid. We're safe here.'

A sound like a yelp came from one of the cells, and they both froze. Javani had been dimly aware that a couple of the cells were occupied – a pair of caravan guards in the first, one bandaged and moaning, one inert, and what she'd taken as two more of the same in the second. In her shock and grief, she'd paid them little enough attention, but now it became clear that one of the occupants of the second cell had kicked the other. As Javani watched, she did it again, kicking at his leg as he sat sprawled on the groaning pallet, then gesturing with a series of sharp, all-too-comprehensible hand signals. The man yelped once more and moved his hands to respond, and she kicked him again.

'Be still, my sister!' the man cried, rubbing at his injured leg. 'Control your fury, lest it consume you and burn this place to glass.'

'We are *in* a *cell*, Aki,' the woman replied, timing her kicks to her words. 'We are *locked* –' she aimed a particularly emphatic kick – '*up*.'

The man rolled away from her, at last out of kicking range. She jabbed with her leg anyway. 'A situation that is merely transitory, momentary and brief. A simple misunderstanding, to be clarified and remedied at the first reappearance of those in command.'

'Aki, they will hang us. Those accursed ungulates have sealed our deaths.'

The man turned, aghast. 'Why would they do such a thing, my sister? It is a crime against the Goddess herself to kill a poet and deny the world the beauty of his art.'

The woman glared back at him with eyes of depthless contempt. 'Why do you think, you asinine dolt? We are *outsiders*, and a bad thing has happened in this town. Of course they arrested the first people they saw who looked like they didn't belong.'

Javani shuddered and Ree wrapped her arm around her shoulders, then turned and barked at the cells, 'Whoever you are, seek solace in silence, or gods help me I will see you hanged myself. The kid and I have too much to deal with to put up with . . .' she gestured with her free hand '. . . whatever this is.'

In a small, shameful part of Javani's mind, the thought occurred that her aunt was being rather more affectionate, rather more understanding than usual. All too logical, given the circumstances, but the small, shameful part coughed and whispered, 'Wouldn't this be a good time to ask for something?'

'Ree?' Javani held her aunt's jacket tight, her face pressed to her shoulder. 'Ree? Can we go? Right now, far away from here.' She tried to make it seem off-the-cuff. 'Can we go west?'

'We can't go anywhere right now, kid. Not until we know it's safe to do so.'

'But then? Can we go west? To Arestan?'

Ree pushed her gently away and gave her an appraising look. 'You want to try crossing the Ashadi?'

'Nobody crosses the Ashadi,' Javani said reflexively. 'There are tigers.'

'There are not,' Ree replied, brows pinched in puzzlement.

'Oh, it was just something that . . .' Javani tailed off. Something Moosh used to say. Oh, Moosh. Oh, no. She felt tears returning, building hot beneath her eyes, her throat locking tight. No, not again. Not yet. There had to be a way to make something good come from all this horror. Somehow.

Javani sucked at her lip. Her anger was returning, a boiling rage of impotent frustration and sadness, fury at Moosh's savage and stupid killing, at these people who made such weighty decisions for and about her without having the decency to tell her what in hells was really happening. And behind the anger burned a curiosity, a tremulous, secret hope, that maybe there was something intriguing to be discovered about herself.

She glanced back at her aunt. She had to tell her, she knew. She had to tell her about Moosh's killing: about who, and about why. She realised she was afraid to. What if Lazant's story was true?

What if it wasn't?

Siavash stared at the ruins of the caravan in despair. He'd barely begun his foot wash at the rooms that Ulfat had arranged before the rising sounds of panic and destruction had brought him scurrying back, half-shod. The dust was settling, the dead and wounded being dragged away, and gradually the picture in the square was becoming clear.

It was hard to escape the conclusion that he was ruined. All his planning, all his work and calculation, wiped out in . . . in . . . whatever this was. The accounts Ulfat had brought were varied and ever less credible, but one thing they seemed to agree on was that the giant Horvaun had been at the centre of things. She was gone now, either dead or fled for all he could tell, but he recognised the bodies of the dark-clad bunch that had accompanied the caravan north as they were dragged to the square's edge.

'Ulfat,' he said again, but then found nothing to say beyond it. Most of the caravan wagons had suffered some measure of damage – one had the blood-slick corpse of a camel buried in its flank – but it was the looting that had sunk him. The moment the square had become a battleground, the rules of polite commerce had suspended themselves, and anyone within grasping distance of his merchandise had made off with whatever they could carry. He wouldn't have been at all surprised to discover his own staff among the beneficiaries of this Irregular Trade Opportunity, and in many respects he couldn't blame them.

A sad gaze around the baking, shattered square gave him little hope for restitution. The town's denizens had made for their homes and slammed whatever doors and shutters they could, and many more were in the process of leaving the walls altogether, no doubt claiming that their bundled silks, chains of pearls or spice jars were merely family heirlooms, brought to market for the day but returning unsold from an overabundance of sentimental attachment.

Ulfat shuffled and coughed beside him. More than anyone, Ulfat knew of just how much Siavash had had riding on this final stop. He was no doubt pondering the dimming prospects of his own continued employment, let alone the notion of a comfortable dotage, now galloping off over the horizon like a whipped horse.

Siavash contemplated wailing and rending his garments, then reconsidered. He'd already lost so much; why ruin an otherwise functional outfit on top of it all? He had other clothes, of course, brought in chests by the servants to the boarding rooms; perhaps there might yet be profit to be made in the trading of aspects of his wardrobe . . .

His eyes alighted on the last wagon in the row, ostensibly undamaged but visibly ransacked. Its side panelling, however, was intact. And if the panelling was intact, then perhaps the items he'd so carefully packed away inside were—

'You! You are the merchant?'

For a moment he thought the Horvaun had returned and his heart came to a sudden and complete stop. Then he matched the words to the voice, and the voice to the hooded and hunched figure before him. A small man, gesturing at him with knobbly, blistered fingers, their tips scarred and stained.

Siavash's heart restarted, and he straightened and puffed out his restored chest. 'I am Siavash Sarosh,' he began.

'Guvuli, wait there and touch nothing,' snapped the newcomer, addressing someone over his shoulder. 'Merchant, my name is Abishantarayan. We corresponded. Do you have my packages?'

Siavash deflated, and gestured with a sad hand at the devastation in the square. 'I could not tell you, master. My stock is blood-soiled, smashed or scattered to the winds. You are welcome to search the remains for your goods.'

The little man was staring at him intently. 'These,' he said in a low growl, 'you would miss. As I said, *we corresponded*.'

Understanding dawned in Siavash's battered mind. 'You— you are . . .' he lowered his voice, 'the purchaser of the *special goods*?'

The man nodded, fast and graceless. 'And do you have the *special goods*?' His sneer mocked Siavash's earnest furtiveness, but he didn't let it subdue his rising mood.

Siavash looked back to the last wagon and its pristine side panels. 'I believe so, indeed and in truth.'

The little man offered an unpleasant grin. 'Guvuli!' he called over his shoulder again, and gestured towards the last wagon. 'That one, you useless, hairy pig-bastard.' He continued to mutter in a low voice as a broad, bearded and mail-clad man limped into view. 'Thicker than baked shit, the bunch of them.'

'What happened here, Master Merchant?' rumbled the new man through his thick beard. 'We were down in the teahouse, missed the ruckus. This place smells like an abattoir.'

Siavash could hardly summon the energy to shrug. 'A dispute, of sorts, it seems. Settled with camelry.'

The hooded little man sniffed, his ravaged fingers tapping against his sharp chin. He had a foreign cast to him, Siavash thought, although his speech had little trace of accent. Perhaps he came from the other side of the mountains? You met all sorts at the edge of the world. 'Get the packages, Guvuli, and get them aboard our magnificent conveyance. We'll have what we need. And don't fucking whistle.'

The bearded man glowered, but he nodded. Before he set off for the wagon, he turned to Siavash. 'Might want to think about leaving the immediate vicinity for a time, Master Merchant. Things around the Guildhouse can get a little . . . *hectic* in the afternoons.'

'Of course,' Siavash said with a resigned bow. 'The customer is always right.'

Javani could tell that Ree was forcing herself not to pace. Her aunt's fists clenched and unclenched, and she'd laid out and counted her bolts three times on the barrel-top, tweaking their alignment with urgent, incessant jabs of her fingers. Despite her overwhelming shock and sadness, it was hard for Javani to avoid picking up on some of the older woman's barely suppressed frustration. The obvious question that Ree wasn't voicing itched at Javani: where in hells was Kurush?

Sounds drifted through the high, narrow windows from the courtyard beyond, the clomp and jingle of manoeuvring horses, stomps and calls. The panic was over, now came the clean-up. They were probably due a guard change soon.

A guard change. A sudden lurching thought occurred to her.

'Ree—' she said in a hoarse voice, her throat still sore from weeping.

Her aunt's attention snapped to her. 'Yes, kid? Are you ready to tell me what happened? The full story?'

A savage rectangle of brilliant daylight flooded the chamber as the door opened. Ree swept up the bolts and turned to face it, stuffing them into her jacket. 'About fu—'

Guild guards entered, and in numbers. They came with muttered curses and a heavy clinking, clustered uneasily around something they kept within a girdle of spears. Javani's eyes were narrow against the harsh outdoor light, one hand raised, and with a gasp she recognised the giant chained in their midst, hunched beneath the otherwise-normal-height ceiling.

The southern woman, the White Spear. The Guild guards had captured her, which was a relief, but Javani found herself horribly close. They drove her unresisting into the end cell, beyond that of the bickering siblings, and she sat down on the creaking pallet, manacled wrists before her, forearms resting on her knees, and looked up at Javani. Her pale eyes were utterly expressionless; she simply stared. The guards, their job done, bustled out in a flurry of muttering mail.

Javani felt very hot and very itchy. 'We have to get out of here,' she mumbled, then, louder, to Ree, 'We should leave. This place. Now.'

Ree was staring at the giant Horvaun in the cell. 'Was this one of the ones who meant to do you harm, kid? Who killed your friend?'

Javani shook her head, urgent, uncontrolled.

'Then who is she?'

Lazant's words in the alley returned to her, unbidden. 'The White Spear,' Javani recited. 'A notorious mercenary killer.'

The Horvaun didn't react. Her gaze was locked on Javani, but there was no malice in it, no feeling at all. Just a blank, relentless stare.

To Javani's surprise, Ree stepped into the path of the gaze. 'Whitespear, is it?' she said. 'What are the terms of your contract? Who's your broker?' She tipped her head forward, staring down the mercenary from beneath implacable brows. 'Why are you here? Answer me.'

The man in the cell was on his feet, slim fingers wrapping the dark iron bars. 'Excuse me, fair maiden,' he said, gazing at Ree as if seeing her for the first time, 'but I notice you have a most particular scar. May I trouble you for your name?'

Ree kept her eyes on the mercenary. 'I told you once. Shut up.'

He fell silent, but he remained where he was, and he seemed to be watching Ree very intently. Ree's eyes were still locked on the Horvaun; Javani was the only one to notice.

Light bloomed in the cells once more as the door opened again. This time, Ree held the Horvaun's gaze for a moment, just to show that she could do it all day, before turning to face the new arrival.

'Kurush. You took your time.'

The Acting Guildmaster swaggered into the cells at a leisurely pace. He was clean of travel dust, his face washed and breastplate gleaming, and carried what looked like a goblet in one hand, one from the old Guildmaster's private set.

'Mistress Ree. I do so hope I didn't keep you waiting.'

Ree's ire had too many targets. She narrowed her focus on Kurush alone, turning away from both the black-armoured mercenary and the mute but gawking man in the cell.

'You're here now, that's what matters. I need to talk to you about—'

Kurush's palm went to his shining forehead. 'Where are my manners? I need to make some introductions.'

Javani felt a tingle in her chest, a tightening, a pre-fear. This was all wrong. 'Ree—'

Her aunt's back was to her. 'Oh really?'

Kurush stepped to one side and gestured to the doorway with a flourish of his goblet. 'Ree the horse-farmer, may I present to you a young man of impeccable breeding and manners, ambassador of his kingdom and newest patron of the Kazeraz Guildhouse, and, I'm proud to say, a close personal friend: His Royal Highness, Prince Zakir Lazant of Shenak, rightful heir to the throne of the King of Kings.'

Javani's heart dropped through the floor.

NINE

The first gentle clinks of spurs echoed from the smooth stone of the cell walls. 'Lazant,' Javani breathed, trying to move her arms, her legs. 'Lazant.' Her voice was little more than a wheeze.

The clink was suddenly loud in her ears, deafening, and the scorching daylight at the chamber's end was coalescing around a well-proportioned, unhurried silhouette. He was holding a matching goblet. 'Lazant!' Javani gasped.

Ree's attention was fixed on the doorway and the approaching man-shape, but she angled her head towards Javani. 'This is him?'

She could only squeak in response.

Ree snatched up the crossbow and began to crank it.

'Please, my good man,' came Lazant's warm tones, twisted in charm towards Kurush. 'There is no need for honorifics.' Then, commanding, over one shoulder: 'Khalida.'

Moosh's killer was with him.

Zakir Lazant stepped into view, his handsome features lit with delight, his arms spread wide, goblet balanced in one hand, just as burnished and oiled as Kurush. His eyes gleamed as they settled on Javani, trapped at the cell block's end. Cold-eyed Khalida was two paces behind him, one decorated hand resting on the bone hilt of an all-too-familiar knife.

The man in the cell started. 'Master Lazant,' he called, 'over here!

It is Aki and Anashe, your faithful and efficient guides, blameless victims of a most dreadful muddle and confusion—'

Lazant ignored him, his eyes for Javani alone. 'Hello again, my child,' he said in near-perfect Serican. Beyond him, Javani registered the White Spear rising to her feet, eyes burning, hands reaching, but Javani could not lift her gaze from the beaming Shenakar.

Ree stepped in front of her, blocking his view, the crossbow cranked and loaded, held loose in her hands. 'Charmed, I'm sure,' she said with a brittle smile. 'And now our introductions are complete, perhaps you'd like to explain yourself, man of Shenak?'

'Child,' Lazant said, stretching to talk past her aunt. 'Come over here now. Let us end this before more are hurt.'

Ree flexed the weapon in her arms. 'Don't talk to her, talk to me, golden boy. I'm unfamiliar with every nuance of courtly custom in your kingdom, but around here we generally do what the person with the crossbow says.'

At last, Lazant allowed his gaze to fall on Ree, his moustache tweaked at its edges, a picture of saintly indulgence. He stared at her for a long moment, appraising. 'Mistress . . . Ree, was it? The . . . horse-farmer.'

Ree said nothing. A muscle in her cheek twitched.

'As I said to your child—' the man began.

'She's not mine.'

'Ah. But you are the girl's keeper.' He didn't break conversational stride. 'I represent the nation of Shenak, and the kingdom is in grave danger. There are those who believe the child has a claim to the throne of the King of Kings, and while she lives, the kingdom could be plunged into a grisly and endless war of succession, costing countless lives, destroying decades of peace, bringing only ruin.'

Ree's head jerked, tilting to one side. Javani tensed. She'll laugh, she thought. She'll find the very notion of me being a queen ridiculous. Right?

'You are mistaken,' Ree said, her voice razor-edged. 'You have the wrong child.'

'I do not believe that is the case.' Lazant took another step forward, and Ree snapped the crossbow level with his chest. He raised one empty palm. 'Please, put down the weapon,' he said. 'I have no quarrel with you, or any other. Do as instructed and you may walk away, return to your farm and your horses. It is with the greatest regret that I travel here on this business, but it is necessary. It is necessary to end one life to save thousands. This is the highest duty. The fate of a kingdom is at stake, its people, its purpose. But I take no pleasure in this grim task.'

'Liar,' Ree spat.

The man in the cell cleared his throat. 'Did I perchance mishear, or did he say your name was Ree, and you are a keeper of horses?'

Everyone ignored him.

'Please. Step away, farmer, and turn this tragedy into a boon,' Lazant said, his voice mellow and polished, weighed with empathy. 'Go back to your animals. Khalida will make restitution for the child. It will be best for everyone.'

Behind him, Khalida flicked open her thick belt. Sewn within it glittered silver ingots, visible for an instant before the belt was refastened. Javani saw Kurush's eyes linger, and the Acting Guildmaster licked at dry lips.

'Listen to the man, Ree,' Kurush called. He'd already moved to one side, behind a column and out of direct bowshot. 'Shenak is a rich kingdom, and it knows how to reward its friends. You want to stay a dirt-farmer at the edge of the world for ever?'

Ree didn't look at him, the crossbow now pressed to her shoulder, pointed at the dead centre of Lazant's gleaming breastplate. 'He's lying to you, Kurush. He's grotesquely wrong, and he's mendacious with it. I hope for whatever he promised you, you took your payment up front.' In the cell, the woman kicked her brother again.

'Please, I assure you I speak the truth of gods,' Lazant replied, the smile still lingering beneath his moustache. He was impossibly reasonable. 'It gives me no pleasure to hunt children, nor to drag my people to a desert armpit like this. But I do my duty, horse-farmer. I do my duty as a prince of Shenak, for the good of the kingdom.' He leaned around Ree again and addressed Javani directly. 'Now you must do yours, my child. Come over here. Yours is a thankless role but it will be quick, and you will feel nothing. Play your part and this ghastly saga ends. Refuse, and your end will be no different, but it may . . . take longer. And you will have company.' He gave Ree a pained look, the smile replaced by a regretful grimace.

Javani looked at him, the oiled moustache, the shining armour, the ornate-hilted knife at his belt; at Khalida moving sideways, hand on her own knife; at Ree swinging the crossbow from one to the other, trying to keep both in the sights. At the posse of Guild guards now arriving in the doorway, marshalled by Kurush's frantic signals. At the massive White Spear, still silent and immobile in her cell, her manacles taut and creaking. At the two figures in the end cell, now engaged in a heated, hissed, argument, accompanied by furious, knife-sharp gestures.

I don't want to die, she thought. I've hardly even lived. I didn't ask for this, nobody ever gave me a choice. Ree never gave me a choice. It's all so unfair.

Shoot them, Ree, she wanted to say, wanted to scream. *Shoot all of them and let's get out of here.* As if her aunt would ever put a bolt in anyone.

A noise from outside fixed her attention like a lance: a soft two-tone whistle, transcending the jittery gloom of the cell block, echoing around the oblivious adults. Was that what she thought it was? Was she the only one to hear it? Her earlier thought returned at a gallop.

'Uh, R-Ree,' she stammered, her voice scratchy and far too quiet.

Ree's attention was split between the advancing Shenakar, and the new guards muscling in behind Kurush. 'A little busy here, kid.' Then, louder: 'Kurush, tell your royal friend to call off his hound and stand aside. The kid and I are walking out of here, or he's going home in an urn.'

'You know I can't be doing that, Ree,' Kurush called back from behind the column. 'Besides, you're always saying the kid's not yours – what's the harm? Take the silver, it's a good trade.'

Ree dropped the fistful of bolts back onto the barrel top. 'I'll save one of these for you then, that sound fair?'

'You know you won't get more than one away, Ree. And like as not you'll cut nothing but stone.'

'Bold words for a man cowering, Kurush. You know what kind of crossbow this is?' Ree called. She slapped the weapon's flank. 'This is one of a strictly limited number made by a friend of mine in the workshops of Arowan, and I can assure you it is phenomenally effective. Want to see what a broadhead will do to that tin plate of yours?'

'I tell you, my sister, this is divine providence! She wills it!' The man in the cells was now yelling.

'Ree? Hey!' Javani tried to make herself heard in the growing clamour. Ree had to be fooling nobody, they'd know she was bluffing as surely as Javani did. Wait, was that another whistle? It was so hard to tell over the noise of the advancing guards and the thunder of her pulse in her ears. 'Ree!'

Lazant was still trying to talk past Ree to her, his face lined with affected concern. 'Please, child. Come over now, and let the suffering end. It will be very much worse if we must come to get you.'

Ree spoke through the corner of her mouth, the crossbow swinging in her grip. 'Don't worry, kid, I won't let them take you. We'll get out of here, then they won't see us for dust.'

I don't think it's going to be up to you, retorted a little voice in Javani's head, and the only person who doesn't seem to realise that is you. She was already calculating with another part of her fevered brain, shuffling along the wall. If the windows are *there*, then the shared wall is *there*, meaning the overloaded section would be right . . . over . . .

'Ree, what time would you say it was?'

Ree almost looked around. 'What?'

Javani was moving faster now, sliding crabwise along the wall, ducking down behind the barrels. For a moment she caught sight of the White Spear, staring back from her cell. Without obvious effort or acknowledgement, the giant Horvaun placed her black helmet over her great pale head. 'Ree, listen, you need to listen!'

This time Ree did look around. '*What*, kid?'

Lazant gave a heavy sigh. 'This is taking too long.' He waved a gauntleted hand towards Kurush. 'Do what you must, Guildmaster.'

Something like a thunderclap echoed around the cells, and the building shook. As one, eyes looked up to the narrow windows, which seemed to be trembling. Khalida's bone-handled knife, somehow now in her hand and snaking towards Ree, hovered in the air.

'What in all the gods—' said one of the guards, then the side wall blasted apart in a shock of flying stone. A wave of force blew out from the wall, laying waste the ancient stonework, smashing the cell bars out of view and blazing the sight from Javani's eyes. She flung herself to the earth as the blast punched her ears and rattled her bones, shaking her organs to jelly as it passed through her. Fist-sized chunks smashed against the columns and the walls, felling two of the guards who had been directly opposite the blast. Javani clamped her hands over her ears as chunks of splintered stone ricocheted around the cells and a pulsing wall of dust flowed over her.

In another moment it was over, the sensation returning slowly to Javani's battered nerves, along with the realisation that the ringing in her ears was the only sound in the world, aside from the soft creak and clomp of falling stone. Bright streaks of extraordinary colours blotted her vision, and she couldn't be certain whether her eyes were open or closed. The cell block seemed very much lighter than before.

'Ouch,' she tried to say, but coughed stone instead. Hard and prolonged. As her spasms subsided, she heard other coughs, and moans and whimpers, commotion from the courtyard beyond, shouts and bells. A number of people in proximity were in distress, and the air was full of their cries as well as choking smog.

Javani managed to sit up, feeling as though she'd fallen a very long way without going anywhere. The ringing in her ears had not subsided, and everything sounded vaguely underwater. More furious blinking and an oblique view brought just enough focus to make out a ragged hole in the cell block wall through which daylight poured. The bars of the near two cells had been blasted clean away, the rest of the block was lost to her in a miasma of swirling dust, now lit brilliant by the shaft of afternoon light from the hole, enough to render it impenetrable. Things were moving back there: she heard the clunk of shifting stone, the groan of metal under strain. Water was dripping from somewhere, drifting in a shimmering curtain of spray across the gash in the wall, floating incongruous rainbows above the carnage.

At last her brain caught up. The Guvulis were robbing the Guildhouse. They'd blown the strongroom. They were executing *her* plan. And she needed to get the fuck out of there before the whole block came down on their heads.

You really overcooked that one, Movos Guvuli.

Still blinking colours and shapes, Javani wafted thick air from before her eyes. 'Ree!' she called. Her aunt had still been in the open when the blast hit. She might be injured. She might be dead. '*Ree!*'

'I told you it would take two blasts, you witless apes. Quickly now, load it up, get it all on the wagon!' The voice came from somewhere beyond, out in the courtyard, echoing off blasted stone. Shantar, the alchemist. Javani tried to parse the scene of devastation before her in the cells. Figures were slumped at the chamber's edge, surely guards. It was hard to detect movement in the shifting walls of dust that drifted before her eyes. She began crawling around the shredded ruin of the barrels towards where Ree had been, praying that her aunt was alive.

A blackened shape lurched out of the drifting dust ahead, suddenly massive in the shaft of daylight from the courtyard. Javani froze. The shape looked one way, then another, and began moving towards her.

Javani began to crawl backwards, retreating towards her corner.

Before her, beyond the ruined barrels, Ree staggered to her feet, her crossbow lost, one hand on her head, the other clutching her scabbarded sword. She was whirling, groggy and panicked, blind to the giant shape's approach.

'Ree!' Javani cried in warning, but the huge figure snapped its invisible gaze to her. Javani ducked back to her corner, cursing herself.

Ree mumbled something as the figure approached her, tried to draw the sword. The figure merely pushed her to one side, into the rubble and out of view.

'Someone!' Javani squeaked. 'Help!' The shape stepped over the barrel-wrecks and into focus, and Javani found herself staring back at the White Spear. Somehow the woman seemed even more massive in the confines of the ravaged cell block, seeming to fill it in each direction. The pits of her battered armour were plugged with dust, and dark streaks marked her skin. Her dark visor was flipped, giving her an extra face above her own, upside-down and inverted. Javani couldn't stop staring at it.

'Girl,' she said in ponderous Serican, her voice like distant thunder.

Javani only shook her head.

'Girl of . . . prince.'

Javani shook her head again, her entire body trembling uncontrollably.

'Come, girl.'

The White Spear took Javani's arm, then hoisted her up and against her hip, holding her like an infant. On some level Javani was deeply insulted. The White Spear turned and began stomping through the rubble, Javani held tight against her. As they reached the tear in the wall, Khalida reared out of the dust cloud, the bone-handled dagger in her hand. The White Spear belted her backhanded against the wall and continued on her way. Khalida's head made a hollow thunk as it bounced from the stone, and she did not rise.

'You're . . . you're not going to kill me?' Javani said as the woman clambered up over the rubble towards the streaming rent in the courtyard wall.

The pale southerner frowned. 'No.'

On top of everything else, the lingering ringing in her ears was driving Javani to distraction. 'Can you speak more than one bloody syllable at a time?'

The White Spear paused, nodded once, then resumed her heavy pace. Javani was ready to scream, for a good number of reasons, but then the Horvaun spoke again.

'By all means, if that is your preference,' she said in clear and fluent Serican, as she and Javani stepped through the riven wall and into the vast courtyard beyond. Her cumbersome speech had vanished like morning mist. 'Do you know who I am?'

'Wait, how come you can talk now? Properly, I mean.'

The armoured wagon stood at the courtyard's edge, two figures at its rear, loading heavy sacks that issued from the blackened and smouldering chasm in the stone. Guards lay scattered around it, probably dead, certainly unmoving. Javani took all this in without really processing it; it seemed no more unusual than anything else that was going on.

'I have always been able to talk. Properly,' the giant woman replied, stepping carefully down through chunks of blasted stone. 'But sometimes it pays for people to consider you less than you are, and a certain slowness of speech can help some to presume a certain slowness of thought. It is always better to be underestimated than the reverse. I ask again: do you know who I am?'

'You're the White Spear,' Javani said. 'You're a mercenary killer.'

'I am a contract operative,' the woman corrected. She had a pronounced accent, unlike any Javani had ever heard, sharp vowels and pinched consonants. But her speech rattled along with perfect clarity. 'And you are my contract.'

A guard came running into the courtyard, pike in hand, alarm and confusion fighting to be uppermost in his expression. The White Spear diverted to pass him and cracked him across the back of the head. He dropped without a sound. She was making for the ravaged outer gate.

'What do you mean?' Javani asked, finding herself clinging to the woman. Where was Ree? What had happened to the Shenakar?

'I was engaged by the council of viziers of Shenak to find you,' the White Spear said in galloping Serican. 'And bring you back to Shenak.'

'Not kill me?'

'Of course not. You are a scion of the ruling house, a princess by blood.'

'What?'

'You are the heir to the throne. It is sealed and certified. My clients mean to see you wear the crown of the King of Kings.'

'*What?*'

'Step no further, Horvaun.'

Javani turned to see Zakir Lazant barring their path. If he'd looked a little travel-worn before, proximity to an impromptu act of demolition had done his decorum no favours. Blood darkened one side of his face and his moustache was matted with dust. His sabre was still at his side, but in his hands he held a set of slim and murderous daggers.

'Let us be reasonable. Turn over the girl and I will see you paid double your customary fee.'

'No.'

'Triple. I am a man of my word.'

'No.'

'Then you must die with her, which is a shameful waste.'

The daggers whipped through the air and the White Spear turned, shielding Javani with her broad back. Clangs and bangs marked the daggers' impacts, and the White Spear grunted and bared her teeth. 'Wait here,' she said, placing Javani down, then spun around to face Lazant, her great pale braids swinging beneath the lip of her helmet.

The Shenakar drew his sabre. 'Guards! To me! The prisoners are escaping!'

A few of the guards who'd survived the blasts or come from elsewhere came shuffling out of the gloom, lining uncertainly up alongside Lazant with swords and pikes raised, blocking the path to the gate.

'Take them!' Lazant cried, sweeping his sabre down, and the guards charged. The White Spear charged right back. She met the first with a leaping sweep of her mailed fist, driving him sideways, then caught the pike of the next and swung him around on the end of it, flinging him into his comrades. She batted away a sword-stroke with a forearm, then kicked out her attacker's knee, before grabbing the final guard by his breastplate and hurling him across the courtyard into a thick pillar.

Lazant stood alone, his sabre in hand. The White Spear advanced on him.

'See you again *very* soon.' He grinned, then turned and ran. A moment later he was out of sight around the corner.

Javani felt her whole body unclench. She was very thirsty and her mouth tasted of blood. From somewhere behind her came more shouts and a low rumble. She couldn't bring herself to turn. She had no interest in watching a building collapse.

The White Spear dusted her gauntleted palms and adjusted her visor, her face disappearing within the black shell. 'Now we can go. We will travel south with the caravan, then overland to the east. A ship is waiting for you. I will keep you safe.' That background rumbling was oddly familiar. It was really getting loud now, and Javani felt a tremor in the earth beneath. Had the blasts cracked the earth? The White Spear turned her head and extended one hand to her, her pale gaze locked through the depths of the visor. She had to raise her voice a little over the noise. 'There are formalities, but those who engaged me were clear. Within the year you will be queen—'

Eight horses hauling the Guvulis' enormous wagon roared into Javani's eyeline, swinging wide in an arc, the vehicle sliding sideways, and knocked the mercenary from view beneath its heavy wheels. Javani screamed again.

'Kid! Kid!' It took Javani a moment to hear the voice over her own screaming. Ree was on the driver's bench, hand outstretched. 'Get on, quick!'

Cries and shouts came from the courtyard's far end, where the Guvuli brothers had realised that their wagon was gone.

Javani stood immobile with shock. 'But—'

'Come on, kid!'

Then arms were around her, lifting her up and forward, and she thought the White Spear must have returned, and felt a sharp and unexpected pang of relief. But it was only Ree, jumped down from the bench, her arms wrapped around her niece.

'Let's go,' Ree said in a low, fierce voice, and levered her up onto the wagon, leaping up alongside. She cracked the reins and they were rolling, swinging the wagon wide around the courtyard, lining up for the gate.

As they wheeled, Javani saw a pair of figures stagger from the blackened blast hole in the Guildhouse wall, one supporting the other, her shoulder beneath his arm, using a discarded spear as a walking stick. The brother and sister from the cell. The woman looked left and right, but the man, despite apparent grogginess, had eyes only for the wagon. He lurched forward, dragging his sister with him. Javani yelped.

'Faster, Ree!'

'What do you think I'm— Shit, guard!'

The last remaining upright Guild trooper in the courtyard was ahead of them, moving for the horses, and they were nowhere near up to speed. All he had to do was halt the lead team and the others would fall in right behind.

A spear hit the side of his helmet, glancing away with a shrill clang that seemed to reverberate around the ravaged courtyard, and leaving a bright groove in the otherwise tarnished metal. The man rocked for a moment, one arm extended, then his eyes rolled up into his head and he dropped from view.

'Might we trouble you for a lift?' came a voice from beside the bench. The woman was jogging alongside the accelerating wagon. 'Remaining in this place seems ill-advised.'

'Where's your brother?' Javani blurted in shock.

The woman narrowed her eyes, as if surprised Javani knew of her companion, then nodded towards the rear of the wagon. 'I took the liberty of loading him already. He has endured a dispute with a hunk of flying masonry and is more of a burden than usual.'

Ree leaned across. 'Hop on, fast. We're getting out of here.'

With a nod, the woman dropped back, and a moment later Javani heard a distinct thump from behind her. 'What are you doing? We have no idea who—'

'They took care of the guard, kid. And we're in no position to choose our allies right now.' She snapped the reins again and bawled at the horses. A moment later, they were through the broken Guildhouse gateway and tearing down the street, the brown buildings flying past in a blur. Ree bellowed and called as they raced, screaming for people to get out of the way, and they cantered through the mostly cleared square and off down the main street clipping almost nothing.

'Gate's coming up.' Ree's knuckles were white on the reins. 'Hold on!'

Javani gripped the bench as they thundered down the street towards the gatehouse. The guards were slow to react, uncertain of what they were seeing, unable to believe that a wagon would be barrelling at top speed down the street towards them with no intention of slowing. Ree's howls at them to move were buried beneath the wagon's roar, but realisation dawned just in time. The gate guards threw themselves from the wagon's path as it rocketed past, throwing up a great plume of dust.

Then they were out, free of the town and onto the desert road, and Ree was whooping and yelling and crying with triumph as they travelled out towards the plains.

Beside her, Javani hugged herself to the bench and felt only doubt.

TEN

Movos Guvuli stood with his hands on his head in the desolated courtyard, staring open-mouthed after the vanished wagon. At his feet lay the torn ruin of a sack spilling uncut gemstones and lumps of ore. From all around came alarm bells and shouts, the moans of the injured and crump of collapsing stone.

'She . . .' he said, working his jaw. 'She took the damned-by-gods wagon. She took our ride. She took our *haul!*'

Beside him a pile of rubble righted itself and sat up. A mountain of black steel shook its head, displacing a great cloud of pulverised yellow stone. 'She took the girl,' it rumbled.

Movos took an involuntary step sideways. There seemed no end to this sudden run of unpleasant surprises.

The mountain removed a dust-battered helmet, revealing a pale and rigid countenance and thick cables of sun-bleached hair. It pushed itself to its feet like a creature rising from the sea and began dusting itself down. 'This . . .' it said, gesturing to the blasted hole in the cell-block wall. 'Was you?'

Movos nodded slowly, his immediate shock forgotten, displaced by the sheer strangeness of the enormous foreigner.

'Then . . . Thank you.'

Movos looked around for Shantar and the others. He'd told them to get out at the first sign of trouble, to make it back to the safe house in town with what they could carry. This counted as trouble, all right – they were beyond signs and confronting it head on, and at high speed. But they hadn't made for the gates, or even into the courtyard. He shook his head. They didn't listen. They never listened.

Squeals and screaming issued from inside the strongroom's new entryway. Movos recognised Shantar's nasal screech, like nails on slate. He was demanding the guards unhand him. Movos swallowed against a throat drier than a shallow creek bed in high summer. It was over, in the turn of a coin, in the theft of a wagon, in the surprising number of guards who had been congregating in the cell block, in stark defiance of what the urchin had told him of their shift patterns. That fucking kid. What had he been thinking, going hand in glove with a child? And a stupid one at that.

'Well, shit,' said Movos Guvuli.

The mountain tapped him on the shoulder with a hand as wide as his thigh. Movos vaguely registered that she was female. 'Should not stay here,' she said, and nodded towards the open gates. The Guildhouse bell was clanging so hard it risked tearing itself loose, no doubt summoning reinforcements from the town walls and the surrounding territory. 'There is not long.'

Movos cast a long, hard look at the blasted wall, the ruined sack, the wide, deep wagon ruts in the dusty earth, and spat uselessly. From somewhere inside the cells came the rushing thunder of the ceiling collapsing, followed by a sudden and towering billow of stone-dust.

'I am inclined to acquiesce.'

Kurush sipped rosewater and pressed a damp cloth to his head. The bleeding had stopped but it was still very sore, and the ringing in his ears felt as if it was there for ever. He coughed occasionally, and each time seemed to expectorate gobbets of phlegmy dust.

From his seat on the steps, he surveyed the ruin of the courtyard, the collapsed wall, the fallen gallery and shattered columns, the smoking wreckage on the yard's far side. Early reports suggested the breaching of the strongroom and the attempted robbery of its contents, but it was hard to know how much had been taken. Harder still given his late predecessor's approach to record keeping, which had always enjoyed a distant if cordial relationship with reality.

Kurush pushed the stained cloth against his head again and winced. Reporting the day's events to the Guild would be no easy task. Perhaps there was a way to conceal the losses, especially given the gaps in the official record, but concealing the fuck-off great hole in the side of the Guildhouse was going to take something spectacular.

The Shenakar prince was approaching the steps, looking, if anything, more dishevelled than Kurush. His eyes glowed with fervour, a near manic smile on his handsome features, and Kurush straightened and pushed the cloth out of sight behind him.

'Your highness. Are you hurt?'

'The prisoners escaped, Guildmaster,' the prince said. It was a statement, but Kurush felt as if he was supposed to respond. Behind the prince, his lieutenant was following with unsteady steps, a discoloured bandage wrapped around her head and covering one eye, something bundled in her arms.

'The assault on the Guildhouse was, uh, an unexpected complication—'

The prince pressed his gauntleted hands together at his chin and took a long breath, then smoothed his dusty moustache and smiled again. 'It is no surprise. The path of the divine is strewn with obstacles, and only faithful execution will stay the course.'

'Huh?'

'I am being tested, Guildmaster, assessed for worthiness. This time, I will not fail. Mother always said I was too quick to give quarter. Not this time.' He fixed Kurush with a gaze that burned with zeal and something more besides. 'I must request an extension to our arrangement. Today's events are no way to end this tale.'

Kurush smiled, relieved that the man wasn't about to up and return to Shenak in a huff, with Kurush's part unpaid. Kurush wasn't much inclined to let the man go anywhere unless he'd siphoned enough Shenakar silver to patch up the Guildhouse and more besides. His predecessor had left the Guildhouse records with more holes than one of his moth-savaged old shirts, and the part of becoming Guildmaster where Kurush got to start his own tidy store of profit seemed ever more remote. 'Of course, your highness. Although you should be aware that my resources are, uh, momentarily diminished by circumstance. This will, uh, necessitate something of an increase in, uh, operational expenditure.'

The prince's smile returned, this time with some genuine warmth. 'That will be no issue. Prepare a column with your best trackers. We cannot let them escape into the wilds.'

Kurush winced again. 'It's going to take a little time, your highness – the caravan's arrival, the state of the . . . uh . . .'

The Shenakar's eyes were unblinking voids.

'I'll, uh, see to it,' Kurush finished.

'I have no doubt that you will, my friend,' the prince replied.

My friend. That was more like it. Friends got paid. Kurush inflated.

The Shenakar lieutenant stepped forward and murmured something to the prince, then proffered the bundle in her arms. He reached out and tweaked aside the ruin of her half-cloak to reveal the bundle's contents.

'This, I believe, may prove useful,' said the prince, blowing the dust from Ree's mechanical crossbow.

'We can't make for the farm, it's the first place they'll go.' Ree was talking, almost shouting over the thunder of hooves and heavy wheels. Javani was barely listening. Her mind was whirling like a tornado.

The White Spear had said she was a princess. That they were going to make her queen. Or kill her. Like they'd killed Moosh. Oh, Moosh . . .

'Don't worry, kid, the place will be safe in Edigu's hands. He'll see to the animals and lie low if the time comes. Hells, he could run the place without us if he wanted. No, our primary issue is that this wagon leaves tracks a mile wide, so we need to head somewhere the tracks won't stick.'

'You mean to travel into the desert?'

Javani started to find the woman from the cells leaning through the gap in the canopy, kneading at the muscles of her upper arm. The bright desert light revealed the sharp-featured face and close-cropped scalp of a woman somewhat younger than Ree, but certainly not young by Javani's estimation. Up close, it was evident that her clothes (and likely those of her brother) were little more than wrapped strips of drab cloth, tightly bound around her limbs and body and secured with a network of straps and pouches. It looked practical, but a nightmare to change in and out of. She was chewing something.

'That I do,' Ree confirmed without looking around, as if she'd been talking to the woman all along.

'These horses cannot run like this for ever. I hope you know what you are doing.'

'That I do.'

'My sister,' came a slurred voice from behind them, 'we left our weapons, our equipment. In the prison. Cells. We should go back.'

The woman spoke over her shoulder. 'No, we should not go back. I am unsure whether this fresh stupidity is the result of your injury or your customary dull wits, but now is not the time to indulge it.'

'Usually our weapons are within reach when we escape,' came the mumbled reply.

Javani turned. 'Usually? How often has this happened to you?'

Ree clicked her tongue. 'Be useful. Are we being followed?'

The woman turned again and bellowed into the back of the wagon. 'Brother, rouse yourself from your stupor! Are we pursued?'

Various clonks and shuffles came from the wagon's rear, loud over the roar of the wheels. 'I see nothing!' The man's voice, the one she called brother. 'The land is barren, nothing but . . . that is, there is . . . I cannot . . .' There came another crash. 'My sister, my words are gone. The injury! I am . . . wordless!'

Ree gave a heavy sigh. 'Are we being followed or not?'

The man appeared, his head popping through beside his recoiling sister like puppets in a show. Beneath short braids, his face was well-worn but handsome, to Javani's eye, and looked similar enough to the woman's to confirm a relation. His clothing was near-identical, the same neutral wraps, but for the necklace of charms that dangled briefly at the top of his chest before he tucked it back within.

'Sister, my words! How am I to compose my works without vocabulary, without lexicon? I am bereft, I am shorn and impoverished, my very—'

'Sounds like you have plenty of words,' Javani volunteered.

'By the Goddess, you are right! I am restored! The light shines upon me again. Once more shall the desert echo to the sounds of—'

The muscles of Ree's jaw were standing proud, casting deep shadows. 'Are we being fucking followed?' she said in a voice just loud enough to be heard over the wagon, her tone enough to cut the man's rambling short. He ducked back through the canopy.

'I see nothing behind but drifting dust,' came his voice a moment later.

'Good. Names.'

'Anashe,' said the woman, still leaning through the gap.

'And the idiot?'

'My brother, Aki.'

'Younger?'

She shook her head, and Ree rolled her eyes.

'My sister, that is hardly a fitting introduction,' Aki proclaimed, his head reappearing. 'Given the distance we have travelled, the weight of our quest – we must use words of consequence, befitting—'

'Is this normal?' Ree asked Anashe, her attention still on the bleached road.

'I regret so.'

'—to wit, I am Aki, called the Gale, and my sister is Anashe, called the Shadow. I am but a humble warrior-poet, charged by the Goddess of All Creation to—'

'He also claims he can smell water,' Anashe muttered.

'Why are you called those things?' Javani asked Anashe as her brother rattled on. 'Gale and Shadow.'

Anashe's mouth tweaked into a half-smile. 'He is called Gale because he makes a lot of noise, and leaves a mess in his wake.'

Aki snorted. 'And she is called Shadow because she dogs your footsteps and disappears at night.'

Javani's half-smile matched Anashe's. 'That sounds pretty slick.'

Aki frowned. 'It is not supposed to. It is denigrating.'

'I don't know,' Javani said, 'it sounds good to me. Mysterious.'

'For someone who calls himself a poet,' Anashe chuckled, 'you'd think he would have better command of his tongue.'

Aki stiffened. 'It is no mere thing to denigrate in multiple languages. In our home tongue, she is called far worse, and deservedly. She is most denigrated!'

'What tongue is that?' Javani asked as Anashe cuffed her brother.

Aki flicked at his sister then waved a hand in an expansive sweep. He seemed much recovered from his daze. 'One from far from here, far beyond these lands and their peoples, none of whom has travelled as we have.'

Javani's curiosity was well and truly piqued. 'Did you come from the west? Over the Ashadi? Do you know a way, the location of the secret pass? You have to tell us, you have to show us—'

'Soft, little one, softness and tranquillity,' said Aki, one palm raised. 'We did not come from the west, but from the east. Far, far to the east.'

'Oh.' Javani deflated.

'But we came a roundabout route,' Anashe supplied, as if trying to soften her disappointment.

'And I have many stories from our travels, such stories!' Aki beamed. 'Are you a lover of stories, little one? Of tales of gods and demons, kings and—'

'Stop calling me "little one",' Javani growled. 'It's demeaning.'

'You are little,' Anashe responded mildly, 'and there is one of you. Do you have another name?'

'Javani.'

Aki and Anashe looked at each other and sniggered.

'What?' Javani's face was getting hot, her back itchy. 'What?'

'Charming as this is,' Ree broke in, half turning her head. 'Can we perhaps concentrate our efforts on escaping vicious murder for a little longer? We need to put as much distance as possible between us and the town before Kurush and his friends find their collective arses with both hands and get on our trail. It's not like we'll be hard to spot, even for a piss-poor outdoorsman like Kurush.' Great yellow plumes marked the wagon's progress, drifting into the clear afternoon air, while before them the landscape began to flatten and blanch. The great salt desert beckoned. 'Can we lose some weight? What's back there?'

'Looks like . . .' Aki began, then, 'by the Goddess!'

Ree yanked the loose canvas aside. 'What is it?'

'Sacks of riches. Metals, gems, ingots . . . a fortune.'

'Throw it.'

Aki's mouth opened and closed. 'But . . . But . . .'

'Aki, if that is your name, we are travelling at speed into a desert in a heavily loaded wagon. The lighter we are, the further we'll get. That treasure is of no use to us if we're dried bones in the sand, right?'

'But . . . But . . .'

'Throw it! The sooner the better, or our tracks will be glinting in the sun.'

Tears in his eyes, Aki began dragging the sacks to the back of the wagon, and with prayers for forgiveness heaved them out and into the rising dust. Anashe went to help.

'Can we—?' Aki began.

'Yes, if you can carry it, you can keep it,' Ree snapped. 'But no complaining later.'

'There are some little barrels here, underneath,' Anashe said. 'They may be water or supplies. Odd, they're reinforced—'

'Don't open them!' Javani was up off the bench, hand outstretched.

Anashe had the sabre poised, ready to lever the lid from the keg. 'What is the matter, little one? We need to know our supply situation.'

'I think that's blasting powder,' Javani said, feeling a new coat of sweat across her skin. 'They were hoarding it, for the break-in. One spark and we go up like the cell-block wall.'

Anashe slowly lowered the sabre. 'Should we throw this as well?'

They looked at Ree, who was attempting to keep the horses steering a path along the ever sandier trail. 'Better not,' she called back. 'Bad if it goes up when we throw it, maybe worse if it doesn't.'

'I am not sure I am comfortable travelling into a desert in a wagon full of smouldering demon-fury,' Anashe said, her brows lowered.

'It needs a spark or flame, or an alchemical reaction,' Ree replied. 'Heat alone shouldn't ignite it.'

Javani turned slowly back to Ree. 'How do you know?'

Ree didn't look at her. 'I've had some experience.'

'You've had a lot of experience.'

Ree ignored that. 'Do you want to talk us through your intimate knowledge of who was hoarding what for which break-in at the Guildhouse?'

Javani cleared her throat. 'Where was it we're going?'

'There's an old settlement at the edge of the desert, a watering hole the nomads use. Tends to be first port of call for the proselytisers when they head out civilising.'

'The what?'

'The missionaries, kid. The ones who believe it their divine mission to go out and inflict their religion on blameless others.'

'Oh. And there's water there?'

'Should be. And often supplies – the nomads tend to leave alms for future travellers every time they pass through. They call it "deferred hospitality".'

'That's . . . nice of them.'

'They're a good bunch, kid, with sensible customs. Just misunderstood. Unlike the Mawn of course, who are all-too-well understood.'

'This watering hole . . . won't anyone chasing us know we've gone there?' Javani said.

Ree cracked a grim smile. 'Two reasons why they might not.

Reason the first: there are several places like it within half a day's hard ride of the town, we could be heading for any of them.'

'But our tracks—'

'*Won't* be an issue in a few hours.' Ree nodded to the eastern horizon, which at last Javani noticed was dark with swirling amber cloud, rising into churning, black-veined columns that advanced like a wall of spearmen.

'Is that . . . ?'

'Reason the second: a summer storm, right on cue. We'd better hope these poor ponies can get us to shelter before it hits. Anything that gets caught out in it is going to be scoured from the face of the earth.'

The horses ran on, into the teeth of the rising wind, and Javani pressed her hands to her ears and tried to quiet her treacherous thoughts.

ELEVEN

Movos watched the bodies swing in the breeze, creaking and twisting, limp as grain sacks bar the occasional twitch. They'd got the gibbet up fast, although only a few people were in the square in the midday heat. Normally he got quite a kick out of hangings, but it was different when the danglers were his brothers. Too slow to escape the strongroom, now speedy victims of the Towering Insecurity of Acting Guildmaster Kurush.

Of course, 'Guvuli Brothers' had always been something of a misnomer: they had not been brothers by blood, but by vocation and circumstance. Their brotherhood had been forged in the mines, hacking at rock with tools that might as well have been made of flint, learning expensive and lasting lessons in the early days of blasting, before the Guild had swept all before it and the notion of an independent miner became as fanciful as a veil-dancing sky-dragon.

'Should not stay here,' rumbled the enormous mercenary from the alley beside him, the woman who had dragged him from the Guildhouse courtyard and his brothers' fate. The White Spear. He owed her more than he could repay, yet felt no debt or obligation. He was without means or purpose, now surviving by habit alone. No, that was untrue. He had a purpose.

Movos clenched his fists, feeling the two fingers of his right hand curling into his palm beneath his thumb. He had compiled a list of those whom he considered were due a bout of consequences, and the Acting Guildmaster was near its top. As was the white-haired woman who'd wrecked the heist and made off with their score. A reckoning would follow, and Movos Guvuli would be its engine. Then he could pass from the earth and join his kith.

'Guvuli. Now.'

Movos took one last look at his brothers, mouthing his respects to each in turn, even the vile Shantar, then pulled his hood low and turned to follow. They should have listened. They never listened.

Shantar was dead. His brothers were dead. The dream of a god's fortune was dead. 'What are you going to do?' he muttered as they left the square behind them.

'Outside Guildhouse. Riders preparing to hunt the girl. I hunt the riders.'

The urchin. Suddenly the kid was special – who could have known? She'd been in the wagon, racing off out of town. The wagon that contained the riches they'd already liberated from the Guildhouse vault. The wagon that should be as easy to track as a stampede of incontinent mouflon on a snowy day.

There was life in the dream yet.

'You need a local guide?' said Movos Guvuli.

Acting Guildmaster Kurush squinted up at the mounted prince, one hand shading his eyes from the sun's glare.

'Are you sure about going out there, your highness? Most people heading out the way they did tend not to come back, for one reason or another.' He paused. 'Mostly because they die,' he added, in case it hadn't been clear.

'Duty commands it,' the prince replied. Ree's monstrous crossbow was strapped beside his saddle, within easy reach. 'A probability of demise is not sufficient. I must bring back certainty, I must bring back proof, or the fantasy of this claim will live on in the hearts of conspirators.'

'Proof? What, uh, manner of proof will you be looking to acquire, your highness?'

'What else, Guildmaster? The child's head.' He smiled so easily when he said it.

Kurush nodded and covered his frown with his shading hand. 'Of course, of course. Well, you know your business best, your highness.' He nodded to the other riders assembling in the barracks yard. He'd lost a lot of active staff to the day's events, from the slaughter in the square to the explosive attack on the Guildhouse, and the strain on his labour pool was beginning to show. Many of the gathering riders carried the marks of their convictions plain on their faces, and it occurred to Kurush that had they not been sent north and into Guild employ, many would elsewise be dead or imprisoned. And such a waste that would have been.

'Our best scouts are at your disposal, those that know the desert like, uh, well, they know it.' Increasingly, Kurush felt he was having trouble with his words. He'd never struggled to bandy with rivals and acquaintances in the past. Perhaps it was the pressure of acting up in front of the foreign nobleman. Perhaps it was the knock to the head he'd taken. Either way, Kurush felt like he was swimming against a rising tide of expectation, fighting to keep his head above the water.

'The crown of Shenak thanks you, Guildmaster. Khalida! Make ready, my Shade, we shall soon be away.'

The prince's lieutenant rode up alongside him, her bandage replaced with a wide-brimmed hat. Strapping still covered one eye. The Shenakar had at last reclaimed the remainder of their baggage and supplies from the packs on the late camels, which had taken a while to sort from the other wreckage as the square was cleared. At her saddle, as well as packs and rolls, was strapped a double-tipped spear, a fearsome head at each end: one bladed, the other with a nasty point. Kurush imagined it needed to be packed pretty carefully to avoid mishaps.

They were not the only ones to retrieve fresh equipment. To Kurush's relief and delight, the caravan's consignment of new Guild weaponry had survived the havoc largely unscathed. He watched with a satisfied glow as the milling riders picked over the crates and cases, the unrolled canvas bundles, their nestled contents gleaming in the high sun.

'What're these?' one of the riders asked, leaning over a long, lacquered crate packed with what looked like desiccated little shells, pale, soft and hollow. She was slack-eyed and sallow, despite the sheen of her bracers and greaves beneath her long coat. There was a pretty good chance she'd survived the day's events thus far through an unwillingness to leave the teahouse until forced. He thought he recognised her as a confederate of Enx's, the vicious little hunter who'd ridden for Nilam until Kurush had nosed ahead in the race for the permanent Guildmaster position, whereupon Enx had found his way onto the Acting Guildmaster's detail like a rat burrowing into a dry-walled storehouse. Kurush did not trust Enx or his team a jot, but then that was true of the bulk of his riders. Their inherent untrustworthiness was what made them so effective, he told himself.

'Ah!' cried the plump merchant who loitered around the crates as if tethered to them like a feast-day bladder. Kurush could only regard the man's generous gut with envy. He guessed the merchant hadn't yet been paid for the consignment; seeing to that was nowhere near the top of his list of priorities, nor might it ever be. 'These are the former cocoons of silkworms, from beneath—'

'No, jackal-pederast, what are *these*?' snapped the rider, lifting something that looked like half a crossbow out of the crate, a few ancient cocoons drifting free. It seemed to have too many wheels and cogs.

'Of course, indeed and in truth,' burbled the merchant, 'these are the very latest issue from the fabled workshops of Arowan: hand-bows!' He reached out and took the weapon from the woman with deft fingers. 'See how it folds and unfolds, stores several bolts, and look! Once unfolded, it can be cranked with one hand and . . .' He turned and loosed the weapon into the chipped mudbrick wall behind him, where it made a satisfying thump. 'It repeats! Just crank again, and it is ready to shoot.'

'Doesn't look too powerful,' the rider muttered, the corner of her lip curling. Her face bore two marks; Kurush recognised the nearer one as murder through robbery. A woman after his own heart.

'When shot from a moving horse, bolt after bolt?' The merchant was leering, as if such activities featured somewhere in his daily existence. 'It is not power that will carry the day, but volume . . . and surprise!' He loosed another bolt, which skidded along the mudbrick and disappeared somewhere into the dust. A chunk of wall cracked and dropped, bursting into powdery lumps on impact. Kurush had to acknowledge the merchant's showmanship, if nothing else.

The rider nodded. 'I'll take one. And a sword.' She shook her head. 'Fifteen years ago there weren't this many swords in the whole of the expanse. Wasn't even this much metal.'

The merchant beamed ever wider as he nodded for a flunky to collect a sword. 'Fresh from the southern forges, the apex of crucible steel! Rolled—'

'Why are they all curved?' The woman turned the blade in her hand. 'What's wrong with a straight blade, like we had down south?'

'Mistress, these are sabres! Up here, you have the horses, you have the height, and you have the reach – the slash is your greatest asset! Shall I demonstrate? Ulfat, come here, bring the mule!'

'Uh, boss?' Berev, Kurush's own right-hander, was at his side, fractionally heralded by his pungent reek.

Kurush bared his ivories at the patiently waiting Shenakar and hauled the shorter man to one side. 'I told you already, you need to call me Guildmaster in front of the prince, understand?'

Berev frowned, heavy eyebrows bunching like scorched ferns. 'I thought you was just acting so, though, boss. Latif said—'

'Latif doesn't know shit from sugar. Call me Guildmaster. Acting or otherwise, I'm in charge.' He flashed another grin of maximal sincerity towards the waiting prince and his lieutenant. Despite his warmth, he could imagine a note of impatience in the twitch of the young prince's moustache. 'Especially in front of *them*.'

Berev nodded, his cow-like eyes devoid of understanding. 'You got it, boss. Guildmaster.'

Kurush let out a hot breath through his nose. His head was still thumping. 'Was there something you wanted, Berev?'

'Oh, uh, yeah.' Berev beamed, and pushed something metallic and fist-warmed into Kurush's palm. 'Thought you might like this, seeing as you're Guildmaster, like you said.'

Suppressing his initial reaction for the benefit of his royal observers, Kurush opened his hand. 'That's . . . the Guildmaster's seal. Where in twelve hells did you find this?'

'In the strongroom, boss. There was a second chamber, guess it was hidden, or walled in, or something. Found it in there with a stack of records and other stuff.'

Kurush swallowed. 'Records? What kind of records?'

'Hard to say, boss. Guildmaster. They was mostly burned to ash in the brouhaha.'

Kurush pulled at his bottom lip with his teeth. While the seal was a stellar find, and would look both elegant and imperious on its chain around his neck, a hidden room of hidden records – and no doubt hidden treasures – was bad news. His predecessor had been skimming more than the expected volumes, that much was clear. How big could the discrepancy be? Big enough for the Guild to have noticed? There was leeway, it was understood, but it was no secret they came down like a mountain on anyone who flagrantly took the piss.

'Boss? You look troubled. You don't like the seal?'

'Seal's just fine, Berev. But I'm thinking we may be at risk from a visit from an auditor.'

'Sounds bad, boss.'

'It would not be my preference, for certain.' How soon could one reach them? Before they'd had time to repair the damage, cover the losses, extract a little more irregular taxation from the homesteaders? Before he'd had time to milk the Shenakar of his kingdom's wealth? Kurush swallowed again. What if one was already on the way?

This necessitated a change of plan. He stepped away from Berev, masking his panic with another no-doubt dazzling grin.

'Your highness, given our previous discussions, the mention you made of the, uh, diplomatic allowances from your kingdom? Well, given my seniority and expert knowledge of the region, I was thinking perhaps an advancement of our discussions concerning an, uh, *ambassadorial* role—'

'Of course, Guildmaster Kurush. Once our business is concluded here, you would be welcome to return with us to take up such a post. A man in such a position would require a significant stipend, reflecting his level of authority.'

For a moment, Kurush felt his doubts lift, the tide of anxiety recede. Not just Guildmaster in the arse-end of nowhere, siphoning handfuls of uncut gems and extorting penniless farmers. A position of nobility in a civilised nation. All he had to do was wait things out here, in safety and comfort, while the crazed nobleman chased ghosts into the desert to his satisfaction. And when he finally returned, Kurush would go with him: Ambassador Kurush, with a Significant Stipend. He was rising now, floating above the waves of unease that had assailed him.

'Now, mount up,' the prince said. 'It is only fitting that the Guildmaster should ride with us at the head of the column. We must not lose the trail!'

'Of course, your highness,' murmured Acting Guildmaster Kurush, as the waters closed over his head.

TWELVE

'This is the watering hole?'

'It was, kid.'

'Oh. I thought it would be greener, you know, an oasis.'

'There are trees, kid. What more do you want?'

'Trees that don't look like they carked it decades ago, and now haunt the spot where they died? Aki, how's your nose?'

'What? What about it?'

'Can you smell any water?'

Ree reined in the wagon behind a battered sandstone wall, out of the fierce wind and sun. The horses were lathered and champing, grateful for the rest but desperately thirsty. Javani watched them with sad eyes. They weren't the only ones.

The watering hole had shrunk away to almost nothing. It sat in gloomy shade beneath a series of descending rocky ledges, unclear whether any actual water lurked at the pit's foot. On the uppermost ledge, surrounded by drooping trunks fringed with pitted and faded leaves, stood the skeletons of buildings, small, rude and wrecked, their stones loose and scattered.

'What are those?' Javani asked, gesturing to the ruins. Some were marked with soot and char.

'I'm guessing that was a temple to one of the new gods,' Ree muttered as she climbed down and set about unhitching the frothing team. 'And those were dwellings.'

'What happened to them?'

'Mawn, or bandits, or maybe internecine conflict. This is the only water for a distance in any direction, I imagine that might have aggravated any differences of opinion on matters spiritual.'

'There's water!' Aki called up from the pit.

'Did you smell it?' Javani called back.

His head appeared at the rocky shelf's edge. 'Indeed I did. I trust I was never doubted.'

'Not for a moment,' Ree said, then slung him the horses' lead ropes. 'Now get these poor animals down there and let them drink before they expire. We can worry about ourselves after that.' Ree's head tilted. 'You all right, kid? What's wrong? I know we've been through some, well, horrible shit today, but we're clear now. We'll be all right here, really.'

Javani nodded, but her eyes stung, sand-scuffed, wind-bitten and ill-used. She felt she'd be crying if she weren't so dehydrated. Her voice came out all scratchy: 'Ree, we need to have a talk.'

'I thought we had that talk already. Did that Peri girl tell you something odd? Her mother has some funny ideas about anatomy, I can—'

'Ree! Not about that.' Javani was too hot, too tired, too thirsty, too wrung out to deal with it all. She wanted to sleep for a year in a cool spring. 'They tried to kill me! They killed Moosh! They cut his throat in the street.'

'I know. I'm sorry, kid, I really am. He was a sweet, simple kid.'

'He could be so . . . *annoying*, but he was my friend. They shouldn't have killed him.' Javani was fighting back tears now, sprung from some hidden reserve. 'It's not a crime to be annoying.'

'And by the gods, if it were, how many would be lined up before the gallows ahead of that little man?'

'Why are you making a joke out of all this? My only friend is dead and we've been chased into the desert by his murderers!' And I might just be a princess, she added to herself, who should be lining up for her throne, and perhaps you might have mentioned that sooner?

Ree sighed and rubbed at the scar on her temple. 'Old habits, I'm afraid, kid. Call it a coping strategy. I'm sorry.' Ree put a hand on her shoulder. 'You're right.'

Javani sniffed, caught off-guard. 'About what?'

'We do need to have a talk. But this isn't the time. We're barely ahead of the storm. Let's go down and have some water, get the horses settled and ourselves dug in, then we can take stock, all right?'

'All right,' Javani replied, but part of her believed not a word.

'It appears someone camped here recently, in the last day or two,' Anashe said. 'There is . . . spoor, and discarded packs. They also dug two graves.'

Ree was chewing something as she hammered canvas between the wooden bones of one of the old huts. 'Rest moved out?'

Anashe nodded. 'Wagon tracks going north-east, towards the salt. The tracks vanish quickly.'

'Another bunch of robe-wearers gone civilising.' Ree shook her head. 'They might as well have just dug all the graves here and saved themselves some time.'

Aki returned from checking over the greatly relieved and resting horses. 'What is the discussion? I detect a dramatic level of animation to my sister's nostrils, this must be good.'

'Just counting our blessings,' Ree said without looking up.

'Ah, the greatest source of blessings is of course the Goddess, and they take many forms, best represented as a hierarchy of—'

'You never introduced yourself,' Javani said quietly.

Ree frowned, still focused on the canvas. 'Huh?'

'They told us their names, I told them mine, but you never told them yours.'

Ree stood, with a sigh. 'Ree,' she said, with a thumb to her chest.

'We know who you are,' Aki said, his tone changed, acquiring a sort of . . . reverence?

'We overheard your conversation in the cells,' Anashe added quickly. Javani spotted a sharp look to her brother.

Ree's attention was barely on them, distracted by the wind-whipped material, pulling at her half-completed fixings. She resumed her ministrations. 'And what brings you all the way out here? What's your trade?'

Again Javani saw Anashe glare at her brother, warning in her eyes. 'We are specialists,' she said, before he could volunteer anything further.

'What does that even mean?' Javani sighed.

'It means we are specialised,' Aki said with a guileless grin.

Javani rubbed her grimy fingers over her face, dragging at herself in exasperation. 'Are you trying to break my mind? I have had a pretty upsetting day and it feels like you—'

'We are currently between employers,' Anashe said, looking slightly pained. 'But previously we worked for an . . . irregular outfit in the south. In Arowan.'

Ree was wearing a half-smile as she fiddled with the blackened timbers, one eyebrow raised. 'You're contractors? I wasn't aware free companies persisted in Serica's great capital.'

'More of an . . . independent agency,' Aki said. 'Specialising in, ah, retrieval.'

'Ah,' said Ree, pausing her work to look up, a smirk on her face as though all her suspicions had been confirmed. 'And what is it you're here to retrieve?'

Aki took a deep breath, poised to extol, but again Anashe got there first. 'Something that can wait.' She looked to Javani. 'We heard what was said in the cells. The prince of Shenak came all this way to kill you?'

Javani nodded, her lip trembling, and Anashe bowed her head. 'I am doubly sorry. If we had known . . .' She closed her eyes tight and shook her head. 'You are truly so important?'

She shrugged helplessly. 'Apparently I'm a threat to his kingdom.'

'Then good for you,' Anashe replied, her eyes open and burning with intent. 'Everyone should be a threat to something.'

'They . . . they killed my friend, because they thought he was me.' Javani felt her emotions rising, her voice cracking. She was struggling to keep herself together, to stay upright, although evening was still some way off. The day's events had hit her like a stampede. 'He wasn't a threat to anyone.'

Aki took a step forward, one hand on his chest. 'I, too, am sorry for the tragedy of his demise. Had my sister not delayed us—'

'Aki, by the Goddess!'

'Anashe, you know the truth of my words. Had we set out when—'

'Our bones would bleach in the deadlake.'

'You conject, my sister, you speculate!'

Javani put up her hands. 'Please! I've had a long day.' She turned to her aunt. 'I'm going to go and lie down. Ree. Ree?'

Ree was staring at the siblings, a corner of canvas tight in her hand, her expression unreadable, deaf to Javani's words. She'd apparently been staring a while.

'Ree?'

Her aunt snapped to, then immediately switched back to her task. 'Get that end anchored down, kid. When this thing hits it's going to rip through here like the wrath of the gods, and anything that's not secured is going to go tearing off with it.' The canvas was already whipping away from her, and she gritted her teeth and yanked it back. 'We do *not* want to be left in the open.'

Reluctantly, Javani did her best, her fingers numb and her body spent, the tongues of their makeshift shelter dancing out of her grip. But her mind whirled without cease, Moosh's face, his words, his body, the grinning Shenakar prince, the gleaming blade, the blurred and choking aftermath of the explosion at the Guildhouse, and then the White Spear, cradling her like an infant, carrying her to safety . . . to her destiny, as Queen of Queens. Until Ree had 'rescued' her.

She shot her aunt a bleary look of meaningful scrutiny. In the cells, when Lazant had made his claim, she hadn't laughed. She hadn't scoffed or spluttered, blindsided by the ludicrous notion of her niece being the heir to some faraway kingdom. She had only accused the man of lying. She'd told him he was wrong.

But she hadn't been surprised.

The hairs stood up on Javani's arms, despite the day's implacable warmth.

'Why are the scouts returning?' The prince reined in his horse, his moustache flared in puzzlement.

Kurush looked at the darkening horizon. A plummeting sensation filled his stomach. He was well below the water now and sinking fast. 'I believe I may have an inkling.'

The first scout was waving his bow, shouting something lost over the rising wind.

'We need to turn the column around,' Kurush said, finding it suddenly hard to swallow. 'We need to head back.'

'Why?' The prince gazed at him with earnest eyes. 'Guildmaster, was I not clear in the crucial nature of our pursuit? Why would we pause our search?'

'Your highness, strength of their sign notwithstanding, we're not going to catch them before that storm catches us. If we're out in the open when it hits, it could do us a serious disfavour. We could lose both men and horse, strand ourselves—'

'The fate of a kingdom is in the balance, Guildmaster! We cannot allow ourselves to be discouraged by a little inclement weather. We must press on. We cannot lose them. Duty commands!'

'Uh, your highness, were we to break for the town now, return fresh in the morning—'

'Has the wind taken your ears, Guildmaster? I am a prince of Shenak, driven by royal duty. When I command, others must obey. If you wish that diplomatic posting, you will be among them. Onward!'

With a heart of lead Kurush watched the prince and his lieutenant ride on, tongues of wind whipping grit into his eyes. 'Not like you can command the fucking weather,' he muttered to himself, then signalled the column onwards.

* * *

'We're in luck, our predecessors didn't clear the place out, and left a few things themselves.' Ree slung two refilled waterskins into their shelter, a burned-out hut now shrouded in swathes of rough canvas that had to be older than Javani.

'Not an abundance of nutrition, though,' Anashe replied, poking under empty, sand-flattened sacks. 'We could always eat my useless brother of course, although he will be stringy and liable to stick between the teeth.'

'That is an outrageous suggestion, even in jest!' came Aki's voice from the old temple next door, where he was trying to settle the horses. 'To even joke about such a thing—'

Anashe mimed his chatter with the snapping of her hand. Javani was too tired for any of it. 'And what about later?' she grumbled. 'After the storm, assuming none of us get eaten? What then? We just go home?'

Ree sat on an ancient, blackened timber with a sigh. The wind was getting really strong now, lashing strands of her sand-stained yet gleaming white hair across her face, rasping their exposed skin with a wash of fine dust. Javani knew this was just a prelude. 'No, kid, we can't go home. In fact, we need to start assuming that we no longer have a home.'

Although in the depths of her weary bones Javani had suspected this, to hear her aunt say it out loud like that, so bald and brutal, still brought tears to her eyes. 'But . . .' she spluttered, trying to fight it, feeling like she ought to, 'but . . .' She tailed off. There was nothing more to say.

Ree said it anyway. 'Edigu will mind the place. The animals will be fine. And he'll know when to hide if he needs to.' She took a breath. 'Maybe he'll even finish the feed-store.'

'Then where instead? Across the desert, after the missionaries?' She expected a no. There was nowhere else to go but west into Arestan. All she had to do was get her aunt to admit it.

Ree shook her head. Anashe was watching them from across the rocky pit, ostensibly foraging for supplies, her face impassive but her eyes black and alert. It was like being watched by a hawk.

'Let's be honest with ourselves,' Ree said. 'We are hunted. By these Shenakar, and – thanks to that shit-weasel Kurush's near-miraculous absence of spine – now by the Guild as well.' She rubbed her hands down her face, leaving grubby streaks, and for a moment Javani felt a pang of sympathy for Ree, for the farm she'd been building, that she'd worked on from dawn each day, to see it all ripped away. Then she remembered Moosh, and the people trying to kill her, and the sympathy redirected itself squarely back towards herself. 'We're also hunted by whatever this White Spear character is, and whatever she wants.' Javani stayed quiet, but she pressed her lips together so tightly that they went numb.

'We can't go back to the town, or the farm, for obvious reasons. We don't have the supplies or the mounts to cross the salt,' Ree went on, 'and we're too far north to cut below the deadlake . . . but . . .' Something in Ree's tone made Javani push herself a little more upright. '. . . There are ways out, south through the narrowlands. And I know where we can get supplies to make the trip.'

Javani sat forward on her nest of packs. Supplies for the south could just as easily be supplies for the west. 'Where? You said it yourself, we can't go back to Kazeraz.'

'There are . . . caches, dotted around the region. Hard rations, travelling gear, even some weapons. Long-lasting stuff, as much as possible. Well hidden.'

'Then how do you know where they are?'

Her aunt didn't meet her eye. 'Because I put them there.'

For a moment there was only the growing howl of the wind, and the creak and snap of its attentions on their rickety shelter.

Ree forestalled Javani's questions with a chop of her hand. 'Just in case, all right? For a . . .' she glanced up at the darkening sky '. . . rainy day.'

'Did you know this would happen?' Javani felt very hot. Her clothes were suddenly too tight. 'Did you know people would come for me?'

Ree was shaking her head, her hands waving side to side in disjointed sympathy with the movement. 'Of course not, kid—'

'Why didn't you warn me? I could have . . . Moosh would still be alive!'

Ree pinned her with a glare as hard as diamond. 'I did not foresee this, kid. And maybe I should have, and for that I am sorry. But there was nothing I could have told you, believe me.'

'I don't,' Javani muttered into her chest.

'What's that?' Her aunt's eyes seem to glitter in the gathering gloom.

'Nothing.'

The gaze lasted a moment longer, Ree's eyes narrow and hard, and then her stare faded like spring mist as she relaxed. 'We need to reach one of the caches, and, assuming it's still intact, we'll have the supplies we need to get us through the narrows and into the plains, a stab closer to something resembling civilisation. From there we could go anywhere – south across the fort line, into the protectorate, east across the expanse, you name it.'

Javani perked up again. This was it. 'Or west? To Arestan?'

'What?'

'We could cross the Ashadi, there's a way, a secret pass. We could make a better life in the west. All we need to—'

'Kid, drop it. Nobody goes over those mountains for a reason. No, not tigers. If there were an accessible pass this side of the narrows, it would be more than common knowledge by now.'

'But—'

'Hush and listen.' Ree sketched in the sand with an animal bone. Javani thought it was an animal bone. It was quite long. 'Town's here. We're half a day in this direction, north and east. Pursuers likely here, here or here. These jaggies are the mountains, here's the river, plains this way, salt and deadlake here and here.'

Anashe was suddenly back with them, peering over Ree's shoulder. 'Most artistic.'

Ree went on. 'The storm is going to wipe our tracks and drive anyone on the trail back to safety. By the time it passes, it'll be night, or as close as makes no odds. That gives us a clear run at dawn tomorrow –' she dragged a long groove through the yellow earth

'– south. We skirt the town, and make for the canyons on the trade road. There's an old watchtower at the neck of the narrows. I left a cache there.'

'But that's back the way we came!'

'No arguments.' Ree gave Javani a warning look. 'It's unexpected, and the storm will have cleared the trail. We take the safe route out of here, leave our hunters guessing, and never look back. Understood?'

'*We must be prudent*,' Javani mumbled sourly into her sleeve.

Ree ignored it. 'Once we're back in the protectorate, we can blend in somewhere new until this threat passes, and not make the same mistakes again.' This last part seemed to be directed to herself.

'You will run?' Anashe said. 'Back south?'

Ree nodded, looking back at the woman with an appraising eye. 'And you, specialist? What are your intentions?'

Aki returned from the horses, his proud swagger a testament to his success in bedding them down. 'We will be at your side, come what may,' he proclaimed. 'For—'

'South works for us,' Anashe interjected. 'We will go with you, if you will have us.'

Ree nodded again, her eyes flicking from one to the other, something inscrutable in her gaze. 'We're in no position to choose our allies,' she murmured.

'But first we must survive the fury of the Goddess,' Aki intoned. To Javani's blank look, he gestured up at the sky. It was almost black overhead.

Ree stuck her head over the topmost ledge, peering over the sandstone wall into the darkening desert. 'The windbag's right. Let's get inside, folks. We are out of time.'

Javani climbed up beside her, looking over the wall on tiptoes. The sky to the east was gone, replaced by a wall of pulsing sand as tall as a mountain, blotting out the world. It was rushing towards them with terrifying speed. She shrieked and sat back down.

Ree offered her a hand and nodded towards their shelter. 'After you,' she said. Then, after a pause, 'Where's my crossbow?'

THIRTEEN

Ree hunkered in one of the burned-out huts with the kid curled beside her, both wrapped in blankets, while Aki and Anashe did their best to mind the horses in the presumed ex-temple. The wind's howl and the rip of churned earth at least precluded any uncomfortable conversations while they sheltered, but Ree knew it was a reprieve and nothing more. The kid was asking a lot of questions, about things of which she had every right to know the truth. Ree had always known that one day would bring the Conversation; she'd just never imagined it would be under circumstances like these.

The storm blew out its fury after a time that seemed unquantifiable. Ree had been huddled in place as it raged, locked and brooding, then Javani was shaking her knee and gesturing. She realised the shriek of the wind was gone, leaving an oppressive, orange-hued groaning in its place. Somehow, she'd nodded off during the turmoil. The storm was not over, but it no longer felt like they were about to be scoured from the earth by the fury of the gods.

'Ree?'

'Yeah, kid?'

'Why are you so . . .' She tailed off, little face scrunched in concentration. Ree swallowed, dreading what might follow. '. . . *Relaxed* with those two? Normally you treat anyone we meet with a level of suspicion that would shame a jackal with a fresh carcass. You treat them like old friends. Or old acquaintances, at least.'

Ree relaxed, but only a little. 'What can I say, kid? I feel like . . . I feel like I know them.'

'You've met them before?'

'I don't think so.'

Ree crawled over and peered through the bundled canvas at the hut's edge. The day was gone, the low sun somewhere in the north-west through cracked cloud and blasting sand, the air blooded and thick. For a moment, Ree wondered if they'd died in the storm, that this was the vestibule of the first of the hells. As a notion, it lingered.

'The horses are well,' came Aki's voice from the next building, 'if a little stained.'

Anashe's head appeared through the building's black-framed window-hole. 'He sang to them. For the whole time.' She shook her head. 'By the Goddess, the noise!'

Javani followed Ree out of the hut, shaking the sand from her blanket in a great cloud. 'Storms are pretty loud when you're in them, I guess,' she said.

'Not loud enough,' Anashe replied with a grimace, and ducked back inside.

'The Goddess blessed me with projection,' Aki said, wading through the orange drifts down towards the watering hole. 'I can make myself heard in the most strained of circumstances.'

'More's the pity,' Ree muttered. She spat sand and tried to clean fine dust from her ears, but ended up merely moving grit around. 'Aki, indulge me. Tell me more of this agency you worked for.'

He paused, halfway towards the water. 'This very instant? I was looking forward to—'

'Now.'

He turned to face her, legs and one side of his body crusted with blown sand. 'It was a small thing, a curio, a trifle, but independent of spirit and endeavour, possessed of a zeal for—'

'Aki, listen to me. There exist people who are charmed by grandiloquence and sesquipedalianism. I am not one of them. When I ask you a question, I expect an answer that is both short and to the point. Delivering otherwise risks incurring my wrath, which is already wild and abroad this evening. Do you understand me?'

'Yes,' he replied with a brilliant smile.

Ree found herself half-smiling in return, shaking her head at the insanity of it all. 'You may be the most annoying person I've ever met,' she said, 'and I've met some types.'

'My thanks,' he said, still smiling. 'It is flattering to be recognised for one's talents.'

She rubbed at her eyes with the heel of one hand. 'Shall we try again? Tell me more of this agency. How big is it? What is it an agency of?'

'I cannot speak to its size,' Aki said carefully. 'We worked primarily in isolation from other operatives. The agency is run by a southerner, known only as the Commodore.'

'That's intriguing, and we'll come back to it. What was the manner of your work?'

'Principally? Retrieval, as we said.' He kept a straight face.

She smiled at that. 'I see.'

The kid hadn't followed. 'Wait, what's an agency? What's retrieval?'

'Theft to order, kid, for something too small to call itself a company.' Ree barely glanced at her, her attention on Aki.

'Our engagements were far more than mere—' he began, but she cut him off.

'Why are you here, Aki?'

His eyes became serious. 'For you, Ree.'

She shifted back, leaning slightly away from him, her smile gone. 'You are here to retrieve me?'

'No, not at all – we are seeking you out, because—'

Anashe emerged from the old temple. 'Aki, what nonsense do you impart?'

'It is time she knew, my sister. We cannot—'

'By the Goddess, Aki, it is not the time for your stool-water! It will never be time for—'

'My sister, you cannot merely shout down all those who disagree as if they are dust on the wind! The world is full of disagreements, and if you cannot—'

He broke off, eyes wide with outrage, then did something with his hands. Ree's gaze snapped back to Anashe, who was responding in kind, furious miming in the swirling orange evening. It hit her all at once.

'Gods' breath,' Ree whispered, 'you're her children.'

The kid looked blearily from one sibling to the other, still wreathed in her sandy blanket. 'What? Whose children?'

Ree shook her head. 'A long time ago, I rode with a good friend. For a long time.' She blinked, rocking as if dazed. 'I think these two are her kids.'

Before them, the siblings continued their vicious, silent argument. Yet now when Ree looked at them she felt something beyond exhausted irritation. She felt a sense of obligation, and familial warmth. Her gaze slipped smoothly to Javani.

'And they came here for you?' the kid said. 'Why?'

'I'm sure they'll tell us, once they tire of squabbling. Right now, we all need feeding. At least there's grain for the animals, care of our missionary friends. Why don't you have a snooze? You must be worn to the bone. Once the storm drops a little more, we'll get a fire going, see what we can cook up for ourselves. And watch out for cobras when you're napping, they're out and about at this time in summer.'

'I always do,' Javani yawned. 'How is there even anything to burn out here?'

'Ratty weeds can grow in the harshest climates, kid.'

She pouted. 'I feel like that's a dig at me.'

Ree only smiled, one eyebrow raised. From over her shoulder came the sound of Anashe pushing Aki into the watering hole.

The storm had ebbed, the wind's howl little more than a grudging murmur, the western sky bloodlit by sunset and sand. Ree watched Aki and Anashe gathering fuel for the fire, each acting with precision and a sort of affected mutual indifference, as if the other's mirrored actions were mere coincidence. She watched Anashe in particular, now keyed to what it was that so tweaked her memory. Her movements resonated with mental images that were over a decade old.

'You two not getting on?' Ree kept her voice low, mindful of the kid dozing upslope.

Aki snorted. Anashe concentrated on meticulous assembly of the firepit. 'We travel together only from habit and efficiency,' she said.

Ree leaned forward. 'And are you who I think you are?'

Aki paused, then sat elegantly down to face her. The fire prepared to her satisfaction, Anashe sat down opposite her brother and watched Ree with deep black eyes. 'What do you mean?' Aki said at length.

Ree looked to each in turn. 'Tell me of your parents.'

'They are dead.' Anashe spoke quickly, but flat-voiced, without emotion.

Aki looked at his sister. 'Anashe, I believe it is time to tell what we know.'

Anashe let a long breath go through her nose. 'Very well. Yes, we know who you are. Yes, although you do not know us, you knew one of our parents.'

'Your mother. Kwayedza.'

She nodded. 'The Commodore told us you rode with her. That you were friends. Until the point of her death.'

Ree sat back and looked off to one side, over the dunes, the blue moon-scattered hills to the expanse of plains beyond. Memories circled her, ready to be recalled, relived, but she pushed them away.

'Yes,' she said, maintaining her gaze a moment longer, then turning back. 'Do I also know this Commodore?'

'The Commodore seems to know you,' Aki said, 'and told us where you might be found.'

Ree's eyes narrowed. The possible mutual acquaintances between her and the siblings' mother were a shallow pool. 'We rode together? With your mother?'

They nodded. Well, that about confirmed it. Ree chewed at her lip in distaste. This so-called 'Commodore', one of her old colleagues from her own freelancing days, should have known better than to keep tabs on her location, let alone hand out pointers to any old pair of professional thieves come rolling in from the east. Once all this nonsense had blown over, she was going to send a very nasty message south with some precise instructions on where and how its rolled-up form should be inserted.

'On what information was I to be found?'

The looked at each other and offered a joint shrug. 'The Commodore is tied into much of the freelancing network of the lower protectorate,' Anashe said. 'Much of what we retrieved for the agency could be considered privileged, and we were not alone in these efforts.' She sighed. 'My brother, in place of material payment for our work . . . traded for this knowledge.'

'We know so little of her,' Aki chimed in, his eyes shining in the evening light. 'She was banished when I was an infant, Anashe little more than a babe-in-arms. Our father was executed soon after. We were raised among family, but . . .'

'We always intended to find her,' Anashe finished. 'When we were grown.'

'But by the time we made it all the way west,' Aki said, then his voice caught. He could only shake his head. 'We know so little of her,' he repeated, in a voice like cracked glass.

Ree felt Anashe's gaze locked on her. The woman affected indifference but there was hunger in her eyes.

Ree felt her own throat tighten. She'd worked so hard to forget, to keep distance from her life before, from the memories, from how it ended . . .

Still the shame stung.

'Get the fire going,' she muttered. 'Then we can talk.'

Ree stared at the kindling flames and stifled a yawn. She was still shocked that she'd slept during the storm; that would never have happened a few years ago. Then again, she wouldn't have felt a dozen niggling aches across her body, the stiffness in her shoulders and knees, the pain in her hand, the waves of fatigue that rolled over her with ever-greater frequency. Ree knew she was getting old, and she did not care for it.

She pushed it all to one side and leaned forwards. 'You wanted to talk, specialists? Start with this: what can you tell me about the Shenakar? You must have travelled with them for weeks.'

The siblings looked up from the incipient fire in shock, Aki's mouth wide, Anashe's nostrils quivering. Now Aki had pointed it out, Ree couldn't ignore the magnificent animation of the woman's nose; while so much of her outward emotion was suppressed, the flex of her snout betrayed her mood every time.

'How—' Aki began.

'You're not the only ones to have been listening in the cells,' Ree replied with a smirk. 'You were the guides from the east? I'm assuming they came by sea.'

He nodded. The bundle behind Ree sat up. 'Then it's your fault they're here!'

'I thought you were asleep, kid,' Ree said sidelong to the bundle.

'It is, and it is not.' Anashe blew steam from her tea mug, a blackened clay cup she'd dug from the sand in one of the huts. Patterns marked its side – another belated gift from the nomads and their deferred hospitality. 'It is their fault they are here.' She nodded at her brother. 'It is his fault we are here.' She sat back with a sigh. 'They came across the water with horses and retainers. The young man and the woman are all that's left now. He's a prince of some sort.'

'So Kurush said. But being a prince of Shenak isn't saying much.'

'How can that be?' the kid demanded. 'Princes are important, aren't they?'

'There are hundreds of them in Shenak, maybe thousands.' Ree rolled her shoulders, trying to chase out the crunches. 'They're big on bloodlines over there, less so on the eternal sanctity of marriage. Makes for a lot of minor princes and princesses.'

The kid rubbed her eyes. 'Eh?'

'Still, the ruling class puts a lot of stock in primogeniture. Primo-primogeniture, if you will.'

'Eh?'

'First-born takes all, without regard for gender or standing. Bloodline above all. It's supposed to make things . . . simpler.'

The kid went quiet. Ree ploughed on, not giving her a chance to voice her thoughts. 'The woman, the one with the eyes and the marks on her arms. I think she's a Shade.'

'She killed Moosh,' the kid sniffed. 'The horrible cow.'

'A Shade?' Anashe had one pointed eyebrow elevated. 'What is a Shade?'

'They're assigned to scions of continental royalty as minders, bodyguards, assistants.'

'Like, their shadows?' the kid said blearily. 'Is that where the name comes from?'

'No. They're trained from an early age, in one of the temples there, to believe their mortal essence has been separated from their bodies, and kept safe in the temple. Their body becomes purely a vessel for the will of their charge.'

'But . . . why?'

Ree sucked at her bottom lip. She was never sure how much of this sort of thing to drop on the kid, but you couldn't keep reality's sharp edges at bay by glossing over them. 'So they can commit otherwise damning acts without becoming irrevocably stained. They need not fear death, as the path to paradise will always be open. Some people think they can drain the essence of others, but we're getting into mad superstition at this point.'

'What, really? Are they actually magical?'

'Hells, no, kid, of course not. But, well, a person can convince themselves of any old hand-wavy mystical shit if they base their identity on it, and their standing in society.'

The kid was staring at her, eyes wide and wet in the firelight. 'When you say "damning acts" . . . would that include murdering an innocent boy?'

Ree blinked hard as she nodded. 'I'm afraid so, kid.'

Aki was staring at the fire. 'A creature with no soul of its own, that feeds on the souls of others, denying them their eternal rest and heavenly reward. There is a word for such a thing.'

Ree rubbed at the scar at her temple. 'That's really not—'

'What word?' The kid was leaning forward in her blanket bundle, still brushing sleep from her eyes.

Aki looked up in puzzlement. 'You truly do not know? What stories were you told as a babe?'

The kid flicked Ree a disapproving glance. 'Tales of war and assassinations, mostly. Political struggles, succession crises, invasions, overthrows. You know, standard stuff.'

'And were they histories or stories?'

The kid squinted, nonplussed. 'What's the difference?'

'Did they have endings? Happy or otherwise?'

She pondered, small face scrunched. 'Yeah, I guess.'

Aki sat back with a satisfied look, as if his point had been proven beyond a scintilla of doubt. 'Then they were stories, their conclusions merely markers in history's thread. History has no end, little one, but the stories we tell are wrapped within it, and some stories are told over and over and over, to begin again as soon as they are ended.'

'And what about death?' Ree interjected, unable to help herself.

He was unruffled, still directing his words to the kid. 'Death may mean the end of a person's story, but not the end of its telling. So long as the story is told, the life remains.'

The kid nodded slowly. 'Ree told me something similar once.'

'But she told you nothing of the gods, the heavens, and those that dwell beneath the earth? How the world came to be, and what is to come at the end of all things?'

'No, none of that.' She shot Ree what she probably considered a withering glare. 'Consider me miseducated.'

Aki's face lit with mischievous glee in the firelight. 'Then let me tell you, little one, of *demons*.'

'Don't give the girl nightmares,' Ree warned with a wave of her finger.

Anashe's tone was so light it could have blown away on the desert breeze. 'And what effect do you expect the day's events to wreak on her sleeping mind?'

Ree took a slow breath. 'Just don't make it worse, Aki.'

'Such a thing would be anathema,' Aki beamed. 'But of course, all tales have a beginning, and there we must start. Come, little one. Let us leave those two to tend the fire and prepare our food, for we are engaged in a far greater endeavour: the sharing of *stories*.'

FOURTEEN

'You are comfortable? Then I shall begin, at the beginning of all things, before time itself.'

'Uh, Aki, is this really—'

'You must know of how the world and its peoples came to be,' Aki continued. 'The oldest stories have been with us for thousands of years; we are inveterate storytellers—'

'Your people?'

'All people. We place ourselves at the story's heart.'

'Why are stories so important?'

The question seemed to shock him. 'Stories are vital, little one. Whether true or not, they tell us who we are, and who we might wish to be.'

Javani coughed. 'I meant, to you. Why are they important to you?'

'I left my homeland long, long ago, but the stories I carry in my heart mean it travels with me still. All I share them with are touched by its soil, will feel the warmth of its sun, hear the rush of its waters, the whisper of its grasses.'

She shook her blanket and sat back against mounded sand. 'We'll see, I guess.'

Aki spread his hands, palms pale in the firelight. 'First, there was nothing, the endless desert of eternal night. Then the Goddess created—'

'If there was nothing, where did the Goddess come from? Who created the Goddess?'

'She is the Goddess of Creation. She . . . created herself. Now, hush, little one, and ready yourself to hear—'

'Does this creation story apply to me, or do I have a different one? In the little temple they always said—'

'We are *all* children of the Goddess. May I continue?'

Javani gestured her permission, suppressing a smirk of her own. It was inexcusably easy to wind Aki up. No wonder Anashe couldn't help herself.

Aki spread his hands again. 'First there was nothing, and then –' he clapped his palms together '– the Goddess created the earth, and the heavens, the moon and stars, and all the bodies of water. She made a god for each, stewards of their realms, the greatest of them Qhodis, who ruled the sky, and Usdohr, who ruled beneath the earth. For a time, they were ignorant of each other, in perfect balance. But each of them was born to power, and craved more in turn. They expanded their realms, pushing against the boundaries, far beyond the intentions of their mother the Goddess – until their realms began to overlap. Thus, the crust of the earth and sky where now we walk became the seam between realms, and there they met.

'And they fought, as gods do.'

'And how is that? With lightning and stuff? Big swords? Beard-pulling? Stinging rebukes?'

'I am beginning to deduce why your adult did not tell you many stories.' He cleared his throat. 'The Goddess rushed to them and separated them before they destroyed each other and the infant earth. She confined them to their realms, never to set foot on the grasses again. But the new earth was now empty, and needed stewards of its own. The Goddess reflected on her mistake: in making them in her image, with all the power that came with godhood, she had failed the first of her children. They had had no chance to learn for themselves the ways of existence, the necessity of work and sacrifice, of love, community and collaboration. She would not repeat her error, and as the new stewards she brought forth the second of her children: us.'

'You and Anashe?'

She saw the slightest twitch at the corner of his mouth. 'Humanity. We are the children of the Goddess, given the domain of this world to nurture and protect it, and all its life. Something powerless, something that could learn its place in the world and the heavens. Creatures of the boundary that needed community and common understanding to survive, to flourish.'

'So far, so good. What went wrong?'

'Why would you ask such a thing?'

'I know how these stories go. What went wrong? The old gods didn't like humanity, right? Did they come back and start slaying?'

'No, no, they remained confined. But . . .' He looked momentarily discomfited, 'Qhodis and Usdohr were indeed jealous of the Goddess's love for humanity, and its dominion over the realm they had lost. While neither could yet walk upon the earth, they could act from their realms. Qhodis sent storms, a deluge, tried to wash humanity away. Usdohr cracked the earth beneath, and poured forth creatures of malice and spite into the world. Evil spirits formed as crocodiles and scorpions and other malicious things, rivers swelled, seas became salty and thorns grew, wars began, and with them, predation.'

He took a deep breath. 'The Goddess could not abide the suffering of her children, and she descended once more from the heavens. She repelled Usdohr's minions and sealed the breaches, leaving his creatures as mindless animals, and locked Qhodis behind a swirling wall of cloud. But she could not stay on the earth without changing it by her very presence, and she could not bring herself to punish them further, which would have meant their destruction – they had been her first creations, and she is a loving Goddess.

'Instead, she offered them a pact: return with her to the heavens to live as family once more, and allow humanity to live in peace on the earth. Show patience, wisdom and learning, and be welcomed into her arms for eternity. To humanity, the same bargain was offered: the promise of ascension, when our learning was complete. The Goddess hoped that by humanity's example, the first of her children would learn a measure of humility and understanding.'

'And did the gods take the pact? I'm guessing humanity still has a way to go on our bit.'

He nodded sadly, his breathing slow and heavy. 'The gods accepted her terms, and departed the mortal realm, leaving humanity to learn and grow and make its own choices. The sky was left without a steward, and remains churning and unruly. The earth fell still, for a time at least.'

'Oh yeah?'

Aki lowered his voice to a bassy growl. 'For Usdohr had played false. Although he had departed for the heavens, he left behind echoes of himself, his agents of expansion: bad spirits that would manifest as dark desire. In this way, Usdohr hoped to corrupt humanity, turning them from the teachings of the Goddess, denying them the chance to ascend in their own turn. Chief among the dark spirits was Xalot, the Scorpion, a creature of spite and spine, horn and stinging tail, with a single staring eye.'

'The cheating bastard!'

'Uh, quite so. The Goddess was anguished, but could not break the accord by returning – that would have invited a revival of the ancient battles that scoured the first days of the earth. But not all of the first of her children had been as Usdohr and Qhodis. Some had thrived, exemplars of all the Goddess held true. It was to those she turned when she learned of Usdohr's betrayal, to Ranu, Besu and Aret: the Champion, the Healer and the Messenger, to rebalance the scale. As gods, they could not maintain their forms to walk the earth, but arrived as spirits, to seek out and battle demonic influence for the soul of every man, woman and child.'

'Come again?'

'Mostly the spirits occupy the world around us, drifting free, but sometimes they can imbue a host with the grace of the Goddess or the desires of the demon. Ranu the champion will walk the earth again, and confront Xalot the Scorpion demon to vanquish it from the earth.'

'How do three spirits defeat an army of demons?'

'It is not for total victory that they fight, but only to beat back the tide. The champions are reborn, time and time again, to serve their roles in the great tale, and each battle won brings humanity closer to learning the last of the Goddess's teachings and achieving ascension. Every demon driven from a host is a step closer to rejoining the Goddess in the heavens.'

Javani sat back, chewing her lip. 'Huh. So it's attrition.' Ree had taught her that word, along with countless others relating to futile military campaigns. 'Keep the demons back long enough to sneak up to heaven the back way. And these last children, the messenger, the champion and the . . . what was it?'

'The healer. Ranu the Champion, Besu the Healer, and Aret the Messenger. The greatest of these is Ranu, Champion of the Goddess, with his holy shield and spear of—'

'You've got that backwards.'

'Excuse me?'

'You've got a healer, a messenger, and a spearman, right?'

'A champion,' he corrected through gritted teeth.

'So your spearman is just the grunt in the front line.' She watched the little twitch below his eye, it was unmissable when you knew to look. 'But a healer is worth ten spears, as they keep others in the fight. So your healer, Bessie—'

'*Besu.*'

'Besu, he's already worth ten times the first one. But. *But*. You know what's worth most on a battlefield?'

'I feel in my poet's heart that you are about to tell me.'

She clapped him on the shoulder. 'Damned-by-gods straight I am. The most important thing on a battlefield, Aki my friend, is *communication*.' She could hear Ree's words echoing in her head, lessons from years ago that had seemed both pointless and irrelevant, but now she revelled in their recall. 'A healer might keep ten spears alive. But a messenger, in the right place at the right time, well . . . they can save thousands.' She sat back, glowing, inflated, irrefutable.

'Well, well,' Aki said, his head doing a series of small, twitching nods, 'stories are all about interpretation, I suppose.'

'So what do we need to do?'

'We must prepare for a night in the desert, I suppose. Be sure to check for cobras—'

'No, no, in your story. People. What do we need to do, to . . . ascend?'

Animation returned to his face, the smile to his cheeks. 'The Goddess instructed her children to learn her teachings, and discover for themselves the truth below, and she gave them a world in which to learn.'

'And what are these teachings? Did the Goddess leave books, or scrolls, or something?'

'They are not teachings of the written word – they are a spiritual discipline, the lessons of the world, of the heavens, of what it is to be a free and loving people. Of what it is to ascend to the arms of the mother Goddess, and be loved in return.'

Javani stared at him from beneath lowered brows, her mouth twisted. 'And how are we meant to do that, exactly?' She rubbed her eyes. The tiredness was creeping back. 'What did the Goddess want in the first place? Why did she keep making flawed children?'

Aki sat back with a sigh. 'It was her nature to make life, and life is complicated – most of all she wanted to raise her children to be good.'

'Tough going, I guess, especially if you're a divinity.'

He nodded sadly. 'She herself was first to admit that she had made mistakes, and to seek forgiveness, and forgive in turn.'

Javani cast a look over to where Ree sat by the fire.

'Hmm,' she said.

They had limited supplies and nothing to drink, but Ree felt almost relaxed as she basked in the fire's warmth, somehow comforting and pleasant in contrast with the day's heat. Tension had left her shoulders, tension that had been there for longer than she'd care to admit. She'd always dreaded an unravelling, a day of reckoning, the avatar of her past coming to claim her back. But now the worst had happened. There was no need to worry about it any more.

'You are smiling.' Only Anashe could make it sound like an accusation. She'd eaten sparingly, maintaining a sort of narrow, quivering vigilance.

'You remind me of someone,' Ree said, lying back against banked sand. 'Not your mother. Someone considerably less fun.'

'You will speak to us of her? As you said?'

Ree looked over to where Aki sat with Javani on the fire's far side, his face and body animated in the telling of some great tale. The kid watched, enraptured, as Aki described the birth of a demon god, with its barbed horn and claws like razors. He fingered his necklace as he talked, making its carved animals dance in time to his words. Poor kid, Ree thought, I've really starved her of entertainment up here.

'Why are you here?' Ree said to Anashe.

'I believe this was discussed.'

'You crossed a continent, perhaps two, put your lives in danger countless times, took shady work for shady types, and bickered all the way . . . to learn something of your mother?'

'We told you. We came looking for her. We were not to learn of her death until the journey was made.'

'What did you know of her? What made it seem . . . sensible, worthwhile?'

Anashe flexed and stretched, then sat back with her arms and legs folded in perfect geometric symmetry. Ree almost shook her head, trying to repair the mismatch of vision and memory. Anashe was her mother, and she was very much not.

'We knew she had rebelled, and been exiled. As we said, we were young when it happened. Very young. Our father died soon after, executed for imagined crimes, or so we believed.' She sat back, her breathing steady. Around them, desert night had fallen, the light faded to strange splashes of vivid colour across the star-strewn indigo of the sky, odd glowing bands marking the lost horizons. Distant animals chirped and rustled, making a life for themselves even in harsh lands as these. 'As we grew, we learned of the truth beneath, the truth both lesser, and greater.'

'What do you mean?'

'When we were old enough, as deemed by our protecting family, one of the aunts revealed the lies we had been told, the tapestry of untruth that was the background to our known world. The truth as the Goddess would have known it. It was lesser, and greater: greater for it was blessed by the real, not the inventions of the mortal; lesser, for the tale it told diminished all it touched.'

Ree cast a sidelong look at Javani. 'How old were you when you were told this, uh, truth beneath?'

'I do not remember. I was a woman, but my brother was not yet a man.'

'I thought he was older than you?'

'He is.'

Ree caught her smirk, and cracked a smile in return. 'Don't tease me, Anashe, I've not yet decided what I'll give you. What was this ugly truth?'

'That our mother had not rebelled. She had been a commander in the old regime, that which was overthrown, when the new order claimed perpetual establishment. The old leaders were executed, she was merely cut and banished.'

Ree nodded, remembering. 'I heard she was a general.'

'So we were told.'

'And your father?'

'He betrayed her. He betrayed them all, and had it not been for him it is unlikely the coup would have succeeded. He fancied himself a man of influence, and sold his family in his quest for self-realisation.'

'I can sympathise.'

'With him?'

'With those he sold.'

Anashe took a long, steady breath. 'Of course, he was marked as a traitor from there. I do not know whether he was killed in revenge, or merely purged by the new regime when he outlived himself, but the result was the same.'

'I am sorry.'

'He was a weak man.'

'I am sorry nonetheless. If we had any booze, I'd offer a toast to better parents.' She did well not to look over at Javani that time.

'I rarely drink alcohol.'

'Yeah, I guessed.' Ree sighed and watched the crackling of the little fire. 'You came a long way for a woman who barely raised you.'

Anashe nodded, slow and precise, then looked over to where Aki and Javani sat. 'It is worse for him. I do not remember her – I have a . . . a sense, maybe, of a person. Scattered memories. But Aki . . . he remembers her. He knew, when she was taken from us. It burns him still.'

'He covers it, but yeah, I see it.'

'To hear our father was no hero, dying for his beliefs, but a feeble traitor who had undone himself and those he was supposed to protect . . . It was like losing her again, and him with her, but with a pain that was worse than a death. You understand me?'

'I do.' Ree was finding it difficult to concentrate, to sit comfortably. Thoughts gnawed at her, prickly and tenacious.

'We vowed to find her again. We failed in that vow. Now we hunt her memory. It brought us to the Commodore. It brought us to you.' Anashe sat forward, staring at the flames herself, not looking at Ree. 'Aki needs to believe that there is another hidden truth, a layer below the layer below. That we could still have come from something worth celebration.'

'He's not the only one who feels this way, is he, Anashe?'

She wouldn't meet Ree's eyes. 'Perhaps,' she said quietly.

Ree nodded to herself. 'Your mother was worth celebrating. I was young when I met her, and she was not . . . I suppose she was our mother when she couldn't be yours.'

'It is . . . pleasing to hear that. But my brother is cursed to be a storyteller, to demand narrative completion. He will reject what does not fit.'

'She gave her life for us, Anashe. She died a true hero.'

Anashe nodded, her eyes glimmering in the firelight. 'It is said that the purest sacrifice is a mother who will die for her children,' she said, the words rough and sticking in her throat. 'It does not dull the pain, but it is somehow sweetened.'

'Does Aki need to hear this?'

'We will talk later. I cannot bear his weeping now.'

'How long have you been travelling together?'

'I am not sure. We have rarely stayed in one place for long, always moving since we lost our parents. We left the rest of our family after we learned of the truth beneath, and have been together since, always moving west, always moving south.'

'That's, what, two decades? Have you always argued?'

'Only when on speaking terms.'

'And then you found the Commodore.'

'And the Commodore found us. We were looking, and the Commodore was willing to be found. An offer of employment followed.'

'For this little agency in the protectorate?'

'Yes. Principally the work of retrieval, as I believe we said.'

'I do like that word. So many possibilities.'

'Then the Commodore told my brother of your location. And here we are.'

'Why now? Why are you here now, at the crest of this chaos? It's too neat for coincidence.'

Anashe pursed her lips in thought, the rest of her body as still as the deadlake. 'Aki had been demanding information for some time, but the Commodore refused. And then, one day, it was offered, as payment for a job.' She placed one finger across her lips. 'Aki insisted on taking a boat up the coast, but we floundered on reaching port, and the urgency faded. But I wonder . . .'

Ree had reached the same conclusion. 'Your Commodore had connections in the freelancing world, kept an eye on open tenders in the Arowan domain. That's where that White Spear character operates from, isn't it?'

'They saw the same tender? That's what prompted the Commodore to tell Aki of your location?' She blinked. 'Were we sent to warn you? Protect you?'

Ree sniffed. 'Or perhaps drive us away and render the endeavour moot.' She shifted her grumbling legs. 'You didn't find it staggeringly coincidental that you were hired to travel to the one fleapit mining town in the expanse you were already trying to reach?'

Anashe sighed. 'Aki considered it a message from the Goddess.'

Ree's chuckle was tinged with bleakness. 'And now you're here, what is it that you want, Anashe?'

'From you?'

'In general. I knew a little of your mother's aspirations. What is it you're looking for?'

'I . . .' She looked around, at the rocky sand, the spangled sky, at the shuffling horses. 'I want my brother to find peace.'

'The only true peace is death, Anashe. Is that what you want?'

'No,' she said, smiling, 'he's not yet annoyed me that much.'

'But what do you want for yourself?'

This time Anashe met her gaze, without passion or challenge, merely implacable. 'I have never wanted children of my own, if that is what you mean. Aki and I have each other, and we have hardly stopped moving since we were grown enough to run.' She broke the gaze, sitting back, taking in the clear majesty of the stars. 'It is understood where we come from that raising a child requires more than a parent or two. It requires a family. It requires balance, some measure of constancy, even in the most itinerant of groups. Aki and I have each other for constancy, and we are not balanced.' She shook her head. 'He would make a terrible uncle.'

'That wasn't what I meant.'

'It was what you seemed to ask.' Anashe's gaze slid over to Javani.

Ree couldn't quite keep the heat from her voice. 'Do you think the kid lacks for something? That I owe her something?'

'I cannot say what you owe the girl, or what she is owed by others. But it is likely something you should consider.' Anashe drew her knees up and into her chest. 'Now, tell me sweet stories of my mother, that I may dangle them before my brother like thread to a kitten.'

Ree stared at Anashe for several heartbeats with challenge in her eyes, then her tension dropped. 'She was a tease and a joker,' she said with a rueful smile, settling back against the cooling rock. 'On one job, she kept slipping rocks into a colleague's pack. Small ones, but frequently, all through the day. Nine hells, you should have heard him whinge! Then, the following morning . . .'

Javani had never been so tired, and yet she could not sleep. Aki's stories had lulled her into something like near-sleep, a state where she couldn't summon the energy to move her arms or legs, but her mind whirled like a dust-devil. She replayed it all, from her fury at her treatment by the Guvulis to the chaos of the camels, to the moment when the soulless monster had murdered Moosh, their flight to the cells, the explosion, the White Spear carrying her out and telling her she'd be a queen. The blur of their escape from the town, the howl of the storm. And now tales of gods and demons around a campfire with people who'd crossed a continent chasing the ghost of their mother. She could hear the adults talking still, murmuring in low voices, the occasional muted laugh, the occasional stifled sob.

She missed Moosh with a sharpness that made her gasp. Nobody else would have listened to her recount such a mad tale, then thought of a way to top it. Nobody else would have sat with her in their little den beneath the town walls behind the stables, that they'd hollowed from the mudbrick using a broken clay jug, and swapped outrageous claims about their origins. They'd both been orphans by the time they met, and if there was one sport they excelled at, it was inventing secret histories for themselves.

Grieving was new to Javani. She'd never mourned her parents, except as a missed opportunity, an abstract ideal. There was certainly no shortage of orphans like her and Moosh in the north; he'd been lucky to have Terbish to take him in, and she'd been lucky to have Ree.

Ree.

Her earliest memories were fractured things, a mass of strange, unconnected places and impressions of people. The only constant through it all was Ree, her single grounding through-line of personal history, of personal identity. Their lifestyle had been peripatetic long before she even knew the word (which was relatively recent, in fairness) and certainly long before she was aware of an alternative. They'd never stayed long in any one place, always living with one eye on the horizon, waiting for the time to come to move on again.

She'd made few friends; not that she wasn't gregarious, but that she kept her connections shallow by design. What was the point in discovering a soulmate if you knew you'd be off with the next caravan that passed through?

Yet out here in mining country, in Kazeraz, with Moosh . . . it had felt different. She'd felt a sense of permanence at last, of groundedness, and that had come squarely from Ree whether she realised it or not. Perhaps it was that Ree herself had felt ready to settle, to anchor herself to a place for the first time in Javani's young life. Perhaps it was that from here there was nowhere else to go; impassable mountains to the west, impassable desert to the north, the rolling, impossible plains to the east, and to the south: their past.

She cracked open her eyes. Ree was wrapped in her blanket by the fire, her scabbarded sword laid close beside her, its fine hilt shimmering in the flickering firelight. Javani knew she prized the sword, it was one of the few things she'd kept close to her in all the time they'd travelled, all of Javani's conscious life. Yet since they'd settled on the farm she'd stopped wearing it, had left it locked in the strongbox in the cabin. If that hadn't symbolised a level of contentment, what would?

And now it was all gone. The delicate little life they'd been building in this new place was over before it had even begun, dying with Moosh on the alley floor.

Ree had once called death another form of parting. Javani thought of the half-friends she'd made and the half-friends she'd left behind, who might as well have died for all her chances of seeing them again, but she knew it was not the same. You can't believe someone is still out there and happy when you've seen him bleed to death in the dust.

The Shenakar killed him because they thought he was the heir. Now they think I'm the heir. The White Spear thought the same. So, am I? Everyone but Ree seems to think so. If I'm not, why do they think I am? What did Ree mean by 'I should have expected this'? What hasn't she told me?

She wondered if she should have been shocked at how readily Ree had taken charge of their situation – unpanicked, commanding, making off with the wagon and driving it into the desert like she'd had a plan all along. Hiding supplies in the rocks and the hills. *I should have expected this.*

Javani thought again of their shared past, of how little she knew of her aunt's time before her. That was the thing about mining country, this far from the 'civilisation' of the protectorate: nobody asked about a person's past; it was bad manners. After all, few people came out here because things were going well for them. Most genuine visitors only came north to sell and exploit, before retreating to safety and comfort elsewhere. Nobody was *from* here – except the nomads, of course, but they'd been chased off by the Guild and its ilk pretty early.

What did she really know about her aunt?

Lazant had said a Serican diplomat took a secret child into the north. Javani was just jaded enough to know that when people said 'diplomat', they meant 'spy'.

She watched Ree's dim shape in the firelight, her mind galloping like a frantic, exhausted pony. All those years travelling ever northward, ever further from the rest of the world. What had they been running from? What had Ree been dreading? *I should have expected this.*

Ree told me my parents were dead. She told me she was my aunt. She's always said it. I don't even know which of my parents she's supposedly related to. Tomorrow, I'll . . . I'll . . .

Sleep claimed her.

* * *

Javani woke once in the night, and briefly. Just for a moment, before she fell back into the welcome embrace of unconsciousness, she became aware of Ree curled beside her, warm against her body. Ree was stroking her hair.

FIFTEEN

Kurush rose slowly from his blanket. It took him quite some time to unwrap himself and shake off the worst of the sand, but he knew that some of it was there to stay. Not yet dawn, and it was to be a day of grating rash in his nethers. He drank sparingly from his waterskin, splashed a little water around his eyes and face in a futile attempt at cleaning away the embedded grit, and sighed deeply. At least he was alive, even if he was destined to spend the next few days scratching at himself.

The storm had savaged their column, sweeping men and mounts off into the desert, scattering scouts and supplies. He hadn't yet calculated the full extent of their losses, mostly because he didn't want to. So much damage, so many dead or missing, in such a short span. An unpleasant conversation with the Guild's auditors now seemed an inevitability. He needed to escape across the water before that happened. He needed the Shenakar to succeed, and quickly.

Kurush hawked and went to spit out a sandy mouthful, then reconsidered. He might yet need the water.

'Boss?' It was Berev, wading across the sand towards him, his remaining teeth glinting in the creeping streaked indigo of desert pre-dawn.

'Guildmaster, Berev. Remember?'

'Sorry, bo— Guildmaster.' Berev scratched at his eyebrow. He was as sandy as Kurush, grains flaking off and drifting in the chill breeze. From over the rise, Kurush heard calls and the stomp and clatter of the column assembling. His heart quickened.

'What's that?'

'The Shenakar,' Berev said, nodding over the dune. 'They're ordering the men out.'

Kurush forged off up the dune, slapping at what he hoped was the last of the visible sand on his clothes. 'The hells they are. The riders answer to me, and me alone.'

His second coughed. 'The prince-man offered half a silver talent to the Guild hunter who brings him the girl's head.'

The muscles of Kurush's jaw bulged. *Fuck*. 'They'll be paid a bonus, sure, but their fees will be processed through Guild channels.' He did his best to stride up the dune, boots dragging up the slope. 'They should at least be waiting for their commander.'

Berev waded after him, his legs shorter and gait stumbling. 'One of the scouts came back. Saw smoke.'

'Smoke?'

'From a cook-fire.'

Kurush's heart was fluttering, a light, giddy feeling up and down his throat. 'Then we've got them treed.' Triumph was in reach.

'Looks that way. Prince-man is sending folks out on foot to surround them, ambush-like.'

'Well, come on then! We can't lead an assault from the rear, can we?'

Javani was the last to wake, which annoyed her. She had dreamed of Moosh, as she'd expected, but not in a useful or therapeutic way. Just sadness and loss, and confusion, and a growing anger at those responsible for the ending of his life and the wrecking of hers. Her mood was unchanged by waking. It was another day, and Moosh was still dead.

Aki was cooking something over a small fire, while Anashe was down by the water, refilling skins. Ree was tending to the horses, re-hitching them to the wagon with murmured words of reassurance. The wagon itself looked packed and ready to go. They all seemed to have been up for hours, while she knew for a fact they'd stayed up later than she had, no doubt talking cryptic nonsense to each other as they seemed to enjoy. Javani resolved that when her time came to ascend to the ranks of the fully-grown, she would strive to preserve a reputation for plain-speaking. Riddles were all very well for maintaining an air of mystery, she supposed, but they were a bloody nuisance if you just wanted to fill in some gaps.

And she had an awful lot of gaps.

'Why'd you let me sleep?' she asked Ree as she passed. 'I could have been helping.'

Ree simply snorted and shook her head without looking around, which did nothing to improve Javani's mood.

'At your age, you need your sleep,' Aki called from beside the fire. 'You have much growing to do.'

'Well, we can hope,' chuckled Ree, and Javani's mood darkened further, especially when Aki joined in.

'Is there food?' she snapped.

'Shortly, little one. Our provisions tend away from abundance, and must be treasured. But by the favour of the Goddess, your comrade Aki excels at the preparation of—'

'You can just say yes,' she muttered. 'I'm going to squeeze the lemon.'

'Go away from the water,' Ree called after her. 'I'm not having you contaminate it for everyone else.'

'Well, yeah,' Javani grumbled back with a sarcastic wobble of her head. 'I'm not a bloody reptile—'

'Go on, then.' Ree waved her off. 'You'll drown your drawers if you leave it too long.' A small smile crept onto her face. 'I remember once, not long before we reached Mahavrik the first time, you'd been quiet a long time. You denied that you needed to urinate, over and over, yet when we arrived and you stood from the wagon bench—'

Javani scuttled away with her hands over her head. 'All right, all right, I'm going, gods be damned!' Cheeks burning, she clambered up between the burned-out buildings, mindful of the drifts of blown sand that lay against anything that constituted a hard surface. The sun was creeping over the undulating horizon as she reached what passed for the outer limit of the settlement, casting the loose ring of stones with gleaming rose dawnlight, the scattered sheets of cloud above glowing copper and gold in the lightening sky. As she squatted down in relative seclusion, removed from the muttered conversation at the waterhole and with only the wind and a few early-rising insects for company, Javani felt something like solitude for the first time in days. Something like peace.

Her mind turned to their predicament. A prince of Shenak was hunting her, determined to stop her ascending to her supposedly rightful throne. A vast southern mercenary had been hunting her – before Ree had run the woman over with a wagon – determined to ensure she ascended to said throne after all. And in the middle, her aunt, dragging them off into a desert with little more than a sackful of secrets, shocked but not surprised that someone had come looking. What did it mean?

And what did she want it to mean?

Javani had been so focused on a new life in the west for so long, away from the heat and the dust and the parched, furrowed earth, the miners and the gamblers and the bandits, that an unexpected alternative had barely registered. But what if they were right, these murderous foreigners? What if she really were a lost princess, and a distant throne was hers to command?

Well, first of all, she needed to be sure the people trying to kill her were far behind them. But after that . . .

A horse whinnied.

The sound puzzled her. It sounded wrong. Too quiet, too distant. From the wrong direction.

Her ablutions complete, she stood. From which way had she heard the sound? The ruined buildings and broken wall complicated matters, maybe, but surely they couldn't make a horse sound like it was somewhere it wasn't. She climbed the last of the rise to the ring of stones and peered out over the dawnlit desert. The low sun cast shadows of farcical length, each ripple and dune before her half-lost to darkness.

She stood for a moment, one hand on the cool stone, peering out over the sands, watching the line of light descending the blurred and distant Ashadi mountains to the west. No sign of a horse. No sign of anything. Perhaps it had been the wind after all. Maybe you didn't just see things that weren't there in the desert, maybe you heard them too – the voices of spirits, the lost travellers—

Something moved.

Javani went absolutely still, her fingers gripping the yellowed stone before her. A dark shape had broached the shadow of a dune, just for a moment, but it had been unmistakable: a crawling figure.

Suddenly she could see them, her eyes adjusted or the light of the rising sun enough to draw out the contrast. Breath catching in her throat, eyes scanning, she marked the tracks, the crawling figures. They were coming from all sides.

She swallowed hard, hard enough to push the bile back down her throat. 'Shit. Shit, shit, shit shit shit shit shit . . . REE!'

Javani ran.

Ree met her at the huts' edge. 'What? What is it, kid?'

'They're coming! They're here!'

Ree half shook her head, frowning, as if she wanted to ask who and how but had already realised the answers, impossible as they should have been. She locked eyes with Javani.

'Get in the wagon.'

'What?'

'Get in the wagon, kid. Right now.' She turned away, making for the horses. 'Aki! Anashe! Time to go!'

'Already?' came Aki's voice. 'But the exquisite breakfast—'

'Right now, you feckless gusset. Bring what you can.'

Anashe was already at the wagon, checking the harness. 'I apologise for my brother. Sometimes he lacks a sense of occasion.'

Ree climbed up on the driver's bench beside Javani. 'Could have finished that sentence two words earlier. You, in the back. Out of sight.'

Javani started to protest but Ree's glare drove her into the wagon's rear. She hunkered down as far away from the fat little kegs as possible.

Satisfied with the horses' rigging, Anashe climbed up beside Ree. 'They found us, then?'

Ree snapped the reins and the horses began their thankless plod, straining to pull the wagon out from the sand and up from the watering hole's dip.

'They did. Aki, push, thrice-damn you.'

'I am not some beast of burden to be applied—' came a protesting voice.

'Fucking push!'

The wagon started to move.

'You were wrong about the storm?' Anashe said, face neutral, as they began to pick up speed.

'I was . . . incompletely correct about the storm,' Ree replied, her gaze fixed on steering the team out of the dip and back to the dusty ruin of the trail. The wind began to snap and whistle through the wagon as they accelerated, the horses' hooves finding the packed earth beneath the previous day's coating of blown sand.

'And your plan?'

'Unchanged. We've just advanced the schedule a little.'

Anashe turned on the bench, staring directly at Ree. Ree's eyes stayed on the trail.

'You're going to run south with them chasing?'

'Nothing else has changed, short of their relative location. You have a bow, or something you can throw?'

'We have only a sword we took from the Guildhouse. It is . . . notched.'

'Then maybe look in the back for something to use as a shield. This could get unfriendly.'

Javani poked her head through. 'What about your sword, Ree? You could lend it to—'

Ree reached around to slap at her hand. 'Nobody touches that sword but me.'

Javani pulled back, feeling the sting of her words more than the slap. 'Then let someone else drive and you can—'

'No.' Ree hunched over the reins, driving the horses as hard as she could. 'Now sit down.'

'I only—'

'Sit. Down.'

Teeth gritted, Javani sat back down. 'Stop telling me what to do,' she muttered.

Ree heard. 'Got something you want to say? Here and now? Because this is not the fucking time, kid!'

Aki's voice came loud from the wagon's rear. 'Riders!'

Kurush watched the wagon peel out from the watering hole with a grunt of disbelief, and a pre-emptive flinch. He could feel the shock radiating from the Shenakar prince like heat from an iron.

'What manner of conveyance is that?' Lazant exclaimed, his head swivelling to follow the vehicle's progress. 'It's as if someone barded a troop transport!'

Kurush could only stare back in mute bewilderment.

'Are you sure these are your best men, Guildmaster? Fate once more throws hurdles into duty's path, and we must overcome,' Lazant said, the slightest tremble in his words as he watched the rising plume of orange dust taint the clean pale blue of the sky. His voice dropped to a whisper. 'Mother always said I lacked determination . . . We shall not be deterred!'

I lost half my best men in a storm that you made them weather, Kurush didn't say. You sent them out half-cocked and competing with each other in near darkness, on foot, scattered across the desert, instead of staying with the horses. You've got them looking to you for orders with your promises of silver, when that silver is *mine*.

Kurush thought of his diplomatic posting, half muttered apologetic reassurances, then turned and roared at the signalman.

'Mount up! Mount up!'

'How many?'

Aki clambered across the rocking wagon, one hand on the struts, maintaining impressive balance despite the thudding impacts of the desert trail beneath them. Javani watched, grumpily, from her corner.

'Two closing, more behind them. They will not be alone.'

'How many did you see in the dunes, kid?'

Javani shrugged, inaudibly, but apparently Ree expected no answer.

Anashe had the sabre across her knees and was checking the blade's attachment to the hilt. 'You know who hunts us?'

'After yesterday? The Guild, the Shenakar, that southern monster, and maybe those bandits we fucked over as well.'

'And which of them do you believe is ambushing our position now?'

Ree was quiet for a moment. 'Kurush is a born thrall. If they're out here now, they bore the storm in the open. They're desperate.'

Anashe squinted. 'Figures ahead, too.'

'What?'

'Stands to reason they'd have cut off the trail, does it not?'

'Shit. Your eyesight is much better than mine.'

'My sister's eyes are better than any – the only shame is what lies behind them!'

'Shut up, brother!'

'Aki, found anything we can use as a shield yet? I don't much fancy getting punctured.'

'There are loose boards here, we could—'

'Do it! And find something to throw. We need to keep them from getting close.'

'We already ejected our surplus, you remember? There is nothing left but the supplies, and those demonic kegs of blasting powder.'

'Not those, not yet. What about your souvenirs?'

'My souvenirs?'

Ree leaned around, fixing Aki with a mischievous stare. 'Some trinkets you kept back from the haul, perhaps. Anything good and heavy?'

Aki's hand leapt to his chest. 'You cannot be sincere, woman! To ask a man as I to discard what few treasures—'

'It's that or we die, Master Gale. Let those bastards take their time lining up their shots – or get aboard us – and our bones are lost beneath the dunes come day's end.'

Aki took a long and ragged breath. 'This is inhuman.'

Ree's attention was back on the trail ahead, but Javani could see her raised eyebrow. 'I'm not sure what you thought you were signing up for, young man, but generally things only get worse before they get better.' She snapped the reins again. 'And that's assuming they get better at all. Ya!'

Anashe rose to her feet at the bench. 'Aki, take the sword and pass me the shielding.'

'Everyone stay low,' Ree called. 'Here they come!'

Movos did his best to walk in the big woman's shadow, but she made it difficult. She stopped, sniffed the air, cocked an ear to the wind, inspected the ground, let the sands run through her great pale fingers. The sun was barely up and already the night's cold was a memory. The land around them was beginning to bake, to glow with packed and reflected heat. For the dozenth time since she'd roused him in the storm's wake, he asked himself what he was doing there, what in the name of the gods he hoped to achieve.

What else are you going to do? came the reply. His brothers were gone. The alchemist, wretch that he'd been, was gone, and with him whatever plans for a future Movos had nurtured these last months. It was a strange thing, to be so unmoored, to have the road ahead torn away at a stroke, replaced with this churning desert of uncertainty and a broad, unfocused hunger for revenge.

Since the abrupt end to his mining days, Movos had ceased being someone who made plans. But the focus and direction of their scheme, the sense of working towards something, had given him more purpose than he'd realised. And now it was gone. He was walking through the desert in the shadow of a giant mercenary because he had nothing else to do and nowhere else to be.

'Are we close?' he asked as she stopped again. Behind him, their pack mule snorted and honked, as frustrated as he was at the constant interruptions. 'Gotta say,' he went on, 'tracking folk through the sand ain't something most will endeavour to undertake, if you catch my meaning. Something of a rarefied calling, the desert scout.'

The woman grunted, then cocked an ear again. Movos mirrored her, but heard nothing but the moan of the wind across the cracked dunes.

'Got a lot of deserts down south, have you? Folks with your complexion aren't exactly renowned for exposure to the hotter climes, if you follow.'

'Tracking is tracking,' she said, and began her walk again. Movos hurried to keep up, feeling the sweat thick against his body already.

'Why are you doing this?' he said, resisting the urge to grab a waterskin from the mule and empty it over his head. He adjusted his hat, flicked sweat from his brow. 'Why are you out here in this insanity?'

'Contract.'

'For the girl?' Movos ran his remaining fingers through his dampening beard. 'Between us, I fear she and her aunt may be a lost cause. Most that travel this road don't travel it back.' Ourselves likely included, he added internally.

'Contract.'

Movos felt anger rising at her laconic answers. It was getting so damned-by-gods hot. 'The contract said get the girl. But what if the girl is gone? What if it's all gone? When do you say, "enough"? When is it all right to . . . to give up?'

The woman stopped, turned, drenched Movos in her shade.

'Give up?'

He swallowed, throat gulch-dry. 'Some contracts can't be fulfilled, right? Circumstances, they change. You have to know when to . . . when to cut your losses.'

She was little more than a silhouette to him, yet somehow he felt the weight of her gaze. 'Only death.'

'Only death?'

'Change of circumstance, to annul contract. Only death.'

'The target's? Yours?'

'Either.'

'But nothing else? Nothing like, like say it being impossible to find your—'

'Impossible is a word of weakness.'

'It's a word of damned-near fact, far as I can see! We're walking into the salt-desert – *walking* – in the hope of tracking some—'

'Perhaps we die. Perhaps she is dead. But we must try.'

Movos scratched at his head beneath his hat, at his beard, smearing the sweat from his eyes. 'But why? Are you gods-cursed? Are your cherished held against your efforts?'

'It is . . . code.'

'Code?'

'Code. Honour.'

'Now that's not a word I recognise.'

She frowned. 'I use wrong word? It means—'

'I *know* what it means, I was being, uh, rhetorical.' Movos removed his hat, flicked sweat from the brim, fanned himself with it. It was fearful hot. 'You're saying that the only thing forcing you to complete this, this ludicrous contract . . . is your own damned sense of pride?'

She gazed down at him, her impassive face almost shaped by an emotion he couldn't name. 'When day becomes night,' she said, 'one must find new guiding star.'

'Huh?'

'What is your code, Movos Guvuli?'

Movos scratched at his head again. It was too hot to think, and her question made his head boil. Unable to meet her stare, he looked down at his feet, to the edge of the trail. Something glimmered back at him in the burgeoning daylight.

'Hey,' he murmured. 'Is that . . . ?'

She stiffened, one hand reaching for the helmet that dangled from her belt. 'Be ready.'

'Huh? For what?' Movos squatted down, brows lowered. He reached out his diminished hand, flicking loose grains away from the gleaming object at the trailside. It looked like a lump of raw turquoise. Just like the lumps he and his brothers had been loading into sacks from the Guildhouse strongroom the previous day.

'I'll be thrice-damned,' he murmured, his eyes lifting back along the trail. A few more gleams had caught the sun, scattered and half-buried. The haul was here, abandoned on the trail. Parts of it, anyway. 'Must have slung it to save weight.' The sun was shining once more on Movos Guvuli.

He reached out his hand again to the lump, probing around it, ready to lift it clear. The pack mule would do. He could fill out its saddlebags, string a couple of extra sacks over it, maybe even waterskins as they emptied. He wouldn't need to keep chasing into the desert after all, if all he needed to do was track along collecting his lost spoils. He began to chuckle as his fingers closed around the lump, a low, giddy thing that started in his belly and travelled up through his chest.

His chuckling stopped. The ground beneath the sand had the slightest tremor. Was that thunder he heard in the distance? Surely there couldn't be another storm rolling in so soon after the last . . .

'Be ready, Guvuli.'

'Huh?' he said, as her hands gripped his shoulders.

SIXTEEN

Javani didn't even see the riders before the first bolts smashed against Anashe's shield of boards. She squealed and ducked low in the wagon's rear as they bounced along, Ree hunched over the reins, Anashe standing over her, legs wide and rigid against the wagon's clatter, the prickled wood outstretched in her hands.

Then the riders had wheeled and were racing alongside, cranking their hand-bows with one glove as they closed. Javani peered left and right: one each side. Anashe swivelled, trying to track which would be ready to shoot first, unable to shield Ree from both.

'Aki!' Javani called. 'Help!'

Muttering something between a lament and a prayer, Aki bounded forward, swung on the canopy's edge and let fly from his hand. Something golden and gleaming flashed through the air, striking the Guild rider square on the forehead as he raised his bow to shoot. He flinched and cried, reeling in the saddle, then his horse stumbled and he was gone, lost in the rising dust cloud that marked their progress to the sky.

The second rider loosed, but Anashe was ready, swivelling the boards in place. The slim bolt punched through but did not clear, its barbed tip coming to rest a hand's span from Ree's head. She flicked a momentary glance at the bobbing metal.

'Bit close, that one, thank you, Anashe.'

'My apologies,' came the strained grunt as Anashe flexed the board in her hands. Her arms and legs were trembling, sweat popping along her skin as she braced against the wagon's thundering transit. 'My brother, your moment!'

'Goddess forgive me,' Aki sighed as he leapt forward again, 'for such callous discard of her bounties.' He flung another of his treasures at the second rider, who ducked. The gemstone sailed over her shoulder and out of view.

Aki wailed.

'Again, brother, should it please you. These boards are hardly reinforced!'

'Would that it were possible, but there is nothing more to throw! Unless . . .' Tears in his eyes, he reached a trembling hand into his jacket.

'Wait!' Javani called, her hand extended. From it dangled Ree's fat blue stone, twirling on its slender chain. 'Use this.'

'Goddess . . .' he breathed, mesmerised.

'Aki!' came Ree's commanding voice.

He snatched it from her grip, swivelled and threw.

The rider's hand snapped up, catching the gem as it flashed towards her head.

'Was that—' Ree barked. 'Fuck! Aki, you witless—'

The rider looked down at the stone in her opening gauntlet. She stared at it, horse champing beneath her. Then without a word she wheeled away and was lost to the dust over the dunes. The trail ahead was clear.

'Well,' Anashe remarked, letting the boards drop on the bench beside her. 'Perhaps we should have—'

A thump at the wagon's rear snapped Javani's attention around. 'Behind us!'

Two horses blasted out of the orange cloud that trailed them, dark shapes first hazy then all too corporeal. Other shapes blurred in the dust cloud behind them. The rest of the Guild riders were on them.

'Aki!'

Aki seemed still in a daze, one hand on a canopy strut, whispering a saga of pain and loss beneath the wagon's clatter.

'Don't let them get level,' Ree cried over her shoulder. 'If one of the bastards has the wit to kill the horses we'll be fucked.'

Anashe sprang down into the wagon and snatched up the sabre from Aki's feet. 'Come, brother, there will be other treats, but not if our blood darkens the sands.'

Aki wiped at one eye, then nodded. 'While I do not dispute the principle, I believe I would be willing to exchange a little blood for the return of my—'

'Aki!'

A rider closed, his own sabre bared and reaching. Javani pointed with a yelp. 'On the left!'

'Which left?' Ree called.

'Mine!'

'Anashe?'

'Ready!'

Ree yanked the reins to the right, and the wagon barrelled across, its wheels driving the rider wide and off the trail.

'On the right!'

'My right?'

'Mine!'

Back came the wagon, but the new rider was ready, pulling back then spurring his horse forward as the wagon slewed past. Anashe leapt to the wagon's backboard, sabre in hand, and slashed at him as he tried to pass. He ducked and swung back, and then the two were swiping and hacking at each other, steel ringing over the constant rumble of hoof-beats and wheels.

Another rider was closing. Javani turned to warn Ree, but he was too fast, racing past the wagon's rear and along the side before she could shout a warning. 'Aki, the side!' she squeaked. He'd already seen the danger, slinging himself out of the back of the wagon and onto the canopy side as Anashe leapt over a clumsy swipe from her rider then kicked him clean from the saddle.

As he bounced away into the dust, Aki reached across. 'My sister, if you please?'

She tossed him the sabre as the second rider closed in on Ree's bench, his own sabre clean and gleaming in his fist. Aki snatched the sword from the air and jackknifed himself up onto the canopy roof, feeling it flex beneath his weight, before bounding with measured strides and leaping from the wagon onto the rider's back. The horse bucked and snorted as Aki wrestled the man clear, arms wrapped, then brought the sabre to bear and cut him from hip to shoulder. Screaming, the rider fell away, but the horse bucked again and Aki struggled to stay in the saddle.

'They are closing!' came Anashe's voice, and Javani turned to see two more riders haring up, sabres primed, Anashe standing bare-handed in silhouette at their approach. 'The weapon!'

Javani leapt to the bench beside Ree. 'Aki, the sword!'

He struggled to control the bucking horse and keep it running beside the wagon. 'I cannot, little one – this recalcitrant *beast!*'

Javani stretched out her hand, grasping for him as the horse tossed and champed. 'Take my hand!'

He made a wild grab, came up short, grabbed at the horse again as it tried to throw him. Javani tried to stretch further, but the wagon hit a rut and almost tossed her from the bench and beneath the wheels. Yelping and tasting sour adrenaline, she grabbed on to the bench and gripped until the palpitations passed.

'They are trying to board us!' Anashe cried. She snapped a kick at one of the closing riders, but as she moved one way the other closed and leapt from the saddle to the wagon. His knife scored the canopy as he grabbed the side. 'I need the weapon!'

Javani's eyes fell on Ree's sword, tucked beside her on the bench. 'Ree, your sword, I'll—'

'No! Don't touch it.'

Javani stared, dumbfounded. Ree's eyes were fixed on the bumpy trail ahead, blind to Aki's struggles or Anashe's battle behind them. 'But you never even use it,' she hissed. 'You just keep it in a box! It looks like a really good sword. Use it!'

'Kid, it's already seen too much use and I don't want to have to use it again.'

'They're going to *kill us!* I mean, maybe not you and the others, but they're definitely going to kill *me!*'

'Ugh, nine fucking hells. Take the reins.' Before Javani could blink, Ree had thrust the sweaty reins into her hands and pivoted away, sweeping up from the bench and bouncing across the wagon floor. Javani watched as she whipped the sword from its sheath, paused, then carved a swathe across the canopy side, slashing ropes and canvas. Javani saw a burst of vivid orange as a ragged stripe of the canopy fell away, taking the boarder with it. The wagon bucked as he fell beneath the wheels.

A thump beside her indicated Aki's arrival, having at last wrestled the horse close enough to the wagon to make the return trip. He was panting and bloodied, the sabre pressed to his chest. A cry and clang from behind them set him moving again, scrabbling off over the bench and back towards where Anashe and Ree were faced with another two boarders, one sword between them. Aki tossed the sabre back to Anashe as he arrived, who slashed at the fingers of the nearest rider then flicked the weapon back to her brother in time for him to cleave the helmet from one who'd strayed too close on the other side. Ree, meanwhile, stood central, her bloodless sword back at her side, her breath coming in great gulps. She'd done nothing but cut the canopy. She looked back at Javani with wide, wild eyes, then beyond her.

'Eyes front, kid!'

Javani turned in time to see two dark shapes directly before the thundering team, then with a double thump that rattled the wagon they were lost beneath the pounding hooves. She screamed. One of the shapes had been the White Spear.

Kurush was riding as hard as he ever had, hard enough to shake his bones and loosen the teeth in his head, yet he could still hardly keep up with the Shenakar ahead. The prince had focused his determination on speed, and his lieutenant had gone with him. Kurush was afraid that if they left him behind, he might never see them again. He'd be marooned in the desert with a dozen casualties and another dozen missing, the Guildhouse strongroom blasted open and robbed, a secret room full of secret records that he wanted nothing to do with. And while none of it was his fault, of course, the auditors were far from certain to see it that way.

Better not to be left behind. Better to finish this business today, here and now. They barrelled forward across the rough ground, now more red dust than sand as they left the desert's reaches behind and closed on the town, dark scrub and blackened trees flashing past as they rode. Their quarry was unmissable, the dirty plume it sent into the clear morning sky could be seen for thirty miles. Riders swarmed around it now, the scouts rallied and charging, the body of their column now catching up in force. Kurush and the Shenakar would be the last to reach them – an unforeseen consequence of picking the best spot to observe their abortive ambush – but all the prince required was the girl's head and his part was done.

Kurush shuddered, despite the fury of his exertion. He willed the thoughts away, focused only on his rewards to come. Royalty. Riches. Renown.

They were closing on the wagon. Not long now.

A hand shot up from between the horses and Javani screamed again. The hand was followed by an arm, then the White Spear pulled herself out from the harness and up to the driver's bench. She was scuffed and streaked with dust but seemed otherwise unharmed. She was dragging something, and as she hauled it up behind her and dumped it into the wagon, Javani was horrified to see it was Movos Guvuli.

'You,' she said, unable to think of anything else.

'Girl,' the White Spear replied. Her ferocious dark helmet was fixed over her pale face, but the cobalt pools of her eyes shone through.

'Nghnnhnnhn,' said Movos Guvuli, who looked as though he'd taken a knock when the wagon ran them over.

'What the— Who the fuck's this?' came Ree's voice from the back of the wagon. 'Aki, to your left – no, your other left!'

'Girl,' the White Spear said again.

Javani couldn't move, her fingers tight on the reins, her arms and body bounced along by the wagon's furious passage. Something moved in the corner of her vision – another rider, pulling up alongside. This one had a hand-bow, levelled and ready to shoot. She stared at the rider, stared at the little bow as it bobbed in sync with the horse's gait, tried to focus her mind on what she was supposed to be doing. There was definitely something she was supposed to be doing.

The White Spear surged past her, throwing herself in front of the bolt as the rider loosed. The bolt plinked and fizzed away into the broken dust, leaving only the faintest of nicks on the White Spear's dark armour. The rider swore and threw down the bow, reaching for the sabre at her side, but the White Spear was faster. She lunged across from the wagon, seizing the rider with a giant hand and heaving the woman bodily from the saddle. She thumped her against the wagon's side, once, twice, then let her drop, swallowed by the swirling orange cloud in their wake.

More riders had caught up with them, surging out of the dust. A volley of incoming bolts thrummed from the side-plating. 'Guvuli!' the White Spear called as projectiles fizzed overhead. 'Guvuli!'

Movos Guvuli clambered unsteadily from the wagon bed, one hand on the back of the bench. Blood was leaking from somewhere within his dark mass of curls. Javani shrank away from him, but there was nowhere to go – the White Spear occupied half the bench, Movos Guvuli blocked any retreat into the back of the wagon, and riders with hand-bows were galloping up alongside. Whatever the Shenakar had promised them for killing her, they were keen to collect.

'Get back,' she squeaked over her shoulder at the woozy Guvuli. 'Get away from me!'

'Be calm, girl,' the White Spear said. 'He is with me. Guvuli, the riders.'

Movos's drifting eyes finally alighted on her, and blinked into focus. 'Just what is it,' he drawled, steadying himself against the canopy strut, 'that's so damned-by-gods special about you, urchin?'

'I wish I knew!'

Another barrage of bolts thunked against the plating. One hit the White Spear's armoured back. Javani yelped and hunched further over the reins.

'Guvuli!'

'Give a man a chance, paleface,' he muttered, then dropped to his knees at the wagon side. He slid the remaining loose boards aside and reached into a space beneath, levering up a set of long metal tubes, apparently lashed together into some kind of bundle. He hefted the bundle in the crook of his arm, one hand beneath, the other gripping a set of cords that dangled from the device's end, and tottered towards the driver's bench.

'Might want to cover your ears, little girl,' he said with a blackened smile, then raised the weapon. 'Now!'

The White Spear ducked, and Movos yanked the cords. A blaze of alchemical light burst from the device in his arms, then with a boom and rattle of cracks it fired a stream of gleaming metal prongs over the woman's shoulder and into the riders jostling behind her. Javani shut her eyes as the acrid stink hit her, just ahead of the cries and screams of the riders as the projectiles punched into their armour and tore straight through. Movos swivelled, a line of ragged holes ripping along the wagon canopy, sending Ree, Aki and Anashe sprawling as they hurled themselves flat, then the slivers of bright metal hit the chasing pack and their line collapsed in chaos.

It was over in an instant. The riderless horses fell away, and for a moment, the world was silent but for the tremendous rumble and judder of the wagon. Movos was chuckling, staring at the weapon in his hand, which was steaming and fizzing and producing a vile stink. 'Gods treat you kind, Shantar, you unlovable turd,' he muttered, then yelped and flung the curled and smoking bundle from the wagon's side.

Javani watched it tumble away into the dust. 'What in hells was *that*?'

Movos was still grinning, sucking at singed fingers. 'A little surprise we packed along.'

The White Spear loomed up, her baleful gaze filling Javani's vision. 'Girl,' she said, 'make for the east road. That ship is still waiting – it will wait as long as it must. I will keep you safe.'

'But . . .' Javani said. 'But . . .'

'Girl, my contract is to bring you to Shenak, and whole. I will fulfil my part, but you must consider yours.'

'What?'

'This is your birthright. You were born to rule – it is your duty. All of us must play our part.'

A dull clunk came from behind, and Javani turned to see Movos reel and put one hand to his bloodied head. 'In all the—'

Ree hit him with the board again and he dropped, falling back from sight into the wagon. She leapt over his collapsing form with a scream of, 'Get away from her!'

The White Spear turned too slowly, still holding the bench with both hands as she loomed over Javani. Ree's kick caught her square in the face, and the follow-up drove into her chest as she raised one hand to shield herself. In an instant, she was gone, lost beneath the wheels in the thundering dust cloud.

'No!' Javani screamed.

'What?' Ree's eyes were wide, and her face was spattered with blood of uncertain origin. 'What did you say?'

'What did you do that for?'

'She was going to kill you!'

'She was only trying to protect me!'

'Then she had a funny way of— Steer, steer! Away from the town!'

Javani turned back to see the trail forking, the horses already leaning back into the climb towards the gates they'd fled through only the day before. She hauled them back across, towards the south road, the trade road. Towards the narrow-lands.

'We take the south road, we can pick up supplies at the old watch-tower and keep running,' Ree went on, sitting down beside Javani on the bench. She was breathing heavily and gleaming with sweat in the rare patches she wasn't caked with trail dust. 'Get to safety.'

'The White Spear was taking me to safety,' Javani snapped.

'What in hells are you talking about, kid?' Ree seemed immediately furious, nostrils wide and quivering. 'What did she tell you?'

'That she was going to protect me, keep me safe!'

'Anything else?'

'That she was going to make me a queen! Back in Shenak! I'm a princess, Ree, she said so. Lazant thinks so, Kurush thinks so, that's the whole reason he—'

'We are not talking about this now.'

'Then when are we? Because—'

'Just do as you're told, will you? Drive the wagon, keep to the south road, and I'll keep you safe. You don't need some massive Horvaun tree.'

'I'm so sick of being ordered around! You're always telling me what to do!'

'You are a *child*, Javani. You can't possibly understand—'

'Then make me understand! How am I ever going to make my own decisions if you never tell me anything?'

'We'll handle that when the time comes, kid, but for now—'

'And when will that be? I've had to do a shit-stack of growing up in the last day or two, or haven't you noticed, Ree? Maybe there's a few things you ought to have filled me in on before any of this happened, do you think?'

That landed. Ree seemed to bend away from her as if she'd been punched, and when she looked back her rage simmered in the wet edges of her eyes. 'There will be time,' she growled, 'but this ain't it.'

'Look out!' came the shout from the back of the wagon, just ahead of a Guild rider leaping down at them from the canopy roof, knife drawn. Ree pivoted and swung, ducking beneath the knife arm and offering a hunched shoulder to the man's oncoming midriff, swinging with him and flicking him over her back and onto the rump of one of the horses. He flailed there for an instant, clawing at the horse's galloping flank, then slipped and slid beneath. The wagon bucked and bounced as he went under the wheels. From somewhere within came the sound of Movos Guvuli hitting his head again.

Ree turned back, one hand clutching her side. 'What the fuck was that? I thought you two had this under control?'

'A thousand apologies,' came Aki's hoarse voice. 'That one slipped through. He crept up the side while we were ejecting his comrades.'

'You'd better be keeping a better grip on my sword than their numbers,' Ree growled.

'There really is quite a profusion of them,' Anashe called back. She sounded out of breath, which alarmed Javani. She'd never seen the woman tire. 'That is the last of that batch, but more will catch us as the horses slow.'

Ree snarled but didn't reply.

'You let Aki use your sword?' Javani couldn't keep the wonder from her voice. 'You really—'

'I dropped it, all right? He picked it up. That's all.'

'Well, this is a big step, I'm proud of you. And Anashe is right.' Javani gestured with the reins. 'The horses can't keep running like this, just look at them.'

Ree jumped back to her feet, one hand on the canopy strut. 'How many more are chasing us?'

'With the dust, it is impossible to know. We cannot be sure we are clear of pursuit, and we are leaving a long trail.'

Ree nodded, chewing her lip in thought, then turned. 'You see the canyon yet, kid?'

'No, not yet. We're a little way off, right, even at this speed?'

'Say when you do.' With that she ducked back inside the wagon, then stuck her head out. 'Or if someone starts taking shots at you again.'

Javani hunched lower.

The trail was narrowing, the desert now long behind them, the red rocks of the narrow-lands rising ahead. They were closer to the mountains, the trail beginning to wind and undulate with the shifting terrain. They rounded an outcrop, the horses frothing and champing against the rocky ground, and she saw the canyon.

'Ree,' she called. 'Ree!'

'How far, kid?'

'Not far!'

'Aim for the middle of the bridge. Right down the middle.'

'What are you doing, Ree?'

'Just steer the damned wagon, kid!'

She steered. The wooden bridge over the canyon was new, and supposedly temporary – installed by the Guild in the spirit of self-advancement until the masons completed their endeavours embellishing the Guildhouse and were free to work on something as humdrum as a stone version. It had satisfied the caravans, at least, shaving a day of mountain trekking from the direct route north. The canyon itself wasn't particularly deep, and the river at its base was a memory in summer as it was, but getting wagons and nervous horses across it without the bridge was a practical impossibility.

Javani had a sudden sense of foreboding.

'Ree? What are you going to do?'

'How's that bridge coming?'

'Any moment now!'

'You two, make sure no riders get close to us. Throw stones if you must!'

'My brother will repulse them with his natural charm.'

'Goddess forgive my imperfections!'

'Here it comes!'

The horses' hoof-beats were a thunderous crash as they hit the bridge, the wagon's wheels a rattling roar in their wake. The bench jumped and shook beneath Javani, almost jolting the reins from her hands.

'Count down to the far side!' Ree shouted. She sounded further back inside.

'What?'

'How long to the other side! Count down!'

'What?'

'Like five, four, and so on!'

'Oh!' Javani blinked sweat from her eyes. The red rock of the other side was rushing towards her. 'One!'

'Oh for fuck's—'

The horses' hooves bit the ground beyond the bridge, and something clonked from the back of the wagon. 'Go, go, go!' Ree screamed. 'Fast as you can!'

Javani turned back as the bridge erupted. The explosion punched out from its centre, ripping boards and struts outwards in a ball of force that lifted the back of the wagon clean off the trail, if only for an instant. Then they crashed to earth again, wheels crunching on loose rock, horses straining, wagon contents in uproar, as debris hurtled down on them. A splintered spar came pinwheeling past, before disappearing down the trailside, as fragments of wood and iron fell like rain.

Javani did her best to calm the horses, who were running in blind fear beyond the limits of their exhaustion and in danger of bursting their hearts. Ree clambered back through, dropping to the bench in a splayed heap.

'What in hells happened?' Javani barked.

Ree waved a slow hand. 'Let these poor bastards slacken off, eh?'

'Are we safe?'

'I'm not much inclined to over-promise on that score, kid. Come on, ease off on the ponies.'

She finally reined the horses into a walk. The trail was climbing again, curling away from the canyon and into the narrows. 'What did you do, Ree? What was that?'

'Take a look for yourself.'

Javani turned, craning around to see. The dark slash of the canyon stood unbridged, broken posts cropped and jutting on each side of a smoking void. Riders had gathered on the far side, first a handful, then more, reining in out of the choking smog of dust and alchemy that cloaked the lower trail. None had made it across.

'Told you it was worth holding onto those blasting kegs,' Ree said, then settled back on the bench with a contented sigh. 'Now keep a look out for the watchtower.' She tipped a hat over her eyes. It looked a lot like the one Movos Guvuli had been wearing. 'I'm going to have a nap.'

Javani was staring open-mouthed. She'd blown up the bridge. Surely there could be no going back now. As she watched, one of the riders began signalling. Before they dropped out of sight around the trail, she saw the group begin to congregate, pulling together. Planning. Organising.

They weren't clear yet.

SEVENTEEN

Kurush's eyes were lost in the darkness of the canyon, picking out shattered remnants of the bridge in a widening spiral. His breath was controlled, long and slow through his nose; his teeth rested tightly against each other without grinding. The reins were secure in his hand, his grip forcibly relaxed. He was not losing control. He was not.

The fucking bridge was gone. The woman had destroyed it. The Guild was responsible for the bridge, and it should have been remade in stone long before now. But his late predecessor had insisted that the Guildhouse works had to come first, the ornate carvings, the towers and pavilions. Even the terracing of the paradise gardens. After all, the wooden version stood up to the infrequent caravan traffic, what was the hurry?

Except the work had already been paid for, the expenses claimed.

Kurush swallowed, his throat unspeakably thick with dust, creeping unstoppably past his mask, gritting his eyes, crusting the inside of his nose. Chasing such a vehicle for so long was an absurdity. And now the fucking bridge was gone, adding a day to the journey into the narrows. They had to catch it. There was no alternative, no recourse. They had to catch the wagon, the prince had to execute the girl, and the three of them would return in triumph to Shenak with her head, the prince would become king – presumably – and Kurush would become a wealthy ambassador.

The Guild would be mollified by his elevation and the new opportunities it presented. They certainly wouldn't pursue him over these minor irregularities. They wouldn't send an auditor to Shenak, after all. Of course not.

But the fucking bridge was gone.

The day was half spent, the horses were tired, the riders were tired – and hardly rested after the desert night and the storm. They needed fresh mounts, and fresh hunters from an ever-depleted roster. They could return to the Guildhouse, scoop up any able-bodied troops who'd somehow escaped their travails so far, send them out on new horses to keep up the trail. Then, in the morning, after a proper night's rest, Kurush would prepare a new column, and—

Lazant was talking. Not to Kurush, but addressing the gathering riders directly. He was more than talking, he was orating, his words at last filtering into Kurush's mind like the dust in his trousers. Kurush gasped. This could not be allowed to stand.

He nudged his horse alongside the prince, maintaining a distance he judged as suitably deferential while allowing for discretion, and cleared his throat. Kurush was no courtier, he knew, but that would come. Once he was introduced to the court of the King of Kings, there would be staff for this kind of thing, advisers and chamberlains and viziers and whatnot, people to draw his bath and tell him which piece of silver cutlery to use for which course. He knew it would be hard, but he was willing to work to learn the ways of court, not to embarrass his patron with his rough frontier ways. Maybe the court would take to him, a curiosity, a novelty, this rough diamond with his swagger and his brutal, effective horsemanship. Perhaps they would flock to hear his tales of life at civilisation's edge, riding down the last of the Mawn scourge, making the expanse safe and the Guild rich. He could picture it, delicate aristocratic women surrounding him, their towering hair adorned with glittering jewels, all of which he could name, all of which he could spin some yarn around as to their origin and extraction. He'd be the talk of the court, so raw, so handsome, the pet project of every underemployed noblewoman . . . perhaps they'd even battle for his affections, duelling each other with, uh, silken fans or waspish tongues. And to the victor, of course, the spoils . . . one of those vizier-drawn baths, this time with company . . .

'Yes?'

Lazant was looking at him.

'You wished to add something, Guildmaster?'

Kurush swallowed again, his throat drier than ever, his thoughts scattered and fled over the horizon. 'Uh, only, highness, that perhaps when orders are to be given to the riders, that is to say, my riders, that ride, uh, for the Guild, that those orders, when it is time for, uh, them to be, uh, said, should be said, uh, by the Guildmaster, meaning, uh . . . me.'

The prince looked at him, his expression unreadable, the corners of his mouth tweaked very faintly upwards. *How is he not spitting with rage at losing the wagon?* Kurush thought. *He should be a rolling ball of fury, but somehow he still seems . . . merry.* There was a near-manic fervour in the man's eyes, a level of positive enthusiasm so at odds with their situation that it suggested to Kurush an alarming level of detachment between the prince and the reality that surrounded them. He knew that self-confidence and optimism were admirable traits, but at what point did you cross a line into something else, something considerably less wholesome?

'By all means, of course,' the prince said brightly. 'Guildmaster.' He gestured to the assembled riders, who were jostling each other to hear what would next be said. 'Kindly give the order to dispatch messengers to the town, to return with fresh troops and horses, to set a party foraging for materials for creating some manner of platform for this bridge, and a third group to take what I am informed is the old mine road in pursuit of our quarry.'

Kurush slowly closed his mouth, which seemed to have dropped open. He faced the riders. A motley but well-equipped collection of hardy survivors, they rode under Guild colours for any number of reasons, but personal loyalty to the Acting Guildmaster was unlikely to be one of them. The slippery Enx would not even meet his eye. 'As his highness said,' he muttered through gritted teeth. 'Get it done.'

'One other thing,' Lazant called out as the riders began to shuffle and split. 'Let this be known: I have increased the bounty. I will now pay one whole silver talent to the rider who brings me the girl's head. An open tender, to any and all. Those returning to the town: spread this news, then return, as fast as you can!'

Kurush's mouth was open again. What the fuck was he playing at? A whole silver talent, to anyone, not just his riders? If that news got out, every bandit, cut-throat and vagabond in the region would join the hunt. It would be chaos. How would Lazant be certain that his triumph was down to Kurush then? That silver was *his* to apportion!

'Uh, highness, I—'

'Indeed, Guildmaster, as you say. Now, before you all depart: will the best climbers make themselves known?'

'Where is this watchtower? The horses are exhausted, I think they've lost at least one shoe between them. We can't keep going in the heat of the day like this.'

Ree sighed and stirred beneath the hat. 'At least this bit is shaded.'

'Ree, I'm serious. What if it's not where you think it is? What if it . . . fell down, or disappeared, or something?'

'Nine hells, kid, relax. It's ahead. Mawn burned it out years back, but there are walls and a well. We'll hole up there, rest the horses, dig up the supplies, get on the road at dawn.'

Javani chewed her lip in sulking disapproval. 'Then what?'

'Then it depends.'

'We still need to have a very serious talk.'

Ree pulled the hat back down. 'I know, kid. We will.'

'But not now.'

'But not now.' She yawned theatrically. 'And if you're going to keep on at me, I'll sleep in the back.' An instant later, she was gone from the bench, and Javani felt oddly alone.

Muttering to herself, Javani steered the plodding horses up the trail. How was it fair that Ree was napping? Javani was the one with people after her, chased from pillar to post for two days now. And now left in charge of steering the team – *not* an easy thing to do at all, by the way, not that anyone had given her credit for just taking over and getting on with it – as they meandered through the high rock walls of the narrows on the south road in search of some mythical watchtower where Ree claimed to have cached supplies like an equally mythical pirate burying treasure.

And what kind of person does that? Drops little caches of travelling supplies in odd places around where they live? Was this a new habit, or had she been doing it everywhere they'd stayed as they'd moved north? How long did they need to rest in one place before it deserved a cache or two? Did she go around and collect them all before they'd moved on, or leave them like the nomads and their 'deferred hospitality'? And why had she never mentioned this to Javani?

Why had she never mentioned any of this?

Well, if she was going to leave Javani in charge, then maybe Javani would put herself properly in charge. She could take the next eastern cut on the trail, make for the distant Kermastar, the great port on the coast, White Spear or no. Or, *or* . . . she could swing the wagon around and take the west road, past the old mines, and make for Arestan over the mountains. The Guvulis had been convinced there was a way through, and if those dung-wits thought they were up to it then there was no reason Javani and Ree couldn't figure their way through. They'd always been a team, no matter how much they drove each other as mad as two porcupines in a sack. Always just the two of them, for as long as she could remember.

Javani sat back on the bench. It was so obvious to her now. Their wandering life, their lack of roots, their progress ever-northward: Ree had been hiding. And what had she been hiding? Javani, of course, the secret heir. And how had she known how to hide so well, to leave little escape routes for herself? Because she'd been the diplomat. The spy. Which meant, of course, that Ree was not truly her aunt, but—

'Your adult has abandoned you?'

Javani jumped as Aki slid through the canvas opening and settled himself delicately beside Javani on the bench. He was grazed and bloodied, and winced as he sat, but he seemed well enough. Considering.

'She decided she needed peace to nap,' Javani muttered, quietly. She suddenly felt no inclination to wake Ree, wherever she slept; here was a chance to ask someone else what they thought of it all, albeit someone who seemed to have a somewhat hazier relationship with reality than most grown-ups she'd met.

'Are you well, little one? A most arresting start to the day, but the Goddess has seen us once more to safety.'

Javani shuffled sideways, allowing him space for his muscular thighs. 'I'm all right,' she murmured. 'Considering,' she added, darkly.

He either ignored it or didn't hear. 'Would you care to hear more tales of creation? Of the wisdom and blessings of the Goddess? Perhaps the trials of the Champion Ranu, with his divine spear of—'

'Do they always possess people? When they, you know, manifest to battle demons.'

His chin dipped, his head bobbing as if riding a strong wave. 'The children of the Goddess do not *possess*, little one. They *imbue*.'

'My mistake.'

'But . . . you are correct, the stories tell of other forms, just as the demon spirits were once animals themselves. Ranu favours the great beasts: the lion, the ox, the elephant—'

'The what?'

'Imagine a moving castle, with a mind keener than most of those who pursue us.'

'I . . . actually, I'd rather not.'

He continued with a wide sweep of his hand. His knuckles were nicked and scratched, and his palm stain-darkened. 'Besu the Healer has taken the form of gazelles, ibexes, zebras – creatures fleet of foot and possessed of care for the herd.'

'What was that last—?'

'A striped horse, little one. Do they teach you nothing in this place?'

She shook her head. 'Nor any other I've been, apparently. What about Aret? The Messenger?'

He watched her for a moment with his wide, round eyes, as if suspecting a trick, before allowing a slow smile to spread across his face. 'Aret takes to the sky: the lark, the swift, the skua . . . and his favourite: the hawk, in the form of which he tore down the red bats of Usdohr, scattering their gizzards across—'

'I get it, thanks.'

He went to go on, but became transfixed by a vast yawn, which seemed to travel the length of his body, his damaged fist unable to cover the great stretch of his jaw, the white expanse of his excellent teeth.

Javani sighed, then swallowed her own yawn. 'Stayed up too late last night, didn't you? Grab a doze in the back with Ree, gods know there's more space there. I'll wake you – both – when this watchtower appears.' Assuming it ever does.

He made to disagree, one hand wagging, then the convulsions of another yawn began and he slithered back through the canopy without another word. A moment later, Javani heard snoring.

So much for asking an adult's opinion.

EIGHTEEN

Javani reined in the exhausted horses before the ruined gate to the watchtower's outer wall. The tower itself was a single structure of perhaps once four storeys, now crumpled and blackened at two. A rough wall still surrounded its small courtyard, nestled against the climbing rocks behind, and through the half-blocked gateway Javani saw Ree's promised well and what had probably once been a stable block.

By instinct, her eyes scanned the tower. It was defensively questionable, but offered a good view down the trail in each direction. They'd see anyone coming . . . if they were coming.

Ree emerged from the canvas and stretched out her arms, making Javani duck, then leaned back over her shoulder. 'You two awake?'

Grunts and muttering came in response. Javani felt doubly tired at the thought that everyone else had been dozing since they'd left the bridge. But they'd been battling to keep her alive, she supposed. And compared to the horses, they'd all got off lightly.

'Pass me my sword, Aki. Immediately. Thank you.'

Javani stifled a yawn of her own. It was late afternoon at most. 'What do we do, then?'

Ree slid down from the wagon to the rocky floor, wincing at the movement, and started walking towards the listing gate. 'Let ourselves in, get what we need, then pretend we were never here.'

* * *

Ree waved the kid on as she dragged back the ruined gate, clearing the way. The wagon entered slowly, the horses at their endurance's end, and Ree directed her to park up by the stables and unhitch them. The kid complied, albeit with a face like a wild pig licking piss off a hawthorn.

'Wakey-wakey, you two,' Ree called, banging on the back of the wagon's side. 'Rest stop.'

Anashe slid down from the wagon without complaint and set about stretching and wincing. Aki emerged in a flurry of yawns, wrapping a strip of cloth around one hand. The kid reappeared from the remains of the stable, her mouth open, already forming her next demand. Ree got in first.

'Kid, rub down the horses and start drawing water. I'll set about retrieving the non-perishables.'

'Wait,' the girl hissed, grabbing her arm and pulling her to one side, away from the siblings.

'Nine hells, kid, what is it? There's stuff to do, and ever less time to do it in.'

'There's always stuff to do! But I've been waiting a thrice-damned sight longer than whatever you buried here.'

Ree rubbed at her chin. 'I'm not sure that's true.'

'Were they telling the truth or not?'

'Who?'

'The White Spear! The Shenakar! The people who have been trying to kill and/or abduct me!' She was struggling to keep her voice controlled. 'Is what they said true? Am I a princess? Were . . . Were *you* the diplomat?'

She was looking up with wide, dark eyes, too much like Ree's own. People always said we had the same eyes, Ree thought.

'Kid, this isn't the time to have this—'

The girl jabbed a finger into her sternum, pushing her half a step backwards. 'You never trust me with anything,' she hissed. Ree flashed a quick glance at Aki and Anashe across the courtyard, who seemed to have found a fascinating pile of bleached timber to inspect. 'You just drag me around like baggage. We've been moving around my entire life, and this is the first place I've ever . . . I had *friends* here, in town at least. I *liked* it. And it's over now, isn't it? Isn't it? Moosh is dead because of something you did.'

'Listen—'

She was crying now, hot tears carving furrows down her dusty cheeks. 'I've finished listening! What if I want to be a princess of Shenak? What if I get back on that wagon, ride out east? There's a boat waiting for me, she said. It'll take me across the sea. To my birthright.'

'Gods' teeth, kid, would you— You think your life would be sweetness, a pawn of scheming factions? Shenakar power games make Arowani politics look like a fucking tea party! You haven't enjoyed the last couple of days? That's just a *taste* of what life in court would offer you – you'd be lucky to make it to your first formal luncheon without getting stabbed, poisoned, strangled or pushed from a high window by someone you swore blind you could trust.'

Javani had gone quiet and still. 'How do you know all this?'

'Trust me, I know.' She immediately regretted her phrasing.

'How? Is it true, then? Tell me more, tell me something!'

Ree put her hand to her brow, rubbed at her eyes. She was filthy with trail dust, and something sticky. 'We will talk. Properly. I swear it. But right now . . .' She cocked an ear. 'You hear that?'

The kid looked at her blankly. 'What?'

Aki looked up. 'Hmm? While you will find few keener hunters, in truth my senses are more devoted to the sphere creative—'

'Hush, brother,' Anashe said, her head tilted. 'For once, stopper your emissions.'

'Goddess *forgive* my imperfections!' Aki hissed, and at last fell quiet.

Snoring was coming from somewhere inside the wagon.

One hand on her sword, Ree signalled for Aki to go around to the far side, then climbed achingly back up herself. The inside of the wagon was carnage – anything stacked or packed had been thrown around in their wild flight, before accounting for the various pitched battles and explosions. One of the collapsed piles near the far end was drawing slowly up and down. It was the source of the snores.

Ree extended her sword and flicked away a pile of loose sacking. A bearded, bloodied face lay underneath, apparently lost to contented sleep. 'Now who the fuck is this?'

The kid's head appeared at the canopy's edge. 'That's Movos Guvuli.'

'The bandit?'

She nodded.

'What's he doing here?'

'He was with the White Spear.' She paused. 'I don't know why. I can't think of any explanation that fits.'

Ree stared at the kid, looked down at the sleeping, battered bandit, then back at the kid.

'We'd better tie him up. There's the remains of a cell on the lower floor, we can sling him in there until we decide what to do with him.'

And in the meantime, she thought ruefully as she watched the kid scooping up an armful of tatty rope, I'd better decide what to do about *you*.

Javani climbed the ancient stairs slowly, Aki at her side, the dazed bandit deposited somewhere on the lower floor.

'I apologise for my earlier somnolence,' he was saying, 'but I can state with great assurance that my intermediary slumber, while distant from a point of full refreshment, has restored sufficient zest to my being that we may now resume.'

Javani's mind was very much on Other Things. 'Huh?'

'The stories. The tales of creation and the children of the Goddess.' His eyes were so bright in the dim stairwell.

Javani rolled her eyes. She was tired, the stairs were flaky and uneven, and nobody seemed to be giving any thought to what *she* wanted. 'Must we?'

He drew back. 'Excuse me?'

'I mean, I've heard it all now, haven't I? The Goddess made gods, the gods fought, minions came out of the earth, crafted from, I dunno, fire or something, taking the shapes of bad creatures like scorpions, but with hooked blades as claws and spears for tails.'

'You do not sound as if you remember it very well. Perhaps I should tell it again.'

'No need, really. I think I've heard enough about the Goddess of Creation, how she left vague instructions for her children, then buggered off back to the heavens. How she left them to fight demons alone.'

Anashe was a pace behind, climbing slowly. 'I see ever more parallels in this tale.'

'At least the Goddess instructed her children,' Javani muttered.

'Kindly do not besmirch the name of the Goddess!' Aki's voice rose in pitch, echoing from the old stone walls. He cleared his throat and tried again. 'Would you care to hear more of the tales? I have many others, some unheard on these shores. I can, for example, teach you the names of all the animals – not the names as you know them, but the true names. The names of power.'

Javani stopped on the curving stairway and turned to him. 'What are your true names?'

'Our names? They are . . . as we told you. Aki and Anashe.'

'And the Gale and the Shadow? That's what your enemies call you?'

Anashe sighed. 'They are names we gave each other. He is the Gale, because he never stops blowing.'

Aki's eyes narrowed, and he let out a sharp breath. 'And she is the Shadow because she is impossible to lose!' He turned and pushed past his sister, stalking off back down the stairway.

'What was—'

'We have travelled together too long,' Anashe said with a weary shake of her head. 'I never thought we would come so far.'

'Why do you travel together, if you argue so much?'

'You've seen him. He cannot be without supervision.'

'That can't just be it. He said you were impossible to lose. That suggests he's tried.'

Anashe ran a hand over her head, over the tight curls, then rested her cheek on her hand, elbow on the crumbling wall. To Javani's eyes, she was all angles.

'I made a promise to the rest of our family,' she said at length. 'It was Aki who dreamed of finding our mother. It was Aki who wanted to voyage west, to cross the Sink. It was expected that I would go too. It was my duty. He knows it, and he resents it.'

'Because he's bigger than you?'

'Because he knows that I do not believe.'

'In what? The Goddess?'

She drew back in shock. 'No, heavens above, no. I do not believe that finding our mother, or at least knowing all we can of her, will . . . will . . . make us complete. Aki does.'

'It must be a hard thing, to know that she loved you but had to leave you.' Javani's eyes wandered to the top of the stairs, where Ree had gone ahead of them. 'But maybe better than the reverse.'

Anashe followed her gaze. 'Maybe, indeed.'

'When I told you my name,' Javani said quietly, her eyes still on the upper floor, 'you and Aki laughed.'

'We did?'

'Don't deny it. I told you to stop calling me "little one" and I told you my name, and you laughed. What does my name mean? Ree hardly ever uses it, she just calls me "kid" the whole time.'

Anashe pursed her lips, looked down at the steps and smiled. 'It means "little young one".'

'What?'

'Or, colloquially, "kid".'

Ree sat heavily on a weathered block of stone on the tower's remaining upper floor. Half a ceiling and a sad, shattered stairway were all that remained of its former climbing glory. She was exhausted, despite her doze on the wagon, and her body ached in new and extraordinary ways. The familiar aches were still there underneath, of course. She realised that at some point over the last few years her thinking had shifted, and that she no longer expected new pains to fade and vanish of their own accord; she added them to the catalogue, and adjusted her expectations.

The kid was in the corner, fussing over a struggling cooking fire, making an utter balls of what should have been a simple task. Ree had put her in charge and had since made no move to help her. It was important for the girl to learn how to start and tend a fire in unfamiliar conditions of course, but beyond that Ree had little faith she could make it all the way across the ruined chamber without her knees giving way and tumbling arse over tit.

Anashe sat opposite her in a sand-swept divot, pointed knees outward. She looked battered and sore, and very dusty; despite attempting to project outward serenity, Ree could see the agitation of her posture, the restlessness of her gaze.

'You secured our guest?'

She nodded, quick, birdlike. 'Although the stones of this place are older than time, and twice as worn. A strong breeze could flatten it, and take us with it.'

'Then we'd better get the tea brewing. How's that fire coming, kid?'

The kid looked up with a sour face, then returned to her ministrations. Still seething over their interrupted discussion in the courtyard, no doubt, as well as her failure to get the fire going. Gods' breath, the girl was exhausting.

Anashe shook her head. 'The people of these plains drink tea in volumes that would, elsewhere, be considered cause for concern.' She stretched an arm and winced. 'This is hardly the climate for warming drinks.'

'You'd be surprised,' Ree replied with a chuckle, leaning back on her stone support. 'Tea has many miraculous powers, and cooling a soul on a hot day is but one.'

Anashe refolded herself, chasing respite from her aches. 'You seem very pleased with yourself.' Her tone was light, its veiled edge unmissable.

'I'd say I had cause, wouldn't you?' Ree felt sudden heat in her cheeks. Anashe's accusatory manner seemed to have a direct path to her molten core. 'With an early start tomorrow, we've seen the last of our Shenakar friends. We're away down the trade road and dust in the wind.'

'Can we outrun them, then?' The kid came wandering over, moving with insulting ease over the strewn stone. Behind her, the fire emitted a thin ribbon of dirty smoke.

'Fire under control, kid?'

'It's fine,' she snapped.

'Get the tea on, then.'

The kid glared at her through narrowed eyes. 'What's the supply situation? Did you find your . . . cache?'

Ree nodded. 'There's not as much as I'd hoped, but more than I feared. Enough for our onward journey.' For the first leg, at least, she added to herself. What follows that, remains to be seen . . .

She turned back to Anashe. 'You rode with the Shenakar. What else can you tell me about them?'

Anashe remained expressionless, her legs now folded beneath her. 'We already told you all we know.'

'Dig deeper, specialist. Think about what you heard from them, when they talked to others, to each other. What they carry, where they came from, how they arrived. We need to know everything.' Just in case.

'The young man is a prince, as we discussed. Came by sea, in a hurry; enough of a hurry to pay silver to the first idiot – and his capable sister – who crossed his path to get him to mining country.' She looked pensive for a moment. 'He said he had to reach someone before others did. I am guessing he meant you, little one.'

'And by the others,' Ree said, one eye on the kid's ham-fisted tea preparation, 'he meant the mercenary and her crew.'

'The White Spear,' Anashe murmured. 'On reflection, it is possible we have heard of her.'

'She arrived with the caravan,' the kid said, steam from the brewing tea drifting past her, condensation gleaming from her young skin. 'There were several of them, all in black, although not armour like hers.' She shuddered at the memory. 'She's the only one left. Why was she travelling with the caravan?'

'Plenty of reasons – supplies, scouts, strength in numbers, and maybe even some silver in the purse for a journey she needed to make anyway. It's not like it's a pleasant or easy trip.' Ree scratched at her scalp. Sand was ingrained in every pore and follicle. 'What do you know of her, Anashe?'

'If it is the person I'm thinking of, she has a fearsome reputation for completing her contracts. Every time. No matter what.'

Ree heard the kid's sharp in-breath from across the chamber. 'Her contract is to make me Queen of Queens.'

'Queen of Kings,' Ree said automatically.

'What?'

'You'd be Queen of Kings, not Queen of Queens.'

'Is that better or worse?'

'It's just how the Shenakar throne works.'

'And hiring mercenaries, is that how the Shenakar throne usually works?'

Ree looked up. The kid had poured the tea and was standing next to her, steaming clay cups in hand. She proffered one, and Ree took it with a grunt. 'I suppose it is.'

The kid passed the second mug to Anashe, who took it with an elegant nod. 'And what about when people come to do things themselves, like Lazant?'

Ree blew the steam from her mug. 'Uncommon. Royals of means don't get their own hands dirty. Most won't even send their own people, or anyone who could draw a line back to them.'

'Deniability,' Anashe murmured.

'Deniability,' Ree echoed, 'of the plausible variety. All the more important when engaging in mannerless acts.'

'Like killing children?' the kid snapped.

Ree could only nod, her eyes on the loose leaf fragments swirling at the brim of the mug.

'And Lazant?' the kid went on, struggling to keep the tremor from her voice. 'He's doing his own dirty work. What does that say?'

Ree was gazing into the darkness of her mug. 'That he's desperate.'

'That's good, right? He's almost beaten?'

Ree shook her head, watching the flicker of reflected light on the filmy surface of her tea. 'It means he has nothing left to lose.' And he's not going to stop unless he's made to.

'But we'll outrun him, right? Tomorrow, we'll set off, we'll be a day ahead, and . . . and . . . then what? What's our plan, Ree?'

Ree swallowed. Her triumphant euphoria from their escape had faded as the inexorable reality of their situation reasserted itself. The day's heat still pulsed from the bright rock outside, an incipient headache with it, and the bitter taste of the tea wasn't helping. 'There's another cache a few miles from the southern exit of the narrows, even with the rot we should have enough—'

'Are you serious, Ree? Are you being serious with me now? Our plan for evading my *brutal murder* boils down to "keep running south and hope to find enough supplies along the road to keep us alive, while hoping our pursuers starve or . . . or . . . *lose interest* before we do"?'

'It's not as bad as that, we've—'

'Even the Guvulis had a proper escape plan, and they're congenital idiots who couldn't find their collective arses with both hands and a map!'

The kid froze, one finger raised, her next emission half-formed on her lips.

'Kid? You all right? Listen, I've been in worse situations, believe me, we'll—'

Javani was already making for the stairs.

'I'll be right back!'

NINETEEN

Movos Guvuli was locked behind an old iron grate that must have once passed for either secure storage or a holding area. His hands and feet were bound in an attempt to discourage attempts at testing the residual strength of the bars, but the rope was ancient and the knots were loose. He was dirty and bloodied, flecks of something in the dark of his beard, but was snoring peacefully, propped against a pile of fallen stone.

Javani watched him for a moment, feeling as if she was intruding somehow, despite the fact that this man was her prisoner. A man who'd dismissed her, cheated her, belittled her, pursued her . . . And now he was at her mercy. The thought didn't make her feel powerful at all.

Movos scratched his cheek with his two-fingered hand, then opened one eye. 'You come to celebrate my incarceration, urchin, or did you just forget the way to the privy? Either way, I don't care, just don't make a mess too close.'

She was blushing, which made her suddenly furious. How dare he embarrass her, after how he'd behaved? She had nothing to be ashamed of.

'It's your own fault you're rotting in a cell,' she snapped. 'You shouldn't have been chasing me.'

He sat straighter against the rubble, fixed her with a dirty, jabbing finger. 'You stole that wagon from me, and the treasures with it.'

'You were going to cut me out of the job!'

'I seem to remember a conspiracy to defraud, as concerns a hitherto-considered game of chance.'

Javani's ire fizzled. 'I feel like we can go back and forth a few times on this one.'

He sat back against the stone, bound hands behind his head. 'Well, I don't exactly have elsewhere to be, in present circumstances.' He scratched at his beard again, eyes downcast as if overcome by a sudden melancholy. 'Since our altercation I've had everything . . . taken away.'

'A man shouldn't risk what he can't lose,' Javani snapped, remembering the menacing of his brothers on poor useless Behrooz.

But he didn't rise to it, just shook his head, eyes still on the drifts of blown sand before his boots. 'Ain't that the truth.'

Javani hovered, uncertain. Movos seemed lost in his own reverie, and while she wasn't exactly rapt by the sparkle of his conversation, it seemed rude to press him, especially given what she was about to ask for.

'You want something from me?' He was looking up at her now, eyes red-rimmed, his voice raw. 'Because if it's all the same, I'd rather be—'

'Yes.'

'What's that, now?'

'Yes, I want something from you.'

'And just what in all the hells makes you think—'

'You had a foolproof escape, right? I mean, it would have to be, if it was going to work for you and your brothers—'

'Hey, now!'

'Sorry. But you said you knew how to escape in a way that nobody could chase you. I want you to tell me how.'

He paused, eyes narrowed, lips framing his next word, all thought diverted to attempting to discern her trap. 'Not sure I know what you mean.'

'Come on, you were crowing about it, back in town.' She leaned closer. 'You have a map, don't you? Don't you? The thing I drew on the back of. What's it a map to?' Her heart surged. 'It's a map to the hidden pass, isn't it? The way west?'

His eyes were slits. 'Maybe, maybe not. I'm still not possessed of the full conviction I know whereof you speak.'

Javani leaned further forward, pressing her face against the ancient bars. 'Tell me how you were going to do it. Tell me how you were going to make your hunters think you dead.'

'Why?'

'Why?' She puffed air through her lips. 'Why do you think, you buffoon? Have you noticed a large number of heavily armoured types taking a particularly keen interest in my well-being of late, specifically the ending thereof?'

'And you think you can use my escape plan?'

'It beats getting hunted down on the plains, doesn't it? Or being ambushed in the narrows.'

'Sounds painful.'

'How were you going to do it, Guvuli? What's the secret?'

He smiled then, a wide grin of battered and yellowed teeth. 'And why, girl, should I tell you a thrice-damned thing?'

Javani drew herself up to her full, unprepossessing height. 'I'll let you go.'

He scoffed. 'You think the grown-ups will let you?'

'I won't tell them. I'll cut your ropes, and the key to this grate is over there. You can be gone before they even think to check on you.'

His gaze dropped slowly, the smile with it. 'Gone to where? To what? I lost it all, short of grubbing back through the desert on my knees for the stones you dropped. My brothers are gone, my gang is gone, there's nothing left for me.'

Javani paused. She hadn't expected he'd lack interest in freedom; her biggest concern had been cutting his ropes without him grabbing her trail-knife and doing her a mischief with it. 'There must be something out there for you,' she said, attempting to put herself in the bandit's reeking boots. 'What about before you were in a gang?'

'Huh?'

'Before you were a bandit. There was a before, right? You didn't march straight out of your nursery and into robbing caravans, I'm guessing.'

'There was a before, true.'

'And? What did you do?'

He met her eye. 'I was a miner. A damned fine one. My brothers and I worked the pits for near a decade, came out here with the rush. Before the Guild put down their marker, sewed it up for the free-minded.'

'Is that why you stopped mining?'

He brandished his foreshortened hand, and she flinched back. 'It was this that did me, this and what came with it. Couldn't go down again, couldn't fund anyone else to work our claim. Guild offered meagre terms, and it was that or nothing.'

'The Guild bought you out?'

He barked a crackling laugh. 'Bought implies payment, girl. They did little more than relieve me of my burden.'

'So you became a bandit.'

His brows lowered sharply, as if in pain. 'Well, not in the immediate, as was. We had some misfortunes guarding caravans, for a time, and after a while it seemed there was greater reward in misfortune than in guarding. Especially with the amount the Guild were shipping south.' He spat into the darkened corner.

'What do you mean?'

'I mean, girl, that the Guild is a rig, a mountain-weight worse than any you tried to run on me in the teahouse. They swallow up every glint and nugget that's hacked or blasted out of these lands, and it's folks like me and my brothers who get ground to paste in the process, then tossed aside or left for dead when our usefulness is spent. The goods keep moving on south, a new batch of hopefuls comes north every week, and the Guild keeps . . . swelling. Like a tick. A bunch of fucking silk-tasselled merchants gorging themselves on the blood of honest miners.'

Javani raised an eyebrow. 'Honest?'

He tossed his hand. 'More honest than the Guild stewards sending them, although granted that's a low bar. Still, it's not about honesty, or purity, is it? This is frontier land, and this is where you grind out a new life for yourself, a life where you keep what you earn. You play by the rules and enjoy the fruits of your labours.' He spat again. 'Until the Guild swoops in with talk of permits and process, and what's yours is taken from your hands. You can see why a fellow might be inclined to turn to a spot of banditry, in search of redress.'

Javani sat against the opposite wall, contemplating. Releasing Movos had been a calculated risk, based on the assumption that knowing his secret plan might yet tip Ree to her way of thinking, and letting a potentially murderous bandit run free was still a step in the right direction. She'd not expected to find him so morose, so embittered, so entirely uninterested in his freedom and his future. Maybe this was what happened to people when they passed a certain age.

'Well,' she said, trying to come up with a positive suggestion, 'the Guild up here isn't what it was. Since the old Guildmaster died, things have been pretty shambolic. Maybe there's an opportunity for you there, now that—'

'Kurush,' Movos snarled, rocking forward. 'Guildmaster Kurush is tightening his grip.'

'Maybe he'll—'

'He won't do goose-shit for anyone but himself. Same as all the others.' Movos chopped the air with his half-hand. 'See, girl, this is the part that's so poorly understood by the tin-smiths down south. The power – the power, girl – is *here*. It's with the miners. It's with the workers! The merchants have the coin, but the miners have the strength. No miners, no mining! No mining, no more gold-train. What they pass back along the chain should be a choice, not an expectation. The clerks in the south risk nothing more than numbers on paper, never their bodies, never their blood.' He was breathing hard, eyes wide, small flecks of spittle gleaming in his beard. 'A local leader of true strength could stand up to them, dictate their own terms of trade.'

Javani couldn't see how this translated to a more positive outlook. 'Kurush is a pretty big man—'

'He's the weakest man I ever encountered. That contemptuous fucker hanged my brothers out of cowardice, their deaths to swell his legend. To impress that foreign dandy.' He shuffled forward, wrapped his fingers around the bars. 'Let me tell you something about Guildmaster Kurush, girl. He never worked the mines, never put his life in the hands of his fellows, never dug in the rock with blackened stumps to reach those trapped below. He was born big and fair to the eye, and all his life he's reaped the benefits of what he is, not what he does. He's never learned to make a damned choice, always done what was easy. You think he might change the Guild in these parts? Oh, I can see it changing. But it won't be changing for the benefit of any bar Guildmaster Kurush.'

Movos slumped back into the darkness, his eyes somewhere on the cracked and bleached ceiling. 'I tried to do the right thing, follow the path, and I ended up a robber and a bandit, my brothers hanged. Where were my choices then?'

Javani cleared her throat. 'Maybe—'

'They never listened. Shantar never listened. Be sure to listen, urchin. Too few know the merit of *listening*.' He seemed to be talking to the decaying stone above.

'What?'

'Five men run into a mine, the mine collapses. All are lost. Or are they? Some time later, five dead men cross the mountains with packs full of gems.'

'Wait, was that the plan? What about—'

His head tipped forwards, eyes lost in shadow. 'Just bring me a drink, girl. Bring me something to drink, and I'll tell you the depth of it. Gods know it won't do me any fucking good any more.'

Javani jumped to her feet. She felt sticky with sweat, despite the evening's chill. 'Right. Right. Ree has some old wine upstairs. Don't go anywhere.' She winced. 'Sorry.'

With the kid gone huffing off down the stairs, Ree had somehow been left in charge of the cooking, despite her best efforts to avoid it.

Anashe was perched on the sill of a narrow window, staring

out into the reddening north-western sky. She'd gone uncharacteristically quiet.

'Watching for pursuers?' Ree said, her attention on the state of their food.

'Sunset approaches,' the woman murmured.

'As it tends to, around this time. Do you want to give me a hand with this? I can't tell what's dried beans and what's rat shit.'

'We travelled further than I ever imagined,' Anashe went on. 'Yet still I see no journey's end.'

'That's a no to the rat-shit filtering, is it?'

'Does she like it out here?'

'Excuse me?'

'Was she happy, living here on the edge of nowhere? Ignorant of who she was, where she came from?'

Ree put down the oilskin parcel in her hand and tried to control her voice. 'You don't know what you're talking about. That ignorance is what has kept her safe.'

Anashe chuckled. 'A tremendous plan for the short term, with only the merest potential for catastrophic long-term consequences,' she said. 'Meaning, perhaps,' she gestured around them, 'these.'

'Are you getting at something, Anashe? Forgive me, but my patience has been worn pretty thin by,' she gestured likewise in mocking imitation, 'these.'

'Do you feel you have told my brother all he seeks?'

A muscle in Ree's cheek twitched. 'I don't believe such a thing would be possible. What he's after is more than I can provide.'

She nodded sadly, still gazing out into the darkening evening. 'And still I see no journey's end.'

'What is this obsession, Anashe, this desperate quest? What does he feel learning of his mother will grant him?'

'Does it matter? Can you not simply tell him more and make him happy?'

'At what cost?'

Anashe's brows lowered, perfect lines. 'Cost? What is the cost to giving him his stories?'

'Because the stories cause me pain, Anashe. Do you understand? They hurt me.'

'What manner of pain? Does it grieve you to remember?'

'Not that . . . not just that.' Ree stared down at her hands. 'I am *ashamed*, Anashe. When your mother died I . . . I wasn't there. I left her, and the others, and she died. She gave her life to save people I should have been there to protect. I should have protected her.'

Anashe watched her from the window, still, perfect, not even seeming to breathe. 'Do you think she would have seen it that way?'

'I don't . . . I don't know.'

'I suspect that you do. The truth beneath may be painful, but I believe it can be liberating.' She paused. 'In many things.'

Ree had a finger raised without even realising it. 'What are you insinuating?'

Anashe's voice remained maddeningly light, her tone pure reason itself. 'Don't we all have a right to know where we came from? Even . . . the youngest of us?'

'You don't understand!' Ree wheeled, her fingers grasping empty air. 'Where I come from, the role of . . . it's formalised, it's defined, it's emblematic, it resonates through the ages.'

'Which role is that?'

'*Parent*,' Ree growled. 'And it means nothing! Nothing by itself. Do you know what my *parents* did to me?' She shook her head too vigorously, reigniting the dormant headache. 'What matters is the act: being a guardian, a carer.'

'Yet if you are performing the role anyway, why reject this label, beyond . . . obstinacy?'

Ree turned on the other woman, nostrils flared. 'What does a parent owe a child, is that it? Or what does a child owe a parent?' She pressed her hands to her temples, feeling the throb below her fingers. 'My birth parents *sold me* when I was younger than she is. I was "married" a couple of years later. And I was "widowed" a couple of years after that. I've been on my own since.'

'Hardly alone.'

'For the formative experiences, I was.'

'And you believe you turned out just fine?'

Ree slumped back against the wall with a sigh. 'I can't bring peace to your brother, Anashe. Or anyone else.'

'I don't believe I am asking you to. But you can help him along.'

Ree pushed herself away from the wall, rounding on the woman in the window. 'And what about you? What will bring you peace? You've followed your brother for years across the world, with no agenda of your own?'

Anashe shrugged, a sparse, economical movement. 'What else was I supposed to do?'

Ree goggled, speechless.

'I have always travelled in his shadow,' Anashe went on. 'This may surprise you,' she said, lowering her gaze, 'but I do not make friends easily, and we have rarely stayed in one place for long. This has made the formation of . . . meaningful relationships something of a challenge.'

'I can relate to that,' Ree murmured with a tilt of her head. 'But what drives you? What would you be doing if your brother weren't dragging you across continents?'

Anashe paused, one long finger against her lips. 'Nothing,' she said at last.

'Nothing?'

'Nothing. I would like to sit in comfort, to while away hours without purpose. I would like to learn to play music, to sing, to do both with friends.' Her voice caught, just for a moment. 'I would like to have friends. I would like to drink wine among people I care about, unhurried and unconcerned.' She thought for another moment. 'I would like to like wine.'

'As aspirations go, I've heard worse.' Ree lifted her wineskin. 'You could start on the last bit now.'

Anashe's headshake was polite but firm. 'Not while I am working. Not while I have work to do.'

'So you want an end to work, then? An end to duty and obligation?'

She ran one finger down her chin and along her throat as she looked up at the crumbling ceiling. 'I wish to feel that my work is complete.'

'Now there's a common aspiration,' Ree chuckled, 'but I doubt it's one many attain. Especially from a standing start.'

'I have made little of my adult life, I know this. Once my brother finds his peace, then perhaps I will return to Arowan, and some . . . prospects . . . of my own.'

Ree perked up. 'These wouldn't be professional prospects, would they?'

Anashe's cheeks darkened, and she looked away, returning her gaze to the gathering twilight, then pushed herself down from the window ledge and began a slow walk to the stairs. 'I should check on my idiot brother. He is my family, and we have no one else. Family is important, don't you think?'

Ree puffed air through pinched lips. 'Fine, fine. Your message is received. If you see the kid down there,' she called, 'tell her . . . tell her . . . um . . .'

'I may struggle with a message of such nuance and complexity,' came Anashe's reply as she began to descend, 'but I will do my best to convey its essence.'

TWENTY

Javani had reached the foot of the crumbling stair when she saw Anashe, out in the dusk lit, dust-swept courtyard, sitting cross-legged in contemplation of something before her.

She wandered out. In a patch of dying daylight, Anashe had dragged out a stretch of mottled and ragged canvas on the baked earth, and was laying out items upon it in neat rows. She barely glanced up. 'There you are, little one.'

'What are you doing?'

'These are the weapons we took from those who came at us on the road today. Some we disarmed, others shed their weapons when they did not function.'

'Better than sharing a sword, I suppose. Where's Aki?'

'With the horses once more, inflicting his poems upon them. As if they had not suffered enough.'

Javani looked over the haul: three of the little hand-bows, a selection of bolts, a trio of sabres, and an assorted collection of knives. She'd found a narrow bundle of short bows and a spear from somewhere, possibly Ree's cache, and set them down on the canvas alongside several fistfuls of tatty arrows. Javani pointed to the hand-bows, two with their strings broken, laid out beside a handful of little bolts, most bent or broken. 'I've never seen bows like those before. Before today, I mean.'

'They are produced in the south, to those who can afford them.

I wonder how much of a debt they owe to that crossbow of your adult's.'

'Oh yes. She was pretty angry about losing that.' Javani peered closer at the little hand-bows, past the battered sabres pinning the corners of the canvas. One of the sabres had large dark patches all down its blade. 'They're like miniature versions. All wheels and pulleys.'

'See that little stamp?' Anashe said with a tap of a narrow finger. 'A maker's mark. They're from Arowan, from the workshops of one of the merchant houses. I never expected to see them so far north – they must have been shipped directly here. The dust seems to plague them, which their architects did not foresee. Still,' she continued, her gaze travelling towards the back of the horseless wagon, 'much of their mechanism remains sound. There may yet be a use for them, or their parts.'

Javani watched her stand and walk stiffly towards the wagon's tailboard. 'What do you mean?'

Anashe reached the wagon and leaned against it, all lines and angles in the dying ruby light. 'During my time in the protectorate, I have found myself developing something of a fascination with alchemy, and its many practical applications in my vocation. The hirsute gentleman we acquired today used one such device to create a great deal of space between us and our pursuers. Another such item might prove instrumental for our continued southern journey, and I am given to wonder if any others remain secreted in this vehicle.'

Javani pondered Movos's words back in the town, before he'd roared away in the wagon, seemingly leaving her behind for ever. 'I think that might have been a one-off. He threw it away afterwards.'

Anashe nodded, her mouth pulled together like a cat's backside. 'However, some of the kegs of blasting powder remain.'

'Just don't blow yourself up, all right?' Javani found she'd taken a step backwards. 'We need the wagon, for a start.'

'I make no promises,' Anashe murmured back, and Javani couldn't tell if she was joking. She really didn't seem the joking type.

Anashe pulled herself up onto the wagon's tailboard, then turned. 'By the way, your adult wishes to speak to you. She asked me to convey the message.'

Javani's mouth twisted as she nodded. 'To, or with, I wonder,' she muttered, and turned for the stairs.

Ree was alone at the fire, the wineskin in her hand lying fat against her leg. 'Take a seat, kid.'

'I need some of that wine.'

Ree's eyebrows climbed, stretching the scar at her temple. 'I'm all for getting to know your limits, but I'd say you're still a little young for that level of experimentation.'

'It's not for me.'

Ree ran a hand over her cheek and rested it on her chin. 'Given neither of our specialist siblings seem much inclined towards alcoholic consumption, I'd guess it's for our bound bandit downstairs. Which would suggest you're currying favour with him, if not bargaining outright, which in turn suggests you're aiming to extract the secret of his grand escape plan, presumably with some lunatic notion of pursuing it instead of what we discussed earlier. Am I close?'

Javani felt heat rising all across her body, her fists shaking at her sides.

'Who *are* you?' she near-screamed. 'Just what kind of . . . How do you know these things? How can I trust . . .' She let out a breath, trying to expel the burning heat. 'How much is true, of your life, of what you've told me?' She took another step. 'Is Ree even your real name?'

'Come on, kid, you know me.'

'I don't know you at all. You keep everything from me, you don't listen to me, you don't *value* me!'

'I do all of those things.'

'The hells you do! You're intent on running south, running for ever!'

'I'm doing it *for* you—'

'Are you? It's not what I want! None of this is what I want!'

Ree was on her feet, instant, poised. 'You don't know what you want, kid.'

'Because you never tell me anything!' Javani's voice cracked and her throat constricted, and she knew she was running out of words; tears were stinging the corners of her eyes. 'Right now, all I want is something true from you.'

Ree gazed at her, clear-eyed and steady, then her shoulders relaxed and she slid elegantly back to her perch. 'Take a seat, kid. Maybe it's time we had a talk.'

Javani sniffed. 'Can I have some wine?'

'No.'

Ree watched her with onyx eyes, the tiny flames dancing in their darkness giving nothing away. 'What do you want to know?'

Javani took a long, heavy breath, feeling the air enter her lungs, feeling her body tremble.

'The diplomat in Lazant's story . . . is that you?'

'He has it wrong, kid. He has it all wrong—'

'Just. Answer. Are you . . .' She took another breath. 'Are you my ma?'

Ree's expression didn't change. She watched Javani, unblinking, unmoving but for the firelight glimmering in her eyes.

'This really matters to you, doesn't it?' she said at last. Her tone was almost quizzical.

'Yes!' Javani squeaked. 'Of course it does!'

Now Ree's face became animated, her brows lifting, her mouth wide as she spoke. 'Is it so important? What will it change?'

'What? What do you mean?'

'It's always been the two of us, for as long as you've lived. We're a team, kid, we don't need . . . labels.'

Javani felt the heat rising again. 'No, it's been you, and me as an attachment, an inconvenience. You've always denied responsibility for me, like you were *ashamed*.'

Ree flinched as if Javani had slapped her. 'What?'

'You always say "she's not mine",' Javani snapped, her voice rising. 'As fast as you can, just in case people *for an instant* get the wrong idea. Gods forgive anyone should think we're related.'

Ree was back on her feet. 'I wasn't denying responsibility for you, you goose, I was denying *ownership!*'

Javani's mouth was half open. 'Come again?'

'People talk about children as if they're possessions. I know a little bit about what it's like to be treated as one.' Ree was breathing hard, her chest rising and falling in the firelight, beads of sweat clear on her brow. 'I never wanted that for you. You've been yours since you could walk, since you could speak. You've always been yours. I was only ever a custodian.'

Javani stood for a moment, watching the other woman breathing, feeling her own breath, hot in her throat and chest. 'Well . . . that's . . . In that case, it's time to start treating me like that, and not just saying it.'

Ree shook her head, ran a hand through her matted hair. 'You're right. You're right, kid, I'm sorry.'

'Good. We agree.' Javani cleared her throat, adjusted her shirt. 'Henceforth, I'll be the judge of what matters to me. And I have a right to know who my mother is. So is it true?' She swallowed, her voice thickening, coming out in a whisper. 'Is it?'

Ree stared for a long time at the fire, the light washing over her face, time's lines carved and faded on her features.

'Yes,' she said.

Every hair on Javani's body stood on end. She felt herself swaying. She flopped down on the stone beside Ree, clumsy and wild. It was that or fall down.

'You lied to me. My whole life.'

Ree met her gaze, her deep eyes steady and unapologetic. 'What I did, I did to protect you.'

'Because of what's happening now?'

'In part, maybe.'

'But why not tell me before? It's not like I was any safer, is it? I don't . . . I don't understand.'

Ree was staring into the fire. 'People put too much stock in "parents", in "family". Expectations and lies. Words not deeds.' Javani felt as if Ree was no longer talking to her, but to herself. 'A family is what you make, not what you're born to.'

Javani put her elbows on her knees, her chin in her hands, and considered herself. She'd expected to feel some kind of weight lift, the great pressure of uncertainty flown from her shoulders, to soar on wings of secret knowledge. Instead, now the shock had passed, she felt almost . . . indifferent. Perhaps, she thought, I was so convinced already that nothing's really changed.

'Kid?'

'Do I keep calling you Ree? Is Ree your real name?'

'As real as any I've had. It's what you call me. That makes it real.'

'What were you, before? Lazant said you were a diplomat . . .'

'He's wrong. But . . . I travelled.'

'To Shenak? What's it like?'

'Never there. I hear it's picturesque, though – green, mountainous. They make a lot of wine and brandy there, eat a lot of rice and fish. But their politics are hopelessly complex and they can't help involving themselves in those of their neighbours. Shenak never had an empire. I think that bothers the ruling class on some instinctive level.'

'But what were you?'

Ree sighed, leaning back on her rubble. 'The work I did, and who I was, or am, are two separate things. I did a lot of jobs, some violent with words, some violent with acts. I am me, and always was.'

'You fought?'

'I did. Sometimes.'

'With your sword?'

'Sometimes.'

'Why is it so special? You wouldn't let Aki use it, even when we were moments from evisceration. I swear you care more about it than you do me.'

'That's horseshit and you know it. But . . .' Ree puffed a breath, blowing loose strands of her fringe from her eyes. 'People have been trying to take that weapon off me for almost longer than I've had it, kid, and, well, old habits and all that.'

'Where did you get it?'

Ree rested her fingers against her temples, rubbed across her eyes, momentarily hiding herself from the world. 'It was a gift.'

'From someone you cared about?'

'From someone I hated.' Her hands fell away, and her gaze was distant and bleak. 'But at a time when nothing in my life was under my control, when I had nothing of my own, and my existence, my mind, my body, were at another's whim, suddenly I had a possession.' The corner of her mouth twitched and she snorted. 'He thought it was a joke. But when he was gone, the sword was still mine.'

'Who was he?'

'Someone best forgotten.'

Javani filed that away for later. 'I'd like to have seen you fight with it. You never do anything with it when I'm around.'

'I hope you never have to see it.'

'Why?'

'Because if I'm fighting someone, it'll be a last-ditch effort to stop them getting to you.'

Javani took a long breath in and out through her nose. She could still feel her heart beating very fast, much faster than it should for merely sitting by a fire talking to her aunt.

To her mother.

There was that electric surge, the hairs standing up again on her arms, a strange, hot sick feeling in her stomach. Whatever this was, it wasn't happiness, exactly, but neither was it despair.

'Well, kid? Is that enough truth for one evening?'

'Not yet. Why do you always treat me like a child?'

Ree laughed. 'You are a child, my dear. If I hadn't been looking after you, you'd be a smear in the desert somewhere already.'

'But how can I ever be anything more if you never let me do anything for myself, live my own experiences? I need to . . .' She thought of Movos's words on Kurush. '. . . I need to learn to make decisions, instead of taking the path laid out for me.'

'Kid, those experiences might kill you or break you and I can't lose anything more.' Ree looked away suddenly, past the fire, out through the half-collapsed window into the night. Javani realised with creeping horror that Ree was holding back tears herself.

'All those years, never staying in one place, always on the move . . . Ree, what have we been running from? Aside from defrauded nobles and merchants, I guess.'

Ree cracked half a smile, her gaze still lost somewhere in the night's deep indigo. 'My past, I suppose.'

'Did you know this would happen one day? You said you should have expected it.'

'No. Not this exactly. This . . . has been a surprise.' Her eyes gleamed now, wet and shining. 'But you travel long enough, you leave a wake. And sometimes you're forced to cross it.'

Javani shuffled closer, considered putting an arm around her au— mother, maybe even resting her head on her shoulder. They'd never had a particularly tactile relationship, which hadn't bothered Javani in the past – after all, they were only aunt and niece.

She couldn't do it, it was as if Ree had a wall of force around her, repelling Javani's touch.

'What was it you were expecting, then?'

'A long time ago,' Ree said, readying the wineskin in her hand. She was still staring out of the lightless window. 'Before you were born, I had comrades . . . friends. And I left them.' She drank from the skin, wiped her mouth. 'I asked them to come with me, but they wanted to stay and fight. And they lost.' She drank again, quicker this time. 'I ran, and they lost.'

'What does—'

Ree closed her eyes tight, took a heavy breath. 'I abandoned the closest thing I had to a family, deserted them to their fate. I told myself they were fools and I was the only one thinking straight, thinking of the future.'

She went quiet, and Javani gave her a moment before speaking. 'And were you?'

Ree opened her eyes with a sigh. 'Yes, but it doesn't mean I made the right choice.' She shook her head as if trying to clear it of thoughts. 'I thought I could keep you away from all this, kid, leave this piss-awful, grotesque world behind. All I wanted to do was be left alone to live a life of my choosing, let the south rot away without me.' She went to drink again, paused, let the wineskin droop. 'But everywhere I go it's the same shit, the same chancers, the same human failings wearing new faces.'

'And you're still the same person, right? Terbish in the teahouse once said that no matter how far you go and how fast you travel, the one person you can never outrun is yourself.'

Ree made a face. 'A bit trite for my taste, but there's some truth buried in the horseshit.'

A slow-moving part of Javani's thoughts arrived at last, waving for her attention. 'When you left your friends,' she said slowly, 'when you ran away. Was that . . . was that because of me? Do you blame me for that?'

Ree turned to her, her eyes black and huge. When she spoke her voice was raw-edged. 'Never. Not for a moment.' She coughed, wiped at her eyes and stood. 'You should get some sleep, kid. We've got a lot to do tomorrow.'

'Can I have some booze, then?'

'Of course not.'

Javani threw her hands in the air. 'Then what was the point of all that? So at last you admit you're my ma, but what's changed? You still don't trust me!'

Ree half turned. 'I trust you with the truth.'

'Which you could have told me years ago! Why did you pretend to be my aunt in the first place, if we weren't in hiding? Who were you really protecting with this fiction – me, or yourself?'

Ree's breath caught, and she swallowed, hard. When she turned, Javani was shocked to see tears rolling down her cheeks.

'You're . . .' Ree began, then took a step towards her, one hand outstretched. She rested her palm against Javani's cheek. It felt cold and rough and unfamiliar. How could her own mother's hand feel unfamiliar?

'You're right.'

Javani blinked. 'Huh?'

'You're right, kid.' Another raft of tears glimmered at Ree's eyes, unshed. 'I did it for me. Because I was afraid.'

'Huh?'

'I was afraid of letting you down as a parent. "Parent" has expectations, "aunt" does not. Anything you got from me was a bonus. I'd been trying just to survive for so long that I'd forgotten how to do anything else. I told myself . . .' She took a long breath that trembled at the edges. 'I told myself that a child just needs someone to look out for them. Someone to look up to.'

Javani couldn't think of anything to say. Ree's hand still rested on her cheek, warming now. Javani's own eyes itched with tears, and her chest felt very hot. So what Ree had feared most was failing as a parent . . . to the extent that she'd never even tried at all.

'My own parents sold me, kid. They exchanged my life, and my freedom, for *political advancement*. I never wanted to . . . I couldn't . . .'

She closed her eyes tight, and the tears ran silent down her cheeks. Javani surged forward and wrapped her arms around her mother, buried her head in her chest, as the woman sobbed against her. 'It's all right, I get it,' she said, over and over, and hoped it was true.

'I'm sorry, kid.'

'We'll work it out.' She broke the embrace, took a step back. 'Do I have to call you "ma" now? It seems weird.'

Ree smiled, wiped at her eyes with her knuckles.

'We'll work it out,' she said.

'And if I want to go to Shenak and be a princess?'

Ree ruffled her hair, hard. 'What kind of mother would I be if I let you do that?'

'Can I have some wine?'

Ree sucked her lips against her teeth. 'Ask me again in the morning.'

Javani supposed that was the best she could have hoped for.

* * *

Javani's dreams were strange and elusive, populated with the shapes of ideas over anything she could fathom. She saw Moosh, or something like him, and felt a tide of profound guilt. *I'm so sorry, Mooshie. I wasn't another orphan after all.*

However, her agonies faded, and when she woke, it was with a sense of righteous satisfaction.

The feeling lasted right up until she heard the rocks begin to tumble.

TWENTY-ONE

The rumble and crash echoed from the rock walls around the tower, its ancient stones shuddering, while a rising curtain of dust flooded the open window to the south. Javani stumbled to her feet, woozy and shaken. 'What in all the hells was that?'

As the thunderous echoes died away, other sounds filtered through, sounds to make her guts lurch: the clop and snort of hooves, the jingle of tack and armour. She looked desperately around the chamber. It was barely dawn, a mellow tawny glow in the north and east, stark contrast to the cloying, drifting dark on the opposite side.

'Ree?' she called. 'Anashe? Aki?'

'Here, little one.' Aki was crouched on the southern side, propped on his elbows, staring out into the swirling gloom. 'I will take no offence that mine was the last name you called.'

'What's happened? What was that noise?'

'Come see for yourself, child of the Goddess.' He gestured to the window. 'The earth cracked and shook, and disgorged the minions of Usdohr,' he said, his voice weighed with despond. 'The road south is blocked, and we are ringed by demons.'

'What? *What?*' She ran to the window. 'Godshit!' she squeaked.

The dust was clearing, the sun's first fringes cresting the peaks behind them, and she saw he was right. A great tumble of loose red rock had filled the southern cut, extinguishing any hope of riding any further, let alone driving the wagon through. But worse was closer: the riders were arrayed before the battered wall and broken gate in a wide semicircle, surrounding them, hand-bows and sabres loose and ready, weapons glinting pre-blooded in the dawn's red light. Javani swallowed. 'How many are there?'

'I have counted twelve. More are arriving steadily.'

'They're not attacking?'

He put his palms on the pitted window frame and pushed himself back. 'I suspect, little one, that they do not feel a need. We are hemmed here. We are at their mercy.'

Javani peered back through the window, through the crimson and amber haze of drifting dawn dust, to the centre of the riders' formation. There she saw Kurush, looking slumped and travel-worn, and beside him, Zakir Lazant, the prince of Shenak, taut and imperious in the saddle. 'Then we,' she murmured, 'are in trouble.'

Ree was pacing by the stairs. 'Let's not dwell on who should have been keeping which watch,' she growled as Aki and Javani approached. Anashe was already there, face graver than ever, the lines around her mouth like valleys.

'Usdohr has cracked the earth and sent forth—' Aki began.

'Aki, be quiet,' Ree snapped. 'They simply risked their necks crossing the canyon, then galloped their way in pitch darkness so they could get the drop on us this morning. I never suspected Kurush of such ruthlessness,' she hissed, 'the man's a thrice-born coward.'

Javani pictured the Acting Guildmaster slumped in his saddle, and the haughty man beside him. 'I don't think it was his idea.'

'You could well be right there, kid.' Ree took a hard breath through her nose, her eyes wide, and drummed her fingers together. 'We need a plan, and fast.'

The thought of the riders beyond the wall made Javani dizzy and dry-mouthed. 'Why aren't they attacking already?'

Anashe unfolded from her position at the wall. 'They are waiting for reinforcements. Our intimation is that they have worked a way across the chasm, but the bulk of their force must still be labouring over the crossing. Those before the walls are the advance party; the rest may still take some time to reach us.' Her hand tightened on the sabre at her belt. 'We should engage them now, before their numbers climb. We could put an end to those at the centre—'

'No.' Ree chopped a hand. 'Three of us, against . . .'

'Twelve,' Aki supplied. 'And counting.'

'Twelve, mounted, armed and armoured. Those odds are long.'

'Don't forget me,' Javani said, her voice hot. 'I could—'

Ree nodded, meeting her eye. 'I know, kid. But the odds are *long*.'

'Then what—'

'What was that thing you said about the Guvuli plan?'

Javani's heart soared. 'Travelling west? Through the secret pass?' She realised she'd never gone back to Movos with the wine. Maybe there was still time now, maybe she could still find something to bribe him with for his map, even with the Guild on their doorstep.

'No, not that, the other thing. The way to ditch pursuers is to make them think you're already dead.'

Javani deflated. 'Oh, that.'

Ree was nodding to herself, her palms pressed together. 'Aki, in one of the workshops there are some old archery targets, man-shaped sacks. See if you can dig out one the right size, and find enough un-rotten straw to stuff it with.'

'Ree? What are you—'

'Anashe, remember that stuff we discussed last night? Your ideas? Now's the time.'

The woman nodded. 'I should admit that I made something of a start already, in the name of . . . prudence.' She seemed to wink at Ree, but Javani knew she must have imagined it.

Javani looked from one to the other. 'What are you all talking about? Ree, what are you—'

Aki was back at the window. 'They are waving something. It is . . . it is a black flag.'

Ree stiffened. 'A black flag? You're sure?'

'So it would seem.'

Javani's neck ached. 'A black flag?'

'A temporary truce,' Ree answered. 'A parley.'

'I thought a white flag was truce.'

'No, my dear, that's surrender. And we won't be needing that. That wasp-fart Kurush has given us exactly what we need.'

'What?'

'Time.'

'Guildmaster, do you wish to address the troops?' Even travel-worn and sleepless, Lazant somehow looked impossibly handsome, the golden light of dawn casting his features with a near-heavenly glow. 'Modern military theory lends great weight to the notion that a well-delivered battlefield address can improve both unit performance and cohesion.'

Kurush looked up from beneath heavy brows, trying to fight his face's natural scowl. Fatigue weighed upon him. Both he and his horse had come close to death in their frantic overnight scramble, and out here a rider with no mount was as good as dead anyway. They'd lost others, along the way – to the canyon, to the climb, to a snapped foreleg in a fox hole in the depths of night – all of them known to Kurush, some with something that had approached familiarity, all thrown away by this mad prince's mad quest. But it was a quest that Kurush needed to succeed. He just had to hold on a little longer and see this maniac achieve his goals, then Kurush could kiss goodbye to this armpit of desert and rock, to the threats of Guild auditors and political rivals, and set sail for a land of grapes and green slopes.

'Guildmaster? Are you well? Between us, your focus has become somewhat erratic – are you in need of rest? Perhaps a return to the town?'

'No!' Kurush barked, hauling himself upright in the saddle. 'No, thank you, highness,' he added, feeling fresh trickles of sweat working their way towards his collar. It was barely dawn and he had little enough water left to lose. He'd taken some skins from lost riders, at least. 'I'll address them now.'

He scanned the assembled riders, barely a dozen of them; several were overnight joiners as word had spread of the prince's offer of silver. Non-Guild, non-professional, non-reliable. They looked at Kurush as though he were just another hireling, a faceless grunt in the pay of their benefactor-to-be. He felt his ire growing. It was too damned-by-gods hot.

'Listen up,' he bellowed, but his throat was dry and it came out as a croaking squeak. He waved Lazant's offer of his waterskin away and tried again. 'Listen up!

'In that tower . . . In that tower is our enemy. As soon as they appear, kill them all, and bring the girl's head to—'

'Guildmaster,' Lazant's voice was somehow pitched low and discreet, yet was audible to every rider on the road, 'this is not the correct form of address.'

Kurush swallowed. He now regretted waving the skin away. It was so damned-by-gods hot.

'Perhaps I may be of assistance?' the prince enquired softly, his voice as smooth as honey.

Go on, then, Kurush growled to himself. Tell me what to say. Work my mouth like I'm your fucking puppet, but at least they'll know the orders come through me. He nodded his assent.

To his horror, Lazant nudged his horse forwards, then swung it expertly to face the assembled riders. Stupid, Kurush snarled at himself, very stupid – should have seen that coming. Still, looking the part was no guarantee, he still needed to impress these grizzled cut-throats that—

Lazant's oration was perfect. He trod a delicate line between evocations of duty and more earthy reminders of the payment on offer for what was otherwise a grisly act, somehow leaving the riders with the impression that not only did they stand to make a personal fortune in silver by beheading a child, but they'd also be all the more *noble* for doing it.

Fuck this, growled Kurush's inner voice, fuck this into the sea with a splintered spear. He could just give the order to stab the man now, kill that lieutenant of his, divide up the silver she carried between those present and say no more about it. Take his share and return to the ruined Guildhouse, and the wrath of the Guild . . .

He clenched his jaw and shut his eyes. No. Hold fast. Stay the course. And would the riders even follow his orders, if it came to picking sides? It was so damned-by-gods hot.

'I think that went well, don't you?' Lazant was back at his side, Khalida in his shadow. 'For a pack of vagabonds, they seem a pliable bunch.' He sniffed, moustache twitching. 'Mother always said I lacked rhetorical flourish.'

Enx was impressed. He'd stuck with the column of Guild hunters through the storm in the desert and the crazed overnight ride through the narrows, not from any particular sense of duty or devotion, but because he had a healthy interest in his bodyweight in silver and an increasing expectation of getting his greasy hands on at least a portion of it. Additionally, chances to abscond had been few, but it wasn't like he'd been really trying.

He adjusted his breastplate and shifted in the saddle. That little speech by the foreigner had given him quite the renewed focus. Now the blood thrummed in his veins, his heart thumping against the burnished steel at his chest. The child was on the other side of those broken-down walls, and she was so, so vulnerable. Her head would be his, and the silver would flow.

His hands twitching in anticipation, Enx watched the one-eyed Shenakar lieutenant pass her prince the monstrous crossbow they'd dug from the blasted cell block, the one the girl's keeper had claimed could ventilate Kurush's breastplate. The lieutenant murmured something to the prince, and he nodded, pressing the weapon to his shoulder and sighting alongside it.

'Have the scouts seen any sign of that black-armoured mercenary, Guildmaster?' he brayed to Kurush. 'She has proven something of an obstacle to this point, and I would care to test a theory.' He clicked the crossbow's trigger, producing a satisfying clunk from somewhere in the device's inner workings.

'None reported, highness,' the sullen Acting Guildmaster replied.

'Let us remain prepared, nonetheless,' Lazant said, passing the weapon back to his second. 'I have no wish to be caught out again. Very good, my Shade. Please see what else you think it will shoot.' He turned to Kurush with an easy, guileless smile, which seemed a dark reflection of the man's own mood. 'But before the violence, Guildmaster, there must be talking. Will you join me for the parley?'

'Aki, Anashe. With me.' Ree was already striding toward the stairs. The siblings followed, cowed by her tone. Javani trotted afterwards, leaving the upper floor empty but for discarded tea mugs.

They marched straight out into the still cool and shaded courtyard. Javani's gaze kept flicking to the stubby wall, to the broken gate that barred it, thinking of the riders on its far side. Occasionally a horse whinnied, but they were otherwise silent, leaving only the noise of the wind moaning through the red rock of the narrows.

'Last chance to change your minds, specialists,' Ree said, her eyes hopping from Anashe to Aki and back again. 'It's not you they're after, you could walk out of here, or just wait it out if you wished.'

Anashe shook her head, a single, rigid gesture. 'We stand by our word.'

'Besides,' Aki added, 'I foresee a rich vein of challenge in the likely persuasion of our outward aggressors that we have curtailed our former loyalties.'

Ree stared at him, unblinking, her eyes hard as gemstones.

'Which is to say,' Aki went on with a cough, 'they may have a hard time believing we are no longer in your service.'

'You know, Aki,' Ree said, 'sometimes it's possible to say the simple version first.'

'I cannot be blamed for the poetry of my soul,' he protested, 'any more than the great sun can be blamed for casting light and warmth on us all.'

'At least the sun packs it in for half the time,' Ree replied with one eyebrow raised.

Anashe cut in. 'I fear we are straying from the purpose of our discourse.'

Aki grinned. 'I could hardly have put it better—'

'Indeed,' Ree muttered. 'You've affirmed your commitment, and you'll take your own consequences from what follows. Now you know what your tasks are. Get them done while I'm outside the gate.'

Despite his previous animation, Aki's face was sombre. 'It will be done. She wills it.' Anashe nodded along with him.

'Good. Get to it. I'll buy what time I can out there, but we have to assume that our truce will be shorter-lived than a fart in a firestorm.'

Javani stepped from the shadow of the doorway. 'Wait, you're going out? Alone?'

Ree glanced up. 'I am, kid.'

Javani advanced. 'Are you . . . You can't go out there! They'll kill you!'

Ree's tone was almost tender. 'And if I don't, they'll come in here, and they'll do for all of us.'

Javani walked the last few steps to where Ree stood. 'What do you think they want to talk about?'

One corner of Ree's mouth pulled back in a sardonic half-smile, crinkling the old scar at her temple. 'I imagine our friend the prince will make some waffling speech about duty and hard choices and the necessity of performing unspeakable acts so that his kingdom might see peace and so forth, then demand that we hand you over in exchange for the sparing of our lives.'

Javani swallowed. She couldn't think of anything to say.

Ree put one hand on her shoulder. 'Don't fret, kid. It's all bollocks either way. Our friend Lazant has a mean streak a thousand strides wide, and I'm sure the thought of our collective murder stiffens his breeches. But he feels the weight of Propriety.'

'Propriety?'

She nodded, eyes narrowed, the crinkles at their corners ever deeper. 'He's making a show of being a good little prince, and this is part of the theatre. Magnanimity, offers of mercy, demonstration that he is, in fact, the reasonable party.' She put one hand on her chest. 'And we are the emotional, irrational monsters, who refused his noble entreaty and put the fate of a kingdom at risk. Like I said: bollocks.'

'You're going to refuse?'

Ree's eyebrows pitched like a temple roof. 'Nine hells, kid, of course. I'm just going to take as long as I can to do it.'

'Aren't you worried he'll hurt you?'

'Beneath a flag of truce? That would be . . . indecorous. Now get your skinny little arse back inside and out of sight – the last thing we need is for you to give one of those jumpy fuckers a clear shot at you.'

Ree signalled to Anashe, then looked back at Javani as she walked towards the gate. 'I'll be back soon.'

Javani backed inside the dark of the tower, one cheek pressed to the cold stone, and watched her mother disappear.

TWENTY-TWO

Javani's legs took her to the back of the tower, away from the brightening courtyard, the outer wall, Aki's thumb-heavy activities at the wagon. Her arms wrapped her, despite the morning's growing warmth; she felt sick and light-headed, and the back of her mouth tasted funny. What was Ree doing, going out there? A flag of truce, with the man who'd murdered Moosh? Had she taken leave of what little sense she had?

It was so unfair. She'd finally chased out the truth of her parentage, the truth beneath as Aki might have called it, and cast her relationship with Ree in something that might qualify as a new light. She still hadn't processed her thoughts, decided whether the knowledge that Ree was her mother was a good thing or not. She hoped it was. She wanted it to be. But there was so much anger, so much resentment. Lied to from birth! And despite what Ree had claimed about it being for her own protection, she'd made her admit that the one being protected all along was Ree. Or at least, it had been, but now she'd wandered out beyond the rickety gate and into the teeth of a dozen Guild cut-throats, and there was a substantial chance that things would go tits-up and they'd never get to have a proper—

'You never came back.'

Movos Guvuli lay propped in the corner of his cell against the wall, much as he'd been when she'd last seen him. The only change was the smell, which was considerably worse.

'Did you get my drink? Just 'twixt us, girl, I've a gullet like a year-dry gulch.'

Guvuli. She'd forgotten. Again. Ree's nebulous plan came roaring back, along with her tremulous hope of a better one. She stopped, put one finger against her teeth. Ree was outside, the siblings working at whatever mysterious tasks she'd set them. Javani was devoid of adult supervision.

'Tell me how you were going to get away, all the way away, and I'll let you out right now, bandit. It's your old mine, isn't it? The Old Scar. You're . . . you're faking a collapse, right? Tell me how you were going to do it.'

He rubbed at his eyes with grimy hands and pushed himself upright against the wall. 'Covered this, girl, I've no—'

She waved an impatient hand. 'Yes, yes, all very sad, aimless and unjust. But aren't you forgetting something?'

He scratched at himself with his two-fingered hand. 'What?'

'Didn't you say that the Guild drove you out of business, then hanged your brothers?'

His fingers paused, his thick brows lowered. 'And?'

'What about your revenge?'

His head tilted back, small dark eyes peering from under the thunderous brows. 'My revenge?'

'Your revenge. Because outside this tower, even as we speak, is a posse of Guild riders, and they're led by Guildmaster Kurush himself. Seems like a fine time to be planning an evening of scores.'

'Why would I wait to the evening?'

'No, no, even-ing. To make even. Even the score. Just tell me how to set off the collapse, I'll free you now and help you find a weapon.' She went for her last throw. 'There might even still be a wineskin somewhere upstairs.'

Movos's eyes were distant, and his lips moved in silence. Javani bit at her lip to keep her smile from escaping. He was going to go for it, it was written all over his face. Of course, actually getting him out of the tower without making things worse would be a challenge, but—

The back wall wobbled with an unmissable thud. Puffs of sand and old stone dust rose into the air. Javani and Movos turned to look.

'Huh?'

The wall wobbled again, then one of the cracked stone blocks buckled inwards and fell to the floor. Points of gleaming daylight shone through its gap from beyond. Another thump set more stone tumbling, until a great fissure collapsed inwards in a plume of rising dust, leaving a jagged slice of red rock visible through its shattered outline.

'What in nine hells—'

Through the dust plume stepped the White Spear.

Javani took a step back, hands at her temples. 'Gods have mercy,' she gasped, 'seriously?'

The White Spear stepped down onto the fallen stone blocks, then into the low room. Her armour was pitted and dented, her dangling hair was matted, and great dark streaks decorated her from helmet to boots, but she seemed to move without visible difficulty. She scanned the room, head turning slowly, then nodded to Movos.

'Guvuli.'

'Whitespear,' he nodded back.

'That . . . That wall . . .' Javani couldn't form her words. 'I thought it was solid rock . . . back there.'

The White Spear shook her head. 'No. Erosion.' She took a step forwards, towards Javani, who shrank instinctively back. 'We should leave now.'

Javani put up one hand. 'This is . . . This is *not* a good time, mercenary.' She gestured behind her, to the courtyard doorway and the wall beyond. 'There's a whole mess of Guild types outside the wall, and unless I can make something happen in the very near future, they're going to ride on in here and slaughter the lot of us.'

'I am well aware of this,' the White Spear replied, easy, conversational. 'Some of their number had the same idea I did. I met them scouting the ridge.'

'What?'

The White Spear turned back and reached out through the rent in the wall, then dragged in a battered corpse. It was wearing a Guild breastplate. Javani shrieked.

'There are four more,' the White Spear said. 'It was not prudent to leave their remains where they might be discovered, so I brought them down the cliffside with me.'

'You killed . . . five people?'

She inclined her head. 'Between me and the fall, yes. But they intended to kill you, which runs counter to the letter of my contract, so I was left with very little choice. Please do not be disheartened.'

'Dishear— I am not disheartened, mercenary, I am horrified!'

'You would prefer them to be standing in my place?'

'That's . . .' Javani clenched her fists. 'That's not what I meant.'

'Then please collect whatever supplies you require, and let us be away back up the cliffside before the outer wall is breached. Do not fear if you cannot climb, I will carry you.'

'No.'

'You wish to climb unassisted? It will be risky.'

'No, as in, no I'm not going.'

The White Spear took another slow step forward. She really was huge, more so in her great chunky armour. She seemed to fill the low room, blotting out all around her.

'Girl,' she said, 'it is a matter of time until the forces beyond the wall exhaust what patience they have for waiting, and enter this place in numbers, with the sole objective of your exsanguination and decapitation. The prince of Shenak has already offered a silver talent to the rider that brings him your head. Do you know how much that is?'

Javani shook her head, suddenly grateful that it was still attached.

'It's a fucking mountain-load of silver,' came Movos's voice from the cell. 'As in, a man could dig out a whole mountain and not ever collect so much.'

'Thank you, Guvuli,' the White Spear said with a nod, which he returned amiably enough. Her gaze fell back on Javani. 'You understand the importance of a prompt departure.'

'Your contract is to keep me alive, right?'

The White Spear took another step. Javani guessed she'd be able to lunge forward and scoop her up if she wished, but as yet she made no move.

'And deliver you to the court of the King of Kings.'

'But I need to be alive for you to do that, right?'

The White Spear's mouth twisted. 'Yes.'

'So number one objective for you is to protect me.'

'Yes.'

'And I'm staying here. So you'd better get ready to keep me whole if those riders break the gate.'

The White Spear's head tipped forward like a bull and her hands rose. 'I could simply *take* you—'

'And climb all the way back up to the ridge with me kicking and screaming on your back? Good luck with that. It'd be a lot easier if I cooperate.'

The hands paused. 'You would cooperate?'

Javani's heart was beating very fast. The light-headedness had returned, and now it felt as if words were tumbling out of her mouth without passing even briefly through her brain. 'If you help me now, if you help *us* . . . I'll go with you, willingly. After.'

The big woman's head rocked back, her chin raised, pale eyes narrow. The tattoo on her cheek flexed and pinched. 'After?'

'When it's safe. When Lazant is . . . gone.'

Oh Javani, came a voice in her head, what have you done?

Kurush watched the gate open with a mixture of exhilaration and dread. Out stepped Ree, looking dusty and dirty yet somehow upright and proud, her manner alone enough to set his teeth on edge. Beside him, the prince shifted in his saddle, then leaned forward to check the seating of the monstrous crossbow one more time. 'Khalida,' he murmured, 'stay ready. We cannot be certain the rules of decorum will be observed.'

The woman at his flank gave no visible reaction, but Kurush felt that something passed between them nonetheless. He'd come to resent the way they communicated, in half-sentences, gestures, even facial expressions – each seemed to have perfect understanding of the other's intentions. For a long time he'd wondered if they were lovers. He thought of Roshana, the ambitious daughter of his late predecessor, of their own brief relationship, which he might charitably have termed 'tempestuous' had he been poetically inclined. Given that he had spent most of his time in Roshana's company – and no small amount of time outside it – trying to guess at her thoughts, he'd ultimately concluded that the prince and Khalida were not, in fact, carnally acquainted.

Which left only the conclusion that they had a miraculous professional understanding, a notion that infuriated him all the more.

'Are you coming, Guildmaster?'

Lazant had dismounted and was looking up at him in placid expectation. The lack of expression on the man's face told its own story; Kurush could smell his withheld judgement. He marshalled an insincere smile of his own and slid down from his mount, settling the sabre at his hip.

'Wouldn't do to keep our guest waiting, highness.'

'Indeed, Guildmaster.' Lazant offered him another bright, open smile. Kurush hated the smiles almost more than anything else. 'Indeed. Mother always said that manners are the mark of true nobility.'

They met a few paces before the gate, surrounded on all sides by Guild riders, withdrawn to a distance that could tenuously be considered discreet. Ree launched proceedings from a poor footing by performing a swaggering bow as the prince approached, her nose almost touching her shin.

'Acting Guildmaster,' she said as she rose. 'Are you going to try introducing us again, or are we beyond that level of pretence?'

Lazant's face had remained impassive, almost beatific, but Kurush was struggling to contain his own seething resentment. He was supposed to be in charge, the Guild riders answered to him, the Shenakar were mere observers. He should have got to speak first.

He drew in a long, dusty breath through his nose, pointedly

ignoring the woman at the gate, and turned to Lazant. 'Your highness,' he said, 'this is Ree. Still a dirt-grubbing horse-farmer.'

The angled sun made deep hollows of the prince's cheeks. 'I am grateful for a clearer light than our last meeting, within the dark of the Guildhouse.'

Ree was gazing back, her expression kept slightly unfocused. 'I seem to remember a passel of blades, and an urgent expression of demands.'

'I regret the urgency.'

'But not the demands?'

'You have clear sight of my purpose, my stakes are no mystery.'

'Indeed. Hence our current discourse.' Ree shifted her hips, standing sidelong. Lazant had shifted likewise, and the two faced each other like duellists. Kurush looked from one to the other, his uncertainty growing, and with it his anger. There was some kind of dance taking place here, some kind of ritual, and it was a mystery to him. What had the Shenakar said about Ree being a former diplomat? She seemed clued in to some kind of conversational two-step that was leaving Guildmaster Kurush on the sidelines.

'Hey,' he said, 'hey!'

They turned. Lazant's expression was blank, but Ree raised one eyebrow. Kurush swallowed, gestured towards the gate. 'Where's the kid?'

Ree's eyebrow flexed. 'Elsewhere, this morning.' She resumed her sparring pose, Lazant lined up before her. 'You requested this parley, prince of Shenak.'

'I did, Mistress . . . Ree, was it?'

Ree inclined her head.

'A local name?'

'Depending on the locality. Say your piece, prince of Shenak, while I keep my peace. Although I hazard I could wager a weight of silver on its mettle.'

Kurush's thick brows lowered. Wordplay irked him more than insolence, and insolent wordplay was enough to set steam from his ears.

'Very well, Local Ree.' The prince began walking in a small arc; opposite him, Ree matched his progress, as if the two of them were in slow orbit around a nondescript patch of blown red dirt. Overhead, buzzards circled, matching their progress with indolent ease, their distant cries ringing from the crags. 'I wish you to be clear on my purpose, and my dedication. You know I represent the throne of Shenak. You know my business is the very preservation of peace and order within the borders of my kingdom.'

'Yet your acts since arriving could hardly be described as peaceful.'

Lazant put one hand on his breastplate, the tips of his gauntlet leaving little bright streaks. 'Another regret. If I may – you *are* the child's mother . . . yes?'

Ree didn't hesitate. 'You have the wrong child. I have told you from the beginning. She is not who you seek.'

Lazant's moustache pulled wide in a benevolent smile. 'Then allow me a polite rephrasing. You are the woman in the reports, a practitioner and traveller, former consort to my late cousin?'

Kurush's eyes moved from one to the other. Ree was holding Lazant's gaze, eyes now in full focus.

'It's possible.'

'You are familiar with engines of state, and the nature of courtly politics.'

'More than I'd prefer.'

'Then you will understand that even the potential existence of a secret heir puts my kingdom, indeed the entire region, at tremendous risk. Unless I can excise that potentiality, Shenak may fall into civil war. Thousands, tens of thousands of lives could be lost, and countless more irrevocably ruined. A nation destroyed.'

'Yet still you speak in potentials. You have no way to know the future, prince of Shenak. Perhaps if you were to return home and simply declare no such heir exists – that you have checked, and are satisfied – your troubles would be over. We will swear that she will make no claim, never even come within a month's travel of the kingdom's borders. I could write you a declaration to that effect.'

Again, Lazant's indulgent smile stretched the gaunt beauty of his features. 'I fear you are not as familiar with the workings of the Shenakar court as you believe. You cannot believe that will suffice, not with a kingdom on the line.' He pursed his lips, his head tilted. 'Yet I can see why my cousin chose you.'

'I did my own choosing, prince of Shenak. Still do, when the occasion demands.'

'But your choice has brought us here.'

'She is not who you seek. I can't say it plain enough: you have made a mistake. Return home in satisfaction.'

'The throne of Shenak does not make mistakes, Mistress Ree.'

'The throne of Shenak murdered the wrong child in an alleyway.'

One hand was on Lazant's chin. 'An error, perhaps, but forgivable in the circumstances.'

'Not by me.' Ree came to a sudden stop. 'What is your goal here, prince of Shenak?'

Lazant ceased his movement likewise. 'My goal?'

'In calling this parley. You can't think to convince me to hand over the girl for you to slaughter her like a festival hog.'

'Perhaps not.'

Ree's eyes narrowed, flicking from him to Kurush, to Khalida, to the ring of riders. 'Then what game is in play here, little prince? Do you simply desire a moment with a more sparkling conversationalist than our Acting Guildmaster, or are you looking to drag and delay?'

Kurush's eyes darted up to the ridge behind them, and she caught the movement. She whirled. 'I think we have enjoyed enough of each other's company. This audience is at an end.'

Kurush's jaw clamped tight. It was too early yet, there'd been no signal from inside, no screams or sounds of combat. Ree was already turned, making for the gate.

'Mistress Ree,' Lazant called after her, 'permit me one last courtesy: to return your gift of plain speaking. At the conclusion of this parley, my indulgence will be spent, and I will do what I must to protect my kingdom. There will be no further intercessions. I would hate for you to misjudge the level of my devotion.'

'You have the wrong person, prince. Return to your kingdom,' she snapped. Kurush looked back at the ridge, at the rippled sheets of red rock that rose behind the old tower. He saw no movement. They needed more time. His hand dropped to his belt.

'Stop!' Kurush bellowed. 'Take not one more step, Ree.'

Slowly, she turned. 'Acting Guildmaster,' she said, eyes on the weapon in his hand. 'Do you, by some chance, want something?'

'Guildmaster Kurush, what are you doing?' Lazant hissed. Behind him, Khalida had taken two steps forward.

'Know what kind of crossbow this is, Ree?' Kurush snarled. 'This is a mechanical hand-bow. Fresh up from the workshops of Arowan, came with the caravan.' He waggled the weapon, brows furrowed in concentration at remembering her words from the Guildhouse cells. 'Small bolt, limited range, but I can assure you at this distance there's no weapon more comprehensive.'

'I know what it is, Kurush, you pox-riddled oaf. Your merry goons were shooting them at the wagon on the ride here.'

He didn't let her get to him. He wouldn't. 'Then you'll know to stay where the fuck you are.'

'Guildmaster, this is most impertinent. You cannot draw a weapon on her.'

'Camel-shit, this is just like at the Guildhouse. You had a dozen blades on her then, I'm just picking up the rope.'

'That was not beneath a flag of truce.'

Kurush took a bullish step forward. 'Well, I don't see a fucking flag now, do you?' He gestured with the hand-bow towards Ree. 'There's no one out here but us, and protocol is as I decide, thrice-damn it. I'm Guildmaster! Think anyone is going to raise a disputation on my fucking manners?'

Lazant's voice was warm oil in his ear. 'Indeed you are, Guildmaster. But—'

'These men answer to me! All of you answer to me!'

'So they do, Guildmaster, but we are in no hurry here. We can allow her to return to her scant fortifications at her leisure, it will make no difference in the end.'

Kurush took another step towards Ree, the hand-bow levelled at her sternum. 'I'll make her call the girl out,' he said. 'She'll do it, because if she don't she'll die right here in the dust. Hear that, Ree? I give the order, those riders behind me drop you like a lame mule. Think on that, why don't you?'

Ree was staring back at him, lips pursed. Unmoved. Brazen. Insolent.

'Call out the girl,' Kurush snarled.

TWENTY-THREE

'Little one!' Aki's voice preceded him from the stairway. 'Your adult is in— By the Goddess!'

He came to a skittering halt, hands fumbling at his belt, searching for something he could use as a weapon. When he found nothing, he snatched up a chunk of loose rock and brandished it over his head, other hand extended.

'Get away from her, Whitespear!' he called. 'Or I will fell you where you stand. Javani, run to me, run to me now.'

The big mercenary looked back at him with blank eyes, then turned to Javani, eyebrows raised.

'I'll handle this,' Javani said with a calming hand. 'Aki, relax, Mistress White Spear is helping us now.'

Aki's eyes were wide and darting, the rock trembling above his head. 'Helping? Why would the most fearsome raider in the south, the Implacable Slaughter herself, be lending assistance?'

Javani bit her lip. 'Because I've promised to go with her once Lazant is, I dunno, removed.'

'And what will Ree say to this, do you wonder?' Aki retorted. 'I do not see her clement acquiescence on the horizon.'

Javani set her jaw. 'It's not up to her. We can talk about it when she comes back.'

Aki blinked twice, and the stone sagged in his grip. 'That was what I was . . . Ree is in trouble. I went up to finish dressing your facsimile, as instructed – I will need your jacket as well, when it pleases you – and saw from the window. The Guildmaster has her at the sharp end of a hand-bow and looks to be waving a fond farewell to his senses.'

'What? What do you mean?'

Aki dropped his rock and spread his hands in useless supplication. 'Kurush will not let her depart the parley. He looks like he wants to kill her instead, or use the threat of so doing to force you into the open.' His eyes drifted past the mercenary to the battered corpse that lay half through the rent in the wall. 'By the Goddess, is that . . . Did they—'

Javani waved a hand. 'Yes, yes, they tried to come in via the cliff under cover of the parley. The White Spear met them on the ridge. But what are we going to do about Ree? Can we charge them and free her?'

'Little one, we are but two here, three if we include your new friend. They will cut her down, or us, the moment we throw open the gate.'

'What is there to discuss?' the White Spear rumbled. 'Leave the woman.'

'I'm not leaving her!' Javani cried. 'She's my mother!'

The White Spear turned her implacable pale gaze on her. 'What is the relevance of that statement?'

Aki took a step forward, puffed up like a bull turkey. 'A mother is a sacred being, to leave one's own mother to die—'

The White Spear's brow twitched, making the spear tattoo jump. 'A mother is a familial relationship, a result of successful breeding, and confers no special aura or significance.'

Javani pulled herself up to her full height, still somewhere around the White Spear's midriff. 'Maybe you'd feel different if you'd had children yourself.'

Again, the brow twitched, the spear dancing. 'I had many children. Most survived, and became part of the clan. It was long ago now, and when I had performed my duty for the clan, I chose my path, and came north.'

'You left your children behind?'

'I left my clan behind, some of whom I had birthed.'

Aki was staring, incredulous. 'And what if they need you? How will they find you?'

The woman's pale face rucked in utter incomprehension, and she stood in silence for a moment, before simply shaking her head.

'Well, maybe your children don't need you any more,' Javani snapped, 'but I need Ree. I'm not leaving her, and if you—'

'Very well.' The White Spear cleared her throat with a rumble like a distant avalanche. 'What is this facsimile you were dressing?'

Aki scratched at the back of his neck. 'A ruse, a creation of straw and sacking, to sow confusion in the ranks of their hunters.'

'Bring it to me.'

'What?'

'Hurry now. Before the chance is lost.'

Aki returned a moment later, the archery target floppy in his arms. It was, to be charitable, unconvincing. The White Spear stared at it for only a moment. 'Only a simpleton would be taken in by this. Child, remove your jacket.'

'But you said only a simpleton—'

'Quickly, if you wish to save your birth parent.'

Javani shrugged off her jacket, only to find the White Spear had plodded back to the rent in the wall, where the corpse of the Guild climber lay. She crouched beside the body, and with a short knife and nimble fingers swiftly removed his outer clothing and armour, then extended a hand for the jacket.

Trying to hide her discomfort, Javani complied. It could be her, she supposed, from a distance. He was slight, and they had similar hair. She tried not to look at the man's face.

'Wait! My sister prepared a little surprise,' Aki said as the White Spear scooped up the body and began roping it to herself, 'in case they should get too close.' He'd removed something from the sacking, and passed it to the mercenary with careful hands and murmured instructions.

Then she was ready to go. The giant southerner turned one

last time. 'We have an agreement, girl? Once this peril is resolved, you will accompany me to Shenak without complaint.'

Javani swallowed. Her throat tasted of burning bile. 'Once this is over, if you still want me, I will.'

The White Spear nodded. 'Then keep your head down.' And with a great sweep of her arm, she disappeared through the hole in the wall and was lost from sight.

Javani counted ten breaths, trying to slow her heart's gallop. 'Aki, hitch up the wagon. I think we're going to need it very soon.'

He stood there for a moment in mute surprise, as if trying to decide whether he should be taking orders from her. The ferocity of her expression seemed to tip the scales, and he bolted from the room.

'You've done it now, girl,' Movos Guvuli chuckled from his cell. 'Luck of the gods go with you, you're going to need it.'

She whirled on him. 'You,' she snapped, 'need to get out of here too. Come on, get up. Take ownership of your own life, will you? Go out and get your revenge, or go back to mining, or even robbing caravans if you must, but do *something* with the gift of an independent existence. You've got the rest of your life ahead of you and it's yours to control.'

Whatever effect she'd had on Aki rolled straight through to Movos, who pushed himself to his feet with a look she'd otherwise have classed as apologetic. 'Hells, girl, if it gets me from your sniping, I'll—'

'What's the trick, Guvuli? How were you going to get away?'

He gave a weary sigh then leaned forward on the bars. 'You were right, we were going through the mine. We'd race in there with the spoils and trigger a collapse, the entrance comes down, all presumed lost. But we stocked the cavern with supplies. A little time later, out we pop on the far side. Secret tunnel.'

'To the west?' Javani asked, near-breathless with excitement. 'To Arestan?'

'Well, westward, certainly, but you'd have to travel weeks underground to reach Arestan. No, we were taking the pass through the mountains.'

'There *is* a pass!'

He nodded. 'If you go south far enough, there's a way through. Paid a lot for this.' From inside his filthy coat, he pulled a tight roll of canvas. Javani recognised the charcoal markings on its outer face. He held it out to her. 'Here. I'm having a hard time escaping the notion you'll need this more than I.'

She took it, her breath hot in her lungs, unrolling it with the greatest reverence. There, drawn on the obverse, clear markings, peaks and canyons, roads and ravines. And a dotted path, travelling ever south and west.

'There are two banks of kegs, one each side in the entrance tunnel to the mine. Shantar put little caps on them, but they won't do a thing until they're woken. You need to crack the caps on each bank, let the air in, then pick up the spool and get as far away as your little legs can get you before you yank it. 'Twixt us, urchin, we never got to testing the blast, for I hope obvious reasons, so I've no idea if it'll actually work, or what it might do to that cavern if it does.' He scratched at the dried blood that caked his temple. 'You know, now I've come into the ownership of a nugget of perspective, the whole endeavour strikes me as near-unbearably risky. Funny, it really didn't seem that way at the time.'

She tucked the canvas roll inside her shirt, tight against her body. 'From where I am, Movos Guvuli, it's about the best option I've got.'

'Good luck to you, kid. Truly.'

'I'll get the key, it won't take—'

'Relax, girl,' he muttered, then shunted the edge of the bars with his palm. The ancient metal popped from its stone restraint, tottered and fell away. 'I'll save you the trouble.'

'You could have left at any point?'

He let the old rope drop from his wrists, spooling like shed snakeskin at his feet. 'Figured I had nowhere else to go. You go on, now, make your own exit. I'll be taking my own damned-by-gods time.'

'Right. Thanks.' She swallowed, her tongue electric in her mouth. 'What are you going to do now?'

One side of his mouth pulled up in a half-smile, his black beard bristling. 'Whatever I please.'

'See you, Guvuli.'

'See you, urchin. And mind those horses, will you?'

'Call her. You don't call her out, I'll drive this bolt through your skull and piss in the brain-hole.'

The prince was close to him now, moving crab-wise. 'Guildmaster, this is not necessary. The girl will be ours one way or another in a manner that does not require the besmirching of protocol.'

'Fuck your protocol! Out here, this is the frontier! This is the untamed, where the strong rule. And I am strong. I make the rules. And the rules say: call out the girl!'

The prince shook his head, baffled, incredulous. 'Guildmaster, there are rules of decency that should be observed for good reason! You are inflaming a situation that requires delicacy. Mother always said—'

'And what's so fucking delicate, your highness? The need to execute this woman's kid? Like that boy you cut in the alley? Was that a delicate situation, too?'

Lazant went quiet for a long breath, and when he spoke again there was a warning growl to his voice. 'You are overstepping, Guildmaster. I urge you to consider your future and make no further rash acts. You are eroding my faith in your investment in the success of our endeavour.'

Kurush turned to face the prince, keeping the hand-bow levelled at the motionless Ree. 'Consider my future? I'm doing nothing but! You need this as much as I do. This gets us the girl, and gets us all out of here. I'm doing what's best for us all! What's necessary!'

The prince's eyes were very wide, rims of white around the irises. Then he tossed a gauntleted hand. 'My patience is at an end,' he said sadly. 'Khalida!' He began striding back to his horse. Kurush couldn't see Khalida, which was odd as she'd been right next to the prince a moment before. She was probably already back at her horse. It didn't matter. He'd show them he was right. The girl would come out, her head would be his, and he'd present it to the prince in triumph. Or he'd shoot Ree down here and charge the ruin, drag the girl out himself. He was going to win.

He turned back to Ree, still fixed by the line of his bolt. 'Last chance, Ree. Call out the girl.'

She stared at him, then her gaze shifted and she was looking behind him. A small smile broke her impassive features.

'Stop smiling! Call out the girl!' He could feel the line of rage rising up his face, popping new sweat as it came. 'I'm Guildmaster, thrice-damn it.'

'Acting Guildmaster,' she retorted in a sharp little voice.

With a roar, Kurush went to pull the trigger just as something swept his legs from beneath him and he crashed to the dirt. The hand-bow flew from his grip. Coughing and reeling, he tried to roll but something sharp pinned him, a long blade at the end of a black haft, pressing against his shoulder just above the span of his breastplate. Khalida stood over him, framed by the cobalt morning sky, haloed by drifting cloud. Her gaze was entirely blank. She began to push down on the spear.

'There, up on the ridge!' the shout came from the edge of the line of riders.

'It's our—'

'It's the mercenary! And she has the girl!'

Shouts went up, and horses reared and stamped. Lazant's cry cut through them all. 'Two silver talents for the girl's head!'

The pressure vanished from Kurush's shoulder, and Khalida with it, then the sky was obscured by great drifting clouds of dust as hooves thundered away back down the trail. As their echoes died away, Kurush sat up, one hand against the back of his head, one probing the meat of his chest where the spear had pricked him.

He looked up just in time to see Ree bearing down on him, foot drawn back, then Kurush's world went black.

TWENTY-FOUR

Ree burst through the gate, bounding with only a mild limp from the kicking she'd given the prone Kurush.

'Anashe! Aki!' she bellowed, swivelling on the spot, eyes searching the dark of the tower interior, the gloom of the lean-to stables. 'The White Spear has her! How does the White Spear have her?'

Anashe's head poked out of the sprawling stable, her eyes wide with shock. Before she could respond, the kid came trotting into the courtyard's glare, one hand shielding her eyes. Aki travelled beside her.

Ree stared at her in disbelief. 'Kid?'

'Hi, Ma.'

Ree's eyes moved from the girl before her, up the cliff to the ridge, then away into the scorching sky. The conclusion was obvious.

'Aki's straw man?'

'Not exactly,' the kid said, a broad grin spreading across her grubby young face, 'but close enough.'

'How in nine hells did you get the White Spear to . . .' Ree rubbed at her temple. 'Never mind. They'll outrun her fast once the climbing's done. We've got a short time before they realise she's leading them a merry dance and head back this way . . .' She looked back over her shoulder at the gate and the dusty trail beyond. 'Some may leap ahead, they could double back any moment.'

Anashe had emerged from the stables. 'Is there any chance we can clear a path for the wagon on the south road?'

Ree was already cutting her off. 'None. It's worse up close. Even if we cut the horses loose and rode for it, we'll be nowhere before they return. There's only one way from here.'

'Just what I was thinking.' The kid was animated, her hands waving towards the wagon. 'We need to get out on the trail, head back towards the canyon. The road divides, and we can—'

Ree's hand snapped up. 'No. No, kid. I hoped it wouldn't come to this, but it's time to do what we talked about.'

'What? What did we talk about?'

'You weren't around, kid, but you inspired it. Aki, is the wagon ready to go? Don't look at her, look at me. Are we ready?'

'I have . . . that is, I have done what I can to repair the canopy and restore a modicum of the vehicle's plating, and hitched the horses. But—'

'And the other thing?' Ree added meaningfully.

He nodded, eyes grave. 'It is prepared.'

'What are you talking about, Ree? What are you going to do?'

'Kid, we don't have time to go into this now.'

Javani pushed herself between Ree and Aki. Anashe hovered off to one side, watching with sober eyes.

'Ree, I fixed it. Me! I got the White Spear to take off with the body, I saved you—'

'Didn't need saving, kid.'

'And I know how the Guvulis were going to get away. He told me, told me how to cut off pursuit by collapsing the mine entrance. He even gave me the map to the hidden pass, see? If you go south far enough, you can get through the mountains. See?'

'You can't trust a word he says, kid. It's too risky.'

'Then what's your plan? What are you going to do?'

'I'm going to stick that dummy on the wagon with me and ride for the bridge, and in full view of our Shenakar and his hunters, I am going to drive it into the canyon. They see you go over the edge, dead beyond doubt, they know their job is done.'

'*What?*' The kid's cheeks were flushed, and tears welled in her eyes. 'That's a *terrible* plan! It's far riskier!'

Ree put one hand on her shoulder. 'Not for you.'

The girl seized the hand with both of hers, gripping it tight. 'You want me to sit here, undefended, while you throw yourself off a canyon? What if they come back? What if they go down to inspect the wreckage? What if they don't think we're dead?'

'Oh, they'll think we're dead all right. There will be no doubt. But I'll jump clear, and you'll be safe here with Aki and Anashe.'

'No,' Anashe said, stepping forward from the shade. 'I cannot countenance this.'

'Thank you!' the kid exclaimed, her arms wide in exasperation, Ree's hand once more her own.

'You will need someone aboard the wagon to keep them from overrunning you. For the ruse to succeed, they must be close enough to believe the girl aboard, without getting close enough to determine that she is not.'

'Oh by the *gods!*' the kid shrieked.

'What are you saying, Anashe?' Ree asked, ignoring the kid's bellows.

'Aki can stay with the little one. I will accompany you.' She nodded at the wagon. 'I too made some preparations, and it would be . . . a shame to see them unused.'

'Now it is incumbent upon me to protest,' Aki cried, stepping forward himself.

'Is it too much to hope,' the kid muttered, 'that you might be protesting at the lunacy of this plan, or—'

'For you to depart on so deadly an undertaking while there are stories of our mother still to be heard, it is unconscionable . . .'

'I'll take it, I guess,' the kid sighed, her shoulders slumped.

'If you are lost, your stories are lost with you, and with them my chance to know my mother—'

'Aki. Aki, listen to me.' Ree took his hand in hers, meeting his gaze, feeling her hot breath in and out, the canter of her heartbeat, the throb of her battered feet. Why, she wondered, do they all keep looking to me for answers, for meaning, for absolution? I'm just a person, my own life littered with mistakes. And now I'm getting old. 'Do not fear for the stories. Stories spread from us, like ripples in a pool, carrying merrily on once their tellers are gone. Long after we are all food for worms, our stories will travel the world, echoing our deeds.'

He swallowed, his eyes wide and tearful. 'While this pleases me, I must understand who my mother was, it is imperative—'

'How long have you been chasing her memory, Aki? How many stories have you had, not just from me, but from the Commodore, from others on your travels? You already know what kind of person she was. She gave her life to save those she loved. Everything else is ephemera.' She gripped his hand in both of hers, holding his watery gaze. 'Do you understand? Do you realise that you already know your mother, that you carry her in you? That your quest is already complete?'

He couldn't answer, but he didn't look away.

'Now I'm asking you to keep safe the one I love, to be a protector, a guardian to her. They must not reach her. Keep them away, no matter what. Can you do this, Aki?'

He nodded, bowing his head. 'In the spirit of my mother, in the form of Ranu the Champion, it will be done,' he intoned. 'They shall not reach her. She wills it.'

'Good boy. She'd be so proud of you.' She kissed his cheek and pushed him gently away. 'Let's go.'

'You know when he says that,' Anashe murmured, so low that Ree suspected she was the only one to hear, 'he does not mean the Goddess. He means the spirit of our mother.'

Ree nodded. 'I guessed.'

'And Ree,' Aki said, regarding her with wide, serious eyes, 'should you survive this day, I hope that one day, too, you will complete your own quest, and permit yourself to be part of a family once more.'

Ree paused, her brows tight. 'What?'

'Hey!'

The kid reared in her path to the wagon, her voice the pitch of a buzzard's screech. 'Has everyone stopped listening to me again? Have I faded from existence and become part of the spirit world?'

'Kid, there's no time. Stay here. I'll get this done and come straight back.'

'I can help! My idea is better!' Her words became scratchy. 'When are you going to *trust* me?'

Ree felt something hot in her own chest, tasted metal at the back of her mouth. 'When the life to be gambled isn't yours.'

The tears bloomed from the girl's eyes, rolling down her cheeks and leaving dark streaks in the dust that matted her. She grabbed Ree's wrist, snatched up her hand again. 'How can you leave me behind? What if something happens to you? You're the only family I have, I can't . . . If you don't trust me to make decisions for myself, how can you trust me to live without you?'

When Ree spoke, her voice came thick and raw. 'This is the last time, kid, I promise. I get this done, then we chart a new path. Partners.'

She was squeezing the hand tight enough to block blood from Ree's fingers.

'What if you don't come back?'

'I'm coming back, kid. Sit tight. But I've got to go now, or all this will have been for nothing.' She attempted to ease her hand from the girl's grip, then turned her head. 'Aki?'

'Come, little one. We must hide, and wait.' He wrapped her, sobbing, in his arms.

The moment Javani's sweaty grip slipped, Ree wasted no time. She was aboard the wagon in three strides, scrabbling for the reins. The Guild riders had bolted off down the trail, then split; some had abandoned their horses and gone straight for the climb, others would be tracing up the long way around, hoping their speed would make up for the longer distance. She needed to give them sight of the wagon, just enough, draw them into a chase without letting them get close enough to spot the ruse. Or close enough to take her out, for that matter . . .

'Anashe! Is everything aboard?'

The specialist loped over. 'I have loaded a few items that may prove surprising for those who stray too close.' She put one hand on the wagon's side. 'I am ready.'

Ree rubbed at her brow, her eye. It was still sticky with unshed tears. 'Are you sure about this? Aki may need a hand watching the girl.'

Anashe gazed back at her, steady and unblinking. 'You will need help if you are to succeed. It is, I believe, what my mother would have done in my place.'

The hot feeling came rushing back through Ree's chest. 'That she would. But you listen, the moment this gets tight, the moment we face a turn, you are gone, understand? Don't compound your mother's sacrifice on my account, my life isn't worth yours.'

'That is my decision. And the child's might be.'

'Very well. Aki, the gate!'

It took him a long, exasperating period of struggling to pull the thing wide enough. The kid had fled inside the tower, hot-faced and snivelling, but there was no time to go after her, to try to explain, to impress upon her that this was the only way. The last time, Ree had said. She'd meant it, truly she had.

Then at last they were moving, wheeling around the broken courtyard before the broken tower, then with a jolt and a thump they were passing through the gateway and out on to the trail. Ree twisted on the bench, trying to peer over Anashe, past the bundled sacking of the dummy at the wagon's rear, trying to get one last glimpse of Javani, to wave, to say something, to lock eyes one more time with her daughter.

Her daughter.

The chance was gone before she even caught a glimpse, and then they were beyond the wall, cracking the reins and picking up speed, heading down the trail, and towards the canyon.

Enx had always been a good climber. As a boy, he'd scaled the impossible rocky towers that ringed the salt desert, acted as a scout on the lookout for caravans and travellers, ripe for the picking of his clan. As a young man, he'd gone south, and found clambering the irregular urban formations of the city no less rewarding – especially when the occupants of the upper floors assumed that the height of their dwellings would provide some measure of inherent protection from uninvited visitors. Of course, it couldn't have lasted; improper construction had done for him, and a slip and fall had been followed in short order by arrest, conviction and exile, and now long after the wounds had healed, his face bore the markings of a thief and rapist.

But he could still climb, and well – especially when motivated by the prospect of a mine's worth of silver. Even if he had to share it with the three other climbers labouring beneath him, he'd still be set for life, free of the Guild, his transit bond repurchased, the world his mollusc of choice. It wouldn't matter who held the Guild's seal then – they could get through as many Guildmasters as they liked. All he had to do was climb, then kill.

The heavens were shining fondly down on Enx. It was exactly what he was good at.

A crackle of falling stone below him drew his attention. Faranak was right at his heel, sweat sheening her corded muscles, her lips drawn back in a pitted grimace of effort. Enx scowled. He did not like Faranak. He didn't like anyone who wore Guild colours, himself included much of the time.

The ridge-top was close now, the cliff's gradient already flattening. Not far to go. Not long until he was a free man again, a free, rich, man. Enx's own teeth bared in a rictus grin, and he climbed.

Enx scrabbled up on to the ridge only a little ahead of Faranak, hunched and panting, his eyes hungry for the tracks of the woman they hunted. The tracks were broad and obvious, no attempt made to hide or disguise them, and Enx's grin widened. He set off at a run, Faranak still at his heel, silent but for the rasp of her breath and the crunch of her boots on the ridge's loose red earth. Scrub and shrub whipped at them as they ran, broken branches and deep footprints their clear path. From over his shoulder, Enx heard the grunts and gasps of the last two climbers completing their ascent; from the sounds they made, the cliff had wrecked them – Enx and Faranak might yet have their mark to themselves.

Enx considered letting her pass him, driving his trail-knife into her neck as she passed. They were a long way up now, away from the pack and their illustrious colleagues, and those who wore the Guild's gear had acquired a nasty habit of coming to sudden and savage ends in the last few days. Another lost figure up here would hardly invite much scrutiny, especially given the recent upheavals in the Guild's command structure. Heavens, the last time Enx had seen the Acting Guildmaster, he'd been pinned to the ground beneath the Shenakar woman's vicious spear. The chances of a serious investigation into Faranak's mysterious death, over and above the other losses they'd suffered, seemed pathetically remote. And by then he'd be long gone on a silver chariot.

The sun glinted from a dark and massive shape that bobbed ahead of them along the ridge-line, and Enx's thoughts of Faranak's assassination dissipated in an instant. The mercenary ahead of them was wrapped in black steel and almost farcically dangerous.

He'd be a fool not to let Faranak go first.

Enx slowed his pace as they closed on the huge, jogging mercenary, the girl's unconscious form in her arms. The ridge had broadened, joined with a thick mesa rich with wiry scrub, its corrugated edges capped with crumbled peaks lit red-gold by the climbing sun. He needed to hurry this up – they weren't far now from the winding trails that led back to the old mines, and there was a growing chance that some of his horse-bound contemporaries might yet come roaring up the mesa's far side. Enx was resigned to the possibility of sharing his prize with Faranak, should she yet live, and even with the two gimlets who'd made the climb behind them, but half a dozen saddle-monkeys was an unacceptable prospect.

Faranak was beside him, her sabre slung over her shoulder and hand-bow drawn, no longer running but still moving with brisk purpose. He let her edge ahead, reached one hand down to the trail-knife at his belt. Enx had eschewed the sabres at their distribution; he knew he was no sword-fighter, and not one to stay in the saddle for any length of time. His trail-knife though, with a blade as long as his forearm and almost as wide, was a weapon that suited him like an extension of his own body. All he needed to do was close the distance.

The crash of brush and breathless cursing alerted him to the arrival of their two errant colleagues, finally caught up from their ruinous climb. Their appearance no longer irked Enx; the more he considered the giant woman ahead, the more collateral he felt he might need.

They were close now, close enough to make out the scratches and dents in the great black shell of her armour, to see the bobbing of her thick braids, bunched and cabled at the back of her domed helmet. She held the girl before her, the occasional flash of dark hair or a dangling boot visible past her armoured elbows.

Enx signalled for the two new arrivals to draw and crank their hand-bows, then he fell in step behind Faranak. If the mercenary had noticed her pursuers, she'd made no change to her step or course. She continued her bouncing run, leaving great ruts in the dry earth, sending up puffs of amber dust, as the Guild's finest closed in around her.

That was close enough for Enx. Time to chance his arm. He dropped to one knee, squinted past Faranak and aimed the bow at the mercenary's massive back. He couldn't miss. He didn't have that much faith in the bow's efficacy – their great advantage was convenience, not armour-piercing – but it seemed worth a punt, on the off-chance the bolt buried itself in the woman's spine and saved them the somewhat perilous job of murdering her up close.

He loosed, and watched with an inward sigh as the bolt struck the small of the mercenary's back and spiralled away into the dust. He'd expected no better. The heavens had other plans for him, it seemed.

'That's far enough, sell-sword,' he called, attempting to style his failed shot as a warning. 'One more step and we punch through that dome of yours and let the buzzards feast on those pale brains.'

The woman rumbled to a halt, but didn't turn. The girl's boots hung limp in her arms – she had to be unconscious. Enx advanced slowly, attempting to work the crank on his hand-bow unsighted, as Faranak and the two others closed in around the woman with their near-useless bows raised.

'You're going to give us the girl,' Enx called, struggling with the crank as he tried to keep his eyes on the standing mercenary. 'You're going to lay her down and step away, and if the spirit of kindness finds our hearts then maybe we'll let you walk away from this.'

He couldn't get the crank to work, and with a snarl he looked down at the mechanism. As a result he missed whatever the mercenary did next, only hearing Faranak's murmured, 'The fuck is she doing? Gods!'

He looked up in time to see the girl sailing through the air towards them, limbs limp. He had barely enough time to register the flight, and the fact that she seemed to be smoking, then she hit the ground at his feet.

TWENTY-FIVE

The man who called himself Zakir Lazant, chosen prince of the highest house of the most royal court of the King of Kings of Shenak, reined in his mount at the trail's fork. Khalida reined in beside him without pause or question and waited to hear his thoughts. The last of the Guild riders slowed, hesitated, unsure if they should be racing off ahead after their comrades, or if there was something else afoot. Either way, they wished to follow the path that led to the silver, the same as every other gutless and faithless vagabond that they encountered beyond the borders of their kingdom, beyond even the thick rose walls of the royal city.

'Khalida,' the prince said, and she sat straighter in the saddle. It was unconscious, but she would not have stopped herself if she could. It had ever been thus, since their early days together. 'His faithful hound,' as one of the other graduates from the Persimmon Temple had dubbed her. Khalida hadn't killed the woman, but she'd taken the sight from one of her eyes, rendering her useless in their appointed path. The half-blind had been cast out not long after, and Khalida had continued to sit a little straighter at the prince's command. That one of her own eyes was now lost beneath bandages gave her no pause at all.

'Khalida,' he repeated, 'I sense I have acted rashly. That exchange with the woman, and the insensible behaviour of our erstwhile

Guildmaster, have driven me to imprudence. Mother always said I was too impulsive.'

Khalida bowed her head and said nothing. The prince was staring into the drifting dust beneath their mounts, his gaze lost in the whorls of floating powder.

'Mother . . . Mother. Is it possible that I have acted rashly in a greater sense, Khalida? We have travelled across sea and desert in pursuit of this child, to end her life that the kingdom might be spared, but could there have been truth to that woman's words? Would the viziers have accepted a denial?' He pulled at his moustache with one gauntlet, and a crack found his voice. 'Would they still?'

Khalida maintained her silence. She knew better than to answer the prince's rhetoric.

'We could yet return, Khalida, with or without a declaration. State our case as the woman said, that no such child exists, that we return with empty hands but our duty discharged. And Mother would say . . . Mother would say . . .'

Without realising it, Khalida had begun gritting her teeth. She remembered the last time she and the prince had returned empty-handed to his royal mother, the great hunting trip of eight summers before. Zakir had allowed decorum to guide him, permitted others to claim his kills in the order of their standing. On their return to the palace, word of his failure had already raced ahead, and his mother had refused to greet him, turning her back in full sight of the rest of the gathering. Zakir had stood adrift in a sea of whispering marble, snubbed and humiliated, Khalida useless at his side, still wondering where his father was. His mother only deigned to inform him of the man's death several days later.

Both Khalida and her prince had learned from that experience.

Zakir raised his head, taking a firm breath through his nose, his eyes once more burning with the passion of righteousness. 'No. Of course Mother is right: *the only certainty is death*. The child must die, and the claim with her. Only then can we return in triumph, in vindication. Only then will we avoid . . . disappointment.'

He swallowed, suddenly hoarse. Khalida kept her gaze fixed on the restless hooves of his mount.

The prince cleared his throat, blinking hard. 'The mercenary's arrival was a convenience for those we had cornered,' he continued, as if he had never interrupted the thought, 'and there is a non-negligible prospect that a ruse or scheme was involved. We should not devote all the forces we have to a single—'

The explosion lit the hillside above them, and the boom echoed across the rugged hills and rearing red peaks. Khalida snapped her head around in time to watch the debris fall around the billowing bloom of black smoke that rose from the mesa above the trail.

The prince had one gauntlet shielding his eyes. 'Khalida, would you say you saw more limbs in that blast than one person would traditionally comprise?'

'I would, Zakir.'

'I fear our riders on the ridge have been outplayed.'

'I fear so, Zakir.'

He gestured to the hesitant riders, five in all, who were staring up at the smoking ridge with a heady mix of horror and confusion. 'All of you! Quickly, ride with Khalida back to the watchtower. You may yet catch them off-guard. Remember, two silver talents to the rider who brings me the girl's head.'

Khalida snapped the riders to her flank with a gesture and a flash of her good eye, but the silver promise had done the bulk of the work. 'And you, Zakir?'

'I will ride on, try to gather those who went ahead, and those who have come since.' He leaned forward, patting the great mechanical crossbow that nestled at the pommel of his saddle. 'Should she be yet ahead, or somehow pass you, I will be waiting. Ride true, my Shade.'

She bowed her head and offered a prayer of devotion, then with a kick of her heels and an echoing cry, Khalida and the riders went thundering back up the trail.

* * *

Aki stepped back from the well in the courtyard's shaded corner, satisfied. That would be enough water to last the day, and if it came to it, the night as well. He stooped to collect the old buckets, one in each hand, and walked slowly back to the watchtower, trying not to spill.

'Little one,' he called, putting the buckets down inside the cool of the threshold. 'I have brought water. You should drink. We lose much through our tears.'

There came no reply from the bundled blankets at the foot of the stairs. The girl had been huddled there since the wagon had torn out into the bright day, leaving only dust and emptiness in its wake.

'I will tend to our captive,' he told the bundle, and walked one of the buckets to the rear of the tower where the bandit Guvuli was confined.

A moment later, he came running back, bucketless. 'Little one, the bandit is gone! Javani—'

He pulled back the blanket. The straw and sacking dummy gurned facelessly back.

Aki stared.

'Oh, by the *Goddess*—'

Aki ran.

Kurush's head hurt, and he was very thirsty. He went to sit up, then remembered what had happened the last time he'd tried. The memory of Ree looming over him, her boot lashing his face . . . Still prone, he reached a cautious hand to his throbbing cheek and winced. It came away sticky. His whole head was thumping in time with his pulse, and it felt as if his jaw no longer fitted together properly. He went to roll and found that his entire midriff squealed with pain. She'd given his ribs and kidneys a going over too, it seemed.

Kurush snarled into the dust. He already owed Ree more than she could ever survive, but his horizons had now moved to an entirely new plane of vengeance. She wouldn't get far, he knew that. The Shenakar would hunt her, his riders would hunt her, and there was nowhere she could run to in the whole of the expanse that would be safe. All he had to do was catch up before the chance to exact his own revenge was gone. Perhaps he'd make her watch as they took the girl apart, piece by piece. He began to dwell on the precise order and logistics of his retribution, but the thudding pain in his skull reminded him that he was curled in the dust beside an empty trail, and several practical steps yet stood between him and delivering justice.

For a start, he needed to stand up without vomiting, and a tentative early effort delivered inauspicious results. His horse was gone, the trail empty, the watchtower gate wide open. The clouds of choking powdered earth that seemed to hang in the air were clearing, and the wide rutted tracks that curled away from the old watchtower and off up the trail triggered something in his fractured memory. They'd set off in the wagon, the woman . . . but not the girl? The girl was up on the cliff. Or was she? He'd heard voices, footsteps . . . Ree was a crafty snake, there was every chance she'd pulled some kind of shenanigan. Hadn't she manipulated him at the parley, driven him to rage, cost him the prince's favour?

Wincing from the pain in his skull and ribs, hissing with the effort, Kurush began to pull himself along on his elbows and knees. The Guildmaster's seal dug into his abdomen. His hand-bow lay beside him in the dirt and he snatched it up, tucked it at the back of his belt. Soon the pain would pass, soon he'd stand. There were horses somewhere, maybe further up the trail, he could hear them whinny and stamp. Ree's tricks wouldn't save her when the time came. And when Kurush brought the prince the girl's head, two silver talents would be his, and the rest would follow.

Kurush crawled faster.

Kurush approached the horses at the cliff foot slowly, not wanting to spook them and send them galloping off up the trail. They were untied, milling and cropping at the wiry brush at the trailside, all four abandoned in a hurry by their riders; they must have thrown themselves straight up the banked, striated cliff from there in their haste to crest the ridge. He recognised the closest animal as belonging to Enx. That made sense: Enx was a stringy, stabby little climber, he'd have scuttled off up the red rock like a lizard. The others that went with him, good luck to them.

Kurush adjusted the seal at his belt, relieving some of the pressure it exerted on his gut. He was angry at the riders, angry that they'd left him in the dirt while they took to the trail in pursuit of the girl, but he could understand them at least. Two silver talents was enough to turn even a zealot's head, and those who worked enforcement for the Guild were anything but devoted.

He'd take Enx's horse. The little bastard was probably up on the cliff right now, chasing after that black-armoured beast of a mercenary. Odds were sharp that Enx wouldn't be returning for the animal any time soon, if at all. And besides, Enx owed Kurush. He was Guildmaster, gods be damned. They all owed him. There would be a reckoning, once this matter was settled. He'd straighten them out, a parting gift before he set sail for his new life as a courtier and raconteur.

A sound like thunder rumbled from somewhere overhead, and the horses shied and stamped, wide-eyed. They began to shuffle and step, heads tossing.

'Easy now, easy now,' Kurush urged through gritted teeth, arms wide as he inched closer. What in hells was that? It had sounded like . . . like . . .

The animals bolted, the first running to his right, then the others came in a rush. He snatched at them, vainly trying to grab their flying reins, a loose stirrup, then his jaw hit the rough rock and he was prone, arm outstretched, as a fresh shock of agony blew up from his ribs.

'Fuck,' he snarled. 'Gods of piss and pondscum!'

The horses had kicked up more of the infernal dust, and Kurush pushed himself up to his knees, coughing and wiping at his mouth with his no-less-dusty sleeve. Sweat dripped from his eyebrows, stinging his eyes, and everything was stuck to everything else. The seal was digging into his gut again.

Kurush squinted into the drifting cloud. A horse was stopped a little way up the trail, standing not twenty strides from him, its head up and ears twitching. He blinked and squinted again. It was his very own horse, fully tacked and supply-loaded, waterskins slung pendulous from the saddle. It must have wandered up the trail after the others when they set off, the disloyal shit.

Kurush's rough tongue slid over cracked lips. He stood with an inward gasp, then took a slow step, then another, grimacing at the effort. The horse was looking away from him, its reins out of view. He approached it sidelong, keeping away from its rump lest it spook and kick out, but as best out of its eyeline as he could manage. Yes, it was his all right. He recognised his cascade of trophies, and the fresh spur scabs along its flanks. If the damned thing would simply obey, they'd both have an easier time.

He was within four strides when he saw the man's legs on the other side of the horse.

He staggered back, almost slipping over, scrabbling for the hand-bow at his belt.

'Who's there?' he cried, cranking the mechanism with urgent fingers. 'Show yourself, gods damn you.'

The legs stiffened, then slowly they began walking around the horse. Short legs, thick legs, legs with a strange gait, a rolling limp. Familiar legs.

Movos Guvuli stepped around the horse's head, the reins tight in his hand. In his other, the mangled half-hand, he held a small rock.

Kurush raised the bow, angered at the tremble in his grip. 'Walk back from the horse. That's my horse, a Guild horse, and I'll be taking it.'

Guvuli stared back with glittering eyes. Dried blood crusted one side of his squat, hairy face, and trail dust powdered his mass of curls. 'I let her go, she's apt to up and bolt like her pals.'

Kurush felt heat rising in his cheeks, the back of his neck popping sweat. How could he sweat more than he was already? He swallowed again, although it did nothing to shift the dust that coated his throat. He was so close to the waterskins now, he could almost reach out and grab one. 'You'll release it or I'll put this bolt through your neck and take the reins from your dying fingers.'

Guvuli's teeth were as bleak as his smile. 'You a man who fancies his aim with one of them little bows? Word is you're as like to punch a hole through our friend here –' he patted the horse with the hand that held the reins – 'as my good self.' He'd not yet stepped clear of the horse, and the animal's movements were still wild and unpredictable.

Kurush found he was snarling again.

'Pass me the reins, then, you fucking pirate.'

'No.'

'What in hells do you mean, no?'

'In the sense that I'm disinclined to be handing over any animal to a man who calls a fine mare like this "it", or treats her so poorly. I found this young lady running free, and I'm minded to return her to the Guildhouse in town. Hardly more than a day's ride from here, unless I take the roundabout route. Could be there's a reward for her safe return.'

Kurush could feel a vein thumping at his temple, threatening to burst clear of his skull and drench the cliff side in his blood. He rammed his hand beneath the breastplate, dug around and dragged out the Guildmaster's seal. 'You see this? You see this, bandit? I'm the fucking Guildmaster. That animal is mine, as are all the others that bear the Guild's brand in these parts. Give me what is mine by right!'

'I'm quite aware of your station, *Guildmaster*.' Guvuli spat the last word. 'Or did you forget your public delight in ordering the hanging of my brothers?'

'And I'd do it again!' roared Kurush. 'I'd string up a thousand of your kind in the Guild's name, parasites and vexations all. A justified act of cleaning.'

Guvuli's thick eyebrows dropped, his eyes like glittering gems in darkness. 'Seems to me right now that the only difference between parasites like me and parasites like you is that seal in your hand.'

'That,' Kurush replied with a vicious grin, 'and this.' He raised the hand-bow.

He didn't even see Guvuli's hand move, but the rock whipped through the air between them and whacked into Kurush's throbbing skull. With a cry he dropped the seal, his hand flying to his temple as he flinched away, waving the bow in Guvuli's direction.

Then the horse twisted, and his bleary view was filled with rump and tail. Before he could move, before he could stagger clear, Guvuli whistled and two iron-shod hooves smashed into his breastplate.

Breathless and gasping, Kurush reeled, the bow flying from his grip, spinning away into the rocks at the cliff's foot. He crashed sprawling back to the dust, breastplate buckled, at least one rib broken, honking like a wild pig on a lance. There he lay groaning and spitting blood, as the bandit slowly led the horse back around towards the trail, then began adjusting the stirrups.

'Wait,' Kurush croaked. He sucked in a halting breath and tried again. 'Wait, Guvuli.' He raised a scuffed hand towards the bandit. Out of view, his other hand inched towards where the hand-bow had fallen, skittered into a narrow crevice in a pile of loose rock. 'I could ride with you. We could ride together.'

Guvuli checked one stirrup, then moved to adjust the other. 'I think not, Guildmaster. Strikes a man as hardly fair on this poor girl, no less for this accursed heat, yes? Besides, those other beasts won't have run far, a skilled tracker could find one without too great a distress. Worst case, town's a couple of days' walk from here. Follow the creek beds, you might even find some water along the way.'

Kurush stretched his grasping hand further. The crevice wasn't that deep, the bow couldn't have got that far inside. He couldn't let the bandit leave until the bow was back in his grasp. 'Wait, wait,' he gasped, 'what are you going to do?'

Guvuli checked the tack, then started unstringing Kurush's trophies. Coils of blackened ears spooled in the dust between his boots. 'Do, Guildmaster? I haven't right decided. But I'll be making plans.'

Not if I have anything to do with it, Kurush growled to himself. His fingers brushed the stock of the weapon, and he fought to keep the triumph from his face.

Guvuli's gaze shifted to where Kurush lay, to where his hand was buried in the rock. 'Wouldn't go delving in there were I you, Guildmaster. A fella who sticks his hand in a cobra nest is apt to get himself bit.'

Kurush's hand closed around the bow and his face lit with exultation. 'And that's why— *uff* . . .'

He barely felt it the first couple of times, the merest pricks on the back of his hand, but now he was having trouble keeping hold of the bow, then dragging it clear. His hand was sluggish and distant, and then came the flare of burning agony.

Movos Guvuli led the horse around, then paused, and stooped to retrieve something from the rocky ground. Ignoring the rising, delirious screams of the Acting Guildmaster, he hauled himself up into the saddle with a grunt and clicked the horse forwards.

'Nobody ever listens to me,' muttered Movos Guvuli, and set off up the trail.

TWENTY-SIX

The wind whipped at Ree as the wagon picked up speed, heavy wheels clattering over the dust and broken stone, the whole vehicle creaking and jolting in time to the thunder of the wheels.

'Anashe, you're clear what's required?'

Anashe's voice carried over the punishing noise of the wagon's transit from behind her, where she made her preparations. 'They must think the girl is aboard with us and give chase, but neither discover she is not, nor prevent your exit from the wagon before it reaches the canyon.'

'One silver talent to you,' muttered Ree. 'There's a dip this side of the canyon, just before the drop, and that's where I'll be making my leap. You need to be gone long before then.'

Anashe poked her head through the gap in the canopy, watching the red rock hurtling beneath them. 'You will, perhaps, consider slowing the horses before I do?'

Ree offered her a brilliant smile. 'If the opportunity presents, Anashe my girl, if the opportunity presents.'

'I am touched by your commitment.' She ducked back into the wagon. 'I shall complete my preparations, then arrange the facsimile as if the child is with us, but hidden. They will not get close enough to see the lie.'

'Whatever it takes,' Ree said, her eyes on the jumping trail ahead.

They were almost clear of the walls of red rock, the way ahead opening out with a growing view of the plains beyond. That distant dark crease had to be the canyon. 'Whatever it takes.'

Khalida saw the rising dust cloud above the rocky bluffs long before the wagon hove into view, its wheels a blur and team already frothing.

'Ready arms,' she called to the five who rode behind her in loose formation, and drew up her double-headed spear from its mount by her saddle. The prince had suspected a trick, and from the speed they were moving he'd been right to do so. Even so, they might simply be in pursuit of the child as much as Zakir was, or even making a getaway while the chance was there. Khalida ruled nothing out. The prince had given no orders beyond finding the girl, so she would act with diligence and persistence, and see the job completed.

One of the riders was already surging off ahead, and she ordered him back with sharp words. 'They make haste towards us in that monstrous contraption. Take positions and prepare to match their speed. The girl is all that matters, nothing else.' She gestured with the spear. 'Determine whether the girl is aboard that vehicle. If she is, two silver talents to the rider who brings the prince her head.'

'And if she's not?' One of the riders drawled back, a seemingly genuine question despite the woman's drooping jaw. 'Do we kill them, or what?'

Khalida considered for a moment. 'Find the girl. Kill the girl. For the rest . . . as the fancy takes you.'

'Anashe, you'd better be ready because here they come!' Ree squinted, counting the riders as they curled out from either side of the trail. Four . . . no, five . . . shit, one more. Three either side, matching speed, running ahead and beside, and closing. 'Remember, don't let them get close enough to see the kid's not with us, and don't let them interfere with our escape.'

Anashe leaned forward from the wagon's rear. 'How fatal must our interactions be to achieve this?'

Ree looked back over her shoulder, through the body of the heavy wagon, past Anashe to where the final block of cargo lay tucked beneath its canvas. One way or another, the Shenakar were going to witness the wagon's inescapable destruction on the canyon floor, which meant there needed to be someone around to do the witnessing.

'Try not to kill them, just keep them at a distance. We need them to see what happens next.'

Anashe nodded, her face calm, her body poised and braced against the wagon's pillar. She was so like her mother. 'Should I kill the horses instead?'

Ree thought of Javani, her outraged disapproval at allowing animals to come to harm. She would not like this. 'If you can't just scare them off,' she sighed, and nodded.

The first riders were nearly on them, one haring in from the left, another two riding up behind. Ree caught only a glimpse as the riders ducked in and out of sight. 'Anashe, the rear!'

Anashe was already moving, loping through the wagon's near-empty body, scooping up a pair of the canisters she'd prepared. She cranked the hand-bow she'd adapted, fitting the first little canister into its modified string. It was really now more of a sling. She reached for the heavy candle that burned on the wagon's floor, lit the canister's taper, and strode to the wagon's rear.

The first rider snatched at her shot, sending her bolt well wide of the wagon in an unseemly rush. The second took a moment to aim, levelling his hand-bow on the crossed elbow of his other arm, lining up on the spare-framed woman who loomed from the wagon's canopy.

He took slightly too long. Anashe loosed her canister between the two horses, where it hit the dirt like a thunderclap, blasting chunks of rock and earth into the air and sending the horses reeling. One fell, crushing its rider beneath, the other bolted, bucking in a frenzy, sending the helpless rider to the dust.

Anashe stepped back into the wagon, and set about cranking the hand-bow once more. Another rider burst through the cloud, hunched in the saddle, hand-bow extended and bobbing, closing the distance to the wagon with shocking speed. Anashe dropped to one knee, set down the hand-bow and snatched up the spear she'd laid out. As the rider closed, she jumped up, steadied herself, then hurled. The spear flew from her arm, scything through the air and connecting with the rider's breastplate with a mighty crunch. The woman slumped and dropped from the saddle, and her horse steadily gave up the chase.

With a satisfied nod to herself, Anashe returned to cranking the hand-bow.

A plink from the plated wood by Ree's head signalled a new rider's arrival.

'On my right!'

At least Aki had braced the plating well enough to provide some protection from the sides. The horses steamed on ahead of her, straining and foaming beneath their harnesses in the hot sun. *You poor bastards*, Ree thought, *your suffering is nearly over*. She looked ahead. The canyon was in view now, a crinkled line of darkness in the blasted beige landscape ahead, the red rock falling away either side. *A little more, just a little more*.

Anashe leaned past and out over the plating, shot a hand-bow, then ducked back inside. A crack and a horse's scream followed an instant later, and the rider to their right was gone. A bolt whizzed past Ree's nose, burying itself in the wood of the opposite plate.

She counted. Four riders down, two left, unless . . . She put up a hand to shield her eyes from the glare of the morning sun. The earth ahead shimmered with heat, the canyon seeming to dance, the plains and the mountains beyond wavering as if seen through water. But she knew what she saw. She knew *who* she saw.

'Nine fucking hells,' she growled. 'Second batch ahead.'

This was going to get worse before it got better.

Khalida and the last of her riders ran parallel to the wagon's path, watching its course. Those aboard were defending themselves with gusto, but she'd seen no sign of their target and was inclined to call off the pursuit. They were heading for the crossroads, then presumably down to the half-repaired bridge in an attempt to return to the town. They would find few friends there; although Khalida had left the supposed Guildmaster to die in the dirt beyond the watchtower, she was in no doubt that the Guild would readily provide a replacement who was every bit as amenable to their offerings as the last. Control of the Guild meant control of the town. Those on the wagon would be resolved soon enough. One way or another.

Wait.

There.

Movement, a small head, in the dark of the wagon's canopy, little more than a bundle of blankets. Hidden. Cowering.

The girl was aboard after all.

The incantation sprang to her lips without thought. She marked the child with her words, fixing her in the centre of her mind. So marked, she would be drawn to the child, inexorably, intractably. Now it was only a matter of time.

Khalida hefted her spear and dug in her spurs.

'Ree,' Anashe called, 'on the left!'

Ree yanked the reins, driving the team wide and sending the wagon ploughing across the trail, throwing up a great billow of dust across the oncoming riders. One of the horses stumbled, slinging its rider clear as it turned a hoof, then resuming the chase unencumbered. The last rider pulled wide to avoid the wagon's roll, then surged forward towards its rear.

'It is the Shade,' Anashe said, watching the rider's progress, then ducked back into the wagon body with her modified hand-bow gripped tight. 'She means to get aboard.'

Ree peered through the haze ahead. The second line of riders wasn't advancing; they were lying in wait, blocking the trail down to the damaged bridge. Her mouth pulled in a mirthless little smile. They were going to get quite the surprise when the wagon rocketed past them and flew out over the canyon. And then the *coup de grâce* . . .

'Anashe, we've got a moment or two. Get rid of our last chaser then start planning your exit.'

'Are you sure you know what you are doing?' she said in a voice that barely carried above the wagon's clattering roar.

'As much as anything else I've ever done. Now move. I can slow the team for a moment but don't want to lose too much momentum.'

'Goddess grant you strength,' she said, and ducked back.

'Thanks, I suppose,' Ree muttered, hunching back over the reins. Then, after a moment: 'You too.'

Khalida's horse was flagging, to her disgust. These local animals had none of the beauty and endurance of Shenakar mounts, and once more she rued the loss of those they'd brought across the sea with them, exchanged for those screeching, honking beasts that had carried them across the salt desert. The wagon rumbled on, its stout team pulling with more strength and purpose than the tired nag beneath her could have mustered on its best day. Her nostrils flared. Those horses had been selected for the purpose of hauling the monstrous wagon. If she didn't catch it very soon, she'd have to cut her animal's throat and walk back to Zakir in disgrace.

Khalida did not do disgrace.

She beat at the horse with her spear, leaving shallow gashes on its flank, and the beast squealed and darted forward with the last of its strength, making for the wagon's juddering rear. The dark beneath the canopy, where she'd seen the bundle. The quarry.

Khalida was upright in the stirrups, bent forward with reins in one hand, the spear in the other, praying the cracked and sand-bitten leather would bear her full weight as she made her approach. The horse was fit to burst as the wagon loomed in her vision, the dust from its wide wheels thick in her eye, hair and throat. She couldn't spare a hand to tweak up her dust mask; the choking air would be overcome by willpower alone.

A figure appeared beneath the canopy, not the child but one of the defenders, the woman who'd slung those fire-blasts at the first of her riders. She looked vaguely familiar, and had a weapon in her hand. Khalida wouldn't give her the time to aim. Locking her legs against the foaming horse, she tensed and flung her spear at the woman. She didn't care if it struck home. Whipping the reins against the horse, she at last drew alongside the wagon's tailboard. One leg hooked over the saddle, then she was away, clinging to the wagon's canopy with her knife between her teeth. With a flexing swing she was inside the gloom of the canopy, feet solid against the rocking boards. Behind her, the exhausted horse faltered and dropped, lost somewhere in the driving plume of red dust that trailed the wagon like a divine marker.

The wagon's interior was murky, punctuated by the occasional dusty shaft of light from the slashes or bolt-holes in the battered canopy. The rumbling floor was busy with lumps and canvas-wrapped objects, even the occasional small keg rolling loose. Khalida remained crouched, watching for movement. Her spear lay not far within, and its bladed tip looked darkened. Khalida removed the knife from her teeth and smiled. It looked as if she'd found a mark after all.

The woman reared from behind the canvas, a sabre in her hand, and took a wild swing at Khalida. Khalida read it all the way, launching herself under the blade and forwards, rolling to collect her spear. She stood to find the woman before her, one hand to a bleeding shoulder, the sabre twirling in the other. Khalida's good eye widened only a fraction as realisation dawned: one of the guides, the sister who had led them across the expanse. What she was doing here, why she was defending the wagon, none of it mattered to Khalida. Somewhere in this rocking, shaking darkened shed on wheels was the child she needed. She would have to deal with this obstacle promptly.

As she came at her again, Khalida darted across the wagon, hopping up onto the canvas-wrapped bundle. Some of the canvas moved and her footing slipped, but the guide was wrong-footed by her sudden drop and failed to capitalise. Then the wagon hit a rut or pit in the trail, sending everything within momentarily up in the air, the fighters included, and the guide came down heavily too close to the tailboard. Khalida pounced, powering forward with her spear leading, swiping and jabbing and driving the woman further off-balance. Two more half-blocked parries and she was reeling. Khalida feinted a lunge, then delivered a hard kick to the guide's abdomen. With a cry, she tumbled over the tailboard and disappeared.

Khalida turned, triumphant. The child was somewhere inside this wagon, huddled and trembling, and Khalida would corner her, and finally finish—

Something hard and heavy hit her square in the face, and she pinioned over the tailboard and into the billowing dust.

Sweat was dripping into Ree's eyes, her arms and shoulders ached, her whole body shaken almost to jelly by the wagon's rampaging passage along the uneven trail. The riders ahead were ever clearer in her vision, arrayed in a loose line across the path down to the bridge. They either meant to block the horses or stick enough hand-bow bolts in them and her to render the wagon inert.

Ree pulled her mouth once more into her grim smile. They were in for a surprise when she veered away, and the plated panels either side of her bench would fend off any of those little bolts they sent after her. All she needed to do was barrel close enough to draw them, then leap clear as the wagon dropped over the lip. Gravity would do the rest. Plus the little extra she had in the back.

She craned her neck around. 'Anashe, you'd better be ready, it's time to—'

She saw no sign of Anashe. She'd got out already. Her grim smile took on a more genuine cast, and she realised a part of her inner tension had unwound. Anashe was clear, Aki and the kid were safe back in the watchtower, and she had her audience for the big finish. All she needed to do now was pull it off.

'Come on, old girl,' she murmured to herself. 'You've done more with less.'

'Who are you talking to? The horses won't hear you if you're muttering.' A figure slipped through the awning and squeezed in beside her on the bench. 'I got rid of Khalida, by the way. No need to thank me.'

Ree stared, transfixed, her heart a fist of agony in her chest and a tide of bile rushing up the back of her throat like a volcanic eruption.

'What?' said Javani.

TWENTY-SEVEN

Berev, Kurush's erstwhile lieutenant, sat nervously on his horse, watching the Shenakar prince sidelong. The man was motionless in the morning's growing heat, on foot beside his horse, watching the dust-throwing speck at the foot of the red rocks become a dust-throwing blur. The distance and the haze made it hard to make out much beyond the certainty that a wagon was heading their way, a big one, inevitably the same wagon they'd chased from the desert's edge the day before. Occasionally they'd seen shapes that could have been horses and riders weaving in and out of its rippling trail, but now they seemed to have fallen away.

Berev was part of the group who'd been sent back to town for reinforcements and fresh horses, and had only recently caught up with what remained of the Guild's hunting team. He couldn't see Kurush anywhere, or Enx, or most of those he expected, and nobody would tell him what was going on. They all sat in silence, deferring to the Shenakar prince, so Berev did too. A steady drip of riders was still coming up the trail over the 'repaired' bridge behind them, a mish-mash of mounts and equipment, hunting bows and looted gear, not even a hint of Guild affiliation about them. There was no point asking what brought them. News of the Shenakar silver had spread far.

The Shenakar prince himself just stood and watched, one hand on his long moustache. The sun overhead made dark pits of his cheeks, rigid lines of the muscles of his jaw; even Berev, who preferred a bit of meat on the bone, had to admit he was a mighty good-looking fellow. He didn't even seem to be sweating. Such was the level of his concentration that Berev couldn't bring himself to remove his hat and beat away the insects that buzzed ceaselessly around him. His own clothes were black with sweat, his burnished Guild breastplate thick with trail grime, and it was taking all the willpower he could muster not to guzzle the waterskin at his saddle-point. He was exhausted from the night ride and the morning's gallop on top of the previous day's exertions, he was uncertain to ulcerous anxiety of the location of his Guildmaster and his chain of command, and he was extremely itchy.

The Shenakar moved at last, reacting to something that was lost to Berev's fading eyesight. 'She is there,' he murmured. 'She is there. They deduced the bridge was restored, and they mean to flee across it.'

He pulled his horse forward by the reins, then with a combination of terse commands and a firm hand, he made it kneel. Berev watched in uneasy astonishment. There was something deeply wrong about seeing one of the Guild mounts responding to a foreigner's commands, especially to do something so unnatural. He looked around, mouth half-open, searching for some measure of reassurance in the eyes of the other riders, some agreement that what they were seeing was against what was right.

None would even look, their eyes fixed on the rocky plain ahead. Berev closed his mouth.

The Shenakar drew a long and heavy crossbow from his saddle-mount, a wicked-looking thing of wood and horn and steel and gears, and laid it across the horse's shoulder. Berev watched in mute agitation as he cranked it, loaded it, then sighted along it. The Shenakar gave another sharp command, and the beast before him went completely still. All around was silence, but for the chirping of insects and the distant call of carrion birds.

Berev swallowed, tasting only the dust that coated his mouth, and swept his gaze to the onrushing wagon.

* * *

'What in nine hells are you—'

'It wasn't safe to stay at—'

'How could this be safer? We're—'

'The dummy was unconvincing, they need to see me or—'

'They're convinced enough, just look ahead!'

The bolt slammed into the canopy pillar above Javani's head.

'What in hells was that?' she squealed, recoiling, hands raised.

'Get down!' Ree yelled, pushing her almost off the bench in her haste. 'The bastard, the crossbow-thieving bastard!'

Javani cowered, huddled against her mother. 'I'm getting back in the back.'

'Hang on.' Ree hauled the reins across, pulling the team wide. The wagon began to tilt on its axles as it turned, curling away from the winding trail down to the broken bridge, making instead for the rocky shelf that preceded the canyon's sheer drop. An arrow whistled just wide of where they sat.

'Why would you . . . Argh, kid, you've ruined everything!'

'Why?' Javani was halfway to scrambling back beneath the canopy. 'This was always a terrible plan! You think you're going to jump clear as this thing goes over the edge, that you'll live, that they won't comb the cliffs? That you'll walk back to us afterwards, no water, no mount, no supplies?'

Another arrow whipped through the canopy and out the other side, leaving a jagged rent, and Javani ducked down again with a shriek.

'No,' Ree growled, her eyes fixed on the rough ground ahead, arms locked tight on the reins.

'So what were you thinking?' Javani called back from her prone position on the wagon floor.

A bolt slammed against the armoured panel beside Ree with a thunderous clang, and she gasped.

Javani poked her head up. 'Ree? What were you thinking? How were you going to get out of this?'

Ree was no longer concentrating on the path ahead, but looking down at her leg. Sweat beaded on her brow. 'You need to get off this wagon right away,' she said in a ragged voice.

'Ree?' Javani crawled forward, poking her head through to the bench. 'What is it?'

A dark stain was flooding down Ree's calf. The bolt had punched through the side panel and buried itself in her leg. 'Gods, you're hurt!'

Ree turned her head, and her eyes were wide and wild. 'You need to jump clear. I'll slow the wagon as we reach the shelf, but only for a moment.'

'No! I'm not leaving you!'

'Kid, it's time to go!'

Another arrow whiffled through the canopy, although this time the angle suggested its shooter was out of position.

'No!'

Ree gripped Javani's shoulder with iron fingers. 'Kid, listen to me. You wanted to know how I was going to stop them combing the wreckage? There wasn't going to fucking be any.'

Javani could barely speak. 'What?'

'That's why it was so important you stay behind. That's why I wanted you nowhere near this wagon when the time came.' She wiped at an eye with the hand that held the reins. 'I packed the rest of that blasting powder into the back of this thing, along with one of Anashe's little surprises. We've soaked fuses in oil, all it's going to take is a spark. They won't go sniffing around the remains because when this thing hits the canyon floor it's going to burst like a sunrise, you understand? No survivors!'

Tears stung Javani's eyes. 'You were planning to kill yourself?'

Ree released the grip, waved her away. 'Hells, no! I fancied myself to jump clear at the last. But now . . .' Her gaze returned to the bolt in her leg.

'Can you get free?'

'I'm pinned, kid. Get ready to jump, there's a patch of brush ahead that might break your fall and give you somewhere to hide.'

'I told you, no! I'm not leaving you now, not when you're hurt, not when . . . when . . . when you're finally being honest with me! After how you've treated me my whole life, to throw me away now . . .'

'Throw you away?' Ree looked at her with wide and gleaming eyes. 'How could you think that?'

Javani merely gestured at the wagon, the bolt in her leg, the approaching canyon edge.

'Kid, I didn't intend it but I would die for you, you have to understand . . .' Ree swallowed. 'Remember, the greatest love is a mother giving her life for a child—'

'Horseshit! What happened to being prudent?' Javani snapped. 'Playing everything safe?'

'I *was* being prudent – with you!'

'Hardly,' Javani scoffed. 'You left me alone with Aki, he's hardly godly protection. Only a simpleton would have been taken in by that dummy.'

'I've been trying to keep you safe your whole life, running and hiding—'

'This isn't how you atone for being a lacklustre parent!' Javani yelled. 'Or abandoning your friends, or the specialists' ma, or whatever it was. You can't make up for abandoning people by abandoning me now!' She took a hard-edged breath. 'I want you to be around for me. I want us to get to know each other, properly. I want you to be my *ma!*'

'Kid, listen—'

Javani met her wavering gaze with all the force of her own. 'No, it's time for you to listen, *long* past time. You've never trusted me to make my own decisions, let alone weigh in on yours, yet all my life you've moaned about how important agency is, how important it is to control your own destiny and dictate your own path.' She gestured to the wounded leg, which was bleeding with some enthusiasm. 'Look where following your own path got you.'

Ree's eyebrows went up, and one corner of her mouth went with them. She was beginning to look a little pale. She moved to speak but Javani got there first.

'Stop trying to do everything yourself, and start trusting your daughter. After all, who raised me?' She cracked a flash of a grin.

'Now turn the wagon, right away. Get back on the trail but follow the back route down to the abandoned mines.'

Ree began to shake her head. 'The Old Scar again? Kid—'

'Hush!' Javani scrambled around, peered out through the rear of the canopy. 'They're chasing, and their horses are a lot fresher than ours. We need to get there ahead of them to stand any chance at all. And we can have a look at that leg along the way.'

'But—'

'We stick with your plan, we both die, maybe soon, maybe in a while, but we're gone as a pair, you hear me?' She plucked a tightly rolled canvas bundle from her shirt and waved it under Ree's nose. 'We follow my plan, we might just make it west, to a new life in paradise. I know which I'd prefer. Now turn the thrice-damned wagon!'

Ree swallowed, shook her head, and hauled on the reins.

Dust mask pulled up as high as it would go, Berev gave chase. It was what everyone else was doing. Already both Guild riders and the local irregulars were pulling ahead of him, ahead even of the monomaniac Shenakar and his beast of a crossbow. He still held it, riding hunched, one hand on the reins, the weapon at his shoulder, his wordless pursuit inspiring the others. That or the promise of a mountain of silver, Berev supposed.

Still no sign of Kurush or the rest of the crew, as they galloped after the hulking wagon and its choking trail and the great rock walls closed in alongside them once more. Berev had hoped they'd be making for the plains. He'd have preferred the plains, or even the desert. There wasn't much to look at, admittedly, and the sun could thump you like a bastard out there, but the mountain trails were twisty and steep and he couldn't shake the feeling that something was *watching* him from the heights above.

They were making for the Cut, back around to where the old mines had flared and failed, where Berev himself had once spent a winter hauling ore. Then he'd let his thirst get away from him, been dragged into too many games of tiles with Kurush and his budding crew, found himself drawn to a life that involved strapping on a burnished breastplate and paying meaningful visits to smallholdings over descending into the crushing dark to grub for nuggets. Officially, the pay wasn't as good, but somehow Kurush had found ways to reward them. After all, wasn't that the point of ascending into management?

And now the gods-cursed wagon and its gods-cursed passengers were dragging them back through the red rock, back to mining country. Berev relaxed in the saddle, allowing the other riders to pass.

Then again, he thought, two silver talents was an awful, awful lot.

Berev leaned forward and put the spurs to his horse.

Khalida rolled in dust. She'd lost track of the wagon, somewhere in her violent tumble, and the impact on the speeding earth had jarred and scuffed her, leaving her vessel scraped and bloodied. What was it that had hit her? Something hard and wooden and banded in iron. A small keg?

She'd kept hold of her double-bladed spear at least, wrapped tight in her fist and pressed against her body, and as her bruising progress slowed she bunched her legs and prepared to stand. The woman she'd kicked from the wagon would be out there somewhere in the swirling cloud, but her priority was the vehicle and its passenger. She had to follow it, to catch up. She was already too far from Zakir, too far and failing.

She sprang to her feet, spear in hand, ignoring the protests of the damaged fringes of her vessel. The rumble of wheels and thunder of hooves filled the air, the tracks along the powdered trail were deep and clear, her path of pursuit was obvious.

Khalida stilled her breath, tensed, and listened.

A horse was nearby, riderless and wandering, lost in the cloud. And with it . . . footsteps and soft words. The guide was taking the horse. This would not do. She had to move fast, before the chance was gone. Abandoning caution, Khalida charged.

The woman burst through the dust cloud, the sabre arcing at knee level as she lunged. She'd heard the approach, but it didn't matter.

Khalida swung her spear low and pivoted, turning the worst of the sabre's force and pulling her legs clear as the blade bounced across. She threw out a semi-serious counterstroke with the spear's other end, but her attention was fixed on the drifting amber fog to her right. There, over the departing cries of chasing horse and riders, the soft crunch of hoof-beats. Had the horse spooked? Another rider? One of those thought lost in their initial pursuit?

Unlikely.

The gelding erupted from the swirling dust, streaked and foaming, and its rider leapt, an ancient lance in his grip. But Khalida was ready. Khalida was always ready. She danced backwards on scuffed legs as the lance whistled a hand's span wide of her, and the man landed opposite the sabre-wielding woman. It surprised Khalida not a jot that the new arrival was the brother, although the why of it all was not hers to reason.

They looked at each other sidelong.

'Aki,' the sister exclaimed, 'what are you . . .'

'My . . .' the brother said, his eyes wide, his breathing heavy.

Then, in unison, each said, 'Where is the child?'

Each, in turn, looked up and into the drifting dust cloud, the deep rutted tracks that led on towards the canyon, then lurched away from it.

'They have not . . .'

'Indeed, they have not. Matters appear to have changed, my sister.'

Khalida took a step, then braced to turn.

'Stop her!' the woman yelled, her voice sharp and waspish. The man charged, throwing himself into Khalida's path, the ancient lance in his hand flexing as he whipped it around. The woman circled her, trying to get behind, trying to catch her in their claws.

Khalida glanced from one to the other, then slid her hands to the centre of her spear. With a flick and a twist she unlocked the two halves, and a moment later she had a short, bladed half-spear in each hand. Her talons were free. They would not delay her long.

The man stared at her blades, eyes jumping from one to the other then back to Khalida herself. 'You show yourself at last,' he said, his voice almost reverent in the dying clamour of pursuit. Khalida said nothing, her functioning eye glancing from him to the woman and back. They had travelled together for weeks on their journey to Kazeraz, if without particular closeness, but the notion that she had somehow hidden herself from him was perplexing.

'Xalot, minion of Usdohr,' he intoned, 'creature of spite and spine. Two long and pointed blades, the horn and the stinging tail. I see you, wearing the skin of the Goddess's children. Know now that you have met your doom: I stand before you as the incarnation of Ranu the Champion, fated to return you to the pit below!'

Khalida heard the woman sigh. 'For the love of the Goddess, Aki, shut. Up.'

'Am I not become Ranu of the First, the champion and liberator, confronting the demon?' He shook the lance in his hand. 'Goddess guide my spear of—'

'For once, will you stop your mouth?' the woman near-screamed. 'How is it you can lose the one thing—'

Khalida lunged, flashing out at the woman with her near-sided blade. Despite her cries, the woman ducked away, and Khalida spun to face the man as he struck. She read the thrust as if warned a week in advance: it was a false blow, designed to draw her focus while the woman slashed from behind. Khalida drew back from his weapon, spinning to face the woman as her sabre arced. Once predicted, the strike was easy to parry. Khalida theorised that the two fought as some kind of team. Their stances were mirrored, their styles matched. She would be alert to more of such tricks.

She danced sideways, ignoring the wounded complaints of her vessel, and tracked the man's path, reading his next blow. They would try to strike her together, and the man had reach. That would not do. She half stepped back, then twisted sideways, swinging both talons with great force. They met at the half of the man's lance, snapping it in a swirl of splinters as he tried to bring it to bear on her.

He howled, which surprised her. She'd made no contact with his skin.

The woman drew up short, eyes wide, nostrils quivering. 'Aki, are you hurt?'

'How can I be Ranu of the First without a divine spear?' Shaking his head, he tossed the ruined haft and pulled a long knife from a sheath on his back. 'But perhaps the Goddess will—'

'You are a damned-by-gods fool and you deserve to have this woman kill you!'

Khalida was inclined to agree. The man should never have dismounted, he lost both height and so much more – the ancient lance was not a weapon to be wielded up close. Khalida risked a flicked glance. The wagon was ever-receding. This would *not* do.

The man came in low, as the woman had before him, then drove up from the ground with his long knife extended. There was no chance to block, Khalida could only throw herself backwards as the blade whistled through the thick air where her chest had been. She ducked and rolled, rose once more to batter away the woman's dancing cuts, then swung high with one talon and low with the second to drive the man a step back. It was all the space she needed.

Khalida ran.

TWENTY-EIGHT

The wagon weaved back up the trail, red rock rising on either side. The Guild riders had been slow on the uptake, too puzzled by the wagon's apparent direct line for a drop off the canyon then sudden lurch back to safety to engage in prompt pursuit, but now they were closing.

The kid had the reins while Ree probed at her wound. The bolt had burst through both wood and plating and come to rest most of the way through her calf. Its barbed head hadn't come through clean, however, and enough of its length remained on the exterior that pulling it through seemed distinctly unlikely. She didn't much fancy trying to slip her trail-knife between leg and panel and saw through the shaft – plus it would make removing the thing later that much more of an ordeal.

Assuming there was a later.

On the bright side, the bleeding had slowed to a dull trickle, and she'd done her best to bind around the thing with the cleanest cloth Javani could salvage. The kid was intent on making it to that old mine of hers, the one bandits had supposedly rigged to collapse, because they supposedly had a secret exit through the hillside and enough supplies to wait out the law. She shook her head at the futility of it. But then, had her idea really been any better?

'How is it?' The kid was trying to keep the horses central as the wagon rumbled up the trail, winding between ever-higher formations of red rock. The sun was high now, and they flew in and out of sudden, plunging gloom as the trail twisted beneath the jutting rocks' irregular shade. 'Can you get free? When we get to the mine, we're going to need to—'

Something landed on the wagon, something heavy that bowed the canopy struts and made a sound like a thunderclap. Ree and the kid turned in unison, panic etching their faces. A point of light appeared in the drooping centre of the canopy roof, then widened in a great slash, flooding the wagon's interior with light. Through the slash came a massive dark shape, crashing to the wagon floor like a black steel beetle.

The beetle unfolded, limbs extending, sat up and removed its helmet.

'Gods,' the kid murmured, 'it can't be . . .'

The waving glare from the rent in the canopy roof cast the White Spear in a strange, undulating light, the tattoo down her cheek like a split in her skull. She was dented and bloodied but seemed otherwise whole.

'Stay back, mercenary,' Ree snarled, attempting to grab the sword at her hip while still impaled on the bolt. 'I don't know just what—'

'Ree, relax,' the kid urged, one hand up. 'She's friendly.'

Ree could feel her eyebrow climbing over her skull. 'Friendly?'

'We have . . . an understanding. We're in no position to choose our allies, remember?'

'Kid, what in nine hells did you—'

'Later, all right, Ma? Later.'

Ma. The word stung her into silence. The mercenary clambered up to her knees and shuffled forward.

'You caught up,' the kid said over her shoulder, still steering the seemingly tireless team.

The White Spear nodded. She was breathing hard, sweat-streaked, her armour coated in dark patches and sticky dust. 'After the distraction,' she said in her sing-song speech, 'it was clear that you were not yet safe. I am here to keep you safe.'

'You jumped from the rocks?'

'I had followed your progress from the ridge.' She turned her heavy head. 'Riders are coming up behind, they may catch us soon. Do you have weapons or ordnance?'

The kid gestured. 'My ma packed some blasting powder back there. There might also be a couple of Anashe's surprises left.'

The woman nodded and slid back from view.

'Kid,' Ree hissed, 'what is she talking about, keeping you safe? What did you promise her?'

Javani put up a firm hand. 'Later. All right?'

Ree had no idea what the feeling was that flooded her, but it wasn't merely impotent rage. Some of it had to be pride.

'What in hells was that?' Berev called to the rider next to him, a narrow, toothless woman he thought might be called Goli. They were closing on the wagon now, eating at the distance with every hoof-beat, and already the lead riders were brandishing their hand-bows in anticipation. Berev and Goli were towards the rear of the chasing pack, a group that had to number twenty or more by now, thundering after the wagon in the dust-choked Cut through the mountains' edge.

Goli offered him a one-shouldered shrug, meaning potentially that she didn't know, that she'd missed it, or that she'd not even heard the question. She doubled forwards, spurring her mount, and made to catch up with the leaders. The silver was weighing heavily on the minds of the chasing riders, but Berev found himself content not to be on the front line. It was impossible to be certain through the eye-gritting dust that roared through the air, but *something* had dropped from the rock onto the wagon's canopy and disappeared inside, something huge and dark. Yet the wagon rolled on, unaffected. Berev thought again of his nameless fear, his feelings of being watched from ruck and ridge-top. Were those in the wagon in league with the spirits of the mountain?

Something appeared in the rear of the wagon's canopy, indistinct through the churning haze thrown up by the vehicle's heavy wheels. To Berev, it was too big to be human, black of limb and ferocious of face, a creature of screams and nightmares. The riders ahead of him, however, seemed far from perturbed. Those at the head of the pack gave great cries, spurring forward, surging to close the distance between their champing mounts and the shuddering wagon.

Berev's pulse quickened. If those ahead were unafraid, he should be too. He dug in his own spurs, wiped dust from his streaming eyes as he hunched over the reins. In a moment he'd reach for his hand-bow and get cranking. Maybe there'd be some silver for old Berev after all.

He saw Goli go racing ahead of the pack, her horse flying over the rocky ground; keeping an easy pace for the early pursuit had let her steal a march on the leaders after all. Berev was close enough now to pick out some detail from the hefty figure at the wagon's rear. A bleached southern woman in black armour, oversized but all too human. She seemed to be holding something in one hand.

Goli closed the distance, her hand-bow extended, her aim true. She loosed. Her bolt whipped through the churning air and struck the black-armoured woman in the centre of her chest. Berev's emotions travelled with the bolt, elation at the precision of her strike, a sudden rush of furious envy at the thought of her claiming the reward in its entirety, then relief-muddled shock as the broken bolt fell away into the billowing dust.

Goli rode on, arm still extended, gummy mouth open even as the roiling powdered earth coated her. The woman on the wagon did something with her hand, then hurled the object she'd been holding. In the next instant, Goli disappeared. Berev flinched back from the blast of force that ripped Goli and her horse from view in a shower of rock and glutinous spray. Something that might have been a fetlock went pinwheeling past him and struck the woman to his left. She dropped from her horse without a sound. Other riders shouted and veered, horses screamed as thick black smoke rolled up from the bloodied crater where Goli had, until that point, existed in one place.

'Fast!' cried a rider a little ahead of Berev, a man he didn't recognise, whipping at a mangy-looking plains pony: one of the town drifters who'd come to join the hunt. 'Before she raises another!'

The man galloped ahead on his wall-eyed mount, two similar-looking types in pursuit. Berev's horse had been spooked by the explosion but he was horseman enough to keep it straight and running – the other runners had eased its nerves, as panic hadn't spread through the chasing herd. But now a doubt was in his mind, enough of a doubt that he eased back in the saddle once more, letting the distance grow between him and the weaving wagon.

The three riders got within a dozen strides, waving what looked like spears and axes as they closed, before the black-armoured woman reappeared. Again, she hurled something from beneath the canopy. This time, it hit the lead rider square in the chest, knocking him back in the saddle and sending his spear tumbling from his hand. He had a moment to stare down at the object as his comrades drew level: a smoking keg of blasting powder.

This time, the explosion battered the cliff wall beside them, showering the riders with serrated chunks of red rock and setting a great collapse in motion as the survivors raced to get clear. Berev heard the Shenakar prince's voice as they galloped through the rushing wall of dust ahead.

'Keep back! Keep back from the wagon, you poor fools!'

Convinced he'd survived the immediate danger, Berev rode in beside the prince who had fallen back to a canter. The wagon was drifting ahead of them again up the winding trail, weaving from one side to the other, threatening to smash any would-be passers against the steep rock that rose at either side. He looked back at the pack emerging from the chaos of the falling rock. Their numbers were diminished, but there were still more than enough riders in pursuit to bring the wagon to a necessary end.

Berev grimaced. More than enough riders to want a share of the reward too. Perhaps a little more pack-thinning wouldn't be too terrible.

Another pair of riders came up alongside, then spurred on to catch up with the receding wagon. The Shenakar barked at them to hold.

'No. We are too confined in this gulch. Another of those blasts could block it entirely.' The crossbow stowed on his saddle, he raised a gauntleted hand. 'Hold at this distance. This terrain will not last. When the ground opens,' he closed the hand into a fist, '*surround* them.'

'And this here mountain of silver for a girl's head,' one of the riders called, 'that's real?'

'For the right girl,' the Shenakar replied, 'you will drown in it.'

Berev felt a shiver run through him, through his legs and into his tired mount. At last, his luck was changing.

'They are falling back.' The southern woman's giant, helmetless head jutted through the canopy between Javani and Ree, thick cables of braids swinging with the wagon's movement.

'We beat them? They're giving up?' Javani couldn't keep the hope from her voice.

'No.' The syllable went through her rising optimism like a harpoon. 'They fear the kegs. This path is narrow, they cannot evade.'

Javani looked ahead. They were over the hump now, winding down the mountainous Cut towards the fringe of the plains. Already she saw rising bands of grey, beige and tired green ahead, wavering in the haze. It wouldn't be long before they left the sharp walls of rock behind, then they'd have to cross the rolling sweep of the foothills to reach the Old Scar's canyon. That was open country.

'And when the path isn't narrow?'

'They will come again, likely all at once. You have some kind of plan, I believe?'

'Say,' came Ree's voice from the edge of the wagon's bench, 'if it's not too much trouble, now the immediate danger of being carved into carmine strips has passed, could we do something about the fact my fucking leg is nailed to the fucking wagon?'

The White Spear leaned forward to look, almost smothering Javani in a mass of armour and hair.

'I will attend to this,' she rumbled. Then, after a moment more's consideration. 'It will not be straightforward.'

'You don't say.'

'Do you have something to bite on? You may find it helps to . . . take your mind off things.'

Javani rummaged, finding a torn piece of leather strapping, which she offered as a token to her increasingly pallid mother.

'Here,' she said, pressing herself alongside on the bench, the canvas map in her hands. 'You can look at this. You know, during – to take your mind off.'

Ree took the map with trembling fingers. 'What is this, kid?'

'It's the secret pass, the map. This is how we get west. Through the mine, and over the mountains.'

Ree gazed blearily at the markings, sweat plastering her hair to her skin. 'You don't say.'

'Are you ready?' rumbled the White Spear from over Javani's shoulder. 'It will hurt.'

Ree's smile was weak but fire danced in her eyes.

'Doesn't everything?'

TWENTY-NINE

Fierce sunlight broke over them as at last the wagon burst clear of the winding trail, casting the unfolding ground ahead in sharp relief, every crease in the terrain a hard black line. Foothills stretched before them, undulating, their surface dust pegged by grasses and deep-rooted things. You could hardly call it pasture, but it was enough for the cattle herds, both wild and branded, that roamed over that broken land in the heat of summer. A few creatures dotted the plain now, grazing aimlessly, the nearest looking up in slow surprise at the wagon's appearance.

'I can see it!' Javani called in excitement, hands slick and trembling on the damp reins. 'I can see the Old Scar canyon!'

Ree put a weak hand on her shoulder. Her leg was now clear and bandaged, but her clothes were thick with blood, and she was pale and sweaty, seemingly lacking the strength to resist the wagon's violent motion. 'Good work, kid. Hard part's done now.'

'We just need to get there ahead of them, then we can—'

The White Spear loomed over them once more. 'Here they come. As expected.'

Ree waved her on with a delicate gesture. 'Perhaps you might be inclined to arrest their progress. Explosively.'

Something that was almost a smile bent the spear tattoo on her cheek. 'Perhaps I would.'

Javani twisted on the bench. 'How many more kegs are back there? Are there enough?'

The woman met her gaze with eyes that returned nothing. 'There are more than there will be time to use.'

Javani swallowed. 'Right. Luck of the gods to you.'

The woman's heavy brow dropped in puzzlement. 'My gods grant no favours,' she said, then vanished back within.

Berev rode as close to the prince as he could manage. In the absence of anyone pretending to Guild hierarchy, not only did he seem to be in charge, but he also held the purse strings of whatever reward was coming, and Berev wanted to make sure the Shenakar was unimpeachably aware of his own contribution on ending the fugitives' run. Also, when the man said stop, it was wise to stop, as Goli's abrupt deconstruction had shown.

As they cleared the shadow of the last of the looming, sheer cliffs and rode into the open, Berev saw the prince quicken his pace, moving to a full gallop. Berev spurred his own mount alongside, conscious of the widening line of riders in his periphery, expanding over the rugged ground now freed of the trail's constriction. To his right were some of the Guild riders he recognised, if only by sight; to the left, a collection of chancers and hoodlums, some of their mounts struggling to keep up the pace. Good. Berev pulled down his mask to spit into the blurring scrub. The more they left behind, the greater his share would be.

They were closing on the wagon, already the detail of its torn and ragged canopy clear to Berev's squinting eye. The hill grass, at least, reduced the volume of infernal dust the wagon kicked up into the cobalt sky, and that of the scattering, thud-footed cattle spooked by its passage that were now lumbering into motion in its wake.

The prince slowed their pace once more, the riders either side of him almost managing a semblance of discipline.

'Does each of you remember your instruction?' he called, turning his head one way then the other and raising one gauntleted hand.

A series of nods, grunts and calls came from along the line. Berev felt a tingling in his gut, a hot, sharp feeling of excitement and . . . *hunger*. It was a stroke of luck so many of the crew had ridden through the night; as a result, they had not just the numbers, but also all the equipment they needed to execute the prince's plan.

The prince clenched his fist and dropped his arm. 'Ride!' he bellowed.

The outermost riders galloped away first, then those a little inside, until their line was like an inverted flight of birds. Berev kept his place beside the prince, watching him closely as they once more broke into a gallop, tearing up the distance between the riders and the wagon.

The prince rode hard, bent double, fully off the saddle. One hand gripped the reins, while the other inched forward, towards the great mechanical crossbow.

Berev swallowed, then pulled up his mask. He was about to get paid.

Khalida ran. She prided herself on not just her speed, but her endurance too. It had been several years since she left the marble walls of the Persimmon Temple behind her for the last time, but she had not allowed her vessel to waste. She had drilled and trained, marched and run under heavy load, spent the moments not at Zakir's side delivering his urgent correspondence by hand and by foot. Her vessel was an engine of exertion, honed and fired, and she knew of no living soul that could equal her.

Yet somehow, they were keeping up.

She risked another look over her shoulder as she vaulted a tumble of fallen rock, feeling a sullen burn in her legs, a rawness to her breath that only grew with each pounding stride. It should not have come to this. She should have left them in the dust after the first lighting sprint, and had they burned themselves up in trying to chase, then her long, easy lope would leave them coughing out their lungs as ascent and distance scoured them. Had that thrice-cursed horse wandered in the right direction, they would be little more than memories to her now.

But they were still there. Both of them. She lacked the time to read their expressions, but both were keeping pace and stride, running side-by-side, clearing obstacles in unison. Khalida breathed hard, a feeling like acid growing in her chest. If she did not drop them soon, eventually she would hit her vessel's limits. At that stage, she could only turn and fight, and hope their labours had taken more from them than her.

She shook her head, showering fresh sweat into the baking air. It made no sense. A lifetime of preparation and training, her soul withdrawn so the vessel might exceed mortal limits, to perform her duty at a level no mortal could surpass . . . No one could catch her. No one should catch her.

She cleared a rocky bend in the trail and saw the riderless horse ahead, cropping at a hitherto resilient briar at the trailside.

Khalida's grimace became a grin with only the slightest tweak.

No one would catch her.

Ree swung back around the panel, favouring her damaged leg, and slumped back down beside Javani. 'Give me the reins, kid.'

'You sure? You up to it?'

Ree nodded towards the wagon's rear. 'Think our southern friend could use some able-bodied assistance.'

Javani passed the reins over, and with barely a pause to shake life into her cramping hands turned and crawled back beneath the canopy. The White Spear stood on the shaking wagon-bed, one arm on a pillar, a heavy keg of blasting powder at her feet. She'd uncovered several more on the far side, the canvas bundle Ree had prepared torn clear. The big woman turned her head at Javani's approach, braids dancing from the wagon's rattle.

'They have learned,' she said in her rumbling voice. 'A pity.' The spear tattoo on her face stretched as she offered something like a smile. 'But it was no challenge before, yes?'

Javani nodded, failing to muster a smile of her own. She'd cheerfully have taken a profoundly unchallenging experience over this, any day. 'What can I do?'

The White Spear nodded at the kegs in the corner. 'Roll one to me when I ask.' She knelt to begin work on the keg at her feet.

Javani swallowed, nodded again, crouched down to crawl across the wagon. 'I can do that,' she said, to herself as much as to her companion. 'I can do that.'

'Here they come.'

The riders were in a line, but the leading edges were curling in, encircling the wagon from behind. She counted eight, ten, more, maybe two dozen racing through the wagon's rising trail. Behind them, hazy through the dust, ran a scattered handful of galloping cattle, confused at all the sound and movement of the chase and trying to join in. At the line's centre rode a determined figure, his half-cloak streaming behind him, his hair flowing in the wind.

Javani's eyes narrowed. Zakir Lazant.

'We begin,' muttered the White Spear as she stood. Something sparked and hissed in the wagon's gloom, and a tail of curling black smoke began to rise from the keg. The White Spear stepped to the canopy's edge, braced to hurl the smoking keg at their pursuers.

Javani was still watching Lazant, her eyes fixed on him as if chained. He was fully upright in the stirrups now, the reins flapping loose, in his hands something long and dark, pressed to his shoulder—

Ree's crossbow.

'Look out!' Javani cried, throwing herself down. The White Spear turned as the bolt ripped through the air and punched through the keg in her hands. The keg's far side splintered and split, showering a stream of black powder over the wagon floor.

The White Spear stared down at the ruptured keg. It was still smoking.

'Get rid of it, for the sake of the gods!' Javani screamed.

Almost as an afterthought, the White Spear tossed the ruined keg from the wagon. It puffed into flaming air before it hit the ground, igniting its drooping trail. The wagon's tailboard burst into flame. From behind came the alarmed honks of the running cattle, and the thud of their flight for the distant rise.

'Put it out!' Javani shrieked, 'put it out! There's powder everywhere!'

This time the White Spear needed no prompting. She grabbed at the torn canvas and set about beating the flames, while Javani joined in alongside. The wagon-bed was dusted with corns of blasting powder, a great black smear of it leading towards stacked kegs at the side. If that powder catches, Javani thought, then up go the kegs, and us with them.

'Ree!' she called towards the wagon bench. 'Ree! Are we close?'

She got no answer, squinting through the haze of sweat and adrenaline to the canopy's far end. Was the figure on the bench slumped over? Had Ree passed out, or worse? Were they now—

Some secondary part of her brain that normally kept track of timing the cooking of eggs roared to the front of her consciousness with a thought that was essentially a packaged scream, but which if unpacked would have read 'it has now been enough time for Lazant to crank, reload and aim the crossbow, and you should get down.'

Javani dropped to the wagon's floor with a yelp, trying to squawk a warning as she did so. The White Spear beat at the last of the flames one more time, then something made a sullen clunking noise and she sat heavily down next to Javani.

'Hmm,' the White Spear said.

Javani looked up through soot-covered fingers.

'Hmm,' the White Spear said again. A bolt protruded from the joint of her arm, punched through the previously impenetrable black metal. Javani didn't see blood, but she knew that meant nothing.

'Are you all right?'

The White Spear reached up a hand and tapped at the bolt, then grimaced. 'This,' she rumbled, 'will be expensive.'

Javani stuck her head up high enough to check the rear board was no longer aflame. 'The fire's out, let's get back under cover before he sticks another in us.'

Without checking to see if the woman was following, she scrabbled back away from the canopy's edge, away from Lazant and the crossbow's reach. Despite the great gash in the canopy roof and the slashes and puncture holes in its sides, it still felt safe. Safer than being in full sight of the Shenakar, at any rate.

Something thudded against the canopy's side, a sort of wet, gulping clunk, and Javani got the faintest impression of a bright object as the stitched canvas bowed, then bounced it away. It left a dark mark where it had hit, a sort of . . . scorch mark.

'Oh, gods' shit,' Javani breathed. 'Lamps. They're throwing lamps!'

Fear of the crossbow forgotten, she jumped to her feet and pressed her eye to one of the whistling holes of brightness that adorned the canopy's flank. Two riders, no, three, lamps and torches in hand, two with flames blazing.

She spun around, eyes drawn to the mass of spilled powder on the wagon floor. 'This is bad. This is very bad. White Spear!'

The big woman looked up. She was sitting across from the kegs, looking as though she was about to rip the bolt from her arm. 'Yes?'

'They're throwing lamps at us. Lit ones! They're trying to set the wagon ablaze!' She gestured at the loose powder. 'If so much as a spark hits this, we're a puff of smoke and a big bang, you understand?'

A bolt sailed through the open canopy, whistled between Javani and the White Spear, and left through a new hole in the roof near the front. Another lamp clonked against the wagon's side, this time from the left. Javani put her head in her hands. 'Oh, gods have mercy, this is it. This is it!' She scrambled forward again, muttering and whimpering, feeling tears forming in her eyes.

'Ree!' she called. 'Ree! Ma!'

Ree's pallid face turned to meet her as she reached the bench. 'Good timing kid,' she said, her voice cracked and dry. Her eyes seemed distant, unfocused, the smile beneath them dreamy.

'We're there.'

Above their heads, glass splintered, and the wagon lit with the bright billow of flames.

THIRTY

Javani stared at the flames spreading across the canopy roof, scorching and curling the canvas black as they travelled, then at the spilled powder and rolling kegs beside the giant mercenary on the wagon-bed. The White Spear met her gaze, her pale eyes lit bright by the burgeoning blaze overhead. They would never beat this out in time, not before an ember fell and set the floor's mess alight. The fire spread slowly but implacably. They did not have long.

She reached forward, gripped Ree's shoulder. 'We have to get off! We have to jump!'

Ree's eyes snapped back into focus, taking in the burning canopy, flicking down to the chaos of powder and splintered keg, the punctured southerner at its centre.

'Shit,' she said. Her gaze snapped forward, to where the pale escarpment rose from the rolling hillside, the Old Scar canyon a blackened crack in its side. 'Shit. We're too far, they'll cut us down before we reach it. Stupid fucking leg . . . Shit. Shit!'

As if to underscore her point, a slim bolt from a hand-bow pinged from the panel beside her. Some of the more aggressive riders, not satisfied by merely setting the wagon alight, were looking to finish the job early.

Ree whirled on the bench. 'You,' she called, 'Spear. Your legs still work?'

The woman looked down at the bolt projecting from her arm, then nodded.

'Good, get up here. Grab her and be ready to jump.'

Javani felt her panic leap at her throat, a familiar nameless fear at its vanguard. 'You're not . . . You're coming with us! We're all going.'

'Kid, I—'

'No. Not again, Ree. Maybe we're cut down before we make the canyon, like you say. But you stay on this wagon, it goes up, there's no survivors.' She forced a grin. 'Better odds on foot.'

Ree met her gaze, eyes soft and crinkled at the corners. 'You are one stubborn piece of work,' she murmured, then fixed her eyes on the fractured wall of rock that had risen up ahead of them. 'I'll get us as close as I can.'

She swung the wagon, sharp and sudden, first to the left then back to the right, driving the encroaching riders wide. The flames waved in sympathy to the wagon's surge, trailing it like a brilliant headdress, burning down the blackening arches and adding a taint of choking smoke to the dust trail in their wake.

Something fizzed and hissed from the wagon-bed. Sparks were falling now, the speed of the wagon's travel not enough to throw all the fire's emissions into their wash. The White Spear was up with them, helmet on, scooping Javani into her arms as they passed into the shadow of the wall of yellow rock, the horses foaming and straining, their muzzles blood-flecked.

'I'll swing it, then we jump!' Ree called over the wagon's furious rumble.

Javani was staring at the horses, at the long reins and strapped harnesses that bound them. 'Wait,' she squawked, one hand on the White Spear's uninjured arm. 'I need a knife.'

A knife appeared in her hand, short and sharp, from somewhere on the mercenary's person. The fact the southerner hadn't asked her why she needed it, or indeed anything else, struck her at once as both refreshing and a little unsettling.

'Here we go!' Ree cried and hauled on the reins. The team turned, dragging the thundering wagon after them, turning so sharply over the broken terrain that for a moment two of its heavy wheels left the ground. Behind them, smoking kegs rolled and fire dripped, and something was making an alarming hissing noise.

The wagon straightened and the wheels dropped.

'Jump!' Ree bellowed. 'Jump now!'

'One last thing,' Javani snapped, and reached down to hack the central binding of straps beneath the bench. Already half-worn through, it pinged apart in an instant. 'Now!' Javani gestured. 'And grab her!'

The White Spear leapt, Javani cradled in one arm, Ree bunched under the other. She curled them together as she landed, wrapping herself into a loose, giant ball and springing forward with her knees, cushioning them with her back. They came to rest in a chaotic and battered jumble of limbs, further progress arrested by a resolute wall of shrub, enveloped in rising dust.

The wagon clattered on along the escarpment, belching flame and smoke and heading for a whitegrass-covered rise, its team already beginning to pull clear of their severed bindings. As the wagon crested the rise, first one horse, then another broke free, finally able to cease their merciless run.

Javani held her breath. At any moment, the wagon was going to blow.

'Get up.' The White Spear was on her feet already, covered in dust and definitely more blood than there'd been before. She had a one-legged Ree supported under one arm and was extending a hand.

'We'd better make for that canyon,' Ree said with a blood-toothed smile. She didn't seem capable of standing on her own, the binding at her calf now soaked dark.

Javani looked around. She could hardly see anything through the dust, but she knew the canyon was still some distance. And now the wagon was gone, she could feel the growing thrum of hoof-beats, rising through the ground to shake her bones. The hunters were closing.

She took the hand.

* * *

Berev saw the wagon catch, saw the burst of flame across its canopy, and felt a mix of triumph and despondency. When it didn't immediately burn down or explode, his hope returned. Maybe it would be enough to smoke them out, get them in the open. That was all he needed. Just a clear shot.

He freed his hand-bow and cranked it as he rode, one eye always on the man riding beside him. The prince seemed a gifted horseman, capable of using only his knees to keep his mount true as he stood in the stirrups, cranked and loosed the mechanical monstrosity he'd had strapped to his saddle. It made Berev think of Mawn horse-archers, or at least the stories of them. He'd never got to see one himself, the last of them had been exterminated or driven off before his own journey north, disgraced throwbacks like Enx their only remains. Despite all the chatter down south, a lot of things had been long settled by the time Berev arrived. He'd never really got to experience the adventure of the frontier.

Well, he was experiencing it now.

The prince shot again, cursed, and set about cranking, all without so much as reaching for the reins. Berev marvelled. But then, he supposed, riding a horse no-handed was exactly the sort of thing they taught princes, wasn't it?

The wagon veered, one way then the other, sending the closing riders wide. 'What in hells was that? They'll tip the thing,' Berev muttered, not quite so loud that the prince might hear. If they crashed and broke their necks, he doubted there'd be much silver to come by.

The prince's hand went up once more, and the shouts went down the line. 'Hold off, let the fire work.'

The flaming wagon was heading straight for the bleached escarpment ahead, rocking and bouncing over the uneven ground, sending up a trail of dancing sparks with every shock. The running cattle were long gone now, fled over the crest of the rise at the sight and sound of the flames. Probably for the best, Berev thought – the blundering lumps would just have got in the way. He fought the urge to get closer, to look to finish the job, before the thing went up or collided with the wall of rock ahead. Maybe the driver had taken a hit and dropped out, or huffed too much firesmoke?

No, no, back he stayed. Close to the prince. Obedient. Respectful. Deserving.

The wagon was getting awfully close to the escarpment now. Berev peered through the rising dust and smoke. That dark smear on its flank, wasn't that . . . An old mine was hereabouts, could that be . . . ?

'Your highness,' he called, 'I think they might be—'

The wagon veered again, cutting in with a sharpness that shocked the riders. Berev saw movement in the dust, watched as the wagon righted itself and thundered off up the rise, the flames now licking down the canopy side. He couldn't tell if—

'The wagon bench is empty,' the prince declared. 'They have jumped.' Berev squinted. Presumably princes were also trained in seeing long distances. He suppressed a sigh. How different his life might have been if he'd been born a prince, instead of a tanner's son. He'd be far from the northern wastes, that was for certain.

He looked back at the prince. Yet here he was, the same as Berev. Perhaps being a prince didn't make that much difference after all.

They slowed to a walk, the line pulling in around them as riders drew hand-bows, sabres or whatever they had left. All eyes were on the prince after his proclamation that the wagon was no longer their quarry. His royal eyes searched the scrub at the escarpment's foot.

'There,' he announced, one gauntlet pointing, and the line broke into a trot.

'Come on, come on, we're in the open here!' Ree was snarling, panting and sweating, bleeding from a profusion of gashes and scrapes. Her leg was killing her. Potentially literally – assuming they survived the day, blood poisoning loomed large in her future.

'I am carrying both you and the child,' the mercenary intoned, 'contributing to my relative lack of alacrity.'

'Horseshit are you carrying me, I've got one leg on the ground,' Ree snapped back.

'Ree!' the kid squealed. 'They've seen us, they're coming!'

The White Spear lumbered faster, the joints of her black armour squeaking and grinding with every thudding step. A bolt whistled overhead, another crunched into the branches of the shrub beside them. 'Soon they will be close enough to aim,' the White Spear grumbled.

Ree looked ahead. The canyon entrance was so close now, barely twenty paces. But at the pace they were making, the riders would be on them in half that. And besides, the mine entrance was well inside the canyon, she knew that much.

'Kid,' she said, 'you've got to run.'

'What?'

'Run for the mine. Run now. We'll hold them here.' She patted the short sword at her belt with her free hand.

The southerner spoke ahead of the kid. 'Are you suffering concussion? Did you receive trauma to your head when we leapt from the vehicle?'

'What?'

'You have no armour, one working leg, and your weapon seems to be an antique. They will put three bolts in you from ten strides and leave you to the desert dogs.'

'You know,' Ree retorted, 'you're really not a lot of fun to be around. And my sword is not an antique.'

'It will serve no purpose nonetheless.'

'Then why don't you—'

Something clunked against the White Spear's back and her step faltered, leaving Ree momentarily off-balance. 'What the— What did—'

She peered back around the woman's arm. The line of riders was approaching at a comfortable trot, moving to encircle them. Lazant was at the line's centre. Although his face was dimmed by the escarpment's shade, Ree was convinced he was smiling.

'I believe I have been struck by another of those bolts,' the White Spear said through gritted teeth. 'This is . . . displeasing.'

Sure enough, a fletched shaft jutted from the dark panels at her back.

'They are surrounding us. They will soon cut us off,' the White Spear intoned with heavy syllables. 'You may wish to begin your preparations for your lives' ends. Perhaps some prayers or confessions, if culturally appropriate.'

'No chance,' the kid snapped back. 'It's not over until I say it is.'

Berev was elated. The three figures were trapped at the rock's base, barely a handful of paces from the canyon mouth, and in a few moments the prince would drop his hand and they would charge. Berev would be front and centre, first with the hand-bow, then with the old wave-edged sword he'd failed to replace. The prince would see him, would witness him take the head, would shower him with silver. All he needed was the signal.

A great boom rolled over the plain, echoing from the rock before them like a double thunderclap. Heads turned and horses shied in momentary confusion, before riders prevailed, aided by the rising burst of black smoke into the crystalline sky from the far side of the grassy rise.

'The wagon, course—'

'Wagon went up—'

'—was packed with powder, saw it myself—'

As the echoes died away, the Shenakar prince sat at the heart of his settling line, eyes fixed on the three figures ahead. One big, one medium, one small, the big one occluding the others. It wouldn't matter, not to Berev. That monstrous crossbow he carried could pierce the armour of the southern beast, and the other two would put up no fight at all.

The echoes still hadn't died away. Berev sniffed and cocked an ear. A sound like distant thunder continued in the background, growing not fainter but, if anything, a little louder.

'Hey,' one of the riders said, 'is that . . .'

The ground beneath them had begun to tremble.

'Oh by the gods,' wailed another, wheeling his horse around.

'What?' the prince said, his gaze still fixed on his quarry. 'What is it?'

Now Berev heard it, above the swelling rumble, the squalls and bellows of panic.

Two more of the riders peeled away, making for the escarpment's far end at a gallop. The others milled, paralysed by indecision, waiting to see just what was coming.

A black tide of wild cattle crested the rise like a bellowing wave, and the riders panicked. With a lurching surge of nausea, Berev remembered just why the mines had been abandoned in these parts.

'Stampede!'

Berev's horse squealed and began to pitch and shy, forcing him to hunker and grasp. Around him horses reared and threw their riders, or flat-out bolted without a care for who stayed on. The prince dug his heels into his protesting mount, forcing it grudgingly forward.

'Hold!' he cried over the growing thunder of approaching hooves. 'Control your mounts. Form a line and advance on the canyon!' His voice was becoming lost beneath the sound of the pounding earth, and he seemed to know it, wrestling with the reins to his panicking steed. 'Obey, by the light of the gods! Hold true to your duty!'

Berev tried to obey, but his horse was having none of it. The line of riders was already broken as horses turned to flee the onrushing horde, indifferent to their riders' wishes. Berev hauled on his mount's reins and kicked at it, trying to force the animal after the prince, but it was taking all his strength just to hold on.

The prince urged his horse forward, whipping it with the reins and jamming his spurs into its flanks, and it took another step towards the canyon. The three figures they'd had hemmed had turned and run, making for the presumed safety of the gloomy little box canyon and whatever lay inside. As he wrestled with his horse, Berev had time to wonder what might happen to them should the stampeding beasts take a turn on their trail. No safety to be had then, no sir. He almost smiled, his lips already drawn back in a grimace of effort beneath his mask. He could still do it, he could still get his mount to follow the prince into the canyon. He could still earn his silver.

The honks and squalls of charging cattle were deafening now, the earth beneath them seeming to shudder and jump, and the prince's horse baulked. In defiance of his commands, it turned away from the canyon for the open plain, then made to buck as he tried to heave it back around. As it bunched to unseat him, the rider snatched a curved dagger from his belt and jammed it through the horse's throat, ripping it out in a great arc of crimson horror. The horse staggered and dropped, and the prince leapt clear, the crossbow still held tight. Half-cloak thrown back over his shoulder, he ran for the canyon.

Berev's own horse was likewise out of patience. It ducked then reared, throwing him clear. He landed heavily on a rock, still feeling the snap of the reins torn from his hands, but otherwise numb. He heard the receding hoof-beats of his fleeing horse swallowed by the rush of the stampede, felt the hot trickle of what must be blood down the back of his neck, and watched immobile as the prince chased after the fleeing figures into the dark of the canyon.

THIRTY-ONE

Javani was dragging Ree, her shoulder jammed in the woman's armpit, up the canyon towards the mine entrance. Ree was pale and sweating, unsteady on her feet, the dark stain that flooded down her leg beneath the dressing already attracting curious insects.

'Come on, keep moving,' she grunted. 'The White Spear can't hold off thirty of them.'

'That stampede should have thinned out their numbers at least,' Ree replied with a strained chuckle. 'Why is she helping us, kid? What did you promise her?'

'It's not important right now.'

'I'd say it is, kid. Did you fill her in on your plan? She expecting some kind of payment we'll be in no position to afford? A disaffected mercenary seems an imprudent addition to our woes should we shake this bunch loose.'

'I didn't tell her about the plan.' Javani wiped sweat from her brow with her free hand, leaving streaks of sticky dust. 'I just told her that if she kept me alive, I'd go back with her. To Shenak.'

Ree almost staggered from her grip. 'You did what?' Her breath was coming fast, her words almost slurred together. 'Kid, didn't I tell you—'

'You weren't there! It was that or lose you, or lose myself. You're part of it, Ree. You're coming with me. That's the deal.'

'Well, we'll see about that.'

Javani dragged her forward again, pressing her body against her faltering mother. 'Yes. Yes, we will.'

Ree's sword was digging into her hip, slapping against her thigh with every step. Such a fuss she'd made over that bloody sword, and now here they were, limping for their lives like an arrow-struck, three-legged gazelle, and it was just making things worse.

'Can we lose the sword? It's slowing us down.'

Ree actually growled. 'From my stiffening corpse, kid. Besides, there's a good chance I'm going to need it very soon.'

Javani only shook her head. If that were true, they'd likely both be stiffening corpses very soon. Sweat-streaked and panting, she pushed on.

Berev watched the prince charge into the canyon, still shaking the blood from his knife, watched him sprint after the lumbering trio ahead. The rear figure, the giant mercenary who'd torn up the market square, turned to face him, spreading her arms wide. In one hand was a long-handled axe.

The prince slowed his run, wiped his knife on his cloak and sheathed it at the back of his belt. He drew a long, curved sword from the scabbard at his hip, something like a sabre, its hilt sparkling in reflected light. He still had the crossbow resting against his shoulder, cranked and loaded.

The woman advanced, and the prince tossed his sword aside, dropped the crossbow from his shoulder, and loosed into the centre of her visor.

The first rampaging herd-beast rattled past Berev, between him and the canyon, obscuring his view and showering his stricken form with a spray of torn earth and pale grass. By the time it had passed, the prince had gone, along with his discarded sword. The black-armoured figure lay prone on the canyon floor, two bolts jutting up towards the streaking sky. Another cluster of cattle roared past, and the view was lost.

It was funny, Berev thought, in the moments before the stampede rolled over him and kicked him to pulp. Princes had always seemed so noble to him, so refined, yet that one had spent the last few days paying vagabonds to murder a child. Berev had never expected to have any children of his own, but he'd certainly never planned to kill any either. If this was what princing was all about, maybe he'd been better off not being born a prince after all.

Khalida almost whooped with triumph as she came galloping down off the cliff path onto the open plain and sighted the rising dust ahead. They were much closer than she'd feared, moving along the base of a stubby escarpment at the far side of a rolling sweep of terrain . . .

She squinted.

A stampeding herd, with a speckle of saddled but riderless horses at its crest. No sign of the wagon, or the rest of the riders. Still, the tracks ahead were deep and clear: the cleft in the rock wall was her target. She would not be denied. She had marked the child and would claim her yet, for her prince. For Zakir. She was his to command, her vessel his instrument. She would do her duty, and uphold the will of the gods, and even should her vessel perish, her soul would ascend in triumph.

A cry from behind her. She turned in the saddle, one hand on the cantle. The chasers were still on her, on found horses of their own. She had been foolish not to hamstring or throat-score every aimless beast she passed on her journey. Now the pair were nipping at her dust, and gaining. She had been doubly foolish for taking the first beast she saw. Now it was sweating and blowing, struggling to keep the pace for what had to be the final sprint.

Another few hundred strides, that was all. She just had to keep ahead of them a little longer. And if not . . .

Khalida reached one hand down and tightened the clasp of her double-headed spear.

'There, quick, into the mine!'

Arms and legs burning, Javani tried to quicken her pace, pulling the wilting Ree along through little more than force of will. The great black tunnel into the rock, otherwise unnerving, was now a welcome sight. She was almost close enough to put one hand on the wall, to feel the bracing supports . . . to find the stacked powder-kegs that lay within, awaiting their moment.

'Kid,' Ree muttered, 'duck.'

Javani ducked, Ree going with her. A bolt ripped overhead, losing itself somewhere inside the dark of the mine tunnel.

'Shit of the gods!' Javani screamed.

Ree was looking over her shoulder, eyes struggling to focus. There was a trickle of blood at her temple that Javani didn't remember seeing before.

'He's walking up, about thirty strides. Cranking my fucking crossbow as he comes.' She rolled her head around, eyes snapping to Javani, close and feverish. 'You could leave me here, make a run for the entrance.'

'He'll kill you.'

'Maybe I'll duel him to death.'

'He'll put holes in you. More than that, you'll be on the wrong side when I bring down the tunnel. Come on!'

Javani surged forwards again, dragging Ree with her, stumbling into the mine with one eye over her shoulder, waiting for the next bolt.

As Ree had said, Lazant was walking swiftly, boots sure on the blown earth of the canyon floor, funny little half-cloak thrown over his shoulder and the crossbow in his hands. He was looking straight at her. One corner of his moustache curled upwards when he saw her looking back.

She kept moving forward, one foot in front of the other, head over her shoulder and gaze locked on him. Trusting Ree to steer them, keeping his eye contact, keeping his focus, keeping him from noticing the large figure in battered black armour that had come surging around the canyon's curve, its carapace bristling with fletchings.

He spotted her at the last moment, as he slotted the bolt home and raised the weapon. He turned and leapt back from her outstretched hand, firing instinctively. The bolt thumped into the meat of the White Spear's thigh and she staggered, but not before closing her hand around the body of the crossbow. With a roar, she tore it from his grip and flung it against the canyon wall, smashing the arms and sending its wreckage into the rising dust.

Lazant took another backward step, then drew his golden sword.

'Come on, kid, you're lagging,' came Ree's muttered words, and then they were inside the mine.

The stampede had thrown up a giant dust cloud over a mire of churned and broken earth, but even through the haze Aki could tell the demon's horse was spent. It had already stumbled once and recovered, trying to skirt a mound that could have been a fallen beast or man, and it looked like its remaining strides were fewer than he had fingers.

'My sister,' he called, leaning low over his own tiring mount, 'we have her!'

He was ahead of Anashe, as he generally tried to be, the long knife in one fist and the reins in the other. His horse was nearly as wrecked as their target's, foam at its muzzle and blown in great streaks along its flanks, lathered with the dust-thick air. Anashe followed close behind, her own mount nearing its breaking point, but they were so close now. The rock of the escarpment loomed over them, the narrow canyon a shadowed space in the drifting dust ahead.

The demon's horse fell, but she was already running clear, sliding from the collapsing animal as it crashed to its knees. Aki tried to urge his mount in pursuit but the horse was done, perhaps inspired by the collapse of its colleague, and it stumbled and began its own gentle fall. Aki swung his leg over the saddle and leapt clear as the horse wobbled, then recovered, and slowed to an exhausted amble now free of its demanding rider.

Anashe dismounted too, albeit with somewhat less grace, her fleeting run now faster than whatever her horse could muster. The demon that wore Khalida's skin was into the canyon now, running with her double-headed spear bobbing in her grip, the horn and stinging tail, her ruined half-cloak flapping. Anashe ran along the canyon's right wall, Aki made for the left, ignoring the dust that stung his eyes, his raw throat and burning lungs. He pumped his legs, the limbs so accustomed to running for hours that the sluggish, leaden feeling building within them was unfamiliar and irksome. Were he a horse, he might have been blowing foam by now. He put it from his mind. What mattered was catching Usdohr's minion, and nothing else. What mattered was being the protector to the child, as he had sworn to Ree.

For a moment, as they ran through the drifting dust, he saw figures at the canyon's end, struggling and stumbling, then they disappeared into the darkened tunnel entrance. Aki's heart, already thudding at a gallop, upped its pace. This was the place of the plan, the mine the little one had mentioned. The mine rigged to collapse, with her on one side and their foes on the other.

Xalot-as-Khalida was racing for the mine entrance, arms and legs moving in perfect rhythm like mill wheels. Aki saw the path that drew her, the whip of a story's dark turn. The demon could not be permitted to reach Javani, to drain the soul from her fragile body. They had to keep her outside before the collapse came.

Anashe had reached the same conclusion. 'Aki!' she called, rough-voiced and breathless. 'The mine! She must not reach the mine!'

Perhaps she'd imagined he would catch her with a swing of his blade, or pass her at a sprint and block her path, but he saw the story's only workable path. He leapt, lunged for her with arms outstretched, wrapped himself around her trailing leg and brought her crashing to the ground.

The demon Xalot bounced hard, kicked at him with venom, her second blow breaking his grip and setting her scrabbling free. Her spear had dropped but she snatched it up in time to find Anashe standing before her, the stolen sabre drawn in her hand. She stood between the creature and the path to the mine's buttressed entrance, distant clangs and clanks echoing from its mouth.

Aki rose behind her, a trickle of blood leaking hot from his nose, the long knife before him, its blade notched and scratched.

Xalot-as-Khalida looked from one to the other as they circled. She took the spear in both hands, rotated one end, then the other.

'Stand aside,' she said in a low voice. 'I have marked the girl, and I claim her.'

Aki shook his head. All was as he had rehearsed in his head, all these years. 'You go no further, creature of Usdohr. Know that the Champion of the Goddess of all creation stands before you, and you will be repelled.'

The creature before them released a long breath through her nose, looked up at the pitiless crystal sky. 'You have me confused, easterner. Whatever demon of myth you take me for, I assure you . . .' She lowered her head, raised the spear. 'I am very much worse.'

She lunged and spun, driving the bladed end between Aki and Anashe, then sweeping it around towards Aki's ribs. He blocked and ducked, chasing the spear's blade around with his battered knife, and as Anashe tried to close, the spear's barbed end swished around and towards her.

She jumped back, wrong-footed, then tried again, as Aki advanced once more. The demon's spear jabbed and scythed with frightening speed, her reach and agility keeping the siblings hunched and defensive. Steadily, she was pushing her way around them, hammering them back, clearing her path.

They needed to do something. One of them needed to get behind her, get on her blind side, prevent her from keeping them both at bay with her lethal sweeps. Stopping her was all that mattered. As ever, Anashe saw it an instant after he did. 'Brother,' she cried, 'break her, as she did your lance!'

Aki surged forwards, slamming his long knife against the haft of Khalida's spear, making no attempt to do anything more than batter the weapon in her hands. Three times he struck it, flaking the long metal strips that bound the steel to its placement, notching the wood. Khalida fell back, tried to regain her distance, swivelling the long weapon to face him.

Anashe was already in place, the sabre raised two-handed over her head. With a cry, she swung.

THIRTY-TWO

Darkness enveloped them as they left the shaded canyon behind, scurrying three-legged down the passageway. The mine entrance was low and dim, even from the gloom of the high-sided canyon. Javani had expected perhaps a torch or lantern somewhere in the entry passage, but the tunnel was dark for the first thirty or forty strides before some prickles of light from a chamber ahead glimmered at its end. She was mindful of the creak and scuttle of the bracing timbers overhead; the Old Scar mine had been abandoned since long before she and Ree had arrived in the area, and from the way people talked about it, the hillside might come down on their heads at any time, without any encouragement at all.

'How much further?' Ree's speech was rasping, her breath coming hard as they bustled past the ancient supports. It was so wonderfully cool inside the rock.

'I'm not sure. I think I can see some light ahead, maybe . . .'

'You really know how to set this thing off?'

She remembered Movos's words. 'Yes.'

'Safely?'

Javani swallowed, dry-throated. Urgent sounds followed them, the clash and clang of steel echoing along the tunnel, seemingly louder as they raced. It was hard to ignore the prospect that Lazant was behind them in the tunnel, catching up as he duelled the beleaguered White Spear. She couldn't bear to turn and see that she was right.

Then she saw them, suspicious bulges on either side, dark stacks that butted from the walls in the near-darkness. Javani's eyes were adjusting. That had to be the blasting powder. This was her target. 'Nearly . . . there . . .'

Ree stumbled and dropped from her grip, landing heavily with a gasp.

'Ree!'

Javani made to grab her, haul her upright with her sweating, shaking hands, but Ree just waved her away. 'I can make it, kid. I'll crawl if I have to. Go on ahead, get your powder primed. Do what you need to.'

Javani hovered, uncertain, thinking of Movos Guvuli's words, how long it would take her to crack the caps on each, then unspool the triggers. If she did one side and Ree the other—

'Move, kid!' Ree roared from her crouch, her cry echoing from the walls, and Javani lurched into action. Eyes still adjusting, she ran to the first stack and felt around on top of it until she found spooled cord and what had to be the cap. Half-blind, she cracked it up and open, releasing a little puff of nasty alchemical stink. Coughing and tearful, she fell back, the thin trigger rope in one hand and the other over her eyes and nose, then turned and ran to the tunnel's far side to do the same to the other stack.

The noise of pursuit was ever louder now. It sounded like someone hammering steel on an anvil, heavy, resonant clangs coming in frenzied bursts, gasps and grunts of effort, but no speech or cries. A half-glance down the tunnel, over Ree's prone form, revealed a blur of figures, one slender, one large, silhouetted against the watery amber light of the tunnel entrance. They clashed and swung, merged and parted, and were now definitely inside the tunnel.

One hand pinching her nose and her eyes tight shut, she snapped open the second cap, then traced out the trigger spool as she backed away from the stack. Two stacks, two spools: if the bandit had been right, she held a roaring firestorm of blasting power in her hands. It really didn't feel like it.

Ree was upright, leaning heavily on one wall and favouring her injured leg. Javani made to move to her, but again Ree's hand came up. 'Get that lot unwound, get to where we're supposed to be. I'll catch you up.'

'You'd better.'

Javani walked briskly backwards, spooling out the cords as she went, trying to keep her eyes down, so she wouldn't see Ree's faltering, painful steps, or Lazant and the White Spear trading sparks at the tunnel mouth. The further inside the passageway they got, the more she worried. The idea was to collapse the tunnel with her enemies on one side and her and Ree on the other, not bring it down on top of them. If they got much closer to the stacks, they'd be caught in the blast. If they got close enough, they might notice them and deduce her intentions, maybe cut the cords or douse the ignition reagents . . . That didn't bear thinking about. But could she bring down a mountain on their heads?

'Keep moving, kid!'

She'd come to a stop, but Ree's angry shout spurred her on. Already slivers of thin daylight glimmered from the rough, wide tunnel walls around her. The tunnel opened up ahead, into something far more unconstrained.

She entered the cavern in a backward dash, her gaze over one shoulder, trying to take in her new surroundings. It was wide and high, boasting at least a couple of unlit lamps on wide wooden tables to one side. The other side was a tumbling wall of slipped rock, no doubt the remains of the original collapse that had rendered the mine useless. From somewhere, water trickled, and distant glimmers of daylight filtered down from unseen cracks in the rugged roof. A little pool lay at the cavern's centre, fed by a thin ribbon of water, and Javani spotted bedrolls and blankets, a firepit: signs of prolonged habitation. All were kept well away from the tunnel mouth and the cavern's opposite side, where a musty shaft of errant daylight lit a sort of rock dais containing what must have been Shantar the alchemist's scorched and pitted work table. And beyond the table, a narrow crack in the rock, just wide enough to lead a laden pony: the secret exit tunnel, the path to freedom.

She made for the dais, spooling the trigger cord as she went, trying to keep it taut without setting anything off half-cocked. If she crouched behind the dais, she'd be protected from the blast while still keeping a good view of the tunnel, and anyone in it.

Like Ree.

Her mother was making slow progress, limping with sharp gasps, one hand still to the wall. She was still too far away, too deep in the tunnel. Javani was ensconced now, urging Ree forward with a sweaty desperation that was almost nauseating, the trigger cords held in her shaking, jiggling grip.

'Come on, come on, come on . . .'

Behind Ree she saw the figures, little more than dark shapes in the tunnel's gloom, swinging and dancing and clashing once more. She couldn't look away, the indistinct figures now mesmerising for their imprecision, their fluid and unceasing movements. The smaller blur was Lazant, that much was clear. He would trade swipes with the large blur, ducking and stepping before landing a flurry of his own with a great metal boom, then retreating a few paces up the tunnel at speed before turning to face once more. Thus the pair of them progressed, the large blur in pursuit of the small, the small blur in pursuit of Javani.

She realised she could almost see them clearly now, see the bolts bristling from the White Spear's armoured carapace, see Lazant's half-cloak flowing behind his movements like a sinuous tail. They were past the keg stacks. They were on the wrong side of the collapse. They were getting close to Ree.

Lazant himself noticed this, giving an exultant cry as he spotted Ree limping ahead of him. She didn't turn, didn't react, just kept limping forward. Another ten steps and she'd be in the cavern. Twenty more, and Javani could reach her, get her to safety . . .

'Ree!' she called across the cavern, her words much more fierce and echoing than she'd expected. 'Ree, run!'

Ree didn't look up, but her pace quickened, her bloodied palm fairly flying from the rock wall as she hobbled towards the tunnel mouth. Lazant, though, was moving. He ducked a swing from the White Spear and scuttled away at almost a full run, chasing after Ree with his sword in hand.

Something tripped him, and he fell, just as the cord in Javani's hand spasmed. He'd caught a toe in one of the trigger cords. Javani's gullet rose to the roof of her mouth – a harder step and he could have set off the blast and reduced them all to ash.

Ree was nearly clear, the cavern's light rendering sharp the runnels of sweat at her brow, the deep lines on her face. Ten paces behind her, Lazant jumped to his feet, staring down at the cord that had tripped him. A dozen paces behind him, the White Spear advanced with a rolling lumber, her gait halting, at least one bolt jutting from her leg.

Ree stumbled into the cavern and collapsed to her knees, unable to stay upright any longer. Lazant hadn't yet moved, oblivious to the pained advance of the giant mercenary behind him. He was staring down at the cord. His eyes traced it forwards, out past Ree into the cavern, then backwards. Back to the gloomy stacks, the banked kegs that he and the White Spear had battled past without noticing their murderous capacity.

He flinched, spun on his heel, his gaze snapping back to the cavern, tracing the path of the cords to where Javani lay crouched. Even at a distance, she saw realisation dawn in his eyes.

Ree saw it too. She was on her knees, just inside the cavern, staring back into the tunnel. 'Do it, kid!' she called. 'Do it now!'

'You're too close!' Javani yelled back, her voice almost a scream. 'Get away!'

Lazant looked one way, then the other, then pounced on the cord with his sword in hand, grabbing it and slicing it clean through. One of Javani's hands went immediately slack.

'Kid!' Ree bellowed. 'Before he cuts the other one!'

'Get away! Get further away!'

Whether Lazant heard Ree's shout or noticed the other cord was immaterial. He ran for it, dashing across the tunnel to where the cavern's weak light drew it clear against the dry rock of the tunnel floor. Javani stared at the remaining cord, taut in her hand, and at her stricken mother, too close to the tunnel mouth.

'Ree! Ree!'

Ree was already moving, lunging from her half-crouch, scrabbling for the cord on the cavern floor. Javani watched her hand close around it, saw Lazant fumble with his gauntlet as the cord danced from his grip, then Ree swung her body around and yanked. The cord whipped up and down, and in the sudden terrified hush that fell upon the cavern, Javani heard something down the tunnel crackle, then hiss.

She leapt up from behind the dais. 'Run!'

Ree was trying to stand, trying to lurch clear. Behind her, Lazant was already at a sprint, hurtling up the last of the tunnel. Javani's eyes searched for the White Spear, still labouring in his wake, her pace quickened but nowhere near—

A flash lit the tunnel like an instant sunrise, casting the running figures as slender silhouettes in a dazzle of white-yellow light, then dimmed. For a moment, Javani's heart stopped. Was that it? Had the kegs not gone up after all? Had the mine's damp stone rendered them—

The tunnel's end became a wall of white. A blast of flame burst up and along the passage roof towards them, flaring and surging out into the cavern and leaving a drifting curtain of smoke, while the walls of the passage rocked with a procession of shattering explosions. The force hit Javani like a fist, knocking her back against the cavern wall in incongruous silence, before the roar and thunder reached her a moment later. Great chunks of rock sailed across the cavern, smaller lumps rocketing from the tunnel mouth and smashing away in all directions. Everything shook. Acrid smoke filled the air, seeming to have replaced all the air in the cavern, the smell of fire and alchemy burning at her lungs and nostrils.

For a few heartbeats, there was almost silence; the cavern quiet but for the clunk of falling debris and the whisper of drifting dust. Then came the sound, soft at first, a gentle, creaking murmur, as if the cliff above were sighing. The sigh became a hiss, which became a rumble, and then a wall of falling rock and earth came tearing down the tunnel, filling it in a great wave.

The last thing Javani saw through the smoke-choked cavern air, before the rock slide hit, was the White Spear in the tunnel mouth, struggling to stand, one hand yanking taut the chin-strap on her helmet. Then the tunnel was gone: in its place, a heavy spill of sand-coloured rock and dust, a junior echo of the cavern's already-fallen wall, the smothering atmosphere now clogged with a tide of rising dust.

It was a lot darker, the silvery light from the cracked ceiling now casting down in great thick shafts towards where the little pool had been. Javani pushed herself back to her feet behind the dais, wincing and flinching at the new scrapes and bumps the blast had bestowed upon her. She couldn't see anyone in the murk. Half the cavern seemed to have become loose rock.

'Really overcooked that one, Movos Guvuli,' she muttered to herself, trying to dust herself down. Off to her left, the slim opening in the rock that supposedly led to the secret exit stood unblocked, but dark and hardly inviting.

Her ears were ringing, but it was subsiding, the reverberations of the explosions and subsequent collapse dying away through the surrounding rock. Gradually her hearing returned, and with it, the gentle sounds of settling stone.

There, a scrape, a groan. Someone was moving.

There, another, a cough. Someone else. But which was whom? The odds were that one of the survivors was friendly, the other decidedly not.

She couldn't leave anyone behind.

'Shit,' muttered Javani, and scrambled into the choked heart of the cavern.

The blast shook the mountain, the ground beneath, sent hidden birds screaming from the bleached and withered trees into the clear skies above the canyon. Anashe had seen barely a flash from the corner of her eye, then the world had shifted with the sound of a thunderclap and a torrent of broken rock had burst from the tunnel mouth as if the cliff itself were vomiting.

She swung and missed, her blade crunching hard against the centre of Khalida's spear but making no mark on the furious woman beneath. A savage kick clipped Anashe's knee, and she fell.

From where she landed, she saw a rising cloud of dust billowing forwards, filling the canyon, racing towards them. Mercy of the Goddess, she thought as her leg yowled with pain, not more of this accursed dust . . .

Khalida had turned, no time to deliver a killing blow, only now taking in the mine's collapse and the remaking of the canyon behind them. For a moment, the spear dipped in her hands.

'You see, demon?' Aki said, stepping around her towards where Anashe lay. 'It is over. She is beyond you now.'

Khalida was staring at the collapsed entrance, her chest heaving, nostrils wide, sweat running free down her face. Blood was leaking from the bandage over her eye. She seemed to be trembling.

Aki let the long knife hang loose in his hand, extended the other. 'Your business here is concluded. Begone from this place, return to your lair. Victory is beyond you. Stay, and you risk only destruction.'

Anashe pushed herself to one knee, tested the other and rose carefully to her feet. The kicked knee was discontented; it would bear her weight, but not indefinitely. With luck, it would not have to.

Khalida stood, still staring at the collapsed mine entrance, letting waves of floating particles roll over her, coating her sweat-slick face and hair, dusting her shoulders.

Anashe looked to Aki, brows raised, eyes questioning. *Are we to attack her? Are we to kill her, when she has abandoned the battle?*

Khalida turned slowly. Dust had covered her face, leaving her ghost-masked. Aki took a step back, and the woman's eye gleamed.

'Duty commands,' she growled, 'and I *obey*.'

She lunged.

THIRTY-THREE

It was the cursing that decided it. 'Gods' pox-riddled bollocks,' came a wheeze from one side of the rock slide, and Javani scurried towards it. Ree was coated in slick sand and dust, her bad leg lost beneath a skittering spread of fallen stone. She was blinking hard and rubbing her eyes, trying to sit up. Javani jumped down beside her, fingers probing the stone around her leg.

'Ree! Are you hurt?'

Ree turned towards her, hands dropping from her eyes, then she stuck her fingers in her ears and waggled them, pulling them out with an audible pop.

'More than I was already?' she grinned. 'You've done quite a number on this place, kid.'

The loose shattered rock on her leg moved easily enough, and Javani dug her clear. 'Is the leg all right? Can you stand?'

Ree pulled another half-smile. 'As much as I could before, I reckon.' Beneath the blood-spattered dust, she was still pale and sweat-soaked. They needed to clean the wound in her leg as soon as humanly possible.

Another cough echoed across the cavern through the dust-choked gloom, and Ree's head whipped around. 'The rockfall – did it . . . Who's still . . .'

Javani shook her head. 'I don't know.' The leg was clear, and looked no less battered than before.

'Then let's not dally. Give me a hand up, kid. Let's go.'

They were most of the way to the narrow crack in the cavern wall, Ree's accursed sword digging once more into Javani's side, when they heard the unmistakable sound of shifting rubble, the crunch of loose stone beneath a standing boot. The dust in the air had begun to settle, the diffuse light brightening along with it, and Javani tried to turn to see who was rising. Ree pulled her on, half her weight still on Javani's shoulder.

'Keep moving, kid, we're almost out.'

'But it could be the White Spear—'

'Whoever it is, we're better off without any further conversations with either.'

They reached the fissure. It was wide enough to lead a pack animal down, presumably one laden with Guildhouse loot, but only just. Javani peered inside. It was very dark, and seemed to curl up and to one side, but she thought she could see a faint glimmer here and there. The Guvulis must have been tunnelling the whole time they were planning the heist. She hoped they'd made it all the way through to the far side.

'Ree, you go first.'

'Are you cracked, kid? Get in there. I'll be right behind you.'

For once, Javani didn't argue. She took a deep and dusty breath then walked into the tunnel, forcing herself through the quarried rock towards what she was sure was the faint light of day some distance ahead. She heard Ree's hard breath behind her as she followed, leaning heavily on the rock as she came.

Javani made it about two dozen strides before the ceiling lowered, looming and unpleasant, her hair brushing its cold and rough surface. Ree would have to duck – she might even want to crawl. At least, Javani reasoned, Ree could take the weight off her foot if she travelled on hands and knees. The tunnel kept curving, kept twisting, growing ever darker, and then her hand met something utterly solid.

'What's the hold-up, kid? Something wrong?'

Javani swallowed, her fingers tracing the outline of the rock before her. A wall of fallen stone, chunks of shattered bedrock fallen from the hollowed ceiling, forming a crude but all too effective blockade to the tunnel. The distant light glimmered through gaps, promising salvation on its other side. She grabbed at a lump of stone and pulled it free, dropping it to the tunnel floor. A touch more light, the tunnel clear beyond, but the opening was too small. Far too small.

'Kid? What is it? I'm getting a little bored back here.'

Javani dug around, fingers scrabbling over crumbling stone, trying to shift the pieces around the opening.

'I think . . .' she began, straining fruitlessly to drag a slab across. 'I think the explosion collapsed this bit.' She let her hands fall. 'Gods damn you all, Guvuli,' she sighed.

Ree was close behind her, her hand on her shoulder in the near dark.

'Looks like there's a gap there, kid.'

'But it's too small, you can't get through there.'

'But you can.'

Javani swallowed hard, her mouth tasting of dust and burning. 'Are you . . . What about—'

'Not without dislocating more limbs than I'm comfortable with, no.'

Javani tried to turn in the tunnel, banged her head on the rock, scraped her elbow. 'Ouch, wait, listen! The Guvulis had mining equipment in the cavern, and supplies. We'll go back, get some picks, start clearing this out.'

'It's a nice idea, kid, but you're forgetting our friend back there.'

'It might be the White—'

'It's not.'

The tunnel was silent but for the trickle of distant water. Javani felt a breath of air on her neck, warmed by the midday sun. There truly was a hole in the rock ahead.

'Then we'll go back together and defeat him.'

'No, kid. We've done well, but this is it. Very soon, he's going to work out where we are. Then he's going to come this way after us, and we are in no shape to do much more than block this passage with our corpses. You're going on ahead, and I'm going back.'

Javani snatched at her mother's hand, which lingered on her shoulder.

'Ree, no . . .'

'The only way to stop him following is to hold him up long enough for you to crawl your way out of this mountain.'

'I can help!'

'I can't face a man like that if I'm worrying about you. Get out, get safe, or at least wait by the exit and smack a rock over the fucker's head if he comes burrowing through.'

'This isn't fair! You keep trying to leave me, to throw your life away—'

'No, kid. Everything I've done, everything your entire life, things you know, things you don't, has been to keep you safe. I need you to listen now, because you're young, and because nothing yet has happened to you so bad that it has cracked your childish sense of invulnerability. There is no benevolent god watching out for you, my darling girl. You are not a chosen creature, impervious to harm and misfortune. If you go back into that cavern, you will die. If you wait too long here, you will die. And you will feel damned stupid for it. You *have* to *go*.'

Ree's voice was cracking, her words thick with invisible tears. Javani struggled in the tunnel, trying to reach out to her, trying to grab hold of her to stop her getting away, but Ree kept her at arm's length with a firm grip, holding her in place.

'I can't . . .' she whimpered. 'I won't! We talked about this, you need to stop running away from me!'

'You will, and you'll be fine.' Ree's hand squeezed hard on her shoulder. 'For once, I'm going to run towards my problems. Now go on, get out of here, and live your life. Prove that I raised you well. Make me proud.' Ree pushed her backwards, into the glimmering dark of the tunnel. 'Go!'

Snuffling and weeping, Javani stood in the gloom, then with aching reluctance she turned and began crawling through the gap in the fallen stone.

'Besides,' came Ree's voice through the stones, already receding. 'I might win.'

* * *

Javani's sobs echoed from the rock around her in the claustrophobic dark of the tunnel, only the whistle of warm air on her wet cheeks a reminder that there was any way out of her stone tomb. Even if she made it out the far side, she realised, she'd be alone, without horse or supplies, without . . . without the map. She'd lost the map when they'd leapt from the wagon. It was gone. It was all gone. Weeping in the silent dark, she crawled and clambered, and at last she was through the last of the slipped rock, the tunnel wide again. Enough room to stand, stretch and arch her back, to ease the crick in her neck, wipe the tears from her cheeks.

Enough room to turn around.

Javani was very still in the darkness, hearing only the sound of her own breathing, her own heartbeat, thumping in her ears, making her throat twitch.

'Gods be damned,' she hissed, 'she's my *ma*.'

Ree moved as fast as her injured leg would allow. The meat of her calf throbbed with a terrible anger, and each time she put weight through it the muscle shrieked and stabbed her back. The cavern was clearer now, the sifting dust beginning to settle, the air still thick with the stink of smoking alchemy. She limped as fast as she could from the narrow split in the rock, one hand on the hilt of the short sword that hung from her hip, towards where she'd heard the cough.

It had been him, of that she was certain. Zakir Lazant had been alive when they'd tried to make their escape, and she ardently hoped to find him less so on her return. Her trail-knife was gone, lost somewhere in the frenzy of pursuit, and the surprise knife was just as missing from her sleeve. That irked her. She'd always meant to strap it tighter, but it had never been a good time.

She smiled to herself between the winces of her progress; a grim, sad smile. When had there last been a good time?

The rubble that had flooded from the tunnel had formed a sort of ramp, a great splatter of sand and pulverised stone. She was making for a dip in the debris, a drop in the mounds of piled junk from where she'd heard the cough. She'd marked it, as she'd ushered the kid from the cavern. She'd marked it, because in the depth of her soul she'd feared, no, *expected* that she'd have to return.

Teeth gritted as she placed her weight on both feet, she drew the slim sword from its scabbard. The blade was still bright and clean, even surrounded by so much grime and dust, the engravings along its length glittering in the wan light from the cavern's cracked ceiling. She and the sword had come a long way. She hoped they had a little further to go.

She took a breath, held it, then stepped over the mound with the sword raised.

There was nobody there, living or dead. She saw the imprint, though, the outline of a fallen form in levered scree. He'd been here. He'd moved.

Ree tensed, locked herself in concentration, the held breath burning at the top of her lungs. He could be anywhere, he could be moments away, his own blade high. She listened, strained over the sound of her own urgent heartbeat . . . there. The splash of water.

She turned slowly, jaw clenched, feeling the sweat running down her back, the angry throb of her leg, the slow trickle of blood into her boot. She'd need new boots as well, on top of everything. Her sword hilt was slick in her palm.

Zakir Lazant was kneeling by the little pool at the cavern's centre, and he was staring right at her. He'd taken the time to rinse the dust from his face, his hair and moustache now glossy and dark. He'd even shed his half-cloak and wiped down his breastplate, which shone with a burnished glow in the strengthening light from the cracks above. He was in the process of cleaning his sword.

He stood slowly, wiping down the blade with the ruin of his cloak then tossing it away. He looked clean, healthy and whole. Ree felt anything but.

A charming smile lit his handsome face. 'I was just on my way to find you, Mistress Ree. You had no need to seek me out.'

Ree worked hard to keep her gaze from flicking back to the little fissure at the cavern's end. If he chose to, he could simply run for it and be away – she stood no chance of catching him from where she was. She couldn't let him reach it, to be alone with the kid in the dark. She couldn't.

She began walking towards him, placing her feet with fierce purpose, fighting down the squealing shocks from her injured calf. He knew, though. She could see it in his gaze, a gaze she'd seen from men like him many times over the years: munificent contempt. He pitied her, but would indulge her pointless defiance for the sake of good manners.

Well, fuck him.

He had a surprise coming.

Anashe fought. She fought beneath the drifting curtains of amber dust, swirling around them until the canyon walls were lost, until the concept of time was lost, until the burning ache in her arms and legs, the sullen pulse of her damaged knee, simply ceased to be anything more than distant background, a notion from another era, of limited interest but for archivists. All that remained was the battle, the fight between the sabre in her hand, the blade in her brother's, and the double-headed spear between them.

How she still moved was a mystery she had no mind to interrogate. How the others did, likewise. They had fought without cease, swinging and lunging and blocking and leaping, until Anashe's body felt like half-moulded clay, soft and malleable and draining of strength. The world was orange, the shade of the canyon now filled with slow-settling particles of blown stone-powder from the tunnel's collapse, puffed ever around by the canyon's slow air currents.

She felt she had been locked in an eternal dance with two partners, ever-repeating: step here, parry here, slide here, swing here, and back to the start. Nobody spoke, the canyon quiet but for the barks of their breathing, the ring of colliding steel and the gentle patter of settling stone.

At least she had Aki with her, she thought, when she could raise her mind beyond simply keeping her body moving. It was too easy to forget that their struggle was deadly, that the blank-eyed woman between them intended their deaths. She had Aki, and Aki had her; two against one. Deep down, she knew they would win.

Then her knee gave way.

Anashe stumbled and dropped with a cry, one foot skidding out behind her, hands thrown out. Khalida was on her in an instant, the spear driving towards her, and Anashe threw herself backwards, sweeping the sabre around with numb fingers. The blade bit the spear's haft just as its barbed tip pricked her shoulder, splintering it, bending it wide.

The sabre flew from her hand as the spear snapped, its murderous point fallen from a shallow wound in her shoulder, the remaining length tight in Khalida's hands. Eye wide, she twirled the wood, spinning the remaining blade around. A small smile pulled at the corners of her mouth.

'You shall not have her!'

Aki charged, long knife wild in his hand, driving it forward as Khalida turned. She deflected his swing, driving his blow wide, then kicked out at his trailing leg. He stumbled, losing the knife as he pitched forward with arms outstretched. Khalida turned back to Anashe and drew back the spear. Her smile returned.

She thrust, but Aki was there. Reeling, unsteady on his feet, blocking the blow. Anashe heard Khalida hiss in frustration, try to wrestle her half-spear free, but it looked as though he held it tight.

'Take her, my sister!' he called, voice tight.

Anashe scrabbled to her feet, grabbed for her fallen sabre, pushed herself up almost hopping on one leg. Still Khalida and Aki battled, her grunts and growls suggesting he had the better of her at last.

'I have her, my sister! Be quick!'

Anashe rounded her brother, the sabre raised, and swept it down. Khalida jumped back, one arm raised, abandoning her broken spear. The sabre scored a deep slash down her arm, spraying a fine red mist into the dusty air. She screamed and staggered back, clutching at her wound, her eye wide in fury and horror, flicking from Anashe to her brother and back. Then she snarled, turned, and ran, lost in the whirling dust.

Anashe heard the tired whinny of a horse from the canyon's edge, then the diminishing thud of hoof-beats. She considered pursuit, one-legged and exhausted, one shoulder numb and bleeding freely. Anashe came to a prompt halt.

'Be after her, my sister. Do not wait for me.'

Something in his voice stopped her. The words were his, the sentiment his, but the tone was . . .

She turned, all her weight poured through her good leg.

Aki was leaning back against the canyon wall, a broad smile of encouragement across his battered face.

Khalida's half-spear jutted from his abdomen.

THIRTY-FOUR

Only once Javani crawled back into the cavern did she realise that she had no idea what she was doing. Part of her screamed just to go back, to flee for the narrow tunnel and be away, or try to lie in wait in the darkness for any pursuit, and like Ree had said . . . smack him over the head with a rock.

Maybe she could do that here. There was no shortage of rocks in the cavern, after all. Perhaps there was something left in the Guvulis' old camp she could use, a pick or something, sneak up while he was distracted and smack him over the head with that.

She looked up and swallowed dust, a sudden hot feeling like fire in her throat.

Ree and Lazant stood facing each other in an uneasy mirror of the parley outside the watchtower, but they were not circling. Ree stood with her back to Javani and the supposed escape, her weight through her good leg but trying not to show it. Facing her stood the Shenakar prince, looking inexplicably clean and shiny. Their swords were drawn: hers short, slim and elegant, his long and thin, the jewels at its hilt glittering in the light. He seemed to glow.

She ducked down as slowly as she could. His eyes were on Ree, but needed to move but a flicker to see her skulking in the gloom. As the dust from the cave-in settled, the cavern seemed to be brightening, and the hiding places within it diminished.

They weren't moving, the duellists. She'd heard of duels of honour fought by nobles outside palaces, and the more common sort in the north of one drunk miner calling out another into the baking street before they traded dagger-blows. This one was something else, and it was making her hands shake and her breath come in hot little gasps like a frightened rabbit. Ree was no warrior and her sword was an heirloom, however much she claimed to have fought years ago. Javani had to do something, to help. She couldn't come this far just to watch Ree die at his hands. She couldn't lose her mother now.

'I should say,' Lazant's voice cut through her thoughts like a cleaver. 'I am impressed by your gesture, and would like to afford you the opportunity to withdraw with honour.' He stood in a casual stance, loose-limbed, his long, sharp sword held extended and unwavering. Javani couldn't believe how clean and bloodless he looked.

Ree said nothing. Her own stance favoured her injured leg, but Javani thought her effort to make it look deliberate was very close to convincing. She held out her blade in sympathy to his, but it seemed so small, so pathetic in comparison. By the gods, but his armour shone.

He took a step to the side, unhurried. Ree matched it, staying between him and the crack in the wall. His moustache twitched in amusement. 'I make my offer in good faith. You saw me battle the white ghost as we entered this tomb.' He spread his arms, let the sword dangle from his hand for a moment. 'She was coated in black steel, a born killer. Yet I alone stand before you. Not even out of breath.'

Ree said nothing, and he took another half-step to the side. She matched it.

'That is quite a weapon you brandish, Mistress Ree.' His head was tilted, his own blade slowly rising to level with hers once more. 'Unsuitable for duelling, of course, but a pleasing piece of workmanship. How did you come by it?'

Ree said nothing.

His smile widened. 'Only now do I truly appreciate why my cousin chose you. I understand that these last years have not coddled you, but some strains of beauty are eternal, and there is a spark in your eyes beneath your battered countenance that to my shame I did not recognise before.' He took a small step forwards, his arm bending, his sword motionless in space. 'I never knew him – he lived and died in the Sink, beyond the mountains – but I imagine we had many things in common.'

He took another step, fast and forwards, and Ree hopped back with a muffled hiss. Javani couldn't see her face from where she hid by the dais, but she could picture her rictus of pain. She couldn't keep standing on that leg. Javani needed to do something. But what?

Lazant extended his arm and touched the tip of his blade to Ree's own. 'I make my offer in good faith. You see, I know a little of you, Mistress Ree, although by another name. I know a little of the diplomat, the fallen courtier, the foreign agent, the spy. I know that she sought refuge in the great fortified city of Arowan as it was besieged, and when others gave their lives in its defence . . . she fled.' He gestured with his empty hand towards the collapsed entrance, where the occasional loose rock still shifted and settled. 'I only offer now the same chance again. Step aside, as you have before. Let others resolve the fate of kingdoms.'

Ree let her arm drop, let it hang loose by her side, let her legs buckle. Her shoulders slumped. Javani watched with mounting horror as Lazant's moustache spread wide over his triumphant smile, as Ree seemed to diminish before his burnished form.

Ree rolled one shoulder. Then she rolled the other, then her head around each way. She shook her bad leg, then planted it firmly, and up came the sword.

'Are we going to fight,' she said, her voice sharp in the cavern's stillness, 'or fuck about?'

Lazant's smile crystallised into a wide-mouthed snarl, but still something danced in his eyes. 'As you wish,' he sighed.

He lunged forward in a flash, his sword slicing the air towards Ree's arm. She parried the strike and fell back, steady but limping, ready for his vicious follow-up. Four times he slashed, four times she parried, stepping each time to block his path to the cracked wall, each step more faltering than the last. Then he feinted, flicked his sword to one side and around and lunged, driving its tip through Ree's arm as she turned too far.

She screamed and staggered backwards, blood blooming from her bicep as he wrenched the blade clear. She slapped at the wound with her sword hand as she scrambled unsteadily backwards, struggling to stem the blood-loss while keeping hold of her weapon.

Lazant left her no chance to recover. He darted forward again with two sharp strikes to her torso that she barely blocked, then scored a line across her thigh as she stumbled backwards again. She cried out and collapsed to the rubble-strewn floor.

Javani let out a silent scream into her clenched fists. There had to be something she could do. If she got around the dais, she could find something to throw, something at least to distract him . . . Until he saw her and came after her, and killed her as swiftly as he and his stooge had killed Moosh. And then Ree would have given her life for nothing. Javani swallowed again, tears running hot down her cheeks, locking her throat to stop the sobs bursting out. This wasn't fair. She hadn't asked for any of this. She hadn't done anything wrong, just been born to the wrong person at the wrong time.

Ree was struggling to stand back up, her sword gripped tight with bloodied fingers. Lazant stepped close to her then swung a kick at her head, then at her sword hand as she tried to block it. The sword clattered away from her nerveless fingers. She slumped towards him, hands thumping uselessly against his breastplate, grappling for purchase, slapping around his waist, and he shoved her down and away. She lay before the prince, curled and gasping and completely defenceless.

Lazant took a step back, inspected the tip of his sword. 'Does my prowess surprise you, Mistress Ree?' He reached up and wiped Ree's blood from the blade with his gauntlet. Behind him, the rubble shifted, the loose stone settling. 'Perhaps you had presumed I was a pampered fop, unschooled in martial ways.'

He walked slowly around her, then jabbed the sword into her back – not hard, just enough to draw another bright rose of blood.

'When one is born to rule, one is instructed in many things,' Lazant said, as he continued around Ree's stricken form in a slow circle. 'The academic: literacy, numeracy, poetry, history; the practical: riding, archery, falconry, and of course, bladesmanship; and the political: etiquette, courtly intrigues, how to lead and command, how to send others to their deaths for the good of the kingdom and the glory of the gods. But there are other lessons taught alongside, in the gaps, if you will. The importance of continuity, of consistency, of predictability, of stability. Of the nature of the interpretation, and implementation, of the will of the gods.

'You see, the world is as it is because the gods ordained it thus, and those who seek to subvert their will are worse than heretics. Natural order must be preserved: some are born to serve, others to lead. It is the role of the king to uphold these natural boundaries – the strong shall not oppress the weak, nor the weak the strong. It is incumbent upon us all to maintain equilibrium. I have worked hard to do my part, but others, yourself included, must do theirs.'

He flicked out with the sword and cut a line down Ree's bent leg, slitting the side of her breeches and carving the skin beneath. She cried out in pain, trying to roll away from him, too cut and weakened to regain her feet.

'I gave you every chance to avoid this,' he said with the condescending disappointment of a parent lecturing a punished child, 'but you made your choice.'

He took another few steps, letting the sword-tip rest on her shaking body as he circled her, light and deadly. 'The child will not get far. Once you are finished, I will pursue her swiftly and put this matter to rest. Your truculence has risked my kingdom too many times already.'

Ree rolled and pushed away the blade, scuttled backwards on elbows and bloodied legs, her hands lost beneath her. She raised her shoulders, stared up at him with contempt in her eyes. 'Risks to your kingdom seem to have a lot in common with you not getting what you want.'

His lips pursed, his moustache bunching. 'You are a temporary obstacle, Mistress Ree, a bump in the road. Perhaps . . . perhaps I should let you live, let you see what I shall do. I have worked so hard to reach this point, you could yet behold my glory.'

A bright smile split Ree's bloodied face. 'Worked? What work have you done? Your entire existence is a gift, handed to you at birth.'

His cheeks darkened, his eyes flashing wide. 'I have worked! I have worked harder than any man who called himself a prince of Shenak!'

'And that is a pretty low bar,' Ree chuckled back. 'All you've worked at is your entitlement. Your tortuous path to the throne has relied solely on the misfortune of others.'

'And who do you think arranged those misfortunes?' he roared, his voice booming around the cavern. Behind them, more loose rock shifted and rolled, clattering in echo of his bellow. 'I pushed my boorish nephew down the stairs and onto his birthday dagger. I drowned my uncle in his silver bath. I watched my fourteen-year-old cousin choke on a pistachio. I have organised more poisonings than my chamberlain has winter festivals. None can say I have not worked!'

'Like I said. Entitlement.'

Ree put one hand on the ground and pushed herself up into a crouch, then upright on shaking, faltering legs. Blood streamed from her arm, her leg, the cut in her back. She stood defenceless, defiant. Around the cavern, stones continued to shift, their thuds and clunks sending dull echoes from the walls.

'You think you condescend to let me live?' she said, spitting the words at him. 'You think you have the right to rule over me, over anyone?'

He stiffened, the sword flexing in his grip.

'I am a prince of Shenak,' he snarled, 'and I was born to rule.'

Her voice was low, razor-edged.

'You are just a sad little man, and you deserve no more than anyone.'

He raised the sword, then dropped it again, the anger fading from his eyes as the mocking returned. 'Yes, I shall—'

Ree's voice cut through his nascent sneer.

'It was a man like you who sold me as a child. It was a man like you who selected me like merchandise. Who beat me when I would not submit. Who drove me to poison us both.

'It was a man like you who tried to rule me with poppies and leaf. Who tried to take my choices and my future. It was men like you who tried to hurt me, to kill me, over and over, when I would not behave as they wished.

'All of them failed.'

Ree took a long breath, shifted her weight between her legs, one hand at the wound on her back, one hand pressed to her side. 'And you are less than them all. Can you presume to finish their work, princeling?'

Lazant was so still Javani had to squint to see the tremble in his limbs.

He lunged with a roar, a howl of pure rage, his blade whipping forward in a flash of bright steel. It travelled a line of absolute force towards Ree's chest, unstoppable and lethal. Yet somehow Ree was moving, pivoting on one foot, rising and rolling to meet the blade. It passed through her and her body kept moving, colliding with Lazant, wrapping her arms around him as they both crashed to the cavern floor. They came to rest in a thudding heap, Lazant's blade sticking straight up into the air, gleaming with a streak of hot blood.

Javani went to scream, caught herself, and crammed her wadded shirt into her mouth to bite. Ree wasn't moving. Lazant wasn't moving. The sword wasn't moving. The cavern was silent but for the continued shift and rattle of settling rock by the collapsed tunnel entrance. It sounded as if the cliff above was finally reaching some kind of consensus on its new arrangement.

The human pile at the cavern's centre groaned, and for a moment Javani felt a rush of pure, electric hope. Then Zakir Lazant pushed

Ree's slumped form off him and rose gingerly to his feet, yanking his blade clear as he did so. Ree rolled once and lay still.

Only the bundled shirt that stuffed her mouth kept Javani's shriek from echoing around the cavern.

The man who called himself Zakir Lazant, chosen prince of the highest house of the most royal court of the King of Kings of Shenak, took a moment to look around himself as his breathing slowed. The insolent horse-farmer lay motionless at his feet, her galloping mouth at last stopped for good. His sword was dirtied, and blood tainted one side of his now dusty breastplate. He rubbed at it with a gauntlet, smearing it across the embossed metal. His mouth dipped in irritation. To be so sullied by a woman so ultimately unimportant. Still, the hard work was done. He knew exactly where the child had gone, he had watched the woman emerge from the crack in the far wall from his vantage by the little pool. She would not travel far, and by this stage, ending her life would be little more than a formality.

He sighed at the thought of how much chaos and bloodshed could have been avoided if he had eliminated her in the alley when first he and his cohort had arrived. Such was the price of peace, he knew, but he and his surviving staff could already have been halfway back across the expanse with the girl's head at his saddle-point if only he hadn't been so hasty.

Hasty. Mother always said he was too impulsive. Mother had said much about him, and sometimes even to him. But this would be his moment. This would be his triumph. To return to the royal city, to stride into the great hall of the King of Kings and throw down the girl's head before the cowering, simpering council of viziers. To stand proud over them, his gleaming armour blinding the wretches as they cringed, crushed by the certainty of the failure of their schemes. And there in the gallery, as she always was, resplendent and divine: Mother. She would lift her veil as the path of rightful succession was confirmed, meeting his eye, and she would nod, just once, and he would know. He would know he was worthy. Zakir Lazant would be a disappointment no longer.

But first, he needed to clean himself up.

He rubbed at the blood again, but it didn't seem to be shifting. He sighed again and went to sheathe his sword, already taking a step towards the little pool, then stopped with a wince. Something was wrong with his sword arm.

'Having some trouble, your highness?'

The horse-farmer. Alive. Speaking. She was still on the ground, her clothing now drenched with blood from myriad precisely delivered wounds, but she was propped up on her elbow and she was *smiling*.

A sudden confusion clouded Lazant's eyes, and he half turned to the pool, then back to the woman, brows lowered with a rekindling anger. The woman had pushed herself to her knees now, her breathing coming hard and blood in her teeth and hair, but her brazen smile was undimmed.

'For all your princely learnings, Zakir Lazant,' she said with a cold mirth in her voice, 'some gaps in your education remain. I know things that you do not, because experience beats instruction and we learn hardest from trauma.' She knelt up, looked as if she was going to stand, then rested her injured arm across her good knee. 'For example, I know that Shenakar men of a certain age and station carry a ceremonial dagger with them at all times, usually at the back of their belt . . .'

Lazant's hand jumped to his back, and returned, empty.

'. . . And however glorious a breastplate, it offers no protection to a blade thrust directly up into the armpit.'

He felt the colour drain from his face. His gauntlet snapped to the corner of his chest where the steady stream of blood still tainted his magnificent armour. His eyes widened, his breath coming in sharp snorts through flared nostrils, and when he spoke it was through gritted teeth.

'My own dagger . . . What have you *done?* You will scream for this!'

His gauntlet creaked as he gripped the hilt of the knife in his armpit, but the woman snapped up a bloodied hand. 'No, no, no, prince of Shenak, in the name of the gods don't take it out. That knife of yours has severed an artery, and the only thing that's stopping all the blood pumping out of your puffed-up little body is that blade. Whip it out and you'll spurt like an Arowani fountain, then you'll go very still indeed.'

Lazant's breath came in hard barks and he felt spittle fleck his moustache. He tried to turn, tried to move forward, but was paralysed by the magnitude of his wound. Suddenly dizzy, he sank slowly to his knees, one hand still on the hilt of the knife embedded in his body, then fixed the horse-farmer with a glare of black hate.

'I will see you broken for this, woman. I will see you—'

The woman leaned forward and slapped him, very hard, across the face. The shock of it stunned him mute. 'Be silent. You are already killed, and your story ends in this mouldering cave. You will be silent as the life leaks from you, and you will turn your mind to considering the fault of your actions.'

Incredulous, he moved to speak again and she treated him to another slap. He tried to raise the sword and was slapped. He slumped back on his knees, the fury draining from him, replaced by a strange, wavering feeling that he recognised dimly as dread.

The horse-farmer slowly pushed herself upright, while rocks shifted somewhere behind her. A small stone came to rest by her foot. Her clothes were soaked through with blood, her hair pinked with it, and she could barely stand, but she seemed to radiate certainty.

'More will come in my stead,' the prince hissed, his eyes half-focused. 'They will not let the kingdom fall to chaos.'

'Horseshit,' she snapped back. 'You're out here on your own, prince of Shenak, and this is the end of your claim. You could have avoided all this. You should have listened to me. I've been telling you since the beginning: she is not the child you seek.'

He turned his head, the anger returning to his eyes for an instant. 'The child of my cousin, of yours—'

'My son was born with his cord around his neck, choked blue

and lifeless,' she said in a furious rush. 'I buried him in an unmarked grave a day's ride into the Grey Hills, and I wept for weeks. I found the girl in the ruin of a settlement, raided by Mawn, her family split and murdered in an arc around the smoking buildings. Somehow, they'd missed her.

'I did not.

'I have carried her since, protected her, raised her, but I have never claimed her. Nor will you. Nor will anyone. Now leave this earth with only the certainty that you gave your life for nothing. The world will roll on, and it will do it without you. You will never see home again.'

It was impossible. She was lying. She had to be lying. But what if she was not? What if it had all been for naught? He could feel the life draining from him, his extremities already cold. She had killed him. The horse-farmer had killed him. And for nothing. Lazant stared up at her, his mouth working but no sound coming out, as she slumped down against the rock pile. Then his features contorted into a vicious snarl, and he snatched at the bloodied hilt in his armpit. 'I shall not die alone in—'

A blur in his peripheral vision, something pelting over the rock-strewn cavern floor, and bellowing as it came.

'Don't touch my . . . Ree!'

Lazant ripped the blade clear, sending hot blood jetting from his armpit, and raised the weapon above his head as the child arrived, knee-first, and smashed it from his grip. He gasped and flailed, his vitality drained, and pitched slowly sideways in mute horror. As his cheek hit the cavern floor, his vision dimming, his thoughts became scattered and vague.

As the life left the body of Zakir Lazant, chosen prince of the highest house of the most royal court of the King of Kings of Shenak, he felt nothing but his mother's disappointment.

Javani stood over the expiring prince, hot breath tearing at her throat, and wanted to say something, wanted to yell, 'That was for Moosh!' as the light faded from his eyes. But the words wouldn't come.

She was shaking all over and felt as if she would throw up if she opened her mouth.

Ree looked up, dazed and fading. 'Oh kid,' she said with a shake of her head and a sad smile, 'you're not supposed to be here.'

Javani swallowed back bile, her thoughts in chaos. She'd heard everything. *She's not even my aunt?* Her voice was a ragged mess, much like her well-chewed shirt. 'I'm going to get you fixed up, Ree, I'm going to get you out of here.'

'I believe you, kid. I always believe you.'

Behind them, a large rock rose from the rubble pile and rumbled downwards in a shower of rising dust, and a sand-coated helmet emerged, followed by a pair of enormous black steel shoulders.

'Finally,' Ree muttered, and closed her eyes.

THIRTY-FIVE

For all their faults, the Guvulis had planned ahead. Half-buried beneath rubble and drifts of powdered stone, they found the stores they'd squirrelled for their intended sojourn in the cavern. Enough of it was of a medical nature that the White Spear could set to work without delay or comment, washing Ree's wounds in the least cloudy part of the little pool, applying unguents and binding them with what passed for clean linen amongst the Guvulis' preparations. Ree herself drifted in and out of consciousness as the mercenary worked, hissing and gasping between bouts of somnolence.

Javani couldn't make herself watch, couldn't bear to see the extent of Ree's injuries, the blood-sodden wreckage of her clothes torn away by the White Spear's powerful grip. She couldn't bear to see her mother in such delirious pain.

No, not her mother. Not even her aunt.

Something welled up within her, a hot ball that seemed to swell until it pressed against the base of her throat and she felt she might at once burst into tears and vomit over the cavern floor. She turned herself away, one hand over her mouth, the other pressed to her chest, physically fighting to hold her emotions at bay. She was unmoored again, cut loose from the world, her recent certainties vanished like ash on the wind. She drifted away from the pool, Ree's words playing over and over in her head.

I found the girl in the ruin of a settlement.

I have carried her since, protected her, raised her, but I have never claimed her.

Nor will anyone.

Something tickled at her thoughts, a thin, desperate idea born of baseless hope.

Her foot bumped against an obstacle on the floor, and she looked down. Lazant was at her feet, on his back, his eyes wide. He was staring right at her. His arm was moving.

She screamed.

The White Spear was beside her in an instant, covering the intervening ground with swift, giant strides. Javani found herself pushed to one side, shielded behind the great armoured form, staring at the broken shaft of a bolt that projected from the curve of the woman's dust-streaked, black-shelled back.

'You saw something?' The mercenary's tone was flat, devoid of accusation or doubt.

'He . . . I thought . . .' She stopped, swallowed. 'Are you sure he's dead?'

The woman took a couple of steps, squatted down, then rose with a fat slab of broken stone in her hands. She sidled over to where Lazant lay, still staring up at the cracked and twinkling ceiling, heaved the slab out over his head, and let go.

Javani shut her eyes just in time, but not her ears. The sound was halfway between crushing a walnut and stamping on an overripe orange, both things she'd done in the past, and then and there vowed to never do again. Something warm and wet spattered against her cheek, and she shuddered uncontrollably.

'Yes,' the White Spear said.

Javani, with great reluctance, opened her eyes, but not before wiping her face with her sleeve and very deliberately not looking at what came off. The scene wasn't as bad as she'd feared, but that was largely thanks to the cavern's low light, and the fact that Lazant was untouched but for a large slab of rock where his head used to be. The splatter marks were somewhat lacklustre, probably because most of the man's blood had already rushed from the wound Ree had made at his armpit.

The White Spear knelt down beside the body and began some kind of inspection. Javani cast a glance back to where Ree lay, a mass of tight and bloodied bandages, her eyes closed and breathing steady.

'Is she going to be . . . Will she live? My m— Ree?'

The mercenary looked up, flicked a heavy cable of hair from before her face and over her shoulder. Her sullied braids looked as though they were going to need the mother of all washes.

'Most of her wounds are superficial. She has lost blood, but not beyond the limit. The wound in her leg from the bolt remains the most serious, but it is clean and sealed. You must watch her over the coming days.'

Javani nodded, her throat thick. She watched the big woman work her fingers beneath the golden blood-striped breastplate, flip the headless body onto its side and start on the strapping. Broken shafts jutted from several places in her armour, and she moved stiffly as she worried at the stained leather.

'Are you all right? You have a few . . . holes in your armour.'

The White Spear tutted as a blood-gummed buckle resisted her attentions, and reached down for the sticky and black-bladed knife that lay beside the body. 'I am fine, thank you,' she muttered as she attempted to lever the little knife into the buckle and tease out the leather. 'This armour is very good. Few of the bolts pierced the second layer, and only one the aketon. I shall live, may a thousand grave-blades take the gods of spite.'

Javani scratched at her cheek, brows lowered. 'Why are you upset? Your armour kept you alive, right?'

'The armour,' the woman grunted as she finally worked the strap clear, 'is very good, and because it is very good, it is very expensive. Expensive to commission, expensive to repair. This damage will be ruinous.' She freed the last of the buckles and rolled the corpse the other way to get at the remainder. Javani put her hand over her eyes as one loose arm flapped towards her feet.

'What in the name of the gods are you doing?'

'Salvage.'

'What?'

'I am taking this armour, and his weapons. These I need to fund my return journey, as well as the repairs to my armour.'

'Why?'

The White Spear paused her ministrations and looked up, fixing Javani with a gaze that was neither angry nor accusatory, but contained no hint of warmth or compassion.

'Because,' she said slowly, 'I will be unable to collect my completion fee for this contract.'

Javani went very still, and a giddy feeling told her she'd stopped breathing.

'You won't?' she gasped at last.

The mercenary returned to the straps. They were less blood-ruined on this side. 'My contract was to find and return the heir. The heir is dead, and has been for many years. The contract is void.'

'But . . . you mean . . .'

'I heard her words, as I freed myself. A lone confession to a dying man.' She looked up again, briefly. 'You are not the heir.'

A warm feeling spread across Javani's chest, a fluttery lightness that set her fingers tingling. It was over. Lazant was dead, and the mercenary was leaving. She would not be Queen of Kings, but she'd never *really* cared about being a princess, all she'd wanted was to stay with—

Cold doused her fledgling warmth. It was over because Ree wasn't her mother after all, wasn't even her aunt. Was nothing to her.

No. Not true.

She was gritting her teeth without realising it, her fists tight. Ree was anything but nothing. What had she said? Labels aren't important. What a kid needs is someone to look out for them.

Ree was the person who looked out for her. That was what mattered.

The White Spear stood, the gory breastplate under one arm, dripping straps hanging loose, Lazant's fine sword and scabbard in her hand. Various other items disappeared into the pouches at her wide belt, including the infamous ceremonial blade.

'The exit is clear?' she said, nodding towards the cracked wall.

Javani started. 'You know about that?'

One corner of the woman's lip curled, flexing the tattoo across her cheek. 'I presumed you were making for this place for a reason.'

Javani coughed. 'Um, yeah. Something like that.' She gestured to the distant crevice. 'Rocks have moved around inside, shifted by the explosion I think. The way's pretty blocked for anyone of your, um . . . bigger than me.'

The woman nodded. 'I will remedy.' She put down Lazant's splattered gear and stomped off towards the far wall. Javani was left alone with the body, now stripped of armour and equipment as well as head. She gave it one last look, trying to summon a feeling beyond guilty relief, then padded back to Ree on increasingly aching legs.

Ree was reclined against a loose stack of shattered yellow stone, her eyes closed, her breathing steady. Javani stood beside her not-aunt, not-mother, for a time, watching her chest rise and fall, feeling an incredible longing for something she couldn't describe, the sudden easing of her terrors undercut by melancholy.

It doesn't matter, she told herself. Labels aren't important. Ree saved me, and damned near gave her life away to do it.

But, came the prickly response, it does matter, doesn't it? When you found out she was your ma, that she was where you came from, that feeling you had, that feeling of certainty, of belonging . . . that was what had been missing from your life, and you didn't even know it. And now it's gone, smashed and blown away to nothing like so much crushed sand. She found you, what family you'd had already dead. Early settlers, perhaps . . . Gods, early missionaries? What if you're the child of those ghastly bearded—

'Are you going to just stand there muttering, kid, or can you be useful and get me some water? Gods' mercy, the state of your shirt. I thought you grew out of chewing it years ago.'

Ree was looking up at her, her eyes crinkled, that familiar mocking smile on her lips. Only the splatter on her cheek and the blooded ruin of her clothes spoiled the image.

'S-Sure.'

The Guvulis had left some battered mugs and cooking irons. Javani filled one at the pool and brought it back to Ree, who drank daintily, one-armed.

'Thanks, kid. I could murder a cup of tea, if we're going nowhere for a while. Our big friend gone to see about the tunnel?'

'Uh-huh.'

'Well, there's a comfort.' She smiled again, a warm and genuine smile so steeped in affection that Javani felt tears burning beneath her eyes. She wanted to wrap her arms around her not-aunt and weep until she slept.

'Are you in a lot of pain?' she said instead, trying to keep the emotion from her voice.

Ree's smile faded a touch. 'I'd like to say I've had worse, but between us, kid, I'm not sure I have.' She rolled her head to one side, stared up at the cavern ceiling. 'You know, not that long ago I'd have been able to take him without resorting to antics.'

Javani blinked. 'What do you mean, antics?'

'I mean I'd have been able to cut him down in a straight-up duel, and I'd have looked great doing it.' She gestured with her good arm. 'I wouldn't have needed so much bandaging, certainly.'

Javani put up one hand. 'Whoa, whoa-whoa-whoa . . . Are you saying you *let* him cut you up? Deliberately?'

'I had few options available. I took a calculated risk.'

Javani's hands were in her hair. She'd taken an involuntary step back. 'Are you . . . How could . . . What if he hadn't made a meal of it, what if he'd just flat-out killed you?'

Ree met her incredulous gaze with eyes that were steady and cool. 'Then I'd have been a bad judge of character.'

Javani sat down heavily beside her, head in her hands. 'That's the most incredible thing I've ever heard.'

'It's *called* a gambit, kid. As you well know.'

'Then that thing you did at the end . . . You danced past his sword. You'd been planning it.'

'Took the knife off him the first time I got near enough. The rest was patience.' She made a face. 'And endurance. Still, if there's one thing I've had a lot of practice at, it's withstanding pain.'

The image resurfaced in Javani's mind, Ree swivelling on one foot, whirling in space, and it locked with a host of other memories. 'The sun dances. Those stretches you do every morning. They're sword forms, aren't they? You really were a sword-fighting spy.'

Ree shook her head slowly, lips pulled back tight in suppressed glee. 'And they say all this desert heat is bad for the brain.'

'Do . . . Do you think you could teach me them? When you're better?'

Only the slightest crinkle at the corners of Ree's eyes indicated the change in her mood. 'That depends. Does that steel-covered lunk still intend to drag you off to Shenak? Do I have to duel her next?'

'No, no!' Javani found she was laughing, half at the absurdity of the thought, half at the volcanic overflow of emotion and adrenaline she could no longer contain. 'She's going home – without me. Said the contract was void. Because . . . because . . .'

'Ah.' Ree's gaze softened, and her unbound hand reached out towards Javani. 'Listen, kid—'

The White Spear's head appeared through the rent in the wall, followed by the rest of her. She heaved a chunk of rock off into the cavern, then approached. 'The way is clear. I suggest you leave now, with me.'

Ree looked at her through narrowed eyes, and the mercenary shook her head. 'I have already told the child. My contract is discharged. Only death does this.'

'Could have dug yourself out a little faster, don't you think?' Ree said, with one eyebrow raised.

'You triumphed in the end.'

'I could have used a hand.'

'Where would be the pride and accomplishment in such a victory?'

Ree's smile cracked into a grin. 'I'm so full of both they're positively leaking out of me.'

The White Spear returned the grin with a faint smile of her

own, the closest thing to comity Javani had seen on her rugged face. 'Come. Child, if you will carry the equipment, I will carry the woman.'

Javani looked over at Lazant's blooded gear and shuddered.

'Come on, kid,' Ree said as the White Spear levered her off the ground. 'You're getting the better end of that deal.'

'What about him?' Javani said, eyes still on the prince's remains.

'What about him?' Ree replied.

'Do you think more will come, after him? To look for him, or . . .' she swallowed, 'try to finish his work?'

Ree didn't respond, and for a sharp moment Javani wondered if she'd passed out again. Then she sighed, low and soft. 'I don't know, kid, I really don't. But listen, one thing is certain: that's the end of this one. That weasel-prick acted alone, and his claim dies in this cavern. I'm sure his mother will mourn him, but his fate will forever be a mystery back home. He stepped inside a mountain and was lost. And Whitespear here will be reporting that the hoped-for heir does not exist. The viziers of Shenak will have to look elsewhere for their next King of Kings.'

'You're sure?'

'As sure as the sun will come up tomorrow.' The White Spear had her clean off the ground, cradled in her arms. She looked small and broken and diminished, but her eyes burned with fierce clarity. Javani believed.

'All that said, we probably shouldn't hang around. Come on, kid. Let's get out of here.'

Anashe helped her brother sit, his back against the striated rock, her own body's pains already a distant irrelevance.

'If you give swift chase, my sister, you will catch her before she reaches the mountains.' His breath was steady, his smile broad, but the spear was almost through him. Blood pooled on the baked earth beneath, casting its parched cracks black and spongy.

'As if, brother,' Anashe said, unable to keep the tremble from her voice, 'I would wish to miss a moment of your company.'

With her good hand, she felt around him, testing the limits of the wound. It was beneath his ribs, but angled upwards. Already she detected a bubbly rasp to his breathing.

She began to tear at her own ruined clothes, seeking to make bindings from them, and he put up a gentle hand. 'Please, my sister, do not further tarnish your appearance on my futile account.'

'Do not say it is futile! Do not say such a thing, Aki!'

He rested his head to one side, taking a breath with slight visible effort, then reached a hand inside his jacket. 'I must give you something, my sister.' He produced a small pouch with a heavy dangle. 'I must give you my treasures. Soon, I will have no need for them, and to let them go to waste would be a crime against the Goddess herself.'

'You are speaking nonsense, Aki. Again!' Tears were hard in her eyes now, brimming over and rolling down her sweat-crusted cheeks. 'Why must you always speak such nonsense!'

'Share them with the child, if you see her again.' He pressed the pouch into her hand and folded it closed, then let his head fall back against the canyon wall. Somewhere overhead came a bird's shrill cry, the first sound to penetrate the canyon's claustrophobic stillness Anashe could remember.

'I was wrong, my sister.'

She tried to meet his gaze, but he was staring off into the middle distance, somewhere out over the rolling plain beyond the canyon's mouth. 'Of course you were,' she replied, 'it is your natural state.' Then a sob pulsed out of her, convulsing her as she bent over his reclining form.

'Aki, my brother, my light, my life. Do not leave me, Aki. Do not leave me in this place. The things I said, the harsh words—'

'I was wrong, sister. I thought I saw it so clearly. In our story, I was Ranu, I was the Shield, the Protector, the Champion. But the child spoke true: I was not.'

'Please, Aki—'

He touched his palm to her face, lifted her chin. Already his fingers felt cool against her skin. 'I am not Ranu, I am Aret. I am the Messenger, my sister.'

'Then you cannot leave me – in the great story, the Messenger lives for ever.'

He smiled again, a smile that was both sad and happy, a mix of pride and profound melancholy. 'How else can I carry the message to the heavens?'

'Aki, no!'

'I was wrong, sister. It is you who is Ranu, the Protector, the Champion.'

'But I didn't protect you!'

He squeezed his eyes shut, and when they reopened, tears glistened. 'You have protected me my entire life, Anashe. You allowed me to complete my life's purpose.'

'What purpose? What do you mean?'

'The final teaching, the final lesson from our mother.' He gazed at her through eyes misted with tears, his breath now coming in long, trembling heaves. 'The greatest love – to give your life for those you cherish most.'

Anashe gazed back, fighting against the tremble of her lip, fighting the sobs racking her body. Her voice came out so small. 'Please do not leave me, Aki.'

'I am Aret the Messenger, my sister, and I will see our mother in the heavens. I will tell her everything we did, everything we saw, everything we learned.' His words were getting harder now, the breath puffing from his blooded lips.

'Everything, brother? Even the stupidity?'

A smile crinkled the corners of his eyes. 'Especially the stupidity.'

'My love will go with you, Aki. Always.'

He fell quiet, his breath coming in bubbling gasps, each slower, more drawn-out than the last. Anashe clenched herself to him, wrapped her battered and ruined body around his, wept into the ruin of his clothes.

'Do you see it, my sister?'

She looked up. His eyes were open wide, staring out at something only he could see.

'What is it, brother? What do you see?' Her voice was little more than a choked whisper.

'My words . . . the poetry of my soul. Do you see it rise?' A beatific smile lit his face. 'It was in my heart all along.'

He breathed twice more, then was still.

THIRTY-SIX

They rested in the shade of a bent and spindly tree, just up from where the Guvulis' tunnel – its final passageway smashed clear by the indomitable White Spear – had dumped them into a sunken gully high between two bluffs. Javani sat close to Ree across the gnarled and exposed roots, not quite touching, listening to the slow rhythm of her breath, each steady inhalation and exhalation chipping away at the tension and grief that had been building within her since the White Spear and her caravan had come to town.

The southerner herself had gone in search of mounts – not for herself, as she stressed (and Javani wondered if a horse existed anywhere in the expanse that could have borne her armoured mass . . . Perhaps an aurochs might have been up to the task), but for her now former targets. Fortunately, from their new vantage on the crest of the bluffs, they had a wide view over the rolling plains beneath, on one side the snow-capped peaks of the Ashadi mountains, on the other the pale shimmer of the salt desert. The plains were near-empty but for a still-smoking blur of wreckage a little way from them, and a number of dust-coloured, stocky-looking horses cropping at the waving dry grass. Javani had smiled when she recognised them, all whole, all resting and feeding. She could finally repay their exertions and bring them back to the farm, tend to their needs, give them a home.

The farm. Home.

They weren't going home. They no longer had one. They couldn't return to the farm, couldn't stay in the north. They had to move on. Again. Would they ever find somewhere they could put down roots? Where was there left to go? Could someone with no family ever hope to find peace?

Shut up, Javani.

Even if Ree weren't her mother, weren't even her aunt, she was still the person in her life who looked out for her. Who raised her, who kept her, who taught her right from wrong – according to her own definitions, at least. Who had gone into the wilderness with a baby on her hip, and made a life for them both.

Tears stinging her eyes, she shuffled closer, put her arm around Ree and rested her head on her shoulder.

'Funny how it's still daytime,' Ree said, resting her head against Javani's own. 'Felt like we'd been down there an eternity. I was expecting to be coming out to a sunrise.'

Javani squeezed her, gently. 'I love you,' she whispered.

'I love you too, kid,' came the croaky reply. 'Even when you smell like baked horse-apples. I'm sorry I put you through all that.'

'How much is "all that"? How far back are we going, here?'

Ree chuckled, then winced, stiffening beneath Javani's weight. 'I'm sorry for a lot of things. I think . . . I think I haven't been doing enough thinking, these last few years. Just been following a furrow in the earth, no eye to the sky. It's time I looked up.'

'Yeah?'

'Yeah. And I'm sorry you heard what you heard down there. I didn't . . . I didn't intend for that.'

Javani tried to shrug, which was hard in her position. At least she knew the truth now. The truth that she was rootless, as shorn of family history as Ree herself. Something tickled at her mind again, the small, desperate thought, and this time she had the strength to drag it out into the light and follow it through.

'Ree.'

'Kid?'

'When the White Spear finally dug herself out, just before you collapsed, you said, "finally".'

'Did I?'

'You did. You'd been expecting her, hadn't you?'

She felt Ree's cheek move against her head, pulling back into her sardonic smile. 'Had I?'

Her thoughts were moving faster now, picking up speed like a wagon set rolling down a mountain trail. 'You knew she was there, digging out of the rock, when you had Lazant on the ground. That speech you gave, when you told him he'd been wrong, that wasn't for him, was it? Was it? It was for her. It was to stop her taking me away!'

Her breath was becoming shallow, her cheeks warming as one implication followed another. 'You guessed she'd accept that, over denial to her face – who'd lie to a dying man, after all? And you were right! She declared the contract void, and she's heading back south in a huff.'

Ree wasn't saying anything, but she wasn't trying to shush her, either. Javani ploughed on.

'So everything you said, about me not being . . . about having lost . . . about finding me . . . You made it up. It's another gambit, isn't it?' She swallowed, feeling the burn in her cheeks, the terrible lightness rising through her gut. 'I'm your daughter after all. And I'm really the heir to the throne of Shenak, aren't I? I'm a princess!'

Ree lifted her head and, with the soft application of her good arm, separated herself from Javani's embrace. She met her eager gaze with steady eyes, brows lifted with unending affection.

'Sorry, kid. You're not.'

Javani's heart stopped. For a moment, she couldn't breathe, her thoughts crashing like the runaway wagon.

'I . . . I'm not?'

Ree slowly shook her head, one corner of her mouth pulled tight. 'I know it's disappointing, and I'm sorry.' She leaned back against the bleached roots with tender care, and stared out over the whispering plain.

'Sadly,' she said, shifting her injured arm beneath its strapping, 'your father was a mule-herd.'

If Javani's heart had stopped before, now it did so twice, with such force as to bend her double, eyes popping.

'What?!'

'Life is full of disappointment, my darling girl, and I've done my best to shelter you, but some things are inevitable. You are not a child of royal blood, although your father was an extremely handsome and muscular fellow with tremendous hair, so perhaps there's hope for you yet. You all right, kid? Did you swallow a fly?'

Javani's jaw was moving up and down, her mouth forming shapes, but she had forgotten how it was she was supposed to make words.

'You mean,' she gasped at last, 'that I'm your daughter, for real?'

Ree gazed back at her, and this time she saw nothing but boundless love and boundless mirth. 'How could you doubt it, kid? Everyone says we've got the same eyes.'

Javani shook herself, her cheeks hot, her neck sweaty. 'I just . . . I can't tell if you're lying now, or you were lying then, or . . . or . . . Aaargh!'

'You don't believe me?'

'I don't know! You lie with such ridiculous ease, how can I ever know the truth?'

The mirth in Ree's expression subsided, but the affection remained. 'Well here's my offer, kid: if you want, you can decide your own truth. Choose your story the way you want it, and I'll be with you all the way. You've earned the right. How does that sound?'

Javani tried to bring her breathing back under control. 'I'll think about it,' she said at last.

A whinny from down the slope drew their attention. The White Spear had returned, leading several horses up from the plain. She was not alone.

'Hey,' Javani said, 'is that Anashe? Where's Aki?'

Ree was staring at the last of the horses, her smile frozen.

'Oh. Oh, no.'

* * *

They buried Aki at the foot of an almond tree at the edge of the hills, on a snub-grassed rise that looked out over the plains. The White Spear had suggested a sky burial – dismembering the body and leaving it for carrion birds, a custom apparently practised in hard and high places – but Anashe demurred. They buried him deep in the red earth, in a pit dug mostly by the White Spear, who wore her scarred black armour for the duration. Javani wondered if she had some terrible disfigurement beneath the armour, or if perhaps it was fused to her body by flame or enchantment. Or perhaps she simply had nothing else to wear. Whatever the case, it seemed not to bother her, and it did not bother Javani.

After the burial, the adults sat in a circle in the shade of the hillside and told stories, first of Aki, but then of others, people she'd never heard of, people that Ree and Anashe seemed to know. Even the White Spear joined in, recounting a tale of a Horvaun berserker (which as far as Javani could tell was some kind of hallucinogen-fuelled warrior) she'd known, a bumptious and well-loved soul who once chased a tooth-whale beneath the ice and emerged victorious. The first time, at least.

Most of the stories of Aki involved his own stories, tall tales told to inappropriate audiences, attempts to superimpose narrative structure on whatever chaos surrounded him at the least pertinent moment. What shone through them all was the shape of a man with strong beliefs but good intentions, which Javani thought was far better than a lot of people she'd known.

Javani had not been an official part of the circle, hovering at its edge in Ree's shadow, but gradually she shuffled forwards, and hesitantly at first, volunteered a story of Moosh. She told of his wild tales and inventions, and how he'd very nearly managed to convince Terbish in the teahouse that he'd discovered a novel way of fermenting goat's milk that would triple her yield. Needless to say, it had all ended in tears (and some very upset stomachs), but Javani felt it was important to include Moosh in the ceremony. He deserved recognition and remembrance, and she was gratified to hear the others solemnly promise to add her story to their roster.

She just wished he'd got to meet Aki – she could only imagine the utter nonsense they'd have talked.

Ree told a story of Aki and Anashe's mother, a woman called Kwayedza; from the way Ree spoke of her, she had been somewhere between a war leader and a mother to her and her companions. Anashe sat in silence while Ree spoke, staring at the scrubby ground between her crossed shins. She had recounted most of Aki's stories with a tight, neutral voice, keeping both the humour and the grief at bay for as long as she spoke, but the moment her words were finished, she seemed to collapse in on herself, tears filling her eyes, her body racked with silent sobs.

Javani was sitting across from her, still huddled against Ree, but the sight of Anashe's pain overwhelmed her. She trotted over and squeezed herself in between her and the White Spear, then wrapped her arms around Anashe and held her tight. She felt the woman's shuddering breath, felt her stiffen at the touch, then unclench, allow herself to be hugged, her head on Javani's shoulder. They stayed that way until the stories were done.

The White Spear stood slowly, flexing her armoured joints, now at least devoid of jutting bolt-shafts. 'It is uncommon to partake in a circle without strong alcohol.'

'It's still too early for booze,' Ree said, testing her own damaged leg as she climbed to her feet. 'I'll make some tea.'

The White Spear rotated her head between black-steel shoulders, producing a satisfying crunch. 'I will return to the mine and gather more of the supplies. Perhaps there is alcohol among them. I am unconvinced that a circle counts as such if all the participants are sober.'

Ree looked back at the rising figures, at Javani helping Anashe to her feet, one arm tight around her. A hot little feeling burned somewhere beneath her ribcage.

'I'd say it counts just fine.'

'Where will you go?'

'Hm?'

'You cannot return to your farm, of course. I will return south and deliver my report, but that will be no guarantee of satisfaction in any faction of the Shenakar court.'

Ree's gaze slipped back to Javani, watching her daughter comfort a woman two decades her senior.

'We haven't discussed it yet,' she said, but the giant Horvaun was right. There was no way they could risk returning to the farm, or to Kazeraz. Their time in mining country was done. They needed to be away in short order, and leave no tracks. Zakir Lazant was unlikely to prove their last unwanted visitor.

'And the Shade? Your comrade reported that she fled their battle. Are you concerned that she may return with reinforcements, seeking vengeance?'

'Anashe said she was making for the mountains.' Ree gestured towards the snow-tipped peaks to the west, bathed in afternoon sun, their distant upper slopes green and shimmering. 'Shenak is the other way.'

The White Spear adjusted the knives at her belt. 'Should she be hunted nonetheless?'

'Are you kidding? Nobody gets over the Ashadi. If she makes it to Arestan, she deserves everything she gets.'

Khalida moved as swiftly as the wounds to her body would allow, crashing up slope, her dying mount left somewhere in the foothills beneath.

Vessel! Not body. She had no body, only a . . .

She shook her head. It was no good, a spell had been broken, a wall breached in her mind. When she looked at her cut and bleeding limbs, she no longer saw an imperfect instrument of duty, she saw her own flesh, her own self. The prolonged battle with the chasers, and its sudden, sharp end, the flood of fear she'd felt – existential, *corporeal* – had blasted the veil from her eyes.

Her prince was gone, lost beneath the collapsing mountain.

Her body was her own, and she wanted to *live*.

She was well into the tree-line now, the air already cooler, thick dappled forest on all sides. Birds screeched and chirped around her, larger animals bolting away from her heedless approach, sending boughs and brush swaying in their wake. She had limited supplies and equipment, only what she'd taken from the horse, but she had blades and she had her life. She'd trained in the mountain forests of Shenak, setting snares and hunting game – she had no concern of keeping herself fed and healthy. She would climb the peaks, cross one of the passes at her own pace, descend to paradise beyond. Summer had plenty yet to run; she had time. And she had a fortune in silver talents, each stamped with the head of the King of Kings.

Khalida smiled as she stopped to catch her breath, hands on her knees. Twilight was falling, already the light in the forest deepening, the greens shifting to blue and indigo. She looked down at herself. The bleeding had stopped. She was going to live, and live well.

To her right, a patch of foliage rippled, shifting in a wind she didn't feel. Khalida pushed herself slowly upright, brows lowered in a frown. The leaves were still now, but she couldn't shake the feeling that something had moved them, something large.

Her hand moved towards one of her blades, then she caught herself. What had she to fear in a mountain forest that didn't have more to fear from her? Her thoughts were better spent on planning her new life beyond the mountains, a life of presence, of physicality. A life of visceral pleasure.

The blur burst from the trees beside her, a fast-moving mass that filled her vision at once with stripes—

Then nothing at all.

THIRTY-SEVEN

Ree found Anashe by the makeshift corral, watching the horses stamp and snort and flick their tails at the might of the hot season's insect horde as the fat red sun disappeared behind the western peaks. She passed her a clay mug of tea, rescued from the Guvulis' camp, and then settled next to her with her own, elbows on a silvered boulder that projected from the hillside's crust of pale grasses.

'I know . . .' Anashe began, then tailed off. Her shoulder was tightly bound and she moved stiffly, but she seemed in a far better state than Ree herself, who refused to use a crutch only from pride. Anashe's greatest injury was not to her body.

Ree said nothing, letting the other woman breathe, form herself unpressed.

'I know that the circle . . . replaces mourning, in mercenary custom,' Anashe said at last. She kept her voice neutral, gave only the slightest shake of her head. 'Sharing stories together like that . . . He would have delighted in it.'

Ree nodded slowly. A circle of shared storytelling after a loss, or when a need for collective introspection seized a free company, was the closest thing to an unwritten law in the conventions of freelance soldiery, especially down south. Over the years, she'd partaken in more than she could count, more than she could remember, the events blurring together, but the stories . . . the stories she remembered.

She sipped at her tea while she waited for Anashe to complete her thought. It had been such a relief to find some in the Guvulis' provisions, after all the ructions. A dearth of tea would have been too much to bear. To their credit, the bandits had planned for a short stay and a long journey – there was even plentiful fodder for the horses.

Anashe took a long, ragged breath. 'I have never had to mourn before.'

Ree turned her head, raised an eyebrow.

'When my mother was banished,' Anashe said, the croak in her voice easing as the words came, 'I was an infant, too small to understand, too young to grieve.' She took a sip from her tea. 'By the time we tracked her to the Sink, learned of her death . . . I felt only the loss of an idea, not a person.'

'You can mourn an idea.'

'You can. And I did. But it was not true mourning. I had lost someone I did not remember, someone I had barely known.'

Ree's eyebrow was still up. Her face ached. 'And in your travels, you saw no other death?'

Anashe shook her head. 'We saw death, we saw maiming, we saw catastrophic loss. These are not happy times, Ree, especially for those caught beneath war's millstone in the south. We travelled through misery. But we travelled.

'And we had each other.'

She took another long breath, halting and harsh, then held it until her chest was still. 'He was my constant companion for every day of my life; my only family, my only friend, for more than three decades. And he was a pain in my posterior for the duration.'

A slow tear tracked down her cheek, gleaming in the red light, but she held her composure. 'We came to this place to learn of our mother, as he saw it, to complete her teachings, to gain . . . enlightenment.'

'You told me before that you wanted him to find peace.' Ree remembered her own answer, and hoped that Anashe didn't.

'I believe he got his wish. He lived his truth, and he found his story, and I was privileged to travel in his shadow.'

Ree watched her, saw the corded working of her throat, her rigid posture, the inner strength that kept her upright. She sipped her tea again.

'And what about you?'

Anashe stared out over the horses, looking out past the makeshift corral to where the land rose, and the branches of an almond tree swayed in the evening breeze.

'I have seen so much of this world, yet so little. We moved fast and far, I do not believe I have ever stayed anywhere long enough to see a season turn. My young life is lived, and some of my old, and I have . . . nothing. I have built nothing, I have made nothing, I have loved none but my stupid brother, Goddess enfold him.'

'What about your enlightenment?'

She smiled, a bright crack in her mask. 'Of course. At least I have that.'

'When I asked you before about what you would do if your brother were not dragging you ever onwards, you said "nothing". But is that what you want now?'

'I want . . . I want to start again. I wish to make my own path, live a life of my own.'

'And what's stopping you?'

Anashe turned, her eyes downcast, her unbound shoulder slumped. 'I lack the experience, the understanding of an independent life. I am as a child, dependent on the care of others. Would you permit me to travel with you as I learn, infant that I am?'

Ree laughed, bright and hard. 'That is not true. Not even a little bit.' She reached across, put her hand on Anashe's arm. 'You're welcome to stick with us if you wish, but you don't *need* anyone.'

Anashe looked around the extent of the rising hills and the imposing Ashadi beyond them. 'Where will you go? I have no desire to cross any more mountains.'

Ree looked back to where Javani was, it seemed, drawing pictures in the loose earth with a long stick by their fledgeling campfire. 'We've not yet discussed it.'

'Do you think you can continue to outrun your past?'

'At this stage, I'd settle for outrunning my present.'

'Do you mean me? I have no wish to become your burden.'

'You would be no burden, Anashe.' Ree removed her hand, scratched at her neck. 'But didn't you say you had friends in the city, down south?' She pushed herself to remember Anashe's words. 'Something like . . . prospects?'

Anashe's cheeks darkened and her nostrils flared, and Ree's eyebrows went up. 'Oh-ho! Tell me more how you have loved none but your brother!'

The woman swallowed, covered her mouth with the tea mug. 'I had some . . . fleeting acquaintances . . .'

Ree put her hand as firmly as she could on Anashe's unbound shoulder. 'Anashe, my girl, listen to me. You are not alone. You have friends here, you have the Commodore and the agency in Arowan – and you have your "prospects". You have lived a life of duty, in service of your brother's goals, and that duty is complete. You are no longer beholden to any but yourself.' She tipped her head forward, staring at the woman from beneath lifted brows.

'You know why contractors claim the circle serves as mourning? It's to save time, to let you get on with the next thing. Nobody on this earth can lose a friend or lover and be free of grief from a single ceremony – the stronger the bond, the deeper the loss, and the grief will travel with you for the rest of your life. I carry scars on my heart as deep and jagged as a canyon, and there are moments when I want to do nothing more than scream at the skies for the misery of it all.

'But the circle lets you keep moving. It frees you, lets you carry your scars your own way, and grieve in your own time. We recognise our loss, and although we may never make peace with it, we give it a name. We carry our pain, but we carry it forward.'

Anashe's eyes were misty, her words thick. 'What are you saying?'

'That you must live a life that is yours, not an idea of someone else's. Don't let the idea of your brother take over from the idea of your mother. You've done what you needed, now do what you choose. Go south with the White Spear. Make friends. Exist. Watch a season turn. You have everything you need.' She paused. 'Except coin, maybe.'

A small smile lit Anashe's face. She rummaged for a moment, then withdrew a small, heavy-looking pouch, let it settle on her palm. It produced a gentle clinking sound.

'Aki's final gift,' she said softly. 'Perhaps this was his will after all.'

'He wills it,' Ree echoed with a tight smile.

'He threatened to return, you know.'

'He did?'

'As Aret, the Messenger. In the form of a bird.' She wiped an eye. 'Watch for one that floats around, doing nothing of use, and making a lot of noise. That will be him.'

Ree put an arm around her narrow shoulders, wincing at the movement, her own eyes stinging. 'I'll be sure to give him a wave.'

Movos Guvuli rode slowly towards the town gates, noting the absence of guards with a tingle of what might have been excitement. He'd taken his time on the ride down from the mountains, taking the long way round and camping a night, with regular shaded stops to rest Kurush's poor, battered horse, snacking on the bounty of the former Acting Guildmaster's saddlebags. Kurush had not been a man to skimp on his skimmings, that much was clear.

As he'd walked the horse, feeling the aches in his legs from each sway of the saddle, the throb of the bumps on his scalp, he'd pondered. The Guild in the north were as weak as they'd ever been. The old Guildmaster was dead, his aspiring successor was dead by snakebite (or should be, by now), the Guildhouse had a great rent in its walls, and half of those who rode beneath the seal were scattered between desert, plains and mountains, lost in the chase for that strange little urchin.

Movos smiled when he thought of the kid, then caught himself, then with a mental shrug, let the smile linger. She'd cost him, true, cost him dear and sharp, but she'd freed him from more than the prison of the crumbling watchtower. Movos was bubbling with ideas like a simmering stewpot, and many of them revolved around the exploitation or even expulsion of the Guild's operations, at least in the short term. He wouldn't be the only one to cotton to the Guild's current frailty, its lack of manpower and resources. Others might turn their minds to making their play, once they realised that the Guild lacked the means to hold its claims, to hold its stores, to hold its forces together. Movos intended to be first. He still knew people, miners former and current, loaders and caravan guards, those employed and otherwise. These things had a way of taking on a life of their own, once they got rolling.

Movos's smile had broadened to a grin as he rode slowly along the still rubble-strewn street towards the square. A quick scout around the Guildhouse was in order. A few types might require forcible persuasion to see the merit of his arguments, but he was willing to make sacrifices. They'd thank him, in the end. He just had to get in there before anyone else was able to capitalise.

There were more horses outside the ravaged Guildhouse than he'd been expecting. Considerably more. Bright-liveried riders and foot-types strutted this way and that, their clothes and armour powdered with travel dust, their chatter boisterous, clipped. Southern-accented.

Movos swallowed. Already a pair of guards was approaching, one with a hand raised somewhere between greeting and warning. He didn't recognise either. Movos cursed himself – he was riding Kurush's horse, the Guild's burnished shield still gleaming from its harness. He reached a slow hand to his chest, where the Guildmaster's seal he'd snatched from Kurush dangled on its chain.

'Are you the Acting Guildmaster?' the first guard called. He sounded as if he was from a long way south. 'We have questions.'

Movos muttered a silent prayer. 'You're not the only ones,' he sighed, and slid from the saddle.

They left at dawn without much ceremony, with a few hugs and warm words. Ree watched the short convoy move off down the slope, back towards the plain, and the town. The White Spear strode, vast and tireless, ahead of three of the stout ponies, now repurposed as pack animals and apparently much the happier for it. The White

Spear was smiling. Ree wasn't sure she'd ever seen that before. It frightened her a little.

At the back of the line rode Anashe. She rode with her head high, her back straight, looking dead ahead, but just before she passed down into the valley and out of sight, she turned in the saddle and gave a single wave.

Ree waved back, harder than she'd intended, fresh tears hot in her eyes.

Movos had weighed his options carefully before opting for bare-faced denial. The guards had relieved him of the horse and marched him into the half-wrecked courtyard, where a tall woman with short silver hair and two long scars at her lip stood, surveying the great blast hole in the Guildhouse wall. Movos twitched and scratched at his beard with his foreshortened hand. So far, he'd recognised none of the new folk in livery teeming over the broken Guildhouse, but surely it wouldn't be long before someone familiar took it upon themselves to connect the great hole in the strongroom wall with the stocky, bearded gentleman standing like a stunned ox in the middle of the ruined courtyard. There was, of course, a good chance that they already knew, and that his short dance on the long rope was a looming formality.

The woman turned to him. She was a little older than he was, very weathered, and one of her eyes had a slightly milky cast. The other stared at him, granite-hard, and he felt himself trying to shrink away from her without visibly dragging his boots.

'You are . . .' She consulted a palimpsest covered with goat-hide so worn it shone. 'Kurush?'

Movos felt the guards behind him looming just that little bit closer.

'No, uh . . . my lady?' he ventured.

The clear eye held him firm. 'You are not Kurush.'

'I am not.'

'You arrived, riding what I'm informed is his horse, carrying the Guildmaster's seal that he inherited from his late predecessor.'

'I did.'

'But you are not he.' One corner of her mouth lifted, curling her scars. 'Then who be ye?'

'Movos, your, uh, my lady.' He thought better than to add his family name. 'I came across the man you mention, out on the trail. He'd been snakebit, one hand in a nest. I thought to return his goods to the Guild, where they might be missed.'

She looked him slowly up and down, then fixed on him again. 'But not the man's remains?'

Movos held the stare. He was acclimatising to it, and his sense of immediate danger was ebbing like a drying creek. He no longer had to force himself to ignore the milky eye. 'Didn't want to risk a fanging myself. I'll happily direct anyone you care to send to retrieve him, though. Man deserves a proper send-off, no doubt.'

The woman's mouth twitched again. Was that a smile? 'There, it seems, we have some disagreement.' She looked down at the palimpsest again. 'My name is Ziba Rahdat, Master Movos, and I represent the Chartered Miners' Guild of Serica.'

'In what capacity would that be, Mistress Rahdat?'

'As an auditor, Master Movos. An investigator of irregularities.'

She tilted her head to one side as she spoke, watching to see his reaction. Behind her, the courtyard door opened and two of the new guards dragged a kicking, struggling, spitting something out into the evening light: Nilam, the other Guild captain, right hand of Kurush's predecessor and Kurush's only true rival for the permanent post of Guildmaster. They threw Nilam to the ground, one of them gesturing with her spear that further disagreement would not be brooked. Nilam sat in the dust, snarling in furious silence, blind to Movos and the auditor.

'We are making some preliminary arrests, pending further investigations,' Ziba Rahdat said, her eye still on Movos. Somewhere in the distance he heard the familiar hammering of gallows-work. 'Tell me, Master Movos, do you have any affiliation with the Guild?'

Her mild tone was all the clue he needed. 'None whatsoever.'

'Yet you are a former miner?'

Movos held his face neutral. She'd read him, his limp, his missing fingers, the slant of his shoulders. 'In my day, before I found myself beset. To my misfortune, I fell out of favour with the Guild hereabouts in subsequent developments.'

Ziba Rahdat put one finger to her scarred lip, tapping it gently. 'Master Movos, I find myself in need of assistance. There is much to do, much to examine and explore, and I need someone at my side with a knowledge of this territory, its claims and peoples, crucially untainted by association with the regime under question. I need, bluntly, a source of local intelligence and advice. It will be a hard and demanding position, but it will offer great influence as to how matters proceed in this territory. Few people I encounter are as public-spirited as you. Do you believe you could provide what I describe?'

Over her shoulder, the guards hauled Nilam to her feet, began dragging her off across the courtyard towards the sound of hammering. For a moment, her frantic glare connected with Movos, and her brows lifted in confusion, shock and outrage. Then she was gone, ferried from sight, and to Movos's mind, unlikely to return.

Movos met the auditor's questioning stare, and carefully considered his reply.

THIRTY-EIGHT

Ree sat in the shade of the almond trees, her bad leg propped on a worn old saddle no longer fit to ride, watching the drifting banks of puffy cloud rolling over the blocky blue hills in the distant east. The morning was hot but the breeze had an edge to it, a cooling breath, and somehow the baked and buzzing world around her seemed less still, less stifling. Perhaps summer on the plains would have an end, after all. She ran a hand through her matted hair. It would be a long time before there was any chance of a bath, that much was certain.

The kid came clomping over from the fire pit and sat down beside her, passed her a fresh mug of tea. They sat quietly, watching the dry yellow grass of the stretching plains below shift and shimmer in the wind.

They sipped their tea.

'Will she be all right?' the kid said. 'Anashe?' She rubbed at an eye with the heel of her free hand. 'I mean, I lost a friend I'd known less than a year, and someone I'd known all of three days . . . and it hurts, you know? It burns.'

Ree nodded, keeping her eyes on the hazy horizon.

'She lost her brother,' Javani went on, 'her life's companion, her shadow. How do you recover from that?'

Ree took a long, slow breath. 'The same way as everyone else, kid. With time.'

They sipped their tea again.

'So, have you decided?' Ree asked, her gaze still lost to the east. 'On your preferred truth? What matters to you?'

'I have.'

'And?'

'Well,' the kid said, one hand on her chin, 'as I see it, people make too much of labels. But you want to know what matters to me?

'It matters that you lied. It matters that you kept me at a distance my whole life, for, and let's be honest here, a really stupid reason.' She took a breath. 'Aki told me that stories are important, even if they're not true, because they tell us who we want to be. And I get that, but my life isn't a story. There is such a thing as the real truth, the truth beneath as he might have called it, and it matters.

'Whatever it is, though, it won't change how I feel about you, how I feel about us. I just think it's something I should be allowed to know.' She swallowed, turned. 'So what is it? Which of the stories you told me is true?'

Ree felt a tightness in her throat that surprised her. 'You're sure you want to know?'

'I am. But whether you birthed me or not doesn't matter a hornet's fart next to what you've done for me. You'll always be my Ree.'

'And you'll always be mine, kid.' She felt a lopsided smile pulling at her cheek, and let out a long sigh. 'It . . . was the last one.'

'Huh?'

'The mule-herd.'

The kid visibly deflated. 'I'm *really* not a princess?'

'That's what you're fixing on?'

The kid put up a hand, waved her palm in the morning air. 'I know, I know . . . I was just so sure . . .'

'I'm sorry, kid.'

'I know. Me too.'

'I love you, Javani.'

'I know. Me too.' The kid took several long breaths, staring over her tea out towards the horizon. 'That other stuff you said in the cave, to Lazant. Were you really sold into slavery when you were my age? By your own parents?'

Ree chose her words carefully. 'I was bought and paid for, but not in that way.'

'To the man who gave you the sword?'

'Yes.'

'Did you really poison him, and yourself, or was that a metaphor?'

'I did. Really. Both of us.' She brushed a hand through her matted hair. 'Turned me white overnight, or so the story goes.'

'Who was he?'

'That's for another day, kid.'

'Huh. Keep your secrets for now, but they'll be mine in time. You can't keep me at bay for ever, you know that.'

Ree couldn't keep herself from smiling, despite the pain that gnawed at her. 'That I do.'

Javani slurped at her steaming tea, then put down the mug on the chipped stone beside her. 'There's something else we need to discuss.'

'And what's that?'

'My name.'

'Ah.'

'I'm not delighted about it. Aki and Anashe told me what it means.'

'Ah.'

'Is that all you have to say?'

Ree spread her hands, almost spilling her tea. 'Well, it was . . . a sort of place-holder, to begin with.'

'*A place-holder?*'

'Until you could choose a name of your own! You know, choose your name, choose your path.'

'Maybe I should change it, then! Is Ree *genuinely* your real name?'

'It's the name I chose, and it's who I am to you. I'm not changing it.'

'Huh.'

'So?'

'So . . . maybe I could stand to be Javani a little longer. Until something better comes along.'

'That's the spirit. Maybe we can talk about what happened to my blue jewel in the meantime.'

'Ah. About that . . .'

'Priceless heirloom, you know, worth an absolute fortune. Had it longer than I've had you; always thought of it as my retirement plan. And you stole it from me. You haven't done anything reckless with it, have you?'

The kid produced only garbled croaks of apology. After just long enough, Ree relented. 'Don't tie yourself in knots, kid. I know it's gone. But count yourself lucky that Anashe passed on a little something from her brother by way of a memento. At least he knew how to atone.'

They sat quietly for a while.

'Ree?'

'Fruit of my loins?'

'Where are we going to go? I lost the map.' She gave a rattling sniff. 'To the hidden pass. We can't go west.'

Ree leaned back against the slender tree trunk, and turned to look at the towering western peaks. 'They really say that on the other side of the Ashadi lies paradise, eh?'

Javani gave a sad nod, and wiped her sleeve along her nose. 'Yeah, but nobody goes over them . . .'

'True. But I hear if you go south just far enough . . .' Ree reached into her jacket and slid out a tightly-bound roll of canvas, only a little mottled and bloodstained. Strokes of charcoal marked its back. It smelled strongly of Movos.

'. . . You can go around them.'

Javani packed the plains pony's saddlebags with the Guvulis' kit as diligently as she could, her mind still whirling. They were going west, at last, a new life beckoned, a life in paradise; but more than that, she'd finally peeled back a layer of Ree's onion of secrets. Ree truly was her mother, or was prepared to swear to the gods that she was. But there was more to Ree than that. There was always more to Ree. The more she thought about things, the more questions she found unanswered. If Javani weren't the secret heir, why had Ree been running all these years – what had she been hiding from? Who was the man who'd not-quite-enslaved her, and she'd poisoned to escape? Had he been important enough to hide from? Did he have powerful friends?

She thought of what Aki had said to Ree, just before they'd parted. *I hope you will one day allow yourself to be part of a family again.* So Javani didn't count as a family? Had Aki and Anashe's mother? Did Javani have some relatives somewhere, who knew nothing of her existence?

Javani smiled to herself. They had a long journey ahead. There'd be plenty of time to grind some more answers out of Ree along the way, plenty of time to decide her chosen truth from the results. If there was one thing Javani prided herself on, it was persistence.

Siavash Sarosh was not ruined, but he was hardly as comfortable as he'd have liked. His caravan had not been the triumph he'd predicted, but neither had it been the disaster he'd feared. It had, in sum, been perfectly ordinary, and while for many that might have been a recipe for contentment, when Siavash considered the extraordinary events he'd witnessed, nay, been at the very heart of, it seemed less than scant reward.

He watched the caravan reassemble in the town square, this wretched, forsaken town on the edge of nowhere, with its tumbledown mudbrick buildings and rotting sun-baked walls, and felt a profound melancholy. His voyage north should have brought him sufficient profit to retire – not that he would have done, of course, but simply being in the bracket of those capable of retirement at any age would have been enough for his self-regard – but it had, in the end, produced little worth celebrating beyond a standard one-hop along the east road. Even the very-dark-grey-market materials he'd smuggled along had done little more than salvage his enterprise after the cameltastrophe.

Ulfat signalled that they were ready. With a heavy sigh, Siavash turned and ambled towards his covered conveyance, consoling himself that despite the upheavals, he'd have plenty more trips yet on which to make his greatest profit. Yet somehow the prospect didn't cheer him; the idea of more trips up and down the mine road in his creaking, juddering carriage seemed to weigh upon his soul.

A great shadow fell upon him, blocking out the early morning sun that peeked over the eastern wall. Siavash looked up, blinking, at the massive figure standing over him.

'You need . . . guards?' The woman gestured behind her. Siavash saw another figure in the southerner's wake, a tall easterner, leading mounts and pack animals. She seemed both sad and excited at once.

Despite himself, despite everything that had happened, Siavash smiled. The smile quickly became a laugh, a great gurgling hoot that left him bent double, wiping tears from his eyes. When he stood, the woman was still looming over him, although now a tinge of concern had entered her once-stony gaze.

'Yes, yes,' Siavash said with a beaming smile, 'indeed and in truth. Join the column, and let us be away!'

That should add a bit of excitement to the journey south, he thought to himself as he climbed aboard his covered wagon. Indeed, he reasoned, nestling himself in the cushions and reaching for the nearest decanter as the caravan rolled underway:

What is life, after all, without a zest for adventure?

The morning sun gleamed from the sharp crags of the towering Ashadi mountains, glinting off the glaciers buried in their shoulders, reflecting with scorching glare from the snow blanketing their jagged peaks. Lower on their barren slopes, falling below the tree-line and its thick carpet of oaks, the serrated lines of the mountains gave way to more gentle undulations, and here and there a stripe of white water carved a path through the darkness of the forests.

Lower and closer still, what looked from a distance like a shadow in the tree-covered rock resolved itself to a narrow cleft, a passage between peaks: a pass. And wending its way up the wooded slope towards it, a small column – four stout ponies, laden with supplies, and two figures, one moving slowly, aided by a stick. At last, they reached the crest of the ridge, and the valley beyond spread before them, green and lush and full of promise. Beyond the valley, the countless ranks of mountains reared: vast, implacable, and ridged with darkness.

Far overhead, turning slow circles as if watching over them, flew a hawk.

REE AND JAVANI WILL RETURN

ACKNOWLEDGEMENTS

It seems to be an ineluctable truth that the more books a writer produces, the shorter their acknowledgements get. And while I do love to buck a trend (he typed carefully), I'm afraid I'm going to be following right along the pathway to correlation on this one. To that end, thanks are due to the following people and entities, without whom this book would neither exist nor take the immaculate form it has:

To my irrepressible agent, Harry Illingworth, and the team at DHH;

To my perspicacious editor, Laura McCallen, and the ineffably sublime Natasha Bardon, Vicky Leech Mateos, and Elizabeth Vaziri, and all at HarperVoyager; to the departed but never-forgotten Jack Renninson, without whom none of this would have been possible; to sterling copy-editor Charlotte Webb, and astute proofreader Simon Fox, to luminous artist Gavin Reece, for another jaw-dropping cover;

To the munificent Steve Aryan and the rest of my FantasyCon buddies; to the peerless Francesca Haig, much missed on these shores;

To the army of fantastic and fantastical bloggers and reviewers who have done so much for books past and present – Nils and Beth and the Fantasy Hive, Hiu and the Fantasy Inn, David/LordTBR and FanFiAddict, Michael at TrackOfWords, Mark at

SlowlyRed, Night at SoManyBooks6, and the Brothers Gwynne; to Matt at the Broken Binding, a scholar and a gentleman;

To Adam Iley, who cops the dedication on this one, James G Smith and Laz Roberts;

To my spectacular wife Sarah, who continues to abide, in spite of everything; to my daughters, who continue to be my daughters, for all the good it's done them;

To my parents, one of whom I lost late last year. I'm sorry you didn't get to see this one, Dad, or those that will follow, but I know you'll have been proud no matter what.

Love to you all.

Hitchin, March 2023

CREDITS

Agent
Harry Illingworth

Editor
Laura McCallen

Voyager Editorial Team
Natasha Bardon
Vicky Leech Mateos
Elizabeth Vaziri

Audio
Fionnuala Barrett
Ciara Briggs

Design
Emily Langford
Gavin Reece

Production
Robyn Watts

Marketing
Emily Merrill

Publicity
Susanna Peden